DISCREET

Book One: Childhood's End

Earle Jay Goodman

Also by Earle Jay Goodman

DISCREET – Book One: Childhood's End
DISCREET – Book Two: Growing Pains
DISCREET – Book Three: Round Up

PIONEER SPIRIT – Book One: Overland Trail
PIONEER SPIRIT – Book Two: Indian Affairs
PIONEER SPIRIT – Book Three: Wars and Rumors
PIONEER SPIRIT – Book Four: An Uneasy Peace
PIONEER SPIRIT – Book Five: White Indians
PIONEER SPIRIT – Book Six: Perilous Times
PIONEER SPIRIT – Book Seven: War Drums

Archer – Winged Messenger One
Squire – Winged Messenger Two
Seer – Winged Messenger Three

"...and the desert shall rejoice, and blossom as the rose."

Isaiah 35:1

DISCREET

Book One: Childhood's End

Earle Jay Goodman

Dedication

Boca Raton, Florida
2013

I dedicate this book with love and gratitude to my wonderful parents and grandparents on both sides of my family who raised me on the stories of my great and great-great-grandparents, some of the earliest pioneers and settlers of America's Intermountain West in the mid-1800s;

and, to my friend and advisor since 1973, mentor, and de facto book editor, Edward P. Frey, Esq. – Thanks, Ed;

and, last but not least, to my first real love since 1979, then business partner, then domestic partner, and now married partner, James John Goodman. You are the light of my life. I love you, Jim.

---Earle Jay Goodman

Table of Contents

Prologue: Setting the Stage

On a lazy October Sunday in 2010, two lovers lounged naked in Art's warm condo in west Greenwich Village. Outside, cold rain fell intermittently. Dark-haired Art asked his blond boyfriend, Josh, to tell him about his great-great-grandfather's gay romance back in the olden times.

Josh's bright blue eyes lit up. "Let me grab my laptop in case I need to refresh my memory about any details. Before I left home, I scanned all the old family papers onto my laptop."

Josh placed his computer on Art's big glass coffee table. "Let me give you a little back story – set the stage if you will."

As a graduate student at NYU writing a thesis on American history, Josh had delivered plenty of speeches and lectures over the years. "In the eighteen hundreds, white settlers followed the brave trailblazers of explorers, trappers, and miners of earlier generations. My ancestors joined many others traveling west. They walked, pushed handcarts, rode horses and mules, and drove covered wagons. Later they traveled by rails.

"Industrious, hard-working settlers cleared the ground of native plants then channeled irrigation waters into desert valleys by the sweat of their brows.

"Even the distant and little-known wilderness of Idaho became a state of the Union in eighteen ninety.

"Business followed these pioneers. One of these industries began producing white sugar from sugar beets at the request of Brigham Young, the second prophet of the Mormon Church."

Art nodded. "Um-hm."

"Around the beginning of the nineteen hundreds, a consortium of Salt Lake City businessmen bought raw land in the fertile deserts of the Snake River plains in southeastern Idaho. They wanted to start mass production of sugar beets and refined white sugar. They built enormous factories for the elaborate processing of the beets.

"Into this rugged locale and tumultuous era, a baby entered the lives of two of the original Mormon pioneer families. My great-great-grandfather Leo was born. I'll call him Grandpa Leo for the sake of convenience. He grew up to be one of the last cowboys to drive cattle across the open plains from Texas to Kansas. Railroads and barbed wire fences soon brought an end to the romantic age of the American Cowboy.

"Throngs of white men came to this Idaho wilderness during the Pocatello Land Run of nineteen oh two. That's when the Government opened up the lands of the Shoshone Indian Reservation to settlement by whites."

Josh hopped up. "I need some water. Want one, too?"

Art nodded yes. Josh brought in two bottles from the fridge and sat down. "Any time you need a break, just let me know. Once I get started, I have trouble knowing when to stop."

"Okay."

Josh sat on the sofa with his legs crossed beneath him Indian style. "Grandpa Leo wrote in his journal, I, Leonard Andrew Hayes, was born on the seventeenth of January in the year of our Lord eighteen hundred and ninety-six, but my life really began the day I first met Sean."

Chapter 1: Love at First Sight

On a hot day in August 1910, gangly young Leo rode his pony hard up the dirt lane on the way home from running errands in Blackfoot. He found his father standing at the large open doors of the barn, talking to a tall thin cowboy. Leo pulled up in a swirl of dust and hopped down close beside them. The older man stopped talking and frowned.

Leo glanced bashfully at the stranger, then back to his father. "Hi, Dad. Excuse me fer interruptin', but I just wanted to let ya know I'm back from Blackfoot."

Leo's father turned and spat over his left shoulder. "So I see. And it looks like ya raced the Yellowstone Special train all the way down the road, too. Doncha know better than to ride yer horse so hard, boy? Now take it in and rub it down good. And give it some oats before ya go in fer supper. Ya hear me, boy?"

"Yessiree, Dad."

Leo shuffled his feet and lowered his head, embarrassed to be told off in front of the good-looking stranger. Leo's busy father, Alma, managed the two thousand-acre sugar company farm and ranch they called home. Leo knew better than to waste his father's time. He led the horse slowly around the two men. "Come on, Daisy. Let's get ya in the barn."

When Leo walked by the cowboy, he looked up shyly. *Gee, he sure looks awful spiffy all dressed in black.* "Howdy."

The cowboy glanced over at Alma, then back to his gangly son. He responded with a cheerful musical lilt in his accent. "Hello, me boyo. And what might yer name be?"

Alma shrugged. "Oh, this's me oldest son, Leonard. But we call 'im Leo fer short."

The stranger smiled a fetching lopsided grin. His left side twisted up a little, making a tiny dimple appear on his cheek. His right side bent down slightly. "Hello, Leo fer short. And I'm Sean Michael McKay. Sean fer short. That was some pretty fancy ridin' I saw there, lad. Yer quite the horseman, me boyo."

"Gee, thanks. I love horses and ridin' and feelin' the wind blowin' in my face."

Sean replied with a friendlier smile, nodding his approval. "Ah. A horseman and a poet, too, I see. Or is that just a touch of the ol' Irish blarney trippin' off yer tongue all natural-like?"

Leo stood taller and smiled back as he studied the man in front of him. A black dust-covered hat shaded his charmingly grinning face. The cowboy wore a black leather vest over a black collarless long-sleeved shirt. He had on tight black cotton Levi's with straight legs all wrinkled at the knees and crotch from sitting on a saddle. The young cowhand appeared about twenty, maybe even twenty-two, but he looked fully grown-up in Leo's eyes.

Sean stood firmly planted on scuffed black cowboy boots with broken-in two-inch heels. He rested his tan gloved hands from his thumbs, latched over the top of his chaps' belt. Scratched-up black chaps covered his legs down to his boots. Silver medallions caught the light, sparkling on the chaps as he shifted his weight from one leg to the other.

Leo couldn't pull his eyes away. *This dandy sure don't look like the usual dirty cowpoke. Why even covered with dust in the heat of the day, he looks clean and neat.* Leo glanced down at the big silver belt buckle on Sean's black leather belt. He noticed the bluish gleam of a steel six-shooter on Sean's right hip and a big hunting knife on his left. Leo couldn't help but notice the bulge in Sean's crotch. He looked away quickly, not wanting to give away his attraction to that nice bulge.

"What're ya doin' here on a sugar beet farm, Mister McKay? Ya look like ya should be out on the trail, ridin' herd on some cattle, not bendin' over to pick some lousy sugar beets."

Alma scowled at Leo. "Well, he's not here to pick beets, boy. Hells bells, does he look like a field hand?"

"No, Dad. That's what I was just sayin'." Leo looked down at the ground. "I was only askin'."

Alma spat over his left shoulder and hitched his thumb at the barn door. "Well, mind yer own business, young man. We're talkin' business here, and ya need to get that horse warmed down and unsaddled pronto."

"Yessiree, Dad."

Leo slowly walked away. Daisy followed on the lead reins. He heard Sean call out a lilting, "See ya lay-tuh."

When Leo looked back, Sean winked. Leo ducked his head with a smile. *I loved the way he sang those words. Low-high low-high. See-ya lay-tuh. Must be Irish, like Mom.* People always mistook Leo's mom for English because of her accent, which upset her. She was Irish and proud of it. Leo led Daisy into the shade of the barn. He stopped just inside the barn door to work on the horse where he could overhear the men talking out front.

"Yes sir, Mister Hayes. Ol' man Henderson of the big Lazy H Ranch told me he won't need me fer a month or so, and then I'll be startin' the fall round-up. I'll be drivin' his herd to their winter pastures down south of here, down close to Durango, Colorado, pert near. He said maybe yer ranch could use some help, temporary like, and for me to ride over and offer me services. He said ya don't keep cowhands on permanent, doncha know. I'm good at breakin' horses. I'm right handy at ropin', brandin', and castratin', even though it's not yet that time of year. I'm mighty handy when it comes to mendin' fences and checkin' the outback fer strays that might have got loose and need trackin'."

Sean whipped off his hat and used it to brush road dust off his chaps while he waited for an answer. His left blondish-red eyebrow raised up in a question.

Leo felt quite taken with the tall man's handsomely beguiling face, especially the one dimple when he smiled just so. Sean's hair, somewhere between blond and red, marked him as a fellow Irishman, even if the remains of an old-country brogue hadn't given him away. Leo didn't understand his fascination and attraction to the cowboy. He had trouble focusing on the job of brushing down Daisy's dusty coat.

Sean glanced into the barn and winked at Leo again, which caused him to blush. The boy turned to industriously brushing down the roan's dusty flanks and ducked his red face out of sight.

"Well, I reckon the Utah Idaho Sugar Company can afford a month's wages fer a good range hand. The pay's a dollar a day, cash in hand at the end of the month, and room and board, of course. Ya can take a stall fer yer mount and bunk up in the hay-loft if that's to yer likin' while here at the farmstead. There's no bunks left at the bunkhouse this time of year. Of course, I'll be sendin' ya out to the mountain range soon. Agreed?"

Sean pulled off his riding glove, then slapped his hand against Alma's to seal the deal. "Agreed."

Leo watched from the shadows of the barn, secretly pleased and excited. He hoped he would have a chance to get to know this good-looking buckaroo from the big neighboring ranch.

"When yer not ridin' the range, come in and take yer meals with the family in the stone house up the road there."

Sean smiled, delighted he wouldn't have to cook for himself. "Why, much obliged, Mister Hayes. That would be right nice."

As Leo led Daisy into her stall, he heard horse steps behind him. He turned Daisy loose in her booth with a swat on her rump then closed the gate. Sean walked into the barn with his big hat in one hand, leading his golden palomino.

Leo stepped forward, holding out his hand. "Hey, Mister McKay. Can I help ya?"

"Sure, me boyo. And it would be good to have yer help and yer company while I settle Brown Sugar, here, into his new berth."

Sean's warm lopsided smile lit up the barn and made Leo's heart flutter. Smells of dust, straw, old manure, and stale urine rose around them. Leo walked up and patted the horse on its flank, raising a small cloud of fine white alkaline dust. "Hi, there, Brown Sugar. Yer sure a big boy. What is he, Mister McKay, fifteen hands? Sixteen?"

"Yep. There about. He's a handful, all right, me big beautiful Sugar. And he's just about the best darn cattle horse ya ever could hope to meet, too."

"Have ya really been on cattle drives, Mister McKay?"

"Oh, sure enough. I've been ridin' the trails since I was twelve years old down on me father's cattle ranch in Saint George, Utah. While everyone else tried their hands at growin' cotton and hemp and rice, me pa's family decided to raise Guernsey cattle fer their milk and meat."

16

"Gee, Sean. Yer from all the way down to Saint George in the south of Utah?"

"Oh, yessiree. I went to school and graduated from high school in good ol' Saint George."

"Oh. We only have a high school in Pocatello, one up in Boise, plus the new one in Idaho Falls. Anyone from these parts who wants a high school education usually goes boarder down at The Salt Lake City University. The Pocatello and Idaho Falls High Schools don't take no boarders."

As they unsaddled Brown Sugar, Sean rattled on, making conversation. "To be sure. Ah, Saint George is very civilized, doncha know. I went to Mormon Sunday School every Sunday mornin' and Primary every Thursday. I drove my Mama to Relief Society every Wednesday. Of course, I went to school five days a week. And even with all of that, I still learned how to be a cowboy. That's the only thing I ever wanted to be from the time I could first remember. It's as simple as that."

When Sean pulled his saddlebags off Brown Sugar, Leo spotted a black leather case hanging off the horse's other side. He looked closer, puzzled. "Mister McKay? Is that there a guitar case?"

"Yep. It's not *just* a guitar, though, me boyo. It's a very good parlor guitar made back in ninety-eight. I'll show it to ya sometime, to be sure."

"I just love music, but we don't have no instruments. Mom hums to herself all the day long, but her voice don't carry worth a darn. She likes playing the mouth organ, but she only knows a couple of songs. I'd love to learn to play the guitar and learn how to sing good."

Sean picked up a horse brush. He examined the boar bristles as he tugged the leather strap over the back of his hand, then leaned into vigorously brushing his horse. "Well, I know lots of songs and would be pleased to teach them to ya. Now, why doncha grab another brush and let's make short work of this labor of love at hand here. I'd like to get me face washed, and me teeth polished before yer Mama calls us to supper."

Leo picked up a well-used curry comb and leaned into cleaning the big palomino stallion. "Sure thing, Mister McKay. Here, let me help."

After ten minutes of vigorous brushing, with extra time and energy spent on Brown Sugar's luxurious white tail and mane, they put down their brushes. They both gleamed with sweat on their brows from the exertion. They smiled at each other. Sean winked and nodded. "Thanks. Now, where can a body get a wash up around here?"

Sean took off his spurs and chaps and hung them on wooden dowels set into the stall's rough, plank wood wall. He reached down into his saddlebags and withdrew a wadded old piece of chamois skin. Then he began cleaning the dust and dried horse spittle from his scarred black chaps. He pulled off his vest, removed his pack of rolling papers and bag of tobacco, and pushed them down into his pants pocket. He hung the vest on another nail and methodically wiped it down.

Leo watched, wide-eyed. He had never seen anyone take the time or trouble to tend their clothes so carefully. He and his brothers threw their clothes around wherever they landed, then pulled them on and wore them until the next wash day, and often even then.

"Whatcha doin', Mister McKay?"

"Well now, me boyo, if ya take the time to shammy yer leather goods, they'll always look good and will last much longer, doncha know. It only takes a minute."

Sean leaned down and wiped off his scuffed black cowboy boots. Leo shook his head. He couldn't believe his eyes. Sean caught the look and smiled an impish grin. "Didn't yer Mama ever tell ya that cleanliness is next to godliness?"

"Nope, Mister McKay. I can't honestly say that Mom ever told me that before."

"Well, I happen to believe it, meself. Even when I'm on the trail, I take a minute to stay as clean as I can under the circumstances. And now, if ya would be good enough to show me the way to the well pump, I would dearly like to get washed up thorough like before meetin' yer Mama."

Sean draped his heavy saddlebags over the stall gate and then carefully tied the leather flaps so nothing would fall out.

The two slender young men, one barefoot and one in high-heeled boots, sauntered over to the well pump behind the stone house. Neatly stacked cords of dry firewood stood nearly half as tall as the house, ready for the harsh mountain winter. They would burn it for heat and cooking. The mountain of logs would disappear by spring.

Leo courteously primed the pump by pushing down on the big handle. The effort nearly lifted him off the ground. After a couple of tries, water flowed into the big wood half-barrel catch basin below the iron spout. Sean took off his hat and shirt and hung them on the clothesline running between the pump and the two-holer convenience. Leo's eyes opened wide in surprise. He leaned in and asked in a scandalized whisper, "Mister McKay, doncha wear no union suit under yer clothes?"

Sean grinned and shook his head. "In this heat? Of course, I wear them when it's cold like any civilized body. But remember, in Saint George, the heat reaches a hundred and ten degrees more often than not. Even if I wore cotton long johns, I would've expired from the heat prostration before now, sure as shootin'. No, me boyo, in the summer heat, I wear as little as possible!"

Leo shook his head in wonderment. He thought only uncivilized Mexican laborers didn't wear undergarments. Hadn't Mom told him years ago it was because they couldn't afford long johns? Something like that. He thought he remembered correctly.

Sean grinned as he leaned over and splashed his face, chest, and arms with cold artesian well water. He spluttered and blew enthusiastically every time he rubbed a double handful of water over his face and hair. It made Leo chuckle to hear him enjoying his wash-up so much. When he finished, Sean shook his head like a dog. He smiled broadly at Leo with his eyebrows raised in delight. "There's nothing like clean cold water after eatin' dust, ridin' the trail, so ya gotta take it when ya can get it. Often as not yer dry campin' out on the trail."

Sean's lean, defined muscles glittering in the late afternoon sunlight fascinated Leo. Sean's reddish blond chest hair, covered

19

in sparkling droplets of water, mesmerized him, though he didn't understand why. Sean pulled his fingers through his full head of shaggy hair like a comb, pushing his hair back off his forehead into some semblance of order. The gentle evening breeze of desert air quickly dried him off.

Sean shook out his shirt with a loud snap before pulling it back on with a frown. "What I wouldn't give right now fer a boiled shirt."

Sean sucked in his hairy stomach, then pushed the tails down between the wide belt and his lean torso. He plopped his hat back on with a smart tap. "Well, me boyo. How's about introducin' me to yer Mama, then?"

"Come on. I can smell the pot roast, so it must be gettin' close to supper time. Follow me."

They strolled briskly over to the kitchen door at the back of the stone house. Sean went to step inside, but Leo grabbed his arm and pulled him back around the corner. Leo's Mom stood in front of a rusted wood-burning stove moved outside for her summer kitchen. This kept the heat out of the house so they could sleep better at night. A white canvas tarp hung overhead on ropes to shade the stove. Leo's mother wore her hair neatly braided and piled on top of her head, pinned up with fake tortoiseshell combs. She had ordered them just last year from the Sears, Roebuck & Co. mail-order catalog. Anything she couldn't find at the Blackfoot Dry Goods Store, she ordered by mail-order.

As Leo and Sean drew closer, they found her talking and laughing to herself, stirring a pot of green beans on the cast-iron wood stove.

Leo strode up with a smile. "Mom, I'd like to introduce ya to Sean McKay out of Saint George, Utah. Dad hired 'im this afternoon to do some work on the back cattle range."

Leo turned back to his new friend. "Sean, this is Elizabeth Hayes, my mother."

"Nice to meet ya, ma'am. Boss Hayes kindly invited me to join yer table fer supper if that's all right, ma'am."

"Why, such fine manners. And isn't it a pleasure to meet so handsome and polite a young man if I do say so?"

20

They smiled politely at each other.

Leo's mother gently stirred the already over-cooked green beans. "Supper will be ready in a minute, so just take yerself into the dinin' room and make yerself comfortable and rest a spell."

"Why, thank ya kindly, ma'am."

"Oh! Be off with ya, now. Call me Lizzie like all me friends and leave all that stiff politeness outside with the dishwater."

"Okay, ma'am." Sean grinned brightly, sharing his cute dimple with her. "But only if ya insist, ma'am."

Lizzie chuckled silently while she shook her head. Her whole chubby barrel-shaped body bounced up and down, though not a sound escaped her mouth. She pointed imperiously with the dripping wooden spoon. "Now go sit a spell, and supper will be on the table shortly. Make yerself at home, Sean. Go take a load off, now."

Leo grabbed Sean's arm to lead him over to the kitchen door, but Lizzie called him back. "Leonard Hayes, I see yer Dad comin' in, and he's lookin' plumb knackered out. Now I want ya to go down into the root cellar and fetch 'im a ladle of me new buttermilk. I set it on the bottom step to cool so that he has somethin' to refresh himself with while waitin' fer supper."

"In a minute, Mom, I just want to show Sean where…"

"If I'd have wanted ya to wait a minute before doin' it, I would've waited a minute to ask ya, Leo. Now, just go and do it, pronto!" Lizzie stamped her foot.

Embarrassed and apologetic, Leo pointed the way for Sean to go. "Yes, ma'am. I'm goin' right now!"

Lizzie turned back to stirring the pot, singing softly to herself. Leo took off towards the root cellar on the other side of the house from the wood stack.

When Sean stepped inside the small stone house, he noticed the hat rack on the wall to the right of the door. He hung up his hat and holster, respectful not to wear them in a person's home. Sean spotted a .30-30 lever-action rifle with a long 26-inch barrel hanging on wooden hooks above the kitchen door. He expected Alma kept it loaded, ready for use against any predator, man or animal, that might threaten the family or the livestock.

Sean recognized right away where the woodstove had been. He found himself in a typical country kitchen with a long table of pine boards over X-shaped trestle legs. All manner of stored, preserved, and dried foods sat on open shelves in a big unpainted breakfront. Braids of garlic and onion hung off little hand-forged iron hooks from a ceiling beam. Pots, pans, and lids of various sizes hung on the wall, stored out of the way until needed. Knives stood on their points in a Kerr jar. Wooden spoons and ladles stood on their handles in mustard crocks like flower arrangements on the work table.

He glanced through the other two doors, not to be nosy but to familiarize himself with the layout. One doorway led to the parlor used as a bedroom with a large brass bed and a mounded-up feather mattress. The other door opened into the dining room furnished with a big plank table, benches on both sides, and spindle hardwood chairs at the ends.

Sean relaxed and leaned his shoulder against the wall. He crossed his arms and examined the framed photographs and silhouette portraits of family ancestors hanging on the wall. The young kids scuffled around outside, stomping their boots on the porch to clean off the dirt. Sean softly hummed to himself the popular American ballad about faraway Ireland, *My Wild Irish Rose*.

Lizzie called out the children's names as she ordered them to carry supper to the table. Before long, a small parade of youngsters entered the dining room carrying serving dishes of bread, butter, and roast beef simmering in the gravy of fresh vegetables from their garden. The smells made Sean's mouth water.

The children introduced themselves as they came in. "Hi, I'm Kirby."

"I'm Stanley."

"I'm Lucy."

"I'm Edna, and that's Ralph with the pot roast."

"Hi, I'm Myrtle. I'm the oldest of the girls."

Sean mixed up their names as fast as the kids introduced themselves.

A gamin smell of unwashed youngsters entered the hot room along with the delicious aroma of freshly cooked food. The domestic odors brought back memories of home life to Sean. *Some things never change.* Sean smiled sadly, reminded of his mother and her home-cooked meals in his youth.

Alma Hayes entered, very much the lord of the manor. He took his seat at the head of the table as though sitting on a throne. Alma sipped sweet buttermilk from a large mug with evident pleasure. He opened yesterday's copy of the Pocatello Tribune, picked up that morning with the weekly mail run to Blackfoot, and shook it open to get the wrinkles out.

Leo arrived last. He had washed his face, hair, and hands – and looked much the better for it, too. Sean smiled and nodded.

Alma looked up from the paper. "Lizzie girl. Ya won't believe it. I just found out why we saw smoke up to the north all last week. I don't believe it!"

Lizzie called in from the kitchen, "What was it, Dad? What caused all that smoke?"

"Well, now, it seems that on July the twentieth and twenty-first, says right here, a great fire burned up north, burning over three million acres of forest in the mountains! It spread from Washington across north Idaho and into western Montana. Ain't that somethin'?"

Lizzie carried in a bowl of corn on the cob and set it on the table. "Three million acres of fire? Tarnation! It's a wonder it didn't spread clear down to here."

"Yep," Alma replied, always laid back in his speech. "It's no wonder we saw all that smoke last week. Says right here in the Tribune the wind drove the fire so fast people couldn't even get out of the way and it kilt eighty-six people!"

Lizzie shook her head sorrowfully on her way back to the kitchen for more food. "No! Why that's plumb awful."

Sean frowned. "Why, ya know, sir. I swore I smelled smoke last week, and I kept me eye out fer fire fer several days. I didn't know if those were clouds or smoke up north. I couldn't imagine a fire could make those huge towering clouds, though."

Alma nodded. He put the paper down and took another sip of buttermilk. "Uh-huh. A three million acre fire of burnin' pine trees makes a heap of smoke, and that's fer sure. The smoke probably blew clear across the land, all the way to Washington Dee Cee. Yessiree. That would make one heckuva lotta smoke!"

They sat down to eat just as a dirty white cat chased a black and white roost hen in one door and out the other. The kids all laughed and pointed, nudging each other with their elbows.

Leo pushed his way to sit between Myrtle and Kirby, opposite Sean. Sean looked up with a smile. Leo laughed and pointed at Sean's hair. "Hey, it looks like ya still got yer hat on, Mister McKay. Looky everyone! Mister McKay's wearing a ghost hat bendin' his hair all around his head."

They all chuckled. Sean raised his fist and shook it at Leo, silently promising future retribution. His eyes squinted in mock anger, but his dimple showed despite his pretend frown.

After dessert, they relaxed at the table, leaning against each other with their elbows on the table. They chatted contentedly about nothing important, feeling peaceful and satisfied. A good day's work and play drew to its end.

Leo looked at his father. "Mister McKay brought a guitar with 'im. Would it be okay if he played some fer us? Please?"

Lizzie glanced up at Sean. Her eyes lit up. "Oh, we would just love to hear some music this evenin', if yer up to it, that is. Would ya mind playin' somethin' fer us?

Leo jumped up and stepped over the bench. "I can go fetch it. Okay, Mister McKay?"

"Yes, please, Leo. That would be nice of ya, me boyo. Thanks."

The whole family moved into the parlor. The older kids sat on chairs. The little ones lounged on the braided rag rug. Alma slipped off his work boots and left them on the floor by the bed. Then he leaned back against the headboard with his legs crossed in front of him. Lizzie busied herself in the kitchen, putting things away while Myrtle cleared the table and washed the dishes. Myrtle grumbled she would miss everything. "Why's it always my turn to do the dishes, anyway? It just ain't fair."

"Don't say ain't, dear," Lizzie admonished her daughter. "That ain't proper English."

They looked at each other and smiled at the old joke.

Leo returned, carrying the black guitar case. He looked at Alma for permission then set it on the mattress. Sean strode over, opened the case, and pulled out the guitar. The kids' eyes grew round when they saw the beautiful instrument.

"See here, Leo, this is a parlor guitar. It's a mite smaller than a regular Spanish guitar, but it makes beautiful music. It's perfect fer playing inside a parlor." Sean pointed to the highly polished reddish wood on its back and sides. "This here's called rosewood from Brazil down in South America. Isn't it beautiful?"

The kids all agreed. "Uh-huh. Sure is."

Stanley and Edna set up their usual evening checkerboard on the braided rag rug. Edna drew the red checker, so she made the first move. Little Kirby climbed over and sat in Leo's lap, tired from running around playing in the heat all day. He sucked his thumb and kicked his dirty bare feet against Leo's shins as he watched the activity around him.

Sean gestured towards the neck of the guitar. "It uses the finest gut strings, of course, and these here are engraved mother of pearl inlays on the ebony fingerboard. Ebony grows naturally black to begin with doncha know. This mahogany neck holds everything in place. These tuner knobs have mother of pearl inlay, too. Aren't they fine?"

Everyone nodded in agreement. The Hayes family watched and listened, spell-bound, as Sean slowly tuned his prized instrument. Every eye flicked back and forth, from one of his hands to the other, as he plucked a string and turned a knob. They heard the tone gradually raise or lower in pitch until it sounded just right.

Lizzie came in and sat down in a straight-back wood chair beside the bed. She picked up her sewing kit and began mending a tear in one of little Lucy's simple school frocks.

Sean softly sang *She'll Be Coming 'Round the Mountain* as his clear tenor voice warmed up. The youngsters joined in singing the chorus. They sang with lots of enthusiasm, even if off-key from time to time.

After several songs, Sean ended with a heart-warming rendition of everyone's favorite, *Oh Danny Boy.*

> *When Irish eyes are smiling,*
> *Sure, 'tis like the morn in Spring.*
> *In the lilt of Irish laughter*
> *You can hear the angels sing*

When the sun finally set around nine o'clock, and the air began cooling off, the children quietly drifted off to bed. Lizzie didn't light a lamp or a candle. Leo carried sleeping little Kirby out to the porch and put him to bed, still dressed in his ragged miniature overalls.

Sean bid a quiet goodnight to everyone. He picked up his guitar case and walked to the barn, content with the new job, the supper, and the music. He looked forward to enjoying a quiet smoke before climbing up the loft for a good night's sleep.

Greenwich Village
October 2010

Josh took a break from telling Grandpa Leo's story to make a quick run to the bathroom. When he returned, he snuggled up against Art on the white leather sectional. They sat gazing out over the dark, polluted Hudson River.

Art rubbed his cheek against Josh's floppy hair, enjoying its uniquely masculine perfume. "I know you're writing a thesis, but you never talk about it. What's it about?"

"Well, the title of my thesis says it all. How Male Couples and Groups Shaped the Exploration and Settling of the American West."

"Well, that's sure a mouthful. But it sounds interesting. It's sure a far cry from writing computer code. You deal with people and events in history while I deal with electronics and events in cyberspace. Sounds like a match made in heaven."

"Oh, you!"

Josh turned around and gave Art a quick kiss. His hand settled over Art's nylon-covered manhood. He gave it a little squeeze through the lounging shorts. "I think *this* might be the match made in heaven."

Art couldn't agree more.

They smiled at each other. Josh nestled in to lean back against Art's arm slung over the back of the sofa. His eyes focused on the far distance as he gathered his thoughts.

Chapter 2: Accident

Morning dawned bright and early. Leo's eyes opened slowly. Dramatic sunlight reflected off the sides of small sapling trees. When Alma arrived to take over as foreman two years ago, he had planted them in their barren front yard. Leo rolled over on the narrow bed on the screened porch, nearly crushing poor little Kirby sleeping with his thumb in his mouth. Leo pushed Stanley's leg off his then slid out from under the sweat-soaked sheet. He reached for his coveralls on the chair by the door. Before he pulled them on, he remembered Sean didn't wear his union suit in the heat. The idea appealed to him. He quickly peeled off his grungy gray pee-stained long johns. Leo hoped nobody would catch him naked as he quickly pulled his overalls up over his tingly bare skin. He looped the blue jean shoulder straps over his shoulders and fastened the buckles to the bib before he secured the brass side buttons. He had grown so much this summer the ragged cuffs ended six inches above his ankles. Barefoot as usual, he went to see what his mother had prepared for breakfast.

Lizzie always woke up before dawn. She stirred up the fire in the stove and set a big fourteen-inch Dutch oven to frying sausages. She shredded leftover potatoes and tossed them in. When the kids arrived, Lizzie would break a dozen fresh eggs over everything and let it all cook up into a tasty breakfast. She stood at the stove, talking to herself as she worked. Since she smiled and laughed silently at her private conversation, Leo didn't think it would be polite to interrupt. He quietly walked over to the tin bread box and pulled out a leftover roll to munch on while waiting for breakfast.

Leo caught a glimpse of Sean walking out of the barn with his big hat pushed back off his face and his black shirt hanging unbuttoned out of his pants. Sean carried a towel and a small leather shaving kit as he headed for the well pump. Leo decided to go say good morning, suddenly filled with a yearning to bask in Sean's attention. He strode casually out the back door and met Sean at the pump with a big smile. "Mornin', Mister McKay. Did ya sleep good?"

"Top of the mornin' to ya, too, me boyo. I slept great. And isn't it a fine and glorious mornin' that the good Lord's given us to breath in and enjoy today!"

Sean charmed Leo with his crooked smile, little dimple, and a big wink. Leo grinned back, his heart beating faster and happier.

Leo watched with growing pleasure as Sean flipped his towel over the sagging clothesline and took off his shirt. Leo wanted to see the man shirtless again, although he couldn't have explained why. "Mister McKay, are ya gonna bathe again? Ya just washed up and brushed yer teeth last night, ya know!"

"Leo, me boyo, whenever I don't have to dry camp, I'll wash me face, and shave me beard, and start the day with a clean smile on me freshly scrubbed face. Now, be a good pardner and do me the favor of holdin' me shavin' mirror fer me, will ya?"

Delighted to have an excuse to stand closer to his shirtless hero, Leo accepted the round mirror. "Sure. Glad to help."

Leo slipped the mirror's hanging wire over his hand, so the mirror faced out from his palm. He stood there, watching happily as Sean once again spluttered while noisily washing his face. Sean whisked his wood-handled boar's bristle brush in a small tin travel cup. Then he slapped frothing soap suds over his cheeks, chin, and neck. He smiled with a twist of his closed soap-covered lips. "Okay there, pardner, hold the mirror steady now, so's I don't cut meself and bleed plumb to death before I even get to have breakfast! I may be usin' one of these here new-fangled safety razors from Gillette, but it still has a blade with a sharp cuttin' edge."

Leo laughed out loud while he held out the mirror and stepped in closer. Sean reached out and grabbed Leo's arm to position it at the right viewing angle. Leo gasped in excitement at the touch. Halfway through shaving, Sean looked into Leo's eyes and smiled impishly. "I see yer imitatin' me, not wearin' long johns under yer dungarees this mornin'."

Leo blushed and nodded, squirming at getting caught.

Sean secretly enjoyed seeing Leo embarrassed. "It feels good, doesn't it? Lettin' everythin' hang all cool and natural like, not all bundled up and restricted and overheated."

Sean smirked knowingly, then turned his gaze back to the mirror to finish shaving. While Sean pulled on his shirt, Leo decided to follow his example. He leaned over the washtub, splashed his face, and ran wet hands up and down both arms. "Can I please use yer towel?"

Sean walked over and began scrubbing Leo's face with the towel in both hands, messing up his hair in the process. "Why sure, me boyo. Here, let me help."

Leo laughed boyishly. "I can do it, Mister McKay. I can do it."

They ended up in a tug-a-war with the white flannel towel until Sean stopped and threw his arm around Leo's bare shoulders. "Come on then, me boyo, let's go eat breakfast before it's all gone."

Smiling, they headed for the kitchen door. Leo thought to himself how nice Sean smelled and how good his strong arm felt on his bare shoulders. It had never occurred to him that anyone could smell nice. He had never noticed such a thing before. Everyone had their own odor, each slightly different, some stronger than others, but nothing worth noticing. Not until now.

Sean looked down on Leo's towel-fluffed hair, taking delight in their simple human touch.

Lizzie gave her kids their marching orders while they finished eating breakfast. "And, Leo, I want ya to kill us a chicken and dress it down fer the pot, first thing, 'cause it's gotta simmer all day so we can have chicken 'n dumplin's fer supper."

"Aw, Mom! Ya know I hate killin' and pluckin' chickens. Can't someone else do it?"

"Why Leonard Hayes, whatever in tarnation's the matter with ya this mornin'?"

"It just gives me the heebie-jeebies, is all. I don't like to do it! Please?"

"Oh, stop that silliness right now. I don't understand what yer carryin' on about. Ya take off every afternoon after yer acre of weedin', and ya go huntin' with yer twenty-two, and ya think nothin' of killin' pert near ever livin' creature ya come across. Ya go huntin' deer and dress 'em down at least once a week. May the good Lord bless ya fer helpin' feed this big family. So what's the matter with killin' and dressin' a little ol' chicken, fer gosh sakes?"

Sulking, Leo looked down at the floor. "I dunno, Mom. I just don't like to do it."

"Now stop that right now and git out there and catch a chicken, or there will be no supper fer ya at me table today!"

Lizzie stamped her foot. All her children knew when Lizzie put her foot down, she wouldn't allow any further discussion. Leo bowed his head in sullen reluctant submission and slowly walked out to the yard. A cloud of doom darkened his demeanor and followed him into the sunshine.

Lizzie called out at his retreating back, "And doncha dare choose a layer, neither, Leo! And if ya don't clean every feather off, I'll see ya get the feather in yer dumplin's. So do a good job and be quick about it!"

Smiling kindly, Lizzie watched Leo's shoulders slumping in defeat as he moped away towards the chicken coop. Leo sighed, giving up all hope of getting off the hook. "Okay, Mom."

"Now, Myrtle, I want ya to go out and pick a half bushel of green beans and wash 'em good at the pump before bringin' 'em into the kitchen. We're gonna preserve 'em in salt brine fer eatin' this winter."

Myrtle sat at the table playing with her favorite rag doll, braiding its yellow yarn hair into a semblance of a ponytail. "Okay, Mom. In a minute."

"Now, listen, Myrtle! If I had wanted ya to wait a minute, I would've waited a minute to tell ya. So go do yer chores, now!"

Myrtle pouted, put down her doll, and sulked out the door. "Okay, Mom."

Sean smiled as he reflected on the similarities of family life everywhere. Everyone carried their share of work according to their strength, age, and abilities. People throughout the West, if not the world, spent the better part of their day's activities putting provisions on the table and setting aside rations for winter. Sean thanked Lizzie for breakfast as he walked outside to feed and groom Brown Sugar.

31

Sean noticed Leo over by the chicken coop, holding a head-less chicken upside down by its legs while the blood drained out, waiting for its legs to stop kicking. Blood splattered him and the ground around him. Leo averted his face in distaste. A scowl made him frown as he held his eyes closed tight to protect them from blood flying through the air. Sean chuckled, remembering the first time he had seen a headless chicken running around. It had raised the hair on the back of his neck. *I'm glad I don't have that chore anymore. I've done it enough times, though.* Sean shook his head and clucked his tongue.

Alma stood in the shade of the barn giving the day's instruc-tions and orders to the Chinese headman and Mexican foreman. The Chinese crew boss still wore his traditional ponytail queue and went by the simple name of Ho. Everyone called the Mexican foreman Jefe, which meant boss in Spanish. The middle-aged man walked like an unstoppable bull ruling his workers with an iron fist and a sharp tongue. Alma noticed Sean leaving the house and waved him over to join them.

Sean walked up briskly and touched the brim of his hat in a salute. "Good mornin', Boss Hayes. What can I be doin' fer ya this fine day?"

Alma pushed chewing tobacco under his upper right lip. "Well, now, I was gonna ride into the Blackfoot General Store to pick up a few things we need. But I was thinkin' maybe ya could save me the trip today."

"Sure, and I'd be pleased to help, sir."

"Take young Leo with ya. He'll show ya the way, and he can sign fer the purchases on me trade account. Oh, and ask Lizzie if she has any butter to send in. Johnny, the storekeeper, says he always has standin' orders fer Lizzie's fine churned butter."

"Yessirree, Boss. Ya want me to leave right now?"

Alma glanced behind Sean at Leo struggling to de-feather the chicken. He spat to the side, then grinned. "Just as soon as Leo gets supper ready, ya can be off. It's a little more than a three-hour trip each way at an easy pace. Ya can be back in time fer supper if ya get goin' soon."

"Sure enough, Boss. I'll just feed and saddle Brown Sugar, and we'll be on our way."

Sean strode briskly up to Leo. Leo sat on an old three-legged milking stool with the chicken between his knees, angrily plucking its feathers. Sean grinned at Leo's blood-splattered face squinched up in a distasteful frown. "Hey, Leo, if ya hurry it up, ya could ride in with me to Blackfoot to pick up some stuff fer yer Dad."

Leo's eyes lit up. He sat up straighter and started plucking those feathers like crazy. "Oh! Wait fer me. I'll hurry fast as I can!"

"And, Leo, if ya wanna ride with me, yer gonna have to wash up again and put on some clean clothes. I don't wannna have to smell chicken blood and guts all the day long!"

Sean snickered at Leo's wrinkled nose and angry glare before he turned back to the barn.

Lizzie carefully dumped her freshly churned butter out of the little wood molds for one-pound bricks and neatly wrapped each one in waxed paper. She tucked the packages into a small peach crate and covered them with damp gauze. "Now, see that ya keep this package damp and cool, so my butter don't melt. Ya hear?"

"Yes, ma'am."

They completed their trading at the general store around noon. Sean handed Leo the receipt for Lizzie's butter. "Come on, Leo. Let's go to the saloon and buy us some dinner."

Leo jumped at the offer. Alma hadn't permitted him to enter the saloon before. "Ya have to wait till yer fully growed up, boy. That's no place fer a kid."

Leo found the saloon much quieter than he had expected. Only a couple of farmers and ranch hands sat around talking quietly while they played cards. The boys walked up to the long counter. Sean ordered a draft beer and a cold bottle of sarsaparilla. The saloon followed the time-honored custom of offering a free lunch with the purchase of beverages. After Sean paid for their drinks, they filled their plates with ham sandwiches, pickles, and boiled eggs and sat down at an empty table. Leo looked with distaste at the unwashed tabletop. Sean ignored it, put down his plate, and ate like a starved man.

Halfway back to the farm, the intense end-of-summer sun beat down on them relentlessly. Not a breath of a breeze stirred the air. Dark circles of sweat showed under both boys' arms, drying to a powdery rim of salt in rings on their shirts. Sean removed his vest and unbuttoned the fake pearl buttons on his shirt, hoping to catch a cooling breeze. The desert plain grew no trees to offer even a passing moment of shade.

Around three o'clock, they both heard a train rumbling behind them, approaching rapidly. The glistening steel tracks ran parallel to the country dirt road. The new line ran from Pocatello up above Idaho Falls, then curved east across a tip of Montana. It ended up in Wyoming at Yellowstone National Park, the world's first national park of two million acres of mountain wilderness.

Both boys stood up on their stirrups and twisted to look at the train. A great billow of sooty coal smoke rose rhythmically from a tall black chimney, rising slowly to drift behind the train in the still air.

The sound drew closer and louder. Leo yelled, "Yippee! It's the Yellowstone Special. Let's race her!" He sat down and kicked Daisy in the stomach. "Giddup, Daisy. Let's go. Yay! Yippee! Let's race!"

Not to be left in the dust by an old roan, Sean leaned forward and shouted into Brown Sugar's ear, "Let's go, Sugar!"

Sean tapped his spurs to Brown Sugar's belly. They took off running in a great leap. Laughing, Sean took off his hat and waved it in the fresh breeze of the race. Brown Sugar quickly caught up and passed Daisy.

Leo shook Daisy's reins. "No! Go faster, Daisy! Go faster! No fair! No fair!"

The enormous black steam engine drew up alongside the racers. Leo glanced over at people sitting all prim and proper in their best Sunday-go-to-meeting city clothes only fifteen feet away. He waved his hat, laughing at the passengers. A couple of youngsters waved out the window, pointing at the riders.

Leo and Sean leaned over their horses, urging their mounts to keep up with the train. But the train steadily pulled ahead until the caboose left them behind.

When the riders relaxed back on their saddles, the horses began slowing down. They finally resumed walking at their normal pace. Greasy soot and ash from the train smoke swirled around them in a gray cloud. Sean looked over at Leo and winked. "Nice race, me boyo, to be sure."

"Yeah, but Brown Sugar's a lot more horse than poor ol' Daisy. We didn't have a chance. But, I sure like racin' the Yellowstone Special. That was fun. But. Uh. Mister McKay. Maybe it's best not to tell Dad, doncha know."

"Yep. Mum's the word, me boyo. I understand. But it *was* fun, though, and that's the truth."

Both boys checked the lumpy gunny sacks tied behind their saddles. Finding everything secure, they continued on their way. Finally, they rode up the lane to the barn in plenty of time for supper.

Leo spotted Alma, standing by the corral, talking with a wizened Shoshone Indian elder. The old brave wore a mix of native and white man clothing. An old-fashioned bowler with a single wild turkey feather in the hatband sat atop his long braided hair.

Alma had tied a red and white Indian Cayuse pony to the corral. Little four-year-old Kirby sat on the Cayuse absently petting its mane while he stared at the strange old visitor. Alma had just given the horse to the Shoshone. He now waited patiently in the established custom of an Indian horse trader to see if the Indian gave him the worth of the horse. If he didn't, Alma would take back the horse.

The old man returned the little tow-headed boy's stare. He didn't say or do anything for several long minutes. Finally, the horse trader pointed at Kirby. "Hionsa."

Alma frowned, puzzled. "Hence?"

The Shoshone Indian pointed at Kirby's hair. "Hionsa!"

Alma knew better than to ask the old warrior from the nearby reservation what the word meant. Most elderly Shoshone only knew a handful of English words for trading.

Little Kirby frowned and pointed at his heart. "Honce? Me?"

Another nod set the turkey feather bobbing. "Hee-onnn-se."

"Honce? Hey, Dad. He called me Honce. How d'ya like that! I have me a new name, now."

Alma walked over and lifted newly-named Honce off the sturdy little horse. Kirby reached up and grabbed hold of Alma's jacket. He tugged twice, demanding attention. "Me name is Honce, now, Dad."

The Indian opened a beaded leather wallet and pulled out crumpled dollar bills and a handful of coins. He resented using white man money, but whites didn't barter without it. He began slowly holding out one paper bill after another. Alma stood with his left hand out, palm up, a stoic look on his face. He paid strict attention to exactly how much the Indian gave him without looking directly at the money. When it nearly reached the horse's value, the old Warrior counted out a fifty-cent piece, a couple of quarters, then slowly added two dimes one at a time.

Finally, Alma accepted the payment. He closed his fist over the money and crossed his right arm over his stomach. He opened his empty fist in a flat palm-down gesture and swept his hand horizontally in the sign for 'Good.'

The old Shoshone brave repeated the gesture, then nodded respectfully. Alma gravely nodded in return. The old man walked over to the fence and untied the horse. He hopped up bareback, more nimbly than Leo expected, then rode away content with the trade.

"Howdy, Dad. Hey there, Kirby. We're back from the dry goods store."

Alma looked over and raised his chin, acknowledging their return. Little Kirby ran up and grabbed Daisy's bridle. "Me name is *not* Kirby! Me name is Honce!"

Sean smiled teasingly, a glint in his eye. "Honce? What a strange name fer a little blond Irish boy. And just where did ya find such a grandiose name, lad?"

"The ol' Injun tol' me. He called me Honce!"

"Ah. Well. If the wise old Indian said it, it must be true then. Right, Leo?"

"Um. I guess."

Leo hopped off Daisy and offered Honce the reins. "All right then, um, uh, Honce. Bring Daisy into the stall so I can unload her, okay little brother?"

Happy to help, Honce led Daisy into the barn with a gentle tug of her rawhide reins. For the next twenty years, his family, friends, and foes alike would call him Honce. The towhead's name referred to dry winter prairie grass, the color of his hair.

The following day, Lizzie carried a heavy platter of fried bacon and eggs to the table. "Take some and pass the plate quick before the eggs get cold."

Lizzie went back outside to the stove and pulled some soda biscuits out of the oven. She carried the hot cookie tray with a wad of her long apron back to the dining room. She tipped the biscuits onto another large platter to pass around the table. "Now, listen up, children. I'm gonna drive into Blackfoot fer bolts of cloth. I've put it off far too long. Ya all need new school clothes, and I can't wait, or ya'll be startin' school lookin' like poor beggar children. So, Leo, I want ya to hitch up Daisy to the single buggy and put up the top. And make sure the bumper is clean to carry the bolts. Myrtle, since yer the oldest girl, I want ya to get supper on while I'm drivin' to and from the general store. I'll take baby Bud with me. I can carry 'im on my lap and still drive ol' Daisy. Then ya won't have to mind the baby while ya do yer chores."

Myrtle whined, "But, Mom! What am *I* gonna cook? Why do *I* have to do it? Why can't *Leo*? He's the oldest."

Lizzie gave Myrtle a stern look. "Dad-blame it, Myrtle! Yer gonna cook the supper, and that's that! I'll tell ya the recipe fer a stew, and ya won't have any trouble at all. Now, listen careful like, daughter."

Lizzie shared her preparation instructions in great detail, ending with the sage advice, "now be sure to remove the bay leaf before ya serve it up, as its pointed tip can get stuck in a body's throat. Ya don't never want to serve a bay leaf in a stew! Now, ya got that, daughter?"

Looking a bit bug-eyed, Myrtle repeated the recipe. Lizzie nodded her head in approval. "Ya got it, daughter. Just take yer time."

"Okay, Mom. I'll do my best. But don't be mad at me if it don't turn out tasty! That's all I have to say."

Lizzie smiled then affectionately kissed Myrtle on the cheek. "It'll be fine, Myrtle. Don't fret none. Just follow the recipe."

Around three o'clock that afternoon, Lizzie rode home from Blackfoot, driving Daisy in their four-wheeled single-horse carriage. The leather bonnet shaded her and little Bud but didn't offer any relief from the heat. She held the leather reins loosely in her gloved right hand. The baby sat in her lap with her left arm securely holding him. Lizzie had opened up the baby blanket so baby Bud wouldn't get prickly heat.

Lizzie felt at peace with herself, pleased she had found two shades of blue and white gingham for Myrtle and Lucy's school dresses. She had carefully negotiated the price of her butter and the price of the bolts of fabric. Smiling, she hummed softly to herself. She envisioned sewing school shirts for the boys from the new cotton cloth. *I hope I have enough cotton for the shirts. I don't want to have to go back fer more at the last minute. Lands 'o Goshen, but I don't have enough hours in the day fer everything I need to do to take care of me lovely younguns. And my, but aren't they a lovely brood of kids, though.* She gazed down affectionately at baby Bud, sleeping in her arm, then bent her neck down and gave him a gentle kiss on top of his curly red hair.

About the time she heard the train coming up from behind, she smelled the acrid black smoke blowing ahead of it on the gentle breeze. Then she heard it.

Daisy knew that sound and what it meant. She began trotting a little faster, then a bit faster, and then faster still. Even without Leo giving her the spurs and shouting in her ear, she knew how to race the noisy locomotive.

Daisy soon began running too fast for Lizzie's comfort. The small black carriage's bent iron springs couldn't compensate. The larger bumps nearly bounced baby Bud right off Lizzie's lap. Lizzie didn't understand why Daisy had begun running. She tightened her grip on the lines of the driving reins and pulled back gently. "Whoa, Daisy. Slow down, girl. Easy, girl. Whoa. Whoa."

She shouted, "Whoa!" more loudly and pulled back harder on the reins two times, expecting Daisy to slow down. She heard a thump behind her. The bouncing carriage had bumped out one of the bolts of precious new cloth onto the dirt road. Angry that she would have to turn around for the fabric, she yanked with all her might and shouted, "Whoa, Daisy!"

One of the reins broke.

When Daisy felt the line go loose, she began running full out like when Leo gave her free rein during past races.

Concerned for her safety now, Lizzie clutched Bud to her breast and pulled the single driving rein as hard as she could. She desperately wanted to slow Daisy down and pull the carriage over to the side of the road.

With a long pull of its steam whistle, the Union Pacific Yellowstone Special passenger train pulled ahead. Daisy raced it full steam ahead. One of the ladies in the passenger car shook her head at the careless lady driving her horse so recklessly. The passenger's big wide hat, covered with pheasant feathers and black lace, moved gently back and forth, signaling her frowning disapproval.

Irrigation ditches carrying water to the new farms passed under the tracks and the country road through shallow concrete culverts. Lizzie didn't see the upcoming culvert and ditch until too late.

Lizzie pulled Daisy over to the right. After the train rumbled by, Daisy began slowing down as usual. The two right wheels ran off the road into the shallow side drainage ditch.

The carriage crashed into the concrete culvert with a bang!

The front right wheel dropped into the ditch that crossed under the road and slammed the carriage to an abrupt stop.

Lizzie realized her situation in a flash. Without even thinking about it, she gently tossed baby Bud onto the soft muddy ditch bank out of harm's way. When the buggy slammed to a stop, it sent her flying.

She landed badly on her right ankle.

The ankle bent too far and snapped.

Lizzie screamed and passed out from the excruciating pain.

Daisy struggled to regain her feet. The tack had yanked her back when the carriage stopped so abruptly and jerked her to sit down hard on her rump. The broken front right wheel sank in the deep mud of the big ditch. The carriage wouldn't budge.

Lizzie struggled up from blackness when she heard Bud crying. She tried to sit up to find her baby. "Bud! Buddy baby. Where are ya?"

She sat panting, dazed from flying head over heels and distracted by pain. Then she broke down crying when the pain overcame every other consideration. "Oh, thunderation! Thunderation! Oh, me ankle. Where's Bud? Where's me baby?"

She sobbed desperately. Tears flowed down her dusty face. Her hair had come loose and hung over her face. She tossed her head to clear her vision and looked around frantically for Bud. *Keep calm, now, Elizabeth Heath Hayes. Yer no use to yer baby nor yer family if ya lose yer head. Just stop a minute. Calm down. Think.*

Lizzie panted hard through clenched teeth. "Oh, me ankle! Oh, thunderation, I've never hurt so bad. Not even givin' birth hurt so bad!"

She went to sit up, but the slightest movement caused her ankle to flare up like a knife stabbing in and twisting. Broken ends of bones grated against each other, cutting into her muscles, ligaments, and tendons. She lay still, panting, taking deeper and slower breaths, struggling to regain control over her body. Sweat, dust, and tears covered her face as she crouched in the mud of the earthen ditch.

"Help!"

She knew nobody could hear her but little Bud. She gasped in panic. "Help me, please! Somebody! Help!"

Daisy struggled to her feet. Unable to move the carriage, she stood locked in place. She took a sip of ditch water.

Chapter 3: Rescue

Nearly two long, painful hours passed before Lizzie heard the clip-clop of a horse slowly approaching. Later, when she told people about her accident, she said she waited fully an eternity and thirty minutes for help to arrive. "And if you've already waited an eternity, it's just plumb amazin' how long thirty minutes can be!"

A group of tired Mexican field hands sat all bunched up on the back of a horse-drawn field wagon with their legs dangling over the sides. When the driver saw the carriage listing at a broken angle on the side of the road, he shook the reins to move his horse along more quickly. As he pulled up alongside the carriage, the men jumped off. They spoke rapidly in staccato Spanish. "Where is the passenger? What happened? Why did the carriage stop in the ditch like that?"

"¿Dónde esta el pasajero? ¿Qué sucedió aquí?"

When they spotted Lizzie on the other side of the buggy, they ran over to her, crossing themselves repeatedly, praying they would find her alive.

She tried again to sit up when she heard them, but the movement made her blanch white from pain. Sweat broke out anew on her forehead. The men reassured her gently, in a quieting tone of voice, like speaking to a baby, "Cálmate, cálmate. No moverse. No problemo. No problemo."

Lizzie began crying again as sweat beaded on her face from the intense pain. Finally, she struggled to sob out, "But, me baby! Where's me baby? Me baby!"

The sun-burnt leader of the worker removed his grimy hat and held it between his hands at his chest. He knelt down beside the wounded lady and leaned over to look at her face. "¿Usted tiene un bebé? ¿Dónde está el bebé?"

He turned back to the field hands. "Muchachos, buscan a un bebé. Un bebé falta la señora."

The men scattered, looking around anxiously. Fifteen feet back from the carriage, a young laborer found Bud asleep in the thick weeds covering the damp ditch bank. Bud slept sucking his thumb as though nothing had happened. "Aquí él es. ¡Aquí está el bebé!"

The young man of Aztec and Spanish descent gently picked up the baby. A sweet, caring look came to his weary face as he gazed at the sleeping child. Taking care to support the neck and head, he carried Bud to Lizzie. The workmen crossed themselves, this time in prayers of gratitude for the child's safe recovery. The men smiled happily. "Vea, señora. Aquí está su bebé. Vivo y sano. No se preoccupe. No problemo. No problemo."

Lizzie closed her eyes in a quiet prayer of thanks when she saw her baby alive and healthy. She cried again, but this time, with silent tears of relief.

In Spanish, the boss quietly ordered his men to go to work. Two men released Daisy from her harness and checked her over. On the count of three, the rest of the work gang lifted the buggy out of the ditch. With the iron rim hanging off the cracked and splintered wooden wheel, they saw it couldn't travel.

The crew Jefe gave a long string of orders in Spanish. Lizzie closed her eyes and held baby Bud close to her breast. The laborers, exhausted from harvesting sugar beets in the hot sun, understood the need to rush the hurt lady to her home.

The head man turned back to Lizzie and enunciated slowly, as though speaking to a child, "Me llamo Alberto, ¿Entiende? Mi nombre es Alberto Sánchez. ¿Como se llama usted, señora?"

Lizzie understood enough Spanish to answer. "My name – is Elizabeth Hayes."

Alberto recognized the Hayes name and nodded his head several times. "Ah, bien. Ahora. ¿Es su marido el señor Alma Hayes, el jefe del rancho de..." Alberto struggled to pronounce the foreign English words correctly. "Utah... Idaho... Sugar... Compañía?"

Again, Lizzie spoke very slowly and loudly, struggling between deep, shuddering breaths. "Sí. Sí, Alma – is – my – husband. Do ya understand? Please take me – to Alma Hayes. Can ya please?"

"Ah, sí, señora. No se preocupe. No problemo."

Lizzie didn't understand anything else he said. He told his crew they had to splint her ankle before moving her. Close to fainting again, Lizzie couldn't make any sense out of his Spanish words. She shook her head, closed her eyes, and laid back against the weeds and clover on the ditch bank, trying to will away the pain.

However, his men understood him only too well. They knew applying splints would cause her great pain, but they dared not move her without stabilizing the break.

Alberto looked around for something to use as splints. He couldn't see any sticks or boards close by, so he went over to the field wagon's toolbox. He scrounged around, then removed a hammer and an iron file to substitute for splints.

He tore off a long strip of Lizzie's underskirt then tore it in half again. He carefully worked both strips of bandages under her leg as gently as he could. He placed the hammer and file alongside the twisted ankle. Speaking softly, hoping his tone of voice conveyed his sorrow for causing pain, he slowly pulled the strips of white fabric into tight knots and bound her ankle. "Lo siento muchísimo, lo siento muchísimo. Sorrrry. Sorrrrry."

Lizzie cried out in a loud gasp, then passed out.

Alberto nodded approvingly, relieved she had passed out so they could rush her to the wagon before she regained consciousness. "Ah, ahora. Let's get the Señora quickly onto the bed of the wagon before she wakes up. She won't feel the pain while she is passed out like she is now. Quickly, muchachos, gather around. When I count to three, lift her up and walk her over to the wagon. Ready? One. Two. Three."

The men lifted Lizzie and shuffled her to the wagon. One of the laborers remembered seeing bolts of fabric in the boot of the buggy and ran to fetch them. He gently lifted Lizzie's head and slipped one beneath as a pillow. He placed the others close to each side of her broken ankle to keep it as still as possible on the ride. Pedro, the teenage worker carrying Bud, climbed up onto the bench seat to ride shotgun. He tenderly rocked the little baby. He hoped the child would not wake up crying and disturb its miserable mother.

The group's foreman, Alberto, climbed up, picked up the reins, and started them off at a brisk walk. His weary men followed alongside, walking without a word of complaint. One of them led Daisy.

As they passed the farm buildings of the Pearsall Ranch where the crew lived and worked, one man tied Daisy to the back of the wagon and another climbed on board to be near Lizzie. The rest of the field hands shuffled off to their shanty village for their evening's supper and rest.

During the ride, Lizzie passed in and out of consciousness. She opened and closed her eyes occasionally as she lay dazed, fighting the pain.

An hour's drive past the Pearsall Ranch, they reached the turn-off to the Utah Idaho Sugar Company Farm. When they neared Lizzie's homestead, Alberto sent the man riding beside Lizzie to alert the Mexican camp that the lady of the house had broken her ankle. The man jumped down and loped off towards the tents at the far side of the big barn.

Young Stanley spotted the farm wagon rushing up the road towards their home. He recognized his mother on the flatbed of the open farm truck. "Dad! Come quick. Something's happened to Mom. Dad! Dad!"

Moments later, the whole family came running around to the front of the small stone house. As the horse-drawn field wagon turned off the driveway, Alma ran up to the wagon in a panic. "Lizzie. Lizzie, me girl! What's happened? Oh, hell's bells! Is she alive? Please tell me she's not dead!"

Sean jogged up from the barn when he heard the commotion. He stopped directly behind Leo and placed his hands on Leo's shoulders in a gesture of support.

Alberto unknowingly drove over Lizzie's cherished marigolds and zinnias in front of the house. Alma walked alongside, holding Lizzie's hand.

"No se preocupe, Señor Hayes." Alberto reassured Alma. "La Señora vive. Si. Vive. Alive. Me entiende?"

Alma knew a little Spanish from years of working with the transient laborers from Mexico. He understood. A flush of relief washed through him. He turned and called out, speaking fast in response to the emergency, "Leo, Sean, Stanley, come over and help carry Lizzie inside to her bed. Myrtle, go turn down the covers. Quickly, everyone! Pronto! Pronto!"

Alma snapped his fingers impatiently and glared a fierce stare, willing the boys to move faster.

Alberto hopped down and joined the gringos. They solemnly lined up on each side of the flatbed wagon. They gently lifted Lizzie and carried her to the tailgate as a group. With Bud cradled in his right arm, Pedro climbed down and watched.

Little Honce stood on the porch, shocked at seeing his mother's inert body. He began sobbing. "Mommy! Mommy!"

Lucy ran up and helped support Lizzie's head as the men carried her up the stairs into the parlor. Lizzie's always neat hair hung loose, her braids nearly unraveled, her prized cellulite hairpins lost in the dark on the country road.

The men gently lowered her onto the feather mattress.

Alma lifted Lizzie's torn skirt and looked at the makeshift splint on her ankle. The ankle had swollen tremendously around the top of her muddy button-down ankle boots.

"Oh, hells bells! She's done gone and broke her ankle real bad. Oh, good Lord Jesus in Heaven! I don't know if we should try and take the shoe off or not. Oh, Lizzie, what happened to ya, me girl, me poor darlin' girl?"

Alma stood up. With a stricken look on his face, he gazed helplessly at everyone standing around gaping. He pointed at Leo and Sean with a snap of his finger. "Saddle up quick as ya can. Ride into Blackfoot and bring Doctor Parrish as fast as he can drive his carriage. Now, go!"

Alma snapped his fingers again in urgent imperative to hop to it. The boys turned and ran for the barn. Fear for Lizzie's life lent them speed. Mere minutes later, Alma heard their horses' galloping down the drive. The sound faded into the distance, heading towards town.

"Excuse, please." A middle-aged sun-wrinkled Mexican woman interrupted from the door. She pushed her scarf off her braided hair. Her teenage daughter came up behind her waiting for permission to enter. The older lady pointed to herself, her daughter, then to Lizzie. "We help. I Benita. Daughter Juanita."

Relieved to have someone to help, Alma invited her in with a sweep of his hand. "Yes. Yes. Thanks so much. Gracias. Please come in."

Alma didn't know what to do to help and feared causing further harm if he did the wrong thing. Myrtle sat down on the chair by the bed and held Lizzie's hand, her face pale from shock. With tears trickling down her face, she whispered, "Mom, I fixed the stew just like ya said. But now ya won't never know!"

The older Mexican woman directed her daughter to bring water as she bent to look at the swollen foot. "Shoe." She clucked her tongue off the roof of her mouth three times and shook her head once, sharply. "No good." She had to speak loudly to be heard over the crying children.

The young Mexican holding Bud bashfully walked into the parlor and handed the baby to Alma. Alma held him out at arm's length and looked him over for wounds. When he didn't find anything wrong, he hugged the baby to his chest. He looked at the young Guadalajaran worker's friendly face and smiled weakly. "Thanks. Gracias. Thanks."

Pedro Ortega of Guadalajara nodded wordlessly. He half-bowed as he stepped back, anxious to leave the emotionally charged room. When Pedro turned to go out the door, he stopped short in front of a young Mexican girl entering the bedroom. His breath caught when he glimpsed her lovely face framed with glossy black hair tied up in a bright red scarf. She held a bucket of water by both hands in front of her. They gazed into each other's eyes. She looked down demurely and pushed past him. Her long embroidered skirts and ruffled slips rustled against the floor as she sashayed in. Pedro turned and watched her kneel by the head of the bed. He promised himself he would find out her name as soon as possible.

Juanita tenderly washed Lizzie's face with a worn washcloth and cold well water. She pushed Lizzie's hair up off her forehead and cleaned the muddy runnels of dust combined with her tears. Juanita felt the large dark eyes of the handsome teenage laborer on her and risked a shy glance up from her labors. He stood leaning against the door jamb, watching her. She shyly glanced back down at Lizzie, trying to ignore the bold stares of the attractive stranger at the door.

Benita knelt by the bed and raised both hands to her face as she prayed for help from the Virgin Mary. She crossed herself, kissed her thumb, then leaned down and unbuttoned Lizzie's right shoe. Lizzie moaned, whipping her head from side to side in pain. When the shoe slipped off, Lizzie screamed piteously. The loud sound scared her children. The little ones began wailing helplessly. Little Honce ran over to his father and wrapped his arms around Alma's long legs. He needed to be picked up and comforted.

Holding baby Bud, Alma silently pushed his children out of the room. They went into the dining room, where they huddled fearfully, trying to soothe each other's fears. They struggled to overcome the shock of seeing their vibrant, active mother reduced to moaning in bed, unaware of her children.

Alma sat down wearily and watched the two nurses. Bud slept peacefully on his lap, sucking his thumb, his forefinger curled up over his little button of a nose. The Mexican señora and señorita gently undressed Lizzie and washed her. They pulled her hair into a twisted ponytail and tied it with a linen scarf to keep it off her face. They gently bathed the swollen ankle and then applied cool rag compresses to ease the swelling.

Myrtle stood at the doorway, keeping watch. Tears glistened in her eyes, ready to overflow. Finally, she ran over and resumed her place on the bedside chair. She took hold of Lizzie's hand and gave it a loving squeeze.

A couple of hours later, Lizzie opened her eyes and blinked. She saw Alma and Bud sitting on a chair beside her bed. She closed her eyes, this time not from unconsciousness but in sleep. A hint of color began slowly returning to her pale face. The young girl from Chihuahua attended her, squeezing a couple of drops of water from a clean wet cloth onto her lips. "Good. Good. Sleep. Sleep."

When the sun dipped below the ragged blue and purple western mountains, Alma asked Myrtle to serve her stew to the family. Myrtle worked listlessly, distracted by her mother's condition. Nobody felt like eating at first, but they all ate a little something. The sober family sat quietly that evening at the trestle dining table.

Myrtle carried plates of stew to Benita and Juanita, sitting with her mother. They nodded their thanks.

As darkness came, Alma put little Bud into his bassinette in the parlor. He lit a kerosene lamp in the parlor window as a homing beacon for the doctor. He lit another and placed it outside the front door.

The children came in and quietly said goodnight to Lizzie. She didn't hear them or respond. Alma gave each child a hug of encouragement and love. They trundled off to their beds with heavy hearts.

Around two in the morning, Alma woke up from a nap when he heard horses approaching. He rushed to the front door. Dr. Parrish drove up in his single horse buggy similar to Lizzie's but made of better materials. It had a tufted and cushioned black leather seat. Lizzie's had a plain wood bench. The Doctor's had a much bigger bonnet to protect him as he traveled in all sorts of weather. The Doctor's big strong gelding, Tex, wasn't even winded.

Sean and Leo wearily dismounted then rushed in to check on Lizzie. They feared she might have passed on while they fetched the doctor. When they found her resting easily, they both heaved sighs of relief.

The doctor pulled two bags out of the boot of his carriage and walked in to take over from the Chihuahuan nurses. One bag contained his portable tools. The other carried his medicines in small jars, tins, and cardboard boxes.

Alma put a hand on Leo's shoulder. "Thanks, boys. Now, go tend to yer horses, and the good doctor's, too. Then try and get some rest. There's some stew left on the back of the stove if yer hungry."

Without saying a word, Sean and Leo merely nodded before they walked out to take care of the horses. Too tired to eat, Leo dragged himself to the screened porch and crawled into bed. Sean climbed up to the barn's hayloft and collapsed on his quilts.

Dr. Parrish frowned as he examined Lizzie's swollen, bruised ankle. "Mister Hayes, um, I'm going to have to, um, try and set the broken bones. The trouble is that ankles are tricky to set, especially when they're, um, so badly swollen. Ankles have three different bones involved, and it appears she might have broken the two, um, that carry all the weight."

Clucking his tongue, he shook his head sorrowfully. The Doctor knew Lizzie might not ever walk properly again. He shrugged and rubbed his hands together. Then he opened the medicine bag and removed a brown glass bottle of laudanum suspended in alcohol. Since Lizzie slept, he let six careful drops of the opium tincture drip directly into her mouth from the glass stopper. He would have preferred for her to drink it down diluted in a glass of water.

A painful hour later, he had straightened out the ankle as best as he could. New splints held it in place. He hoped the ankle would heal straight and true.

Dr. Parrish left Alma with instructions she couldn't put weight on the ankle for at least a month. He ordered her to lay still and move only enough to use the bedpan. Then he recommended that Alma buy a lambskin with its fleece to place under Lizzie so she wouldn't develop bedsores. The Doctor quietly gave Benita instructions. They both spoke Spanglish – part pidgin simplified English, and part pidgin simplified Spanish – as they discussed Lizzie's ongoing care.

Dr. Parrish left Alma and Benita with a small supply of laudanum and a yellow box of powdered Bayer aspirin for the pain. He asked Alma to send him five dollars when things returned to normal.

"Thank ya kindly, Doctor Parrish, sir." Alma pulled a five-dollar bill out of his hip wallet. "We really appreciate yer coming out in the night like this. Won't ya please stop and rest a spell before headin' back?"

The Doctor removed his big gold pocket watch from his vest pocket, opened it, and wearily checked the time. "Thanks, but no.

The sun will, um, be rising in just a couple of hours. I need to be back at my clinic in case someone needs, um, to find me. Don't worry. I'm used to it. Good old Tex knows how to get me home even if I fall asleep, um, which I probably will. So, good night to you, Mister Hayes. I will try to come around, um, in a day or two when I'm out making the rounds in the countryside to see how she's mending. Just keep her still, and, um, let her body do the rest. Soak her ankle in rags, wet with, um, Epsom salts, as much as you can. I explained it all to Señora Benita. That's all we can do now. That, and, um, pray."

The doctor drove away into the pre-dawn night.

Alma slumped back against the doorframe, worried sick. He looked at Lizzie, sleeping pale and wan. Finally, he took his pillow and curled up on the braided rag rug to catch a couple of hours of sleep. Benita sent Juanita to her bed in the camp while she sat up, keeping watch for the rest of the night. She worried about the news of the revolutionary war and the bandito, Poncho Villa, down south in her home state of Chihuahua. She feared she might not be able to go home to the countryside near Colonia Juarez at the end of the harvest season. She also worried about Lizzie's recovery.

Sean woke up fuzzy-headed from lack of a full night's sleep. He crawled down the ladder from the hayloft and listlessly fed Brown Sugar. Then he grabbed his shaving kit and towel to start his day. The house seemed unusually quiet, even though it had to be around nine in the morning. He shaved, polished his teeth, and walked over to the kitchen door. He looked in and saw the kids sitting dejectedly around the table. Nobody spoke. Everyone looked glum. Sean forced himself to sound cheerful in the face of all the frowns. "Good mornin', everyone."

Some of the kids replied, distractedly, automatically, "Mornin'."

Sean walked over to the door to the parlor. Alma sat next to the bed holding Lizzie's hand. Alma looked up, with great dark circles under puffy, blood-shot eyes.

"Good mornin', Boss. How's Missus Hayes doin' this mornin', sir?"

"Well," Alma drawled, even more slowly than usual, "The doc said she can't walk fer a month at the minimum. She's come awake a couple of times. But she hasn't said nothin' yet. So, I still don't know what happened to 'er."

Juanita arrived to trade nursing duties with her mother, the bone-weary Benita. They spoke softly in Spanish before they kissed each other on both cheeks. Benita shuffled away to sleep in the heat of the day in the Mexican tent camp.

"Ya know, sir, when I was twelve years old, I went on me first cattle drive. I had the grandiose titles of assistant cookie and trail musician. But, what I'm tryin' to get at, sir, is that I learned how to cook. Nothin' fancy, of course. But I know me way around a wood fire, a skillet, and a Dutch oven. If ya wish it, I could maybe help out today, keepin' the kids fed and out of the house so Missus Lizzie can enjoy some peace and quiet."

"Why... thanks, Sean. That would be... much appreciated."

Greenwich Village
October 2010

Yawning, Josh stretched. "Hey, Art. I'm starting to lose my voice. No wonder. Just look at the time. The sun went down since I began."

Art stood up and arched backward, then forward and touched his toes. "Yep. Time to start cooking dinner. Fascinating story, Josh. I love how you talk with their colloquial accents. It makes everything so much more real and believable."

"Thanks. I've worked on reconstructing Grandpa Leo's story for some time now. I'm enjoying sharing it with someone at last."

Josh walked into the bathroom. Art went to the kitchen.

After washing his hands and face, Josh moseyed into the small gourmet kitchen and grabbed Art in a big bear hug. "Hi, there, you great big gorgeous hunk of meat."

"Hi, there, yourself, beautiful."

After supper, Art asked Josh what happened to Grandpa Leo after Lizzie's accident. Rather than starting a movie, they began a new routine for the young couple: supper, the story of Josh's ancestors, hot sex, and sleep.

Josh happily resumed telling the story of his Grandpa Leo.

Chapter 4: Marching Orders

Two days after Lizzie's accident, Leo ran into the barn. "Sean! Dad wants to talk to ya. Where are ya, Sean?"

Sean leaned out of Brown Sugar's stall and waved. "Here I am, Leo."

Leo rushed over. Sean put his hand on Leo's bare shoulder and tugged playfully at the bib straps of his overalls. "So let's go see if yer Dad has me marchin' orders ready yet. And it's glad I'll be to not work as cookie fer this rowdy crowd of Hayes wranglers and rustlers."

Leo looked up at Sean with a grin, pleased at his touch. Although they had nearly the same height of five foot eight inches, Leo walked barefoot, as always in the summer. Sean wore his two-inch heel cowboy boots, making him stride taller and more manfully. Leo looked up to Sean in many ways.

They entered the house through the kitchen to the parlor, where Alma kept Lizzie company by her sickbed. During their troubles, the hired hands went to the house for their orders and to make their reports. The bedroom parlor had become the farm and ranch operations office.

Lizzie had good color in her cheeks this morning, not the sickly bluish pallor of the past couple of days. The young Mexican girl, Juanita, attended Lizzie. She constantly replaced the moist rags over Lizzie's brow to keep her cool and over the broken ankle to keep down the swelling. She shared the chore day and night with Lizzie's ever-attendant daughter, Myrtle.

Leo and Sean stopped at the door. Sean held his big black Stetson hat in his hands in front of him. "Mornin', Missus Lizzie." He smiled and nodded to Alma. "Mornin', Boss Hayes. What can I be doin' fer ya this beautiful day?"

"Well now." Alma pulled his attention away from Bud, who sat on his lap sucking his thumb and following the movement of a fly crawling on the ceiling with his big blue eyes. "I figure it's time ya started earnin' yer keep around here as originally hired. Not that we don't appreciate yer playin' cookie fer our brood the past couple of days." Alma smiled and nodded his thanks. "But, we still have fences to be mended and strays to be brought in and branded before winter. Are ya still willin' to ride the fences, Sean?"

"Of course, sir. Do ya want me to start today?"

"Well now, by the time ya get yer stores together and line up yer pack mules, ya can be ready to start bright and early tomorrow mornin'."

"Would ya like me to cook today's meals, then?"

"Nope. Just prepare everythin' to do your job out on the back range. Young Myrtle will take over preparin' the food fer the household, now that Lizzie's well enough to give her directions and teach her recipes."

Lizzie opened her eyes and looked over at Sean. She wondered why Leo, standing behind Sean, had such a big frown on his face. "We thank ya fer cookin', Mister McKay. Who could've foreseen a day when I couldn't do me daily chores because of a buggy accident? But, Myrtle can take over now, so ya can get back to yer man's work."

"Yes, ma'am, Missus Lizzie. I'm just relieved to see ya gettin' better and all. Surely it won't be but a week or two, and ya will be up dancin' a jig fer all yer worth!"

"Oh, I'm afraid me dancin' days may be over, but I do feel like I'm startin' to mend. Thanks again fer yer help."

Sean nodded his head.

Lizzie winced when the young nursemaid placed another cool rag over her swollen ankle. Alma noticed. He frowned down at her black and blue ankle surrounded by a sickly yellow bruise. "Maybe it's time fer another drop or two of laudanum, Lizzie, me darlin'."

"No, Dad. Just let me catch me breath and get Myrtle started on the day's chores. Ya know how that medicine makes me drowsy. Once I drink some down, I'll just spend the rest of the mornin' nappin' and dreamin'."

Sean and Leo backed out of the sickroom before turning for the barn. "Hey, Leo, can ya show me where the barbed wire's stored?"

"Sure, Sean. It's in the small locked shed next to the tool shed. The one with the door locked up high so the little kids can't get in and hurt themselves."

They walked up to an old woodshed, nearly a six-foot cube. The hot desert sun had bleached its plank siding and split shingle roof a dull gray over the years. Sean unlatched the barrel bolt latch at the top of the six-foot door. They entered a stuffy dusty windowless storeroom. Sean saw stacks of wooden X frames holding nasty barbed wire wrapped around thick wooden dowels. *I hate workin' with this stuff. A body always gets hurt, no matter how careful. And dynamite! Now, why would Alma keep dynamite here? Oh! I guess they're still clearin' rocks out of the fields. Alma stores dangerous stuff here. No wonder he keeps it locked away from the younguns!*

Sean picked up a small wood box filled with U-shaped steel staples to fasten the barbed wire to fence posts. "Hey, me boyo, where would I be lookin' fer the wire cutters and pliers and heavy leather gloves that a body needs to work with this ornery fencin' material?"

"Why right next door in the regular tool shed. We should find everythin' ya will be needin'. Dad keeps the sheds well stocked. He has the hands trained to return everythin' to its rightful place. A place fer everythin', and everythin' in its place, as my Dad's always sayin'."

"Smart Dad ya got there, me boyo. Takes a lotta work to run a big spread orderly like with good methods and good organization."

Leo smiled proudly as he led Sean to the large tool shed next door. Sean carefully locked the rusty iron slide bolt behind them, securing the dangerous storage shed.

Leo indicated where tools hung neatly ranked on an old plank wood wall. "Here's the different sizes of pliers. And over here're wire cutters. And there's the post diggers and post-pounders. See? We've got everythin' that ya will need."

"Um-hm, looks like yer right, me boyo."

Sean gathered together what he wanted. He put small loose supplies in a used gunny sack that still smelled of clean dirt. Leo took the bags as Sean filled them and placed them by the door. "Um, Sean, I was wonderin'… if'n… ya might not… ya know… wanna take me along with ya. To help out with the fence mendin'. And to keep ya company in the evenin'."

Leo held his breath. He didn't dare move. He only knew he didn't want to be left behind to tend kids and weed sugar beets, not when he could be out riding the back range with his hero and new friend.

Sean turned to Leo and looked him up and down appraisingly. "Humph! Well, I guess ya might be growed up enough to ride with me. But I don't need no homesick pup whinnin' away fer his Mommy and causin' me nothin' but grief on the trail!"

Leo looked up at Sean with his best puppy dog eyes, his eyebrows raised to a point between his eyes in a silent plea. "No, Sean, I promise. I'll be good and I'll help ya and I'll make myself useful and I'll do whatever ya say. Please, Sean?"

Sean chuckled, then reached out and ruffled Leo's shaggy brown hair. "Well, ya gotta get Boss Hayes and Missus Lizzie to agree. If they give their permission, then I guess I would welcome yer company."

"Yippee! Yahoo!"

Leo took off in a mad hurry running for the stone house as fast as his dirty bare feet would carry him. He made an exuberant jump and touched his heels together. "Yippee!"

Leo slowed down at the kitchen door. Little Lucy and Honce, playing in the backyard, looked at Leo like he had gone plumb loco. Leo took a deep breath to compose himself and reviewed what he would say.

Sean followed more slowly. He arrived in time to hear the last of Alma's answer. "Why when I was your age, I was drivin' ox carts, haulin' timber fer the railroad with Pa and me older brothers. I guess ya could handle a couple of weeks away from home, learnin' how to handle yerself campin' out on the trail. Lizzie, ya don't have no problem with 'im goin' away fer a couple of weeks, do ya, me darlin'?"

Leo looked anxiously at Lizzie. She smiled serenely, already floating in the haze of Laudanum's medicinal tincture of opium. "That would be sweet. Have a nice trip, Leo."

Leo spun around to rush out to tell Sean, only to crash into him standing right behind him. They both stumbled until they found their feet, hands on each other's shoulders. Leo grinned and grinned, his eyes big with excitement at the idea of going out on the trail with Sean. Sean smiled back with his lopsided grin, sharing Leo's happiness. Sean looked over at Alma. "Boss Hayes, the boy here can't go out in the desert wearin' only his dungarees. And he'll be needin' a hat and gloves and boots, too, doncha know."

"Well, now, I suppose ya could tighten the belt on me ol' woolies from me wranglin' days. Go check in the barn and see if ya can't find what ya need."

Leo grabbed Sean's elbow and yanked him out of the parlor bedroom. "I know where Dad keeps his ol' tackle. Come on. I'll show ya!"

He pulled Sean, half running and half laughing, out to the barn. They found an old matted pair of Alma's angora chaps in the tack room. Though old, they had long curly sheep's wool on the outside for protection against cactus, sagebrush, and the elements. Leo pulled them off a wooden dowel and slipped them on over his coveralls.

They scrounged around in the discards. Leo tried on different used hats, mismatched leather gloves, work boots, and worn-out cowboy boots. They eventually had Leo fitted out in a mishmashed version of Sean's handsome cowboy attire.

Leo strutted around like a peacock, showing off his new cowboy gear. But, the woolies slipped down off his narrow hips and tripped him up. When he staggered, he lost the wide-brimmed hat. He made a frantic grab for his chaps with one hand and his hat with the other, then froze. He looked up sheepishly. Sean stood with his fists on his hips and a smirk on his face, chuckling at Leo's antics. His eyes sparkled in merriment. "Well now, me fine boyo, we're gonna have to fix these here clothes if ya wanna wear 'em on the trail. We can't be havin' yer britches fallin' down, now, can we?"

Leo shrugged with a blush. Sean shared his roguishly lop-sided smile and raised his eyebrows mockingly. "Here. Give me those woolies. Let's punch some new holes in the belt so ya can cinch 'em up good and tight. Then, go find a piece of ol' leather we can trim and put inside the hatband so it'll stay on yer head."

Used to running barefoot, Leo stumbled when he turned around. He had never worn high-heeled cowboy boots before. He staggered over to the workbench against the wall and scrounged through pieces of old leather bridles and harnesses.

Finally, they had Leo outfitted like a working cowboy with boots and wooly chaps. He wore a long-sleeved collarless shirt, a big bandana tied around his neck, and a big brown hat. The hat's sides curled up while the front and back curled down. Leo held his head up high, proud to be all grown up, and looked over at Sean for approval.

Sean teased him by pretending not to notice. Then he ran over, grabbed Leo by surprise, and knocked off his hat. He scrubbed his knuckles on Leo's sun-bleached hair, making him squirm. Leo laughed boyishly, happy for the attention but frus-trated Sean didn't compliment him on looking all grown up. They broke apart and stood there, gazing at each other with big smiles.

"Ya ready, me boyo?"

"Yep. I'm ready, Sean."

Chapter 5: Riding Fences

Leo had trouble sleeping that night on the open screened porch. His tossing and turning on their narrow bed earned him an irritated elbow from his younger brothers more than once. At first light and first cockcrow, he rushed to pull on his new cowboy gear. He wobbled on his high-heeled boots over to the barn as fast as he could, half afraid Sean might have changed his mind and left him behind. Leo breathed more easily when he detected light inside the barn's open door. He slowed to an unsteady march. Grinning sleepily, he helped Sean load their packs on three big sturdy pack mules. The mules all had long ears, bulky bodies, and horse-like tails.

"Mornin', me boyo. Better get Bluch saddled up. I've almost got us loaded. We need to leave at first light."

Leo's grin faded when he remembered his Dad telling him he couldn't take his favorite horse, Daisy. "Ya know we don't have another horse broken to pull the buggy, Leo. How about ridin' Bluch instead?"

Leo had whined, "That fat old horse?"

Alma had frowned. "So long, son."

Reluctantly, Leo led the mature mare out of her stall. Although disappointed about not riding Daisy, his excitement returned by the time he had Bluch saddled and bridled. After he checked the cinch twice, he stood back and shook his head sorrowfully. *Yer not as pretty as Brown Sugar, but yer gonna be my ride fer the biggest adventure of my whole life.* He looked her over critically. She had dark charcoal gray legs, tail, face, and ears with a lighter mottled gray body. Horse breeders called the coloration Blue, which is why Alma had named her Bluch. She had foaled three times.

Leo shrugged, then led Bluch over to join Brown Sugar and the three bulky pack mules. The mules' rigging included long rawhide lead lines and pack saddles with breeching straps and breast collar straps to keep the heavy packs and panniers in place. The lead mule already had a thick leather blanket on his back with eight heavy spools of barbed wire carefully tied with a rope of braided rawhide.

The second mule had handles of shovels and post diggers sticking up above its head and back. Leather-edged canvas panniers hung off both sides of its back, filled with tools and supplies for mending fences. It also carried the farm's brand, a large iron S inside a U on the end of an iron rod.

The third mule, a chuckwagon on legs, transported their store of food supplies and cooking implements. Each of the three mules also carried two large tarred canvas water bags with corks or zinc twist caps in the top drinking corners. The bags allowed enough evaporation to keep the water cool, although the tar tainted the flavor of the water. The horses also carried tin canteens of drinking water.

Leo and Sean tied on their .22 rifles, saddlebags and gunny sacks of clothing. Then they secured their bedrolls of two blankets tied around a pillow behind the saddles.

"Hey, Leo. Where's the Diamond matchbooks, eh? We don't want to have to reinvent fire while out in the wilderness, doncha know!"

"No, no, I've got a whole box full of 'em in the same bag as the spices and salt."

"Well, that's all right, then."

Sean tied one mule's lead to the other, then tied the front mule's lead to Brown Sugar's saddle horn. He looked over at Leo. "I think we're ready to leave. Oops. Can't forget the guitar, or we'll have no music to while away our long evenings by the fireside."

Sean rushed up the ladder to the hayloft and took a last quick look around to see if he had forgotten anything else. He grabbed the black leather guitar case in his left hand and backed down the ladder with his right hand clutching the ladder rungs.

Sean carefully secured the guitar case to the back of his saddle, inserted his left foot in the stirrup, and flew up into the saddle. With a raise of his head and a nod, he signaled Leo to do the same. Leo grinned and leapt up onto Bluch's back.

Sean turned off the flame in the barn's kerosene lantern. Leo followed Sean leading the pack mules out of the barn at a sedate pace. The sun lit the clouds above the purple eastern mountains a bright lavender. They turned onto the farm road before anyone else stirred in the house.

They headed up the lane toward the end of the farmed land where the barbed wire fences began. They passed milk cows and early farm hands heading to the barn for the first milking of the new day.

Leo couldn't wipe the smile off his face. A tingle of excitement buzzed through him, from his toes to the unaccustomed cowboy hat on his brow. When Sean looked over, he saw Leo's teeth glaring in the morning sunlight. It made him smile, too. He remembered many times he had felt the same way, leaving early in the morning, setting out on a trip to new places and new adventures with friends riding at his side.

When they passed the last outbuilding of the farmstead, Sean began humming the melody to *She'll Be Coming 'Round the Mountain When She Comes.* Leo hesitantly joined in. Then Sean took up singing the words. Together, they belted out the campfire favorite at the tops of their lungs. Their right arms bent at their elbows, pulling on imaginary train whistles every time they sang, "When she comes, toot toot!"

That first day, they mended a couple of loose barbed wire strands along the way. Twice they inserted floater posts to lift sagging wire off the ground. They reached the end of the irrigated fields by evening, far south and east of the farmstead. They rode along the border of the cattle range until the sun began to set.

Sean called over to Leo, "Let's stop here fer the night. There's no water, but it won't be our last dry camp on this trip, I don't suppose."

They both climbed down off their horses a bit stiff. They paused a moment to stretch. Leo's knees ached from the constant movement, and his back hurt from sitting in the saddle all day. He moaned out loud. "Ridin' to Blackfoot and back never left me so sore."

As he helped unload the mules, Leo discovered a seam in his jeans had rubbed a small saddle sore on the inside of his right leg. It stung when he bent over.

They spent their second and third days riding slowly in a southerly direction. They stopped as needed to replace broken strands of wire. They cut down small trees to make fence posts. The searing sun bore down on them mercilessly. The hot desert air sucked away their sweat but didn't cool them off. Every footstep carried them a little higher into the Grand Teton Mountains and closer to the huge Fort Hall Indian Reservation on the ranch's southern border.

Leo noticed bluish-white patches along the northern sides of the tallest peaks, remains of snow that hadn't melted all summer long. The cleared and irrigated fields had given way to sagebrush and cactus, unclaimed virginal desert. They climbed higher and entered foothills, where they came across the occasional small stream. Good grazing grasses, sego lilies, and oak brush grew in the foothills, replacing the bone-dry desert. Their travels became greener and softer the higher they climbed.

Sean looked out approvingly over a grassland nestled in a gentle swale between two softly rounded foothills. He spotted several cows and a couple of half-yearling calves grazing on the far side. "Why, Leo, this land is plumb beautiful, doncha know. Ya wouldn't even know that the desert lay baking just a day behind us, now, would ya, me boyo?"

Leo took a deep breath of the cooler mountain air, nodding yes, content to be riding in these pastoral hills. He looked up at the mountains, blued and misted by the air, where several taller foothills nestled between them and the far-off up-thrust of rugged granite peaks.

Leo pointed over to where a small natural creek widened out. Tall pine trees grew alongside a clump of quaking aspens, taking advantage of the free-flowing water. "This would make a nice place to camp tonight, wouldn't it, Sean?"

"Right ya are, me boyo. Let's make camp here and get cleaned up fer a change."

Grimy from sweating at mending fences and eating dust on the ride, they both longed for a cool bath and a change of clothes. They carefully tethered their horses and mules where they could find grass for grazing and reach the creek for water.

"Here, give me a hand, will ya?"

Sean began unloading the mules. Leo walked to the other side of the mule from Sean and helped lift off the heavy panniers. They carried the bulging saddlebags over and hung them off the ground on a tree branch.

An hour later, they had the mules unpacked and the horses unsaddled. They curried and brushed down the horses. Wordlessly, they worked in tandem, already a well-practiced team. They picked up the pannier holding their food stores and cooking equipment and carried it twenty feet upstream to a flat area by the small pool in the tiny babbling creek.

Leo kicked and cleared an area for the fireplace while Sean assembled a small iron tripod spit to hold their pot over the flame. Leo gathered an armful of deadfall for firewood and laid the fire. Sean fetched the beans he had soaking in a pot with the lid tied shut so the water wouldn't spill out. He hung the pot from the tripod's black iron hook.

Once the fire blazed up, Sean cut up a slice of salted pork to grease the bottom of their cast-iron skillet. He diced an onion and added it to the pan. He pulled the pan away from the flames to simmer. Leo hung their consumables high up in a tall pine tree, so animals couldn't steal their food while they slept.

Leo walked back to the campfire. He stood watching Sean bend over and give the beans a quick stir with a wooden spoon.

Sean looked up with a frown. "Leo, me boyo, ya smell to high heavens." Then he dramatically lifted his arms and pretended to sniff, grinning mockingly. "But then, so do I, doncha know. Hows about we take ourselves a bath in the stream and make a change of clothes?"

"Gee, Sean. I don't think ya smell bad, though ya are a bit ripe, now that ya mention it. But, a bath's a great idea! Let me get the towels and soap from my packs. I'll be right back."

Sean checked the pots and then added a couple of small deadfall branches to the fire. He toed off his boots. Then he pulled off his belt and chaps and left them near his bedroll by the fire pit. He strutted over to the stream. The snowmelt water had cut a bed in the sandy ground about a foot lower than the surrounding grassy pasture. Sean sat on the natural bench ledge, pulled off his clothes, then ran into the creek. Laughing boisterously, he waved at Leo to hurry up and join him. "Yahoo! Hells bells but this water's colder 'n a witch's teat!"

Leo ran over, stumbling as he pulled off his clothes. He laughed at Sean bent over in water up to his knees, scrubbing his bandana between his hands in the running water. Leo threw his clothes on the grassy bank and hopped into the creek. As he waded over to Sean, carrying his mother's homemade block of lye soap, he admired Sean's strong lean body glistening in the setting sun. Leo handed him the bar of soap. "Here, try some of this. It'll help get out the dirt and sweat."

"Thanks, me boyo. It'll sure be nice to have clean clothes next to me skin again, and that's fer sure."

Sean scrubbed the soap against his bandana, then handed it back to Leo. They had their clothes soaped, rinsed, and spread out to dry on the grassy higher riverbank a few minutes later. Sean turned to Leo, holding the bar of soap. "And now it's time to get ya cleaned up, me boyo, and yer gonna love it!"

Leo stepped back, alarmed. He scrambled and stumbled on the slick stone creek bed, trying to get away. "No, Sean! I can wash myself!"

Sean rubbed the soap between both hands until they were slick with suds, grinning an evil smirk. His teeth showed like an attacking ferret. "Come here, me boyo. Ya need cleanin' bad." He chuckled evilly.

Leo instinctively pulled in his elbows and crossed his arms in front of his skinny stomach. He just knew Sean would go for his ribs. Sure enough, Sean grabbed him and slid his slippery, cold hands along Leo's scrawny ribcage, tickling him like crazy.

Leo laughed and jumped around, struggling to pull away. "No! No! Don't! I can't take it."

"Stand still, ya little heathen. Stand still and let me soap up yer filthy hair. Otherwise, yer gonna have to sit downwind from me all the night long!"

Sean pulled Leo up tight against his body, held him close with his left hand, and rubbed the soap all over Leo's scalp with his right hand. Leo stopped fighting and reached up to help lather his hair. He couldn't stop chuckling.

After Leo rinsed the soap from his hair, he grabbed the soap and turned to Sean. "Turnabout's fair play. Now it's my turn."

They laughed together as they stood in the babbling stream, soaping each other up. They both ignored their semi-tumescent state of excitement and took pleasure in getting clean. Finally, shivering, they stepped out of the river bed, picked up their flannel towels, and dried off. Sean rubbed the towel over his hair. "I'm gonna fetch me some dry britches. These aren't dry enough yet."

Leo nodded. "Yeah. Me, too."

They walked over to their saddle bags hanging on the tree by the fire. They pulled on clean pants and then hung their flannel towels over the branch to dry. Barefoot, they strode back to the stream, picked up their damp clothes, and hung them up to dry.

"Ah, this is the life, me boyo, to be sure." Sean sang out in his clear tenor voice, lilting the words as though singing. "Warm sun, gentle breeze, clean water, and dinner cookin' over a hardwood fire. Ah, and now it's time fer a little music to add a bit of charm to the lowerin' of the sun. Whaddaya say to that, me boyo?"

"Oh, yeah. Please sing somethin'. That would be great."

Sean took his guitar out of its case and returned to the fire. He sat on the ground, legs crossed Indian style, and leaned back against a smooth boulder, strumming the guitar as he tuned it.

"Sean?"

"Yeah, me boyo. What is it?"

"Sean, would ya please teach me to play the guitar? I just love music, and I'd do anythin' to learn to play."

Sean stretched his legs out wide and flat on the grassy pasture and patted the ground in front of him. "Why sure, me boyo. Come sit here between my legs, and I'll show ya the basic fingerin'."

Leo self-consciously lowered himself between Sean's spread legs, afraid to lean his bare back against Sean's hairy chest. Sean grabbed Leo's stomach, yanked him back tight, and handed him the guitar. He reached around and positioned Leo's hands on the neck and belly of the instrument. Sean spoke softly in Leo's ear, which gave him goosebumps. "This is how ya hold the guitar, me boyo. Now, just rest back against me, and let me sing ya a song."

Leo slowly relaxed his head back onto Sean's left shoulder. Sean pulled the guitar tight into Leo's lean stomach and played the introductory chords to *Oh, Danny Boy.* Leo shivered with delight when he felt the strumming chords vibrate through his stomach down to his crotch. Sean began softly singing the words in Leo's ear. Leo closed his eyes and drifted into a lovely space he had never visited before.

Sean's clear vibrating voice sang *Danny Boy* softly, intimately, heartbreakingly, just for Leo. *Oh Danny boy, the pipes, the pipes are calling, from glen to glen, and down the mountainside. The summer's gone...*

Leo couldn't move. The vibrations on his stomach from the guitar and on his back from Sean's singing left him spellbound. He hardly dared breathe for fear of shattering the breathtaking enchantment. Softly, sweetly, nearly whispering, Sean leaned over and sang with his mouth touching Leo's ear. *And all my dreams will warm and sweeter be - If you'll not fail to tell me that you love me - I'll simply sleep in peace until you come to me. - I'll simply sleep in peace until you come to me.*

As the gentle vibrations of the last chord dwindled to silence, the boys sat enthralled with each other's company, thrilled with their intimate closeness, totally at peace with the world.

Sean carefully placed the guitar aside on the grass before he wrapped his arms around Leo's bony chest. He gazed at the fire with a gentle smile as night settled around them. Leo leaned back with a peaceful glow on his face as he remembered the music.

Leo took a deep breath savoring Sean's clean, masculine scent. He opened his eyes but didn't want to move away from Sean's warm embrace. He turned his head and looked up at Sean, smiling. Sean looked down at him, smiling back roguishly, the dimple in his left cheek winking in the waning light.

Sean's stomach growled. Leo chuckled. The magical spell dissipated into the evening air like the call of a will-o-the-wisp. Sean pushed at Leo's shoulders. "Methinks it's time fer supper, me boyo. Now get up, and let's finish cookin' so we can eat. Whaddaya say?"

Reluctant to give up the moment, Leo slowly turned onto his hands and knees, then sat up. He looked at Sean leaning against the boulder. "Words fail me, Sean. That was the most beautiful thing I've ever heard. Thanks fer sharin' yer music with me." Leo smiled, leaned in, and whispered in Sean's ear, "I'll never ferget this moment."

Sean whispered back, "I won't either, me boyo."

Then, Sean pushed Leo away. "Give me a hand up, me boyo, and let's tend to the inner man. Then we can relax some more."

Leo stood up and offered Sean his hand. He pulled Sean up to his feet by taking a big step back. "Allee-oop!"

Sean carefully placed his guitar on top of the small boulder. Then he stepped over to the fire and poured the beans into the iron skillet. Next, he added dried chili peppers, salt, pepper, and ground cumin to the beans. He opened a tin of canned tomatoes with his hunting knife and poured the contents into the skillet. He gave it all a stir and moved the pot closer to the hot coals.

"Another quarter-hour, and we'll have ourselves a right royal feast. Let's go check the tethers before we eat, so we can just relax after supper. Whaddaya say, me boyo?"

Hungry as bears, they ate supper that evening with great gusto. "I think maybe we should go huntin' tomorrow. Wouldn't some fresh meat be nice? I think a young doe. Yep. That'd give us somethin' to flavor our meals fer several days. Let's camp here in this beautiful spot fer another night and take a rest break from mendin' fences. Whaddaya think, me boyo?"

"Gee, Sean, I think that would be great. It sure is beautiful here."

Leo glanced over at Sean, watching the flicker of firelight wash over his face and torso. *And yer sure beautiful, Sean.* Then, he pulled his eyes away, looked at his plate, and began eating again. In the silence of his mind, the words of Sean's song haunted him. *And all my dreams will warm and sweeter be if you'll not fail to tell me that you love me.*

Overcome with emotions he had never experienced before, Leo stopped eating. He yearned to be embraced, sung to again, secure in Sean's arms again. He didn't recognize his longing as love. He didn't know how to express his feelings. Slowly, he walked over to the Dutch oven and poured the remains of his plate back into the pot.

Leo walked over and sat down close to Sean. Sean chewed his food, apparently lost in thought, hypnotized by the flickering firelight of the little fire in front of them. Leo crossed his legs Indian style, placed his arm around Sean's neck, then laid his head gently down on Sean's shoulder.

Sean stopped eating. He looked over and smiled peacefully at Leo. His eyebrows rose up in a question. "Is everythin' all right, me boyo?"

Leo snuggled in closer. "Um-hm." He reveled in Sean's warmth and strong muscles. Leisurely, he took another deep breath, memorizing Sean's pleasantly musky, masculine fragrance. "Um-hm."

Sean put down his plate and wrapped one arm around Leo's waist. They sat silently, watching the fire die down to glowing crimson embers.

"Leo, sorry, but we need to stir the fire and add more firewood. Here, let me get up and do that while ya spread our blankets over there beside the fire. All right, me boyo?"

After tending to their chores, they walked over to the stream and relieved themselves. They strolled back to the fire, removed their pants, then stretched out side by side on their old wool blankets and quilts.

Sean opened his arms wide. "Come here, me boyo. Come sleep with me tonight. There, there. Ya've been needin' a hug all evenin', now, haven't ya?"

They pulled each other into a warm embrace. Both took breathless delight in the heat and textures of each other's smooth skin, lean muscles, and soft hair. Sean took Leo's hand and gently placed it on his swollen member. He then squeezed Leo's throbbing erection. "There, there. That's what ya've been needin', isn't it!"

They fell into an intense kiss, a kiss overflowing with affection and love and passion. They fell into each other's hearts and mouths with a sensuality and hunger that surprised them both. The intimacy felt so natural, so pure and right that nothing could stop them.

Sean slowly moved his kisses away from Leo's lips, kissing a trail down his neck and across his chest. He kissed, nibbled, and licked first one nipple, then the other.

Leo watched with eyes open wide in delight. *Oh! I never knew a man's teats were so tender and sensitive. I've gotta remember to do this fer Sean.*

Sean moved lower. He kissed down the center of Leo's ticklish stomach, following his treasure trail lower and lower. Leo wanted to see what gave him such pleasurable goosebumps. His head rose higher and higher as he paid close attention. He made mental notes of exactly what raised his excitement so quickly and dramatically. When Sean's kisses reached Leo's erection, Leo's eyelids drooped in ecstasy. He gasped and squirmed with low moans of exquisite pleasure. At the same time, he paid close attention to what caused such overwhelming excitement. He wanted to give Sean the same thrills.

When Sean roughly shoved Leo's knees up and apart and moved his kissing and licking even lower, and then lower still, Leo's eyes opened wide in astonishment. *I never knew a body could do that. Oh! That's… That's… Oh my!* He couldn't wait to practice on Sean. His mouth watered at the thought. Suddenly he just had to kiss and taste Sean. His passions rose to a fever pitch. He twisted around and pushed his face into Sean's groin. He took a deep breath, then began enthusiastically applying his newly learned skills. They began sucking at the same time, caressing each other intimately as they soared higher and higher. Sean licked his middle finger and slowly inserted it into Leo's clenching bottom. The new sensation sent Leo spasming over the top. Sean happily joined him.

They sat up and hugged their sweaty torsos together. They kissed gently, sharing their breath, sighing in pleasure, love, and relief.

After they calmed down, they lay spent and at ease, shoulder by shoulder and hip to hip. Leo's head rested on the pillow of Sean's strong arm. They gazed up at all the myriad bright stars overhead. A full Harvest moon glowed so brightly it cast shadows from the pine trees around them. Leo's heart overflowed with questions and longings, full of songs and love, near to bursting with happiness and contentment. He twisted a bit and put his left hand over Sean's heart, thrilled to feel life beating in his chest. He caressed the wiry forest of reddish-blond hair on Sean's chest and kissed Sean's cheek.

Leo hesitated, afraid Sean would reject him, or worse, laugh, but he braved on and whispered, "Sean. I think... I think I'm in love with ya. Yer just so wonderful."

To Leo's great relief, Sean hugged him tighter and responded huskily, "And I think I'm fallin' in love too, me boyo. It started the first moment I saw ya ridin' hell-bent fer leather down the lane to the barn, yer face glowin' with life, that first day I arrived at yer father's farm!"

"Oh, Sean."

Without saying anything more, Sean drifted off to sleep. Leo lay there peacefully listening to Sean's soft snores. *Boy, that sure was a lot different from when I first learned about sex.* His thoughts drifted back to when he had just turned eleven. He had begun waking up in the mornings with erections. Hair sprouted above his penis, on his testicles, and under his arms. His growing spurt had added nearly a foot of height in just ten months, with all its attendant aches, pains, and periods of unexplained moodiness and grouchiness. His voice started cracking, which embarrassed him. The sweat glands on his nose grew visibly larger, extruding an oily sweat when he rubbed his nose with his forefinger. He didn't understand anything happening to his body.

Naturally, his parents didn't discuss growing up, sex, intercourse, or secondary sexual characteristics with him. Nobody discussed such things except the older guys on the school playground. Society didn't consider it proper.

As Leo grew drowsier, he remembered back to a warm spring day during fifth grade when Miss Dingle dismissed the class for recess. Everyone raced outside, consumed with spring fever. Old Nicholas pushed his way out ahead of everyone else. Everyone called the big dumb Russian immigrant Nicky. The teachers held him back in first and second grade because he couldn't speak English, leaving him the oldest and biggest student in the one-room school. At least once a day during recess, he shouted, "I'm the King of Bunker Hill!" Truth be known, he was simply the biggest bully on the playground.

That warm spring day had Nicky's blood pumping. He started a game of leapfrog with all the boys. Then he held up his hands to stop them. "Whip! Crack the Whip, ever'one. I'm the head, now grab on and don't let go!"

All the boys hustled to join hands as Nicky took off running. He dodged right for a few steps, then turned left in a huge circle which sent the boys on the tail end running faster and faster. Suddenly he changed and ran in a tight circle, then shot off in a straight line. Leo, one of the smallest boys, ended up last. His feet barely touched the ground as he leaped along. The momentum swung him giddily across the weedy dry grass of the yard. He shouted and laughed gleefully from his speed.

Nicky surprised everyone when he stopped and spun in place. He pulled all the younger boys along behind him into a tightening spiral. Leo danced at the end with increasing momentum. He became afraid of losing his grip and flying off to crash to the ground. But, to his and Nicky's surprise, the momentum spun him around full circle, and he crashed into Nicky.

They both went sprawling.

The other boys stopped running. For a second, Leo felt relieved to land on top. Nicky would have squashed him. But then Billy screamed, "Dogpile! Dogpile!"

All the boys jumped on top of him, crushing him anyway.

Smashed between all the wriggling boys and Nicky's big body, Leo and Nicky both grew noticeably erect. The other boys finally got up and staggered away, laughing and pushing each other on the shoulder. Nicky copped a feel of Leo's erection with a knowing leer before he shoved Leo off. After they got to their feet, Nicky walked over to two of his followers and motioned for them to follow him.

Nicky strutted up to Leo. He pushed out his chest and shoved Leo. "So, Leo. Ya got any hairs on yer prick yet? Huh, do ya?"

Leo blushed and looked down at the ground.

Nicky grabbed hold of Leo and indicated for Tommy, his schoolyard lieutenant, to grab Leo's other arm. Then he snarled out, in a near whisper, "To th' creek, boys. Now!"

The four boys rushed over to the dry creek bed behind the school playground. Scrawny leafless trees and a few pines screened the gully from the school. The older boys claimed it as their hideout during recess. Nicky pushed Leo up against a tree trunk and groped his crotch. "I asked ya if'n ya had hair on yer dick, yet, Leo."

Nobody had ever fondled Leo before. He found himself both scared and aroused, growing harder by the second. Leo glanced up. Nicky's ugly pimples revolted him. He meekly nodded his head yes.

"So, let's see, then."

Leo turned his head, disgusted at Nicky's sour breath. Nicky nodded to his two compatriots. They knew what to do. They rushed Leo and jerked down his breeches and long johns, leaving him exposed to the air. When Leo began struggling to get away and pull up his pants, the boys held him tight. Nicky grabbed hold of Leo's penis, roughly moving his fist up and down. Leo's mind went into overdrive, reeling with emotions and feelings he had never experienced. The attack felt wrong and ugly. But the new sensations on his tender male parts felt unbelievably good – until he shouted and orgasmed for the first time in his life. "Ohhhh!"

Laughing tauntingly, the boys dropped Leo's arms. Nicky finished milking Leo's erection and let go. Leo leaned over and rested his hands on his knees, struggling to catch his breath. He

72

didn't understand what had just happened. Nicky stepped up and wiped his hand on Leo's hair with a smirk. "Now ya knows what t' do with yer prick, doncha? Yeah. Now ya knows."

Nicky and his pack laughed and ran away, leaving Leo with his pants down around his ankles.

Leo stood up slowly and pushed his fingers through his mussed-up hair. He looked at the slick semen from Nicky's hand and gave it a tentative sniff. Leo wiped his hand on his pants, then pulled them up and tied the rope belt. *Wow.* He shook his head as he stood up. *That sure was somethin'. I loved the way it made me feel, but it didn't seem right to me. Huh-uh. Not right at all. That wasn't nice of them to do that to me.*

The rest of the afternoon found Leo depressed and uncomfortable, though he couldn't have explained why. He felt dirty. Yet, secretly, the memory of all the new sensations of surging passions thrilled him.

Making love to Sean sure is a lot different from gettin' jerked off by that nasty Nicky and his pals. With Sean, it's pure music and joy and wonderment. With Sean, it's beautiful. Gee. Now that I'm becomin' a man, my life's movin' faster and faster like I'm on the tail end of a real-life game of crack the whip. Yep, my life's just a game of whip - and I love it!

As Leo drifted off to sleep, he remembered how, once he had learned about masturbation, that's all he wanted to do. But he never found any privacy to pursue such personal pleasures. Occasionally, he managed to sneak off to the hayloft and rub one out as fast as he could. But fear of his father or one of the farmhands catching him deterred him from doing it very often. A couple of times, he had enjoyed a more leisurely exploration of his budding sensuality when he rode out of sight at the swimming hole or when he laid down in a dry ditch far from spying eyes. *But that was never anything like making love with Sean.* With that happy thought, he turned, cuddled up to Sean, and slowly drifted off to a dreamless sleep.

They slept peacefully in each other's arms, all night long.

Chapter 6: Valor

Sean woke up about five-thirty the following day just as the light became noticeable over the purple mountains to the east. He nudged Leo. "Mornin' pardner. Let's get dressed quick like and hike up the creek. Maybe we can find us a deer while it's takin' its first drink. Come on, now. Up and at 'em. And keep it quiet. Let's not spook the wildlife and scare the deer away."

Leo stretched and yawned a big yawn. "I'm awake, Sean. Let me grab my rifle, and I'm ready to go."

They quietly pulled on their clothes and hats. Sean buckled on his sharp hunting knife and Colt .44 six-shooter. *Gol-dang, but I wish I could find me a black holster.* He picked up his hunting rifle and filled the magazine with five live rounds, then shoved extra bullets in his pants pocket.

Leo picked up and examined his old hand-me-down .22 before loading the magazine to its capacity of ten bullets.

Sean waved for Leo to lead the way. They walked upstream on the soft weeds of the creekbed to muffle their footsteps. After about twenty minutes, Leo spotted movement a hundred yards away. He immediately bent over and fluttered his hand low to the ground. They both dropped down to check out the prey without being seen.

A buck and a doe stood in the creek. A younger doe bent down to drink. Leo raised his eyebrows then nodded at the smaller doe. Sean pointed with his chin in a gesture to take the shot if you have it.

Leo knelt and took careful aim. Concerned he would miss and look like a clumsy kid, his hands quivered in overcompensation. He found the deer's shoulder in his gun sight then aimed more towards the stomach. He took a deep breath, pulled the butt of the rifle securely into his right shoulder to steady his aim – and squeezed.

Bam!

The staccato echo of the shot answered back from the mountains less than a second later, only much softer.

Bam!

The little doe dropped at the side of the creek. The buck and larger doe bounded across the stream, leaping in graceful high arcs in their panic to escape. Their white tails stood straight up, a warning flag of danger.

The great white hunters took off at a run then slowed as they drew near the carcass. The doe's hind legs twitched a bit, but it lay dead at their feet.

Sean gave Leo a congratulatory slap on his back. "Clean kill, pardner. Good shot, to be sure."

"Thanks. It is a nice lookin' doe, isn't it?"

"Do ya want to field dress 'er while I go fer the pack mule, or shall I dress it out?"

"It's my kill. I'll dress it out. If that's all right, Sean."

"Sure, pardner. I'll be back in half an hour or so. Be sure to save the heart and liver fer us if ya can."

"Okay, Sean. See ya soon."

Leo withdrew his old Bowie knife with a buffalo horn handle. Then he pulled out a small flat whetstone from his pants pocket. He spat on the stone for moisture and began sharpening the blade. When the blade reached razor sharpness, he tested the edge and pocketed the whetstone.

The young hunter straddled the small doe and flipped her onto her back. He thrust the knife into its breastbone at a sharp angle, just like his dad had shown him over the years. He did it carefully so Sean would be proud of him. After he finished, he looked down at his clothes and frowned. *Doggone it, I got blood splattered everywhere. And here I thought I was bein' so careful like and neat. Oh well. Knowing how Sean likes his cleanliness, I'll just have to wash up again. Doggone it all!*

Leo pulled the carcass over to the stream, took off his boots, and waded in. Using his hands as scoops, he threw fistfuls of water into the body cavity to wash out as much blood and gore as he could.

This's hard work, field dressin' a doe by myself. Sure is a lot easier helpin' Dad or one of the farmhands. But I did it. And I didn't taint the meat nor cut meself, neither. Maybe I am growin' up a bit, after all. Leo smiled when Sean rode up, leading Bluch and one of the pack mules. He didn't want Sean to see him covered in blood, so he leaned down and frantically scrubbed his hands and forearms.

"Hey there, pardner. I see ya finished already. Good job."

Sean slid off Brown Sugar upstream from the doe. He dropped his reins over Brown Sugar's head so he wouldn't stray. He pulled the mule over to the dressed-out carcass. Flies swarmed up from nowhere, attracted by the blood. Leo swatted them away, then splashed the open body cavity with more water, scooped up in both hands.

"Here we go, pardner. Let's put this beauty on the mule and get back to camp. I'll help ya butcher it up. Then we'll put some to smokin' and some to cookin'. It'll be good to have meat in our diet fer the next few days, won't it?"

Sean looked critically at Leo's blood-splattered clothes and face. He wrinkled up his nose and frowned. "Then ya can take yerself over to the creek and apply lots of soap – again!"

Leo shook his head. *I knew he would say somethin' about me bein' a bloody mess. I just knew it! Doggone it all!*

They returned to camp and hung the carcass from a high pine branch, head down to drain the blood. Working as a team, they began carefully carving out the cuts that would make for easy cooking and smoking. They knew most of the meat would go to waste with just the two of them. They didn't need to skin and butcher the whole carcass. Instead, they focused only on the better flank steaks and rib steaks.

Leo stopped a moment, knife in hand. "Sean. I've been thinkin'."

"Yeah, pardner, what about?"

"About last night."

"Yeah?"

"About us being intimate and affectionate and, ya know, touchin' and all."

"Um-hm. And?"

"Well. I was wonderin'. Is that normal fer two guys to like each other that much? I've never heard of guys likin' each other like that before."

Sean thought a moment while his hands worked at carving the meat off the carcass. "Listen, pardner, as ya get out in the world, ya will find different people live lots of different ways from the way yer family lives on the farm. Fer some of us, lovin' a man is natural and good and beautiful. Fer others, only a woman's soft ways can win his heart and fire up his loins. Fer a few others, they can take their affections from anyone, man or woman, under the right circumstances."

Leo stopped working for a moment and straightened up to stretch his back. He frowned in concentration. "But... was it wrong? Was it a... a sin?"

"Well, now. I reckon some would call it a sin. Here now, pardner. Hold back the skin there while I slice away the fat that's holdin' it to the meat. Yep. The way I figure it, every man has to decide fer 'imself what's right and what's wrong. The Mormons and the Catholics, certainly, would consider it a sin. Leastwise, if it's done in public or becomes common knowledge. If it's kept private and discreet, nobody says anythin'. The real religious preach the only reason two people should make love is to make a baby. Here, now. Hold that skin back more and pull a little harder. That's it. Now, the way I figure it, me boyo, there must be a whole lotta sinnin' goin' on in the world. There's surely lotsa men and women sharin' their affections and their bodies with no intention of makin' babies. But, like I said, every man has to figure it out fer 'imself and make his own way in the world, as best he can."

"So... um... you've known other boys and men... um... in the... um... same way as we did last night, that is to say?"

Sean stopped butchering and gave Leo a sympathetic smile. He understood the confusion and conflicted feelings troubling Leo's mind. "Pardner, I've given me heart to a couple of menfolk and to one sweet girl over the years. I've expressed the passions of those romantic urges a few times, too, like last night. But I never did anythin' I would regret. I live my life by the motto, to thine own self be true."

Leo nodded then turned back to the work at hand. "But… um… how did ya know I was gonna be one of them guys that would welcome yer affections, rather than one who wouldn't?"

"Sure, but it's because it just happened all-natural like – an easy, mutual thing, doncha know. I believe if ya have to force a thing, then it's no good. *Then* it's a sin, in *my* mind. But, don't worry, me boyo. Ya still have many years ahead of ya to try different things till ya find out what ya like fer yerself."

Leo's hands stopped working again. He couldn't bring himself to look Sean in the eye. "But, Sean, I think I have found out what I like. And it's you!"

Leo looked up at Sean from under half-closed eyelids, fearing Sean's reaction. Sean gave Leo a warm lopsided smile and a big wink. His eyes danced merrily. "Oh, Leo Hayes, stop bein' all flirtatious like a tart and a flibbertigibbet and help me finish up with this here job of bucherin' before the whole day passes us by. We still have to build up the fire so we can smoke this here deer meat into spiced venison jerky."

Sean turned back to slicing thin steaks out of the doe's flank with a smile on his face. Leo sighed in relief and returned to butchering the doe. "Was that a quote from the Bible or the Book of Mormon, Sean?"

"What's that, pardner? What're ya referrin' to?"

"Ya said ya lived by the motto of to thine own self be true, or somethin' like that, right?"

"Ah, yes. Well, that's a quote from the old English bard, William Shakespeare. It's from a play I studied in high school called *Hamlet*. The whole piece, as I remember, goes something like, um, above all, to thine own self be true. And it must follow, as the night the day, thou canst not then be false to any man. Shakespeare wasn't a Bible prophet, me boyo, but he understood human nature. Besides, I think it's good advice, so I try and live by it. Now, do ya understand?"

"Um-hm. Could ya cut that piece of gristle there? It's not lettin' go of this last piece. That's it. Thanks."

An hour or so later, Sean pointed downstream. "Here, now, pardner. Before ya get yerself cleaned up, how about draggin' the remains of this carcass across the creek and some distance away downwind? Otherwise, the wolves will want to join us fer supper tonight."

"Okay, Sean. Just help me lower it to the ground, and I'll drag it away."

Leo jumped on Bluch bareback and rode away, dragging the remains of the small carcass behind him. When he returned, he went for his lye soap and flannel towel before Sean could say anything. He walked over to where Sean knelt, building up the fire. "I'll wash yer back if ya wash mine."

Leo beamed a mischievous smile when Sean looked up from the fire in surprise. Sean immediately grinned right back and lifted his eyebrows at the idea. His eyes glittered as he unbuttoned his shirt and rose quickly to his feet. "Last one in's a monkey's uncle!"

They raced for the creek, throwing their clothes and boots left and right. They splashed into the stream, dancing and whooping and hollering, soaping each other up and wrestling gleefully.

When things calmed down, Leo retrieved his bloody pants and shirt. He put them in the creek and held them down with heavy rocks so the fresh running water would pound them clean.

Later that evening, they enjoyed a hearty dinner of fried venison steak and onions with beans leftover from the night before. They finished with an apple partially baked in the ashes for dessert. Sean made half a pot of fresh coffee. They sat down with their backs against a small smooth boulder by their campfire. The fire burned low and steady, smoking two dozen long thin strands of flank steak dangling off green twigs stuck in the ground. To make a simple kind of venison jerky, Sean had sprinkled the thin strips of deer meat with salt, pepper, sugar, and chili seeds. By morning, they would have jerky that would last a long time.

Leo smiled bashfully as he remembered how delightfully last night's lesson had ended. "So, Sean. Would ya please show me how to play the guitar? And fer real this time?"

"Sure, pardner."

Sean retrieved the guitar from its case hanging in the nearest pine tree. A gentle breeze came down from the mountains, carrying the perfume of faraway snow and the clean, crisp scent of pine trees. Sean took a deep breath and savored the fresh air, so different from the dusty desert air of lower altitudes. As he walked back to the boulder, he tuned the guitar and then sat down close to Leo. Sean took the strap off his back, put it over Leo's shoulder, and handed him the instrument.

"All right, now. Take the guitar and hold it like I showed ya last night. That's it. Now put yer index finger here, yer middle finger here, yer fourth finger here, and yer little finger here."

Sean patiently positioned Leo's inexperienced fingers on the ebony fingerboard. "That's good. Now, press lightly to hold the strings against those little ribs there, then strum the strings with your right thumb. Like that. Yeah. That's good."

"Gee, that's beautiful."

"That's the C major chord. It's the most used chord. Many songs start and end with it. Can ya remember where yer left hand is and where yer fingers are? Okay then. Let's try the F major chord next. Put yer index finger here…" And so the patient teaching progressed. Sean took things slowly. They stopped when Leo complained his fingertips felt like they were developing blisters.

"Don't worry, pardner. With a little practice, yer fingers will develop just the right calluses so ya can play fer hours. Here, let me take over and play fer a wee bit. I need to keep in practice, too, doncha know."

Sean leaned back with the guitar in his lap. He tucked his left leg under the guitar with his right leg out straight. He began with the chords to the chorus of *When Irish Eyes Are Smiling*. "See, Leo, this is why I taught ya those basic chords. Ya string 'em together one after the other like this, and it makes music. Now, rather than sing the words, I'm gonna sing the names of the chords so ya can follow along in yer mind and learn them. Now listen."

Sean sang the melody to the chord names rather than the lyrics. Leo heard the words in his mind as he followed the tune, *When Irish hearts are happy, All the world seems bright and gay. And when Irish eyes are smiling, Sure, they steal your heart away.*

80

At the same time, he repeated the names of the chords, remembering how they felt in his fingers. Nodding to the beat, he began singing the names of the chords along with Sean. By the third time through the chorus, he knew the names and understood how they flowed to make music.

After the lesson, Sean pulled a beat-up paperback out of his saddlebags. He sat down by the fire and began reading. Leo interrupted before Sean had even read a paragraph. "Have ya read lotsa books, Sean?"

"Um-hm. Hundreds, to be sure."

"Hundreds? Really?"

The only books Leo had ever read were at school. His parents only owned a Bible and a Book of Mormon, which he found hard to struggle through. Reluctantly, Sean put down his book and turned to Leo. "Sure, but I love to read. I've read so many great books by some of the greatest authors in the world. Of course, I can only afford the dime novels, but still. My Dad's little home library of dime novels included important books by really famous authors. And pardner, they really expand the mind, what with their stories of pirates, and wars, and strugglin' to make good. Oh, yeah, to be sure, I love to read a good book, all right."

"Would ya mind readin' to me? Ya know, read out loud?"

"Why, sure."

Sean patted the ground next to him and gestured with a sideways tilt of his head. "Come sit next to me so ya can follow along and practice yer own readin' skills at the same time."

Leo scooted over and sat right up against Sean. He happily slung his arm around Sean's back and placed his chin on Sean's shoulder. Sean held the book propped up on his bent knees, angled to catch the firelight.

They read until the light faded. Afterwards, they relaxed side by side, enjoying the full harvest moon and bright stars in the night sky. The Milky Way glowed in a soft white band across the dome of the inky heavens. Sean pointed low on the horizon. "See there, Leo? There's Orion. Or is it O'Riley? Or maybe O'Brien? Do ya know Orion?"

Leo chuckled and nodded. "Yep. Dad taught me to recognize some of the constellations one night when we was campin' out on a deer hunt. I see him. O'Riley or O'Brien. Real funny, Sean. Real funny."

They took a minute and added more fuel to the fire so it would burn long and low, smoking the jerky all night long.

As they sipped strong black coffee the next morning, Sean inspected the jerky. "Well, pardner, looks like the jerky dried out and got smoked good and proper. Let's pack it away to munch on when we're on the road. Whaddaya say?"

"Okay, Sean. But, I want to taste it first." Leo picked up a ten-inch strand of thin leathery meat and pulled off the end with his teeth. "Um. It's tasty but tough as nails. Gonna take a lotta chewin' to get it soft enough to swallow, but it's real tasty."

"Well, I'm glad ya like it."

Sean stood up, shaded his eyes with his right hand, and looked across the small valley. "See those cattle grazin' across the way, there. Let's go check those calves fer brands and see if we ought to claim 'em as Utah Idaho Sugar Company livestock. Come on. Saddle up. Time to get back to work."

After they checked the tethers on the mules, they saddled up Bluch and Brown Sugar. Sean tied the branding iron to the cantle behind his saddle and checked his pockets for matches.

"All set, pardner. Let's ride!"

They mounted up. Sean led the way at a lively trot across the pleasant grassy swale of their picturesque little valley. Leo felt strong and rested. He took delight in the cool mountain air and the warm morning sun. He thrilled to the movement of Bluch's big muscles beneath him as she warmed to the morning run. He felt more alive than ever before as he willingly followed Sean. The breeze of their passage blew in his face, exhilarating him.

When they neared the small cluster of cattle, they found a dry heifer, two lactating heifers, a yearling, and two calves. Sean slowed to a walk then dismounted far enough away he wouldn't spook the cattle. He walked towards them with his hand held out. "Whoa, there, now. Easy, easy. That's the way. Stand easy, me pretties, and let me check yer brands. Whoa, now. Whoa, there. Stand easy."

Leo sat on his horse and watched Sean go to work.

Sean walked back to Leo and Bluch. "Well, pardner, one of the calves isn't branded, but its ma is, so we need to get it branded all legal like."

Sean looked back over Bluch's withers at their camp, where a wisp of smoke still rose from their fire pit. He calculated the distance. "It's not too far, Leo. I think I'm gonna lasso the calf and lead it to the fire back at the camp. It won't take longer than making a new fire here. Keep an eye out in case they take off runnin' and keep out of the way. I can handle this just fine. Okay, pardner?"

Leo nodded. "Got it."

Sean leapt up on Brown Sugar and pulled the coiled reata off the saddle ties. He gently nudged Brown Sugar towards the small herd. Sean dropped Brown Sugar's reins about twelve feet away from the maverick calf. He set his flat loop to spinning and tossed it over the calf's head. He tightened the lasso with a sharp jerk so the calf couldn't pull loose.

With a deft move, Sean wrapped his end of the rope around his saddle horn. Using just his knees and heels, he communicated to Brown Sugar to back up and take up the slack in the rope. When the calf felt the rope pulling it away from its mother, it dug in its feet and bellowed piteously. The other cattle looked up, their eyes opening wide in alarm. One snorted angrily and pawed at the ground, shaking its head from side to side.

Sean backed up Brown Sugar, then turned and headed slowly back to camp. When the calf resisted the lead, Sean yanked on the rope and pulled it along. It stumbled a couple of times but eventually began following, crying out piteously for help. Its mother followed placidly.

They made an odd parade walking back across the narrow meadow. Sean led the calf at the end of his rope. The mother heifer followed its baby. The other cattle reacted according to their herding instincts and followed docilely. Leo rode flank, twenty feet behind the small herd. They walked at a leisurely pace towards their smoldering campfire.

When they neared the camp, Sean stopped and untied the branding iron. "Hey, pardner. Come take the iron and put it in the fire. Pile on more wood and get it good and hot. I'll keep the tension on the rope, so the little beast doesn't get away."

"Sure, Sean. Here I come."

Leo rode over, took the branding iron, and trotted back to the fire. He hopped down and thrust the iron into the center of the hot coals. He added a couple of medium-sized branches plus a handful of twigs over the coals. They burst into hot flames with a whoosh, forcing him to scramble back away from the heat.

Sean sat calmly on Brown Sugar, watching the cows chewing their cud. He crossed his right leg up over the saddle, looped it around the saddle horn, and made himself comfortable. He rolled a slim cigarette and lit it up while he waited for the iron to heat.

As soon as they stopped moving, the herd closed up into a loose cluster, then bent their heads to eat the lush grass and weeds growing around the camp. The dry heifer sat down and lazily chewed her cud. She watched Sean calmly as he moved Brown Sugar around, keeping tension on the lasso. Well trained as a cattle horse, Brown Sugar knew what to do. They had played out this scene time and again over the years down South on the cattle trails. Sean's slightest movement communicated his desires to Brown Sugar almost telepathically.

Leo picked up the handle of the branding iron and lifted it from the fire. It glowed a dull orange. "This hot enough, Sean?"

"A bit more, pardner. Don't get impatient. If it's not hot enough to burn the mark through the fur, then ya just have to do it over again so the brand will take. And that's sloppy work. We're not goin' anywhere."

Leo thrust the iron back into the fire, then scrambled back away from the heat of the glowing coals. He squatted down and sat on his haunches. His arms dangled off his bent knees as he watched Sean and Brown Sugar moving around, keeping the rope taut. The calf, in the meantime, stopped squalling and moved up to find its mother's udder. With its front legs splayed wide to lower its head, it nursed. Its mother chewed her cud contentedly, mindlessly.

Sean finally called out, "That should be hot enough by now. Let me see."

Leo pulled the branding iron out of the coals and showed Sean the red hot end.

"Yep. Keep it hot, now, till I call fer it."

Sean pulled his piggin' string off his saddle and dismounted with a leap. Brown Sugar knew to keep the rope tight even without a rider. Sean walked down the rope to the calf. His gloved left hand slid along its taut straight line. The piggin' string dangled loosely in his right hand.

As he neared the calf, Sean set the loop on the piggin' string. Then he yanked on the lasso around the calf's neck and jerked it to the ground. It fell on its side with a bellow. Its mother turned around in a hurry, eyes wide with fear. Sean calmly but quickly tied three of the calf's legs together with the piggin' string. He stood up and waved at Leo with a broad sweep of his hand over his head. "Bring me the iron, now. Quick!"

Leo grabbed the hot iron and jogged over to the fallen calf. The mother cow spun around to face this new threat and took a threatening step forward with a snort.

Leo handed off the branding iron like a baton in a race.

Sean knelt beside the calf with his right foot firmly pressing on its belly. His left knee pushed against the calf's stomach to hold it still. Sean pressed the burning hot iron against the calf's flank. It burned through the thick, coarse hair instantly, branding the tough skin of the calf. The calf bellowed as though dying, struggling frantically to get loose. Sean held the brand for three seconds, then casually tossed it to the ground. It burned the grass with a damp hiss and quickly cooled to a dull gray. Sean pulled the slip knot on the piggin' string and backed away. The calf sprang to its feet. Sean released the loop of the lasso. The calf rushed over to its mother.

Before Sean finished coiling up the lasso, the calf stopped crying, took a munch of grass, and began chewing. The heat of the branding had barely touched its tough, thick hide.

To be helpful, Leo walked over and retrieved the branding iron. He waved his hand in front of his face, fanning away the acrid stench of burnt hair. His face scrunched up in distaste. He looked down at the backward S inside a larger U, already cooled to its natural dull gray of rusty forged steel.

The boys didn't want the cows to soil their camp with manure, so they led them back to where they found them. For the rest of the day, they rode up into the hills around the fertile valley, checking for more cattle without finding any. They enjoyed the ride, taking pleasure in each other's company and casual conversation. As the sun lowered to where it nearly touched the hazed blue mountains to the west, they headed back to camp for their last night in the picturesque valley.

Early the following morning, they packed up their smoked venison jerky. The rising sun reflected off high billowing clouds, casting a soft golden glow over the little vale. They both stopped and looked around. The reflected light made the greens of the grasses and trees greener, the blue of the bachelor buttons bluer, and the lavender of the thistles more vibrantly pink against the dark green weeds along the creek bed. Leo felt uplifted, like a man who had come into his own at last. He treasured up in his mind the cool grass of the pasture, the cold bite of snowmelt creek water, and the warmth of snuggling together with Sean at night. *I don't never wanna forget this, not fer the rest of my life.*

They saddled their horses and loaded the mules, ready to go back to work riding the fences. As they stood side by side making a last-minute check of their camp, Leo impulsively hugged Sean and kissed him on his cheek. Sean hugged him back but then pushed him away to arm's length. "Careful there, pardner. Ya gotta be careful about displayin' affection in broad daylight where someone might see ya."

Leo felt like Sean had slapped him. Blushing, he staggered back a step. His hurt feelings showed clearly on his face. Sean saw and understood. "The better part of valor is discretion, pardner. Hasn't anyone ever told ya that before?"

Leo planted his gloved fists on his hips, clearly annoyed. "Nope. Hells bells, Sean, yer the one with all the highfalutin' high school words. I've only just graduated from eighth grade this past spring. I have no idea what in tarnation yer even talkin' about."

Leo felt insulted as well as rejected. He turned away angrily and checked the cinch on Bluch with a hard jerk. Motivated in part by hurt feelings and in part by a spirit of mischief, Leo neatly planted a small jagged rock beneath the back of Brown Sugar's saddle blanket. He placed it where it would poke Broke Sugar when Sean sat down in the saddle. Frowning, Leo mounted Bluch and watched.

Sean swung up onto his saddle. Brown Sugar snickered, reared up, and danced around in a circle, nearly bucking Sean off. Sean leaned forward and stood up in his stirrups, releasing the pressure on the saddle skirt. Sean patted Brown Sugar's neck. "Down, boy. Whoa, boy. That's a good boy." He sat down again and glanced over at Leo. "Wonder what's got into Sugar this mornin'?"

Brown Sugar reared again and nearly threw Sean off his back. Then he bucked out twice and pitched Sean forward with a hard jerk. Sean jumped off and held the reins in his left hand. "Whoa, boy. Down Brown Sugar. Down boy. That's my good Sugar."

Sean inspected his saddle, rigging ring, and cinches. "I don't see anythin' wrong. Maybe there's a wrinkle in the saddle blanket or somethin'."

He dropped the reins, unhitched the saddle, and pulled it off. The blanket slid partway off, dislodging the pebble. Sean heard it fall to the ground with a soft plop.

Sean dropped the saddle blanket, then leaned over and picked up the sharp little pebble. "Now, how the dickens did that get…"

He turned a glare at Leo. Leo's bright grin confirmed his suspicions. "Why, you!"

Sean threw the pebble in mock anger, hard as he could, and struck Leo in the chest.

"Ow. That hurt!" Leo burst out laughing, unable to hold it in any longer.

Disgusted at being the victim of one of the oldest practical jokes in the book, Sean slapped his saddle blanket back on Brown Sugar, then hefted up the saddle with a grunt. He couldn't stay angry, though. When he stood up from cinching the saddle, he burst out chuckling, shaking his head at yet another of Leo's dumb antics.

They mounted up and began the day's journey. Sean turned toward Leo, riding beside him. "Listen, pardner. I didn't mean to upset ya. All I was tryin' to say is we need to, well, be discreet. Be careful like. Use good judgment. Look before ya leap, doncha know. All I was tryin' to say is some folk don't wanna see two guys likin' each other too much. Nobody approves of expressions of affection in public. In private, that's a whole nother matter but not out in the open in broad daylight."

Leo's grin turned into a pout. "Okay. So I gotta think before I hug ya. Well, that ain't what I was feelin' to be right at the time! I don't see why I have to go around hidin' from people. Blazes, but life sure ain't fair, no sirree Bob!"

The mules struggled against their lead reins. They planted their legs and pulled back. Sean yanked hard three times on the lead mule's reins until it took a step and began walking. He turned his attention back to Leo. "Well, pardner, there's a lotta folks that feel the same way, doncha know. They were the men who left the big cities and the churches and the watchful eyes of their women-folk and went west. They preferred to hunt, trap, and explore. They would do anything to get away from endless rules and judgments. They're the men who explored the world and opened up the West back a hundred years ago and more. Didn't ya ever wonder why a body would head out into the wilderness on his own, without womenfolk to help make his life easier? Did ya ever wonder why the old-timers always had their saddle buddies and cronies, their pardners and sidekicks? Did ya ever think about all the great teams of men who went out to live their lives the way they wanted?"

Leo thought about what Sean said as they rode slowly by the barbed wire fence on their left. After they topped the first hill away from the lush valley campsite, the landscape reverted to rocky desert, dry and barren. The sparse grass and short wild oats turned a dry golden straw color. Low lying shrubs of scrub-oak hugged bare outcroppings of granite. A few stunted sagebrushes grew here and there, adding a gray-green color. Tumbleweeds grew, still rooted in the rocky soil. They only saw an occasional snake, lizard, stink bug, jackrabbit, or mouse flickering by, almost out of eyesight. Occasionally a hawk flew up so high it became a speck in the vast blue sky.

"Hey, Sean. Where's the wilderness nowadays? Where do men go now? We don't have a wild west anymore, not like when Butch Cassidy and Buffalo Bill and the mountain men and trappers went west. The whole country's civilized. Farmers have plowed the land and fenced it with barbed wire everywhere ya look."

"Exactly me point, pardner. Exactly me point. It's because we have to live around other folk, all bunched up in towns and cities, farmsteads and ranches, that we have to be careful not to offend others. I grew up in a righteous Mormon family with ties back to Brigham Young and all, but I'm not a religious person by nature. But, the good Lord said, 'Do unto others as ye would have others do unto you.' That's called the Golden Rule, pardner, and I think maybe Christ had it right. That's the truly proper way to live."

They came upon a nearly dry feeder creek and stopped to water the horses and mules. They walked upstream to refill their canteens. Leo washed his face, then stood up and popped his hat back on his head. "Sean, did all the hunters and trappers and explorers like the affections of other men?"

"Well, now, I'm only sayin' that many adventurers could get along as easily without womenfolk as with. And many, I dare say, shared more than the dangers of the road and the stew in the pot, if ya get my meaning?"

Sean wiggled his eyebrows up and down at Leo, which made him chuckle. He knew what Sean meant.

"When yer on the trail drivin' beeves to market, there will be some as do and some as don't like men. There will be some that will welcome yer friendship and others that won't. That's just the variety of human nature, pardner. And nothin' we can do about it, neither. Just be discreet and treat people with the same respect ya want them to show ya back. It's a private thing, after all. I mean, ya don't see married people kissin' and huggin' out on the streets in broad daylight, do ya? No sirree, ya don't! Even a varmint and a woman of questionable virtue don't go at it out in the street like dogs in heat. If ya keep yer affections private, it's none of anybody's gol dang business what ya do after lights out. That's what I say."

"Well, ya sure do say a lot of it, and that's fer dang sure!" Leo laughed at the drop-jawed response on Sean's face. Leo took off trotting ahead, leaving Brown Sugar and Sean behind in the dust. Sean calmly lifted his bandana up over his mouth and nose.

The next night, they enjoyed a simple supper of fried-up canned ham, gravy made with coffee, and a potato baked in the ashes. They snuggled up side by side on their bedrolls. They crossed their arms above their heads and gazed up at the sky. Eventually, they made slow blissful love again.

Chapter 7: Job Offer

Sean and Leo spent the next couple of long hot days mending fences. Sometimes they strung new wire or tightened up old wire that had sagged. Sometimes they replaced fence posts. They developed sore backs from the hard work of digging post holes. Even with gloves, they both developed painful blisters on their hands from stringing barbed wire. Their heavy perspiration dried on their shirts and pants, leaving rings of salt.

On the third morning, they came to a ninety-degree turn in the fence. The tautness and weight of the wires had broken the rotted corner post off at its base, leaving the stump in the ground. They didn't have any more posts. No trees grew within sight for them to cut down and use, so they had to improvise.

"Hey, pardner," Sean concluded after he looked around at the barren land, "I guess we'll have to make a deadman to hold up the fence here."

"What the blazes is a deadman, Sean?"

After dismounting, they both stretched up tall and then leaned over to their sides. Riding non-stop for hours left their lower backs and legs sore from the exercise.

"Well, normally, ya take a big stake and drive it in the ground at a sharp angle, then ya run wires stapled to the post back to the stake and tighten 'em up. But since we're out of posts, we'll have to figure out somethin' else."

Sean carefully stepped over the fallen wires and stood by the broken post, looking around. "See there, pardner? There's a boulder we can use for our deadman. Now, all we gotta do is run the wires. We're gonna need a lever we can leave in the twisted wires after we tighten 'em. So, take the hand saw and cut us two pieces of scrub oak about a foot long. Make sure they're good and strong, Okay?"

While Leo cut the rough trunks of the small bushes, Sean pulled on heavy leather gauntlets. He untied the partial spool of barbed wire from the pack saddle, leaving their last full spool.

Sean stapled the loose end of the wire to the top of the fallen fence post and then wrapped the wire around it as tight as possible.

91

Then he walked the spool over and around the low outcropping of rock and back. He added several more staples to secure the ends. By the time he had repeated this process halfway down the post with another row of wires, Leo had returned with two lengths of scrub oak.

"This is the darnedest stuff! Tough as doornails. It didn't want to be cut fer nothin'. But, here they are. Hope they'll do."

"They look fine, Leo. Give me one and copy what I do. We'll raise that post back up good as new, doncha know."

They each took a stick and walked halfway to the deadman rock. Sean inserted his stick between the top two strands of wire and twisted them around, turning the stick over and over. The top of the post began lifting off the ground. Leo caught on and did the same with the lower double strands of wire. About forty twists later, it became harder and harder to make another turn. The post now stood upright, pulled taut against the wires.

Sean walked back to the post and plucked the top rung of the fence. Good and tight, the wire gave a low thrum. Sean nodded. "Yep. That did it. Now that deadman will hold up this here fence corner fer years to come. Ya see?"

"Good job, Sean. Yer so clever. I never would've thought of that!"

"Just comes from experience, pardner. Once you've seen it done, it's pretty easy to copy, doncha know."

Both boys dripped with sweat running in streaks through the dust covering them from head to foot. They bent over and carefully slithered between the new strands of barbed wire to return to their horses. They removed their heavy leather gloves and protective leather cuffs. Sweat trickled down their backs between their shoulder blades. More perspiration made dark Vs below their belts.

"Gol dang, but I could sure use a wash-up. Wouldn't ya like one too, Sean?"

"Yep. But we only have drinkin' water. Let's move on a bit and see if we can't find a stream before sundown. We'll use the drinkin' water if we have to, but only if we have to."

Leo reluctantly wiped his face with his dirty bandana necker-chief, then climbed into the saddle. "Okay."

As evening set in, they stopped at a sandy stretch of clear ground and set up camp. It took half an hour of scrounging to find enough twigs and brush for a small cook fire. After they laid the fire, Sean stood up before lighting it. "Let's clean up before we start cookin' supper, whaddaya say?"

"Oh, yeah. That sounds good. Too bad we didn't find water."

"Well, grab yer towel and a water bag. I'll fetch a towel, too."

They returned to the fire pit. Their panniers of cooking uten-sils and food stores sat on the bare ground close to the fire. Sean shrugged. "Ah, desert livin'. Ain't it just the bee's knees?" He pulled off his sticky shirt and wrinkled his nose at it. "Ah, fer a boiled shirt." Then he shouted out, theatrically, "My kingdom fer a boiled shirt!"

Leo looked at Sean like he had gone plumb loco. Leo didn't understand the literary reference to 'My kingdom for a horse.' Leo stripped off his sweaty shirt, wishing he had a freshly laun-dered shirt as well.

Sean twisted off the zinc lid of a damp water bag and held a corner of his towel over the pour spout. He tilted it just enough to dampen a corner of the towel. "Waste not, want not. Never use water ya might need. But just a little bit can be a pleasure."

Sean carefully wiped off his brow and cheeks, then his neck. He cleaned his hands and forearms before wiping out his smelly armpits. "Ah. Sure now, and that's better by a long shot."

He turned his towel over and dried off what little moisture remained. Leo copied him move for move.

It took a while to fry leftover venison steaks in a slice of salt pork. Sean added a splash of coffee to the pan to make red eye gravy for the tough, dry meat. It took a lot of chewing, but they were hungry and ate every bite. They wiped their greasy fingers on their dirty Levi's when they finished.

Leo poured coffee into their tin travel cups. Somehow the cup always felt hotter than the coffee. He took a sip. "Gee, that needs some sugar."

Without asking, Leo grabbed Sean's cup. He stepped over to their supplies, searched through the spice bag, then added a couple of pinches to each cup. He stirred the coffees with his forefinger.

Leo walked back and squatted down. He held the cups out level during the move until he sat on the ground with his legs crossed, then handed one to Sean. Sean took a sip, made a face, and spit the mouthful of coffee out on the fire. "What the? Why… that was salt ya put…"

Leo couldn't help himself. He pointed and burst out laughing. "Ha. Ya should've seen yer face. Hahaha!"

Sean tossed the cup aside as he lunged for Leo. "Why, ya little brat. I'll get ya fer that!"

Leo moved his cup of sugar-sweetened coffee aside, but when Sean landed on him with a crash, it spilled anyway.

Sean growled, threateningly, "Why ya no good, trouble-makin', whippersnapper." He roughly flipped Leo over onto his stomach and pushed his face into the sand. "Try to feed me salt, will ya! I'll make ya eat dirt, ya lousy son of a gun."

Leo stopped laughing and began twisting around as hard as he could. Spitting, he struggled to lift his face out of the dirt. He bucked up repeatedly, trying to throw Sean off his back. Sean placed his right elbow on Leo's back just below the ribs and leaned his weight into it.

"No. Don't. Uncle! I give. No! No! Stop!" Leo squirmed frantically to escape the punishment. Finally, he managed to slip out sideways like a crab. He rolled over and leapt to his feet, brushing the dirt off his face with both hands. He darted back out of range.

Sean sat down Indian-style and shook his fist at Leo, shooting him looks to kill. Leo chuckled as he brushed himself off the best he could. "Oh, ya shoulda seen the look on yer face. It was price-less. Priceless, I tell ya."

Leo chuckled softly, pleased with the prank despite the pun-ishment. He walked over to their pile of panniers, retrieved the guitar, and placed the strap over his bare back. His fingers searched for the dominant seventh chord, learned the night before, then strummed the strings with his thumb. After only a few days of lessons and practice, his fingertips had developed little calluses from the guitar strings.

Sean spread their bedrolls on the ground by the dwindling fire. A wisp of smoke spiraled up in the still, warm air. They sat down back to back since they didn't have a boulder to use as a chairback. When Leo's fingers began to tire, he handed the guitar to Sean. Sean started to pick out the melody to *My Old Kentucky Home*.

"Sean."

"Yep."

"I've been wonderin'."

"Yep. About what?"

"About the first time ya fell in love. I don't mean just the sex stuff. I mean when ya knew in yer heart with that funny special feelin' that ya never wanted to be apart, but to stay nearby and help and be held close every night."

Sean smiled warmly, charmed by Leo's struggle to express his romantic feelings in words for the first time. "Well, now, it was, let me see, about nine years ago. I was just a little older than ya are now. I was the assistant cookie on me third cattle drive that fall. We were goin' from southern Arizona all the way up to the railhead at Kansas City.

Sean stopped playing the guitar. He laid back on the quilts, folded his hands behind his head, then crossed his legs at the ankle. He gazed up at the nearly full moon. "I was gettin' too big fer me britches, as cookie told me every day. I wasn't takin' any pleasure from me job of drivin' the hoodlum wagon that carried everyone's bedrolls and extra supplies. The hoodlum wagon is also called a Trail Pup, doncha know. The trail boss gave me that as a nickname. Boy, I sure hated it!

"Then, about halfway along the drive trail, several of the hands came down with diphtheria. We were all real concerned. We were out in the wilderness. Blazes only knows how far from doctors and that new toxin stuff. Or was it ant-tie-toxin? I don't remember. But that new stuff they have to treat diphtheria. So we just had to sit tight and wait it out with 'em.

"The fifth night, I'll never forget it, one of the sickest of the hands, nice guy, Joe Paterson by name, started to strangle and fight his blankets like he was drownin' in a lake. His airways'd grown closed from a false membrane caused by the disease inside the throat. Before anyone could think of what to do, he died from lack of air – suffocated to death right in front of us. Oh, it was a horrible thing to watch. We were all plumb stunned. Made the hair on the back of me neck stand right up to watch 'im die of strangulation like that. Of course, then the other four sick guys were scared to death that they were gonna die, too. We were all nervous, truth be told, fer them cowhands. And fer ourselves, too, not knowin' if we were gonna get infected and take sick and die.

"It was a gloomy group the next mornin' when I rolled out of me bedroll to fix a big pot of coffee fer the hands. One other fellow, a young boy on his first trail, Jesse Josephson, died during the night. And the other three were still real sick, strugglin' just to stay alive, unable to get up and ride. Well, the trail boss set up the remainin' crew on a rotatin' guard and ordered four of the men to dig two graves. I tell ya, there weren't none of the jokin' around that usually greeted our early mornin' breakfasts on the trail.

"After the boss set everyone to workin', he rode out to check on the herd. He found tracks of strays wanderin' away since we stopped movin'. So he rode back to camp and ordered Jackson to take Trail Pup, that would be me doncha know, and go round up the strays. Well, I was so happy, even though it was a sad day, what with two funerals and all, but I was finally gettin' a break. I finally had a chance to show the boss I could sit a saddle and do a real man's job of work.

"Well, I'd had me eye on Jackson ever since the round-up at the Crooked Seven Ranch. He was tall, dark, slim, and handsome as the day is long." Sean pointed at the guitar case. "That there is his parlor guitar, the one I play now."

Leo raised his eyebrows in a big question mark, but Sean ignored him. Leo turned over to lie on his side facing Sean. He propped up his head on his bent arm so he could watch Sean's face as he told his story.

"Well, the Boss assigned me to partner with Jackson after that day. He ordered Jackson to scout fer strays and bring them back to the herd. The cattle had developed the habit of walking the trail. A few of the leaders kept takin' off to find new grazin' grounds. Some of the other beeves just followed the leaders, willy nilly.

"So, anyway, back to Jackson. It turns out his mother was half Cherokee and half French Canadian trader. His father was all Irish from way back. His family had immigrated to South Carolina back in the late seventeen hundreds. My, but he sure got all the best looks and best traits of his ancestors. I swear, he was so beautiful I thought he must have had the blood of elves coursin' through his veins, breedin' true down all the generations from the old world of magic and mystery. He made Black Irish have a wonderful new definition when it referred to manly, masculine beauty. He looked like a thoroughbred Arabian standin' next to a herd of wild palominos. He was so fine. His eyes and smile were like the sun coming out from behind dark clouds after a storm."

Leo laughed, interrupting Sean waxing eloquent as he recalled Jackson's good looks. "All right. All right. I get the picture!"

Sean stopped and smiled ruefully at Leo. His left dimple caught the shadow cast by the moon. "Why, I remember like it was yesterday. After everyone ate their supper and I scrubbed the pots and pans, I would get out me old hand-me-down Spanish guitar. I'd sit close to the fire and entertain the men with what songs and ditties I knew. The men were mighty appreciative. They clapped and whooped and hollered and told me they liked my songs a lot. I always felt flattered when Jackson sat close by, payin' attention, listenin' to me every note and word.

"Some nights, dependin' on who was off duty and what instruments we had, we'd have ourselves a real hootenanny dance. We usually had banjos, fiddles, accordions, harmonicas, and spoons on a washboard. No matter how tired those cowboys were from sittin' in the saddle all day, could they ever dance up a storm! And if we had a caller, we'd get going till late with Virginia Reels, Square Dances, Rounds, and Polkas, dancin' till the cows come home!"

Sean grinned up at Leo as he remembered the fun and excitement of those bonfire dances from his youth.

"But, many nights, I just played a while. Then, when I'd get tired of playin', Jackson would go over to that same guitar case over there and take out his beautiful guitar. He'd sit down and tune it. But when he played, everybody quieted down. They took a seat wherever they could close to him. Nobody said a word. They weren't rowdy, jokin' or gamblin' or rough-housin' like when I played. And, just like everything he did, Jackson's guitar playin' was inspired by the angels. Plus, he had a singin' voice that was pure magic to listen to."

"One night, we had camped away from the main herd lookin' fer strays. He told me his daddy had fought in the Civil War and had raised him on stories of heroes and the horrors of war. Jackson heard about hard marches and freezin' winters with low rations. But mostly, Jackson learned all the songs from the Civil War times. He sang them with passion and love and patriotism. I loved hearing his daddy's stories and then listening to the olden time, familiar songs."

"So, anyhow, we became closer and better friends. And then our feelings developed over the next few weeks into somethin' even more, leastwise fer me. He was an old man, ya know, about thirty-five or thirty-six. I was only a young Trail Pup of fifteen goin' on sixteen, and wet behind me ears, to boot. Jackson was real stand-offish at first. Finally, I had to make it known in no uncertain words that I was truly takin' a shinin' to 'im. Once he understood how I welcomed his attentions, why, he just opened up his heart and his arms and his mind and his soul to me, and I just fell into them, madly, deeply in love."

They both lay there silently. Sean gazed up at the stars and moon, lost in his memories. Leo gazed adoringly at Sean, hoping he would keep talking for the rest of their lives. After a few minutes, Leo touched Sean's chest. "So how did ya' end up with his guitar, anyway?"

Sean turned towards him. A look of sadness fell over his face like a veil. "That's another story, me young Trail Pup, a long story, too. It doesn't have a happy ending, so I think we'll save that fer another day. Okay, pardner?"

Leo nodded silently as he reached over and placed his arm protectively around Sean's hairy chest. He snuggled in closer, which comforted them both. They nuzzled and kissed languidly. As their passions rose, they tumbled together, tenderly, lovingly, until they soared to a climax.

Leo cuddled up to Sean, using his arm as a pillow. *I love how my wonderful Sean smells. He smells like love to me.* They fell asleep like that, happy to be together, peaceful, and contented.

Like all journeys, this short walk-about drew to an end. Leo and Sean spent their last night on the bank of an irrigation ditch. Flat fields of sugar beets spread out before them. They could barely make out the farm buildings as specks on the horizon.

Leo woke up worried. Sean had agreed to report to Henderson's Lazy H Ranch for the fall round-up, then drive a herd of cattle to Henderson's winter pastures. Leo didn't know if he could survive without love in his life now that he had tasted of it. Sean would be away for several months, even if he planned to return. Anger surged in Leo at the thought of Sean leaving him behind. *And why would he come back, anyway? He's not from these parts.*

They drank black coffee for breakfast. The caffeine ramped up Leo's anxieties about Sean's departure even more. They packed up and took off for home.

They arrived like triumphant conquerors to a victory parade of shouting kids running out to greet them, cheering and shouting questions all in a noisy commotion. Geese and chickens squawked and ran away in a flutter, adding to the racket. Barn hands and field hands waved hello. It surprised Leo how happy he felt to see his family again.

Leo jumped down off Bluch and ran over to hug everyone. He picked up little barefoot Lucy and swung her around and around until even he began getting dizzy. When he put her back down on her feet, she wobbled and turned around slowly. Then she hollered in her piercingly high voice, "Leo, ya gotta unwind me! I'm still spinnin'! Ya gotta unwind me!"

Everyone laughed and pointed. Sean's eyes sparkled merrily as he guffawed along with the rest of them. Honce spun himself around enthusiastically, excitedly trying to wind himself up like Lucy.

Myrtle grabbed Leo's hand and pulled him away from the milling kids. "Ya gotta come see Mom. She's doin' a lot better, but she still can't walk none on 'er broken ankle."

Leo pulled his hand loose. "Okay. Okay. Let me put Bluch in the barn, and I'll be right in."

Sean smiled kindly as he took Bluch's bridle. "No, pardner. Go on ahead. Go say howdy to yer Mama. I'll take care of everythin' out here, doncha know."

Smiling, Leo nodded his thanks. Myrtle grabbed his arm and rushed to the back door. "Mom! Mom! Leo's come back. Leo's come back!"

Leo paused outside the kitchen door and took off his hat. He used it to swipe at his clothes, brushing off some of the dust to make himself presentable. He stood at the door of the parlor bedroom and gazed fondly at his mother, sitting up in bed with pillows stacked behind her and a pillow under her broken ankle. She wore a lightweight knitted shawl around her shoulders over a white cotton nightgown. Myrtle had neatly braided her hair and pinned it into a bun with new-fangled bobby pins. Leo wondered if anyone had found her favorite tortoiseshell celluloid combs after the accident.

Lizzie smiled and waved for him to come closer to the bed. "Well, don't just stand there, Leo. Come and give yer ol' Mom a hug and a kiss."

Leo grinned from ear to ear. He bent over and hugged her, careful not to jostle her leg, then tenderly laid his cheek on hers. "Golly, but it's good to see ya, Mom."

"Well, son, I never thought I would have heard meself sayin' it, but I missed ya, and I'm right happy to see ya back, safe and sound. Now, step back a little, and let's get a good look at ya."

Leo stepped back, grinning. Lizzie smiled happily, pleased to see her oldest child growing up. "My but yer turning into a good lookin' cuss, aren't ya? We're gonna have to beat the girls away with a stick, given another month or two. My, my, but just look at ya!"

Leo ducked his head, unused to receiving compliments from anyone, much less his Mom. He didn't know how to respond. He shrugged and sat down on the chair by her bed.

"So, how's the ankle comin', Mom?"

"Ah. It's healin', darlin'. But the Doc doesn't think it's healin' straight an' true. He said I might have a hard time walkin' on it after it heals. But at least the pain is subsidin', and I can sleep of a night. Doc warned me that me dancin' days may be over. He told me to prepare fer the worst an' hope fer the best. I guess that's all anyone can do, anyway, isn't it, son?"

About half an hour later, Sean tucked his head into the room and greeted her in a bright, lighthearted lilt. "Why Missus Lizzie, it's so good to see ya sittin' up. When we left, this was a sick room. But I can see now it's nothin' but a boudoir fer a woman o' leisure fer receivin' her guests in. La dee da, but ain't we posh, now!"

Lizzie laughed silently, shaking her chubby body and rattling the bedframe. She pointed her forefinger at Sean and flicked it in a go-away gesture. "Oh, you! Get out of here with all that woman o' leisure stuff. I'm still recuperatin' from me life threatenin' accident. I'm no woman o' leisure!" She chuckled some more. Leo and Sean smiled happily.

Leo nodded his head up for Sean to take a seat. Just as he sat down, Myrtle sauntered in. Lizzie began giving her directions for preparing dinner. As she left the room, Sean looked all big-eyed at Lizzie and wagged his finger at her. "See? What'd I tell ya? A woman o' leisure, layin' in bed all the day long givin' orders to the servant girls. My, what airs ya have taken on, Missus Lizzie!"

"Oh, off with ya now!"

The kind attention pleased Lizzie, as did the company. She hadn't enjoyed many laughs since her accident. She picked up a quilt panel inside a split-wood ring. She pulled the needle out of the edge and resumed embroidering a red wild rose. She had chosen the rose for her contribution to Mrs. Pickett's friendship quilt. She planned to embroider her name and date around it in a neat, decorative border. She still hoped she would be well enough to attend the quilting bee with her friends.

They chatted while she embroidered. Sean entertained her with the story of the night a wolf slunk into their dry camp and tried to make away with what little salt pork they had left in their food stores. Sean told how he heard the horses snicker in alarm, grabbed his Colt six-shooter, and let off a shot in the air that scared Leo half to death. Sean clapped Leo on his back in a friendly way. "Sorry about that, pardner. Never did apologize fer scarin' ya awake like that. Oh, but ya shoulda seen the look on yer face! That big gray wolf ran hellbent fer leather out of the camp. The horses rearin' and pullin' at their tethers. The mules kickin' out and bayin' in a panic. Oh, what a fine ruckus, and that's a fact!"

Leo ducked his head, embarrassed. Sean hadn't revealed how they had made love an hour before the wolf came to steal their food. They had fallen asleep in the warm night air without bothering to get dressed. Leo had scrambled around in a panic, searching for his boots in the near dark of the waning moon. By the time he came fully awake, the emergency had passed. Chuckling, he looked over at Sean affectionately. "Well. All's well that ends well, now, ain't it?"

As he gazed at Sean, he remembered Sean would depart soon and leave him behind, all alone. His heart sank. His smile faded.

Sean turned his attention back to Lizzie and missed when Leo's smile turned into a frown. "Well, Missus Lizzie, I'm sure glad to see ya on the mend. Now, I best go find Boss Hayes and report on our work. So long, now."

Sean stood up and left the parlor. He grabbed his hat and six-shooter off the kitchen wall on his way out. He found Alma out back by the barn returning from the fields on a frisky tan palomino named Sandy. Sean took off his hat and meandered over to join him. He nodded his head respectfully. "Howdy, Boss Hayes. Here. Let me give ya a hand with yer tack."

He helped Alma unsaddle the horse and remove its bridle and saddle blanket. He gave Alma his report on their trip around the outer fences as they worked. Sean sent Sandy out into the corral with a slap on its rear. "Yessir, we had ourselves a good trip, all around the perimeter. Yer fences're good as new. But now, if I might be so bold. I've gotta question fer ya, sir, regardin' the future of young Leo and what ya might have planned fer 'im."

Alma crossed his arms and leaned back against the barn door. In his laconic way, he leisurely spat out some dark brown chewing tobacco spittle. "Um-hm?"

"Well, sir. I was wonderin' if ya might have plans to send Leo off to high school? He's a bright boy, doncha know. He told me yer school here only goes through the eighth grade and that he's already finished and graduated from the eighth grade."

Alma looked away, a little embarrassed. "That's right. And, no, I don't have no plans to send 'im away to school. I may be boss of over a hundred hands, but I don't make enough money to buy nobody an education. The price of sugar beets is down again, and the big new factory hasn't started turnin' a profit yet. I know, 'cause I already spoke to me bosses, tryin' to see if they might have a scholarship that the company could give 'im. But they said they couldn't, at least not this year."

Alma spat onto the dirt floor of the barn. "Now, why d'ya ask, Sean?"

"Well, I kinda figured it to be that way, Boss Hayes. Mister Henderson told me to be on the lookout fer extra hands fer his fall round-up and cattle drive. I wondered if maybe Leo might benefit from a couple of months of hard work. Since he can't get an education of the book learnin' sort, mayhaps he would benefit from an education of a more practical nature."

"Um-hm. I see. That's mighty kind of ya, Sean. But do ya really see that young pup out on the trail with ya fer weeks on end?"

Sean nodded his head. "Oh, yeah. He sits his horse real good, and he's a natural at helpin' out with all the chores of the road. Leo did right good on the fence mendin' trip, so I figure he would be worth his salt on the trail. If ya don't mind 'im goin', that is."

"Nope, I don't mind. I was just gonna put 'im to work here in the sugar beet fields. I reckon bein' a horseman and cattleman is maybe a step up from bein' a field hand, leastwise in his mind. I take it ya discussed this with 'im, and he's willin'?"

"Oh, no, sir. I didn't want to get his hopes up in case ya were sendin' 'im away to school or needed 'im here on the farm. But I think he'd welcome the job and do all right fer 'imself by joinin' up with me. Do I have yer permission to invite him to join me, then?"

Alma agreed with a nod. "Um. Yep. I reckon that's probably the best thing fer 'im, at this stage of 'is life. And I thank ya kindly fer thinkin' of 'im and givin' 'im a chance to grow up like this. Who knows? Maybe he'll mature a bit and stop all his childish practical jokin'."

"Well, the boy *will* do a lotta growin' up on the trail. That's a given."

The men turned and walked out of the barn. Sean shook his head sorrowfully. "But I don't know if he's ever gonna stop jokin' around. Why, he kept me on my toes back in the hills, to be sure. One day, we ran across some rattlers in the afternoon."

Sean chuckled and glanced over at Alma. "That night, I warned Leo that if he was brave enough to take off his boots, he better be sure and check 'em in the mornin' to make sure no snake had crawled in to make its nest. Well, and wouldn't ya know it, but the next mornin', I tipped me boots out, like I always do on the road."

Sean began laughing so hard he could barely continue. "Out of my boot dropped this long brown thing I took to be a rattler. And boy howdy, did I jump back! I threw the boot away and started diggin' fer me six-shooter in me bedroll. All of a sudden, I heard Leo crackin' up, bustin' a gut laughin'. He pointed down at the ground, and there, sittin' in the dust, was a string of venison jerky we'd smoked a couple of days before. Ha! Did I feel like a fool!"

Alma hmphed with a big grin. "Yer not gonna let 'im get away with that, now, are ya?"

Sean shook his head. "I didn't have a chance to come up with any satisfactory revenge yet, sir, but I sure do plan to. Yessirree Bob!"

Alma went to the house and found Leo sitting by Lizzie's bed. He walked over and messed up Leo's rich brown hair – no hugging or kissing a non-female relation for him. "How're ya doin' there, boy? Ya managed to stay alive out in the wild, I see."

"Yes, sir, Dad. It was real hard work, but I enjoyed campin' out and ridin' and all."

Alma sat on the bed beside Lizzie. "And how're ya doin' today, Lizzie, me girl?"

Sean caught Leo's eye and tipped his head towards the door, inviting Leo to go out with him. Leo stood up. "See ya later, Mom."

The young cowboys walked out and sat down side by side on the front porch steps. "Well, pardner. I'm surely gonna be sad to be leavin' ya here in the bosom of yer family."

Sean patted Leo's back as he pulled his eyebrows down mournfully. "It sure has been nice gettin' to know ya, though."

Leo caught his breath. His chest constricted. Betrayal, abandonment, and rejection hit him like a hard punch in the gut as it all crashed down on him at the same time. He turned a stricken face to Sean and hissed out in a low, strained voice, "Oh, Sean! How am I gonna be able to live without ya?"

Then Leo leaned in and stared fiercely into Sean's eyes. "Didn't it mean nothin' to ya, the affections we shared on the trip? How can ya just say goodbye like it, like it weren't – nothin'?"

Overwhelmed, close to breaking down and bawling like a baby, Leo had to stop talking. He stood up. His right hand rose to massage his forehead as he fought to regain control of his emotions. He stood there stunned, shaking his head, squeezing his temples, bewildered at life's cruelty in bringing this wonderful man into his life for just a few short weeks of adventure and love only to take him away so soon.

When Sean saw Leo's bad reaction to his teasing, he decided he better put an end to it. Then he remembered all the practical jokes, including salt in his coffee and the stone under his saddle blanket. He decided to put the screws to Leo just a bit more.

"So, pardner. I guess yer all relieved to be back home again, safe and sound, right? Back with yer Mom and Dad in the bosom of yer family with good home-cooked food on the table every day? I guess ya will be right happy to stay here and spend the next few weeks bent over in the fields pickin' sugar beets out of the dirt, right?"

Leo glared at Sean like he had gone plumb loco and angrily shook his head no. Leo couldn't speak. He feared losing control, allowing his sorrow and loss to spill out like a broken dam, leaving him helpless and ashamed. He shook his head mournfully, turned, and began walking away from the torment.

"What? Do ya mean ya might be all right leavin' yer family, leavin' this good life behind, and goin' out on the hard cattle trail with me?"

Leo spun around and stared at Sean, trying to discern if Sean were serious or just teasing. Suddenly, his eyes opened wide. His mouth dropped open. "Ya mean? D'ya think? Well, ya mean I might?"

"Well, pardner, if yer willin', I'm hirin' ya on fer me up-comin' cattle drive. It's gonna be a long hard road to travel. Long days of work with a rocky bed at night, if ya get any sleep at all between wolves and stampedes and night watches. But if ya think ya can stand to be away from yer Mom and Dad, I extend ya the invitation to work fer me fer the next three months or so. Now, whaddaya say, pardner?"

During Sean's little speech, Leo's face transformed from hopeless sorrow to confusion, then hope, then overblown excitement. "Yippee!"

Leo flung his arms around Sean and picked him up. He tried twirling him around like he did his little brothers and sisters, but Sean weighed too much. Leo laughed out loud in excitement and glee. "Yippee!"

Alma sauntered out and leaned against the door. He spat into the yard. "Hm. I take it that was a yes, then, Sean?"

Leo spun around to face his father. "Can I, Dad? Can I go to work fer Sean on the Henderson cattle drive? Can I please?"

Alma looked calmly at his son. He took his time. Finally, he nodded. "Well, now. If yer Mom says it's all right with her, then, well, I guess it'll be all right with me."

Leo nearly knocked Alma over as he ran past in his mad dash to ask Lizzie's permission.

Lizzie shook her head sadly. "Oh, dear. If ya go away like that, ya will never be me baby boy, again. Oh, dear. But I guess I can't find it in me to keep ya at home on the farm if yer head is set on goin'."

"Yippee!"

Leo ran back out to Sean on the front porch. Leo paused, pulled back his shoulders, and stood up tall. He walked up to Sean and held out his hand, all grown-up-like. "Sean, ya have yerself a hand fer the duration."

They shook hands formally three times, smiling, both relieved they would not have to say goodbye.

Greenwich Village
October 2010

On the last Sunday in October, Josh and Art slept in, snuggled up under a down comforter. Josh woke up Art with a long, sensual blow job that left them both coming in sheer rapture. They took their time showering, admiring each other's bodies under the spray of body washers and the handheld showerhead.

After a light brunch, Art asked if Josh would like to continue telling Grandpa Leo's story. They went in and sat down in the living room. Art snuggled up next to Josh so they could hold hands.

"The next part of Grandpa Leo's story has him setting out on his first cattle drive. They would make a seven-hundred-mile trip, mostly through barren desert mountains. It took them just over ten weeks from Blackfoot, Idaho, to Durango in the southwest corner of Colorado. They would face a physically demanding trip of long hard hours."

"To put it in perspective, Art. You and I could rent a car in Blackfoot and drive the same route today in about thirteen hours. Plus time for breaks and meals. It took them over seventy days. We would travel encapsulated in climate-controlled comfort. They traveled exposed to the elements day and night in the wilderness. Heat. Rain. Wind. And even cold."

"Driving herds of wild cattle was a young man's job. It aged them quickly. Now, let me tell you about when Lizzie gave Leo the blank book that became the journal of his love affair with Sean."

Chapter 8: Round-up

After Leo's last supper at home, Lizzie invited Sean and Leo to sit down in her parlor bedroom and visit for a while. "Since the two of ya are leavin' at first light, I just wanted a moment to say me goodbye's private like. Now, I promised meself I wasn't gonna cry just because me oldest is leavin' home, but I might just do it anyway. That's a mother's right and duty if ya ask me."

Lizzie used her handkerchief to wipe away a tear as she smiled and nodded her head. Alma sat on the bed beside Lizzie in his stocking feet. He gestured for Leo and Sean to take a seat. Stanley and Edna walked in with the box of checkers, but Alma asked them to play on the dining table tonight. They just shrugged and walked right back out.

Lizzie pointed at the plant stand beneath the window. "Dad, would ya please give Leo his little goin' away present?"

"Sure, Lizzie, me girl."

Alma lumbered over, picked up a small package wrapped in brown paper, and handed it to Leo. Leo looked at Lizzie in surprise. She nodded, motioning with her hand for him to hurry up and open it. Leo untied the string, folded back the paper, and exposed a book bound in cardboard. Two brown pencils fell onto the braided rag rug. Leo leaned down, picked them up, and tucked them in his shirt pocket. He flipped through the book of empty white pages. Puzzled, he looked at his mother for an explanation.

"It's a blank book, Leo. It's a place ya can write a record of yer days and yer thoughts. Ya can make it a journal of yer travels or a diary if ya prefer. It's good to keep track of those things that happen in life, things ya don't wanna forget. It's just fer yer own use, so use it how ya want. Ya can even write down yer most personal thoughts that ya can't share with anybody else."

Leo looked over at Sean. *I'll always want to share everything with Sean.* Sean caught the glance and winked, pleasing Leo immensely.

Alma coughed in his hand. "Yep. Ya can make a note of things ya learn, too. A notebook's a mighty handy thing to have along with ya when travelin'."

Leo thanked his parents for their gift. He shook Alma's hand and leaned in for a quick hug. Then he walked around the foot of the brass bed, leaned over, and kissed Lizzie on her cheek. She pulled him down for a long hug before letting him go.

"So long, Dad. So long, Mom."

"Travel safe."

Lizzie waved goodbye with her little hanky. "Hurry home, son. So long, now."

The two young cowboys strode out to the barn. They climbed up to the hayloft where they had slept since returning from the fence-mending excursion. Leo had trouble falling asleep. Excitement bubbled up inside him at the idea of striking off for unknown adventures with Sean.

Bright and early the next morning, Leo dressed in a hurry. As soon as he pulled on his boots, he ran over to the stone house to rouse Bob. Bob had agreed to ride with them so he could bring Daisy back to the farm. Bob surprised Leo by showing up dressed and ready to go. They left at first light without stopping for breakfast, anxious to be on their way.

Leo rode beside Sean. "But what if ol' man Henderson doesn't take a likin' to me, Sean? What if he says I can't go?"

Sean glanced over at the worried crease between Leo's eyebrows. "Don't worry, pardner. He's not goin' on the drove, so he won't care. You're goin', and that's all there is to it!"

Leo smiled and nodded. Worry still gnawed at him at the possibility of being separated from Sean at the last minute.

By the time the rising sun's heat began making itself felt, they cantered up to the old Henderson ranch house. A gentle breeze carried the smell of coffee and frying bacon. Sean figured the ranch house cookie was serving breakfast to the bunkhouse hands out back at the summer kitchen.

They tied their horses to the hitching post in front of the ranch house. Sean and Bob unloaded the pack mule while Leo unsaddled Daisy. Bob soon mounted up and grabbed Daisy and the pack mule's lead reins. He turned around with a wave and trotted away. "Good luck, Leo!"

Leo waved goodbye. "Thanks, Bob. So long now."

Nodding his head towards the door, Sean led Leo up the steps and knocked briskly. A wizened old lady dressed in black opened the door. With a suspicious squint, she spoke loudly like a deaf person. "Yeah? Whaddaya want?"

Sean doffed his hat and held it between his hands. "Good mornin', ma'am. I'm Sean McKay, and I've come to boss the fall round-up and cattle drive to Mister Henderson's winter pasturage. Is Mister Henderson at home?"

Rolling her eyes up as though saying, 'where else would he be,' the old lady gestured for them to come in. They walked into a large old parlor of rough-sawn pine paneling with a wall-to-wall stone fireplace on the opposite wall. The room had two closed doors cut into the wall on the right and two on the left. The raw log beams holding the low ceiling brushed against Leo's hair. He instinctively ducked safely out of the way. A worn Navajo rug centered a grouping of mismatched chairs facing the fireplace. Giant mounted horns of a Texas Longhorn adorned the rock wall above the mantle. A brass spittoon sat to the right of the firebox next to a stack of chopped firewood.

The gray-haired old lady led them over to the far right door. She pushed it open and gestured them through without saying another word. Sean squared off his shoulders and led Leo into a large, old-fashioned country kitchen. An older bearded man dressed like a cowboy stood flipping flapjacks at a big cast iron stove. Leo heard a loud voice call out, "Come on in, boys. How ya doin' there, Sean? Are ya ready fer this year's fall round-up?"

Leo glanced around at the kitchen. It looked like the original log cabin from when Mr. Henderson's father settled here in the mid-1800s. Roughly squared-off logs chinked with cement formed the walls. Leo looked up at the undersides of cedar shake shingles above the log beams holding up the roof.

Like most houses out in the country, the Henderson family had added to it haphazardly over the years. It had rustic older parts surrounded by fancier Victorian era additions.

"Yes, sir, Mister Henderson. I'm ready. And I brought along me sidekick. He's an apprentice cowboy, Leonard Hayes, son of Alma Hayes of the Utah Idaho Sugar Company Farm over Wapello way. With yer permission, he wants to sign on fer the drive. Leo, this is Mister Alex Henderson, the owner of this here Lazy H spread."

Leo stood tall, hoping to look like a full-grown man, and stepped up with his hand extended for a handshake. "Nice to meet ya, sir."

The old man remained seated while he shook Leo's hand in a firm grip. Leo gazed into a well-worn face, leathery, sunburnt, and wrinkled from the eyes down. Mr. Henderson's hat had protected his forehead and bald scalp, leaving it as pale as a newborn baby. Leo saw a lively sparkle in his eyes, belying his apparent old age. With a polite nod, Leo stepped back.

Mr. Henderson nodded at two chairs at the small dining table where he sat nursing his first cup of coffee. "Have a seat, boys." In a much louder voice, he called out to the nearly deaf cook, "Hey there, Cookie, how's about a couple cups of Arbuckle's java fer these here cowpokes. And where the blazes is me breakfast? A man could starve plumb to death awaitin' fer food round these here parts."

The old cook poured two glazed mugs of black coffee, then plopped them on the table. "Hold yer horses, Boss Alex. I barely just got the gol-danged hands served up out in the summer kitchen. Yer gol-danged griddlecakes are nearly ready fer ya."

He looked at Sean and Leo with a scowl. "I suppose the two of ya are hungry, too, right?"

The sullen old man turned back towards the stove, grumbling. "The youngins're always hungry if memory serves. And it does." Glaring with a frown, the crotchety old cook banged down a crock of maple syrup in the center of the table more loudly than necessary to emphasize his point.

Leo nodded yes with a big smile as he stared hungrily at the pancakes browning on the big wood stove. His early morning ride had given him a healthy appetite. Since Lizzie seldom made flapjacks, Leo considered them his favorite breakfast. Sean and Leo sat down. They stirred teaspoons of sugar into their coffee and then blew on it to cool it down. Sean took a sip. "Yessiree, that's strong enough to strip varnish, just the way cowboys like it out on the trail."

Mr. Henderson trusted Sean's judgment, so he barely interviewed Leo. "Yer hired. I'll pay ya a buck a day plus grub, and I hope ya work hard and earn ever penny of it."

"Yes, sir! Thank ya, sir!" Leo heaved a big sigh of relief he could stay with Sean. He smiled at Sean. Sean answered with a nod and a wink.

Mr. Henderson gave Sean two hand-written lists of names. "This here list is only fer yer round-up crew. This other is labeled round-up and drive."

As they went through the lists, Mr. Henderson commented on the men's various abilities and experiences. He pointed out how Sean would only have a couple of seasoned cowpunchers. "The rest're ordinary ranchers an' farmers, but the best I could come up with."

They reviewed the hand-drawn map to the fall round-up's permanent base camp on the two-thousand-acre ranch's border. After they finished eating, Mr. Henderson leaned back and turned to Leo. "Now, son. The wrangler'll have a variety of mounts fer ya to work with, but if'n ya gets a favorite ya wants to claim fer yerself regular like, then ya have to buy it, or ya can't complain."

Leo nodded politely. "Yes, sir, Boss."

Finally, Mr. Henderson ordered Sean to assemble his crew and take off first thing the following morning. "Time's a waistin'. Time's a waistin'."

They exited through the back door and then strode around the sprawling old ranch house to Brown Sugar and their gear by the front door. Sean led the way back to the big old barn and sprawling corrals. They dropped their bedrolls and saddlebags by the barn door. Sean looked around. An older man hobbled out of the barn, accompanied by a slim young man with bright red hair and tons of freckles. The older gent appeared to have back problems. He walked a bit stooped over. "Hey there, Sean. I see ya made it back."

"Yes, sir, Dick. I'm here and ready to head up the fall round-up fer good ol' Mister Henderson."

"Good ta see ya, again, Sean."

The grizzled, unshaven old man gestured at the teenager beside him. "This here's me nephew, Liam Flanagan. He's from me little sister's ranch just outside of Idaho Falls. This here will be his first cattle drive."

Leo didn't like seeing Liam's eyes grow round as he stared at his handsome new trail boss.

Liam walked up to Sean and enthusiastically shook his hand. He smiled, showing lots of teeth beneath a wispy carrot-colored mustache. "Nice tuh meetcha, Mister McKay, sir. I've grown up with cattle all of me life. I've worked the past two fall round-ups. But me folks wouldn't let me go on the cattle drive till I graduated school. Which I did last spring. I'm so excited to be part of your outfit. If there's anything ya need, just let me know. I'm your man. Uncle Dick, here, has been Old Man Henderson's right-hand man and best friend pert near their entire lives. And I'm lookin' forward to gettin' to know ya and helpin' out in any way I can."

The young cowboy's enthusiasm tickled Sean. *If he were carryin' an apple, and if I were a school teacher, he would be aimin' to be the teacher's pet, fer sure.* Sean merely smiled and nodded politely. "Nice to meet ya, Liam. And this is me sidekick, Leo. Leo, this is Mister Henderson's ranch manager and lifelong friend, Richard Aiden. Everyone around these parts calls 'im Dick. And this's his nephew, Liam."

Liam and Leo looked each other over suspiciously. They nodded curtly but didn't reach out to shake hands. Liam didn't like seeing his dashing trail boss already had a sidekick.

Sean jumped down off Brown Sugar. "Come along, Leo. Let's stow our gear. I need to get Brown Sugar turned out to pasture and meet the rest of the hands. We gotta get things organized all proper like, doncha know."

The four men strolled into the barn. Sean stopped while his eyes adjusted to the dark. "So tell me, Dick, first things first. Who's gonna be our cookie, and where's the chuckwagon?"

The following morning, Sean led a gang of thirty-one cow-boys and five wranglers up into the foothills. Old man Henderson had ordered Sean to assemble a herd of two thousand head for the fall drive.

They rode into a shallow valley watered by a small babbling creek six hours later. Sean stood in his stirrups and took in the lay of the land. He examined a dilapidated corral built years ago for the semi-annual round-ups. "This looks to be the fall round-up camp, Leo. Let's set up camp and go to work."

Sean pointed towards a small stand of quaking aspen trees close by a bend of the creek. He ordered Tommy Boy, their wran-gler, to build the rope fences near the water. The corral had to accommodate their remuda of a hundred seventy-one horses plus four draft mules for the chuckwagon. Then Sean directed young Thomas, their trail cook, to set up the chuckwagon and its trailing pup wagon beside the creek.

During the last cattle drive, Thomas's horse had taken a hard fall, landing on Thomas's leg and breaking his shinbone. Since he couldn't ride or rope while recovering, he had helped their Cookie for the rest of the drive. After he returned to the ranch, he contin-ued working as the ranch's assistant cook, learning the tricks of the trade. He not only enjoyed cooking but discovered he had a natural talent for it. The cowpokes welcomed him as their cookie even though he limped and needed a cane in bad weather.

Sean called the hands together and instructed them to set up camp. They would start the round-up at first light. "Let's get this rodeo started right smartly, now!"

Sean then directed Mick and Slim to check out two hunting rifles from the chuckwagon and bring in fresh game for supper. When Mr. Henderson reviewed the men's abilities with Sean, he had called Mick and Slim crack shots. Sean also detailed ten men to walk the old corral and repair it. He waved over two of the older hands and ordered them to retrieve the two-holer conven-ience seat from under the chuckwagon. They knew where to in-stall it a short walk away from the camp in a small ravine. "And make sure ya take the Rears & Sorebutt Catalogs with ya and leave 'em within' reachin' distance, too."

While Sean gave his men their orders, Liam rushed up. "Is there anythin' special I can do for ya, Boss McKay?"

Sean turned to him. "Maybe Thomas the cookie could use a hand settin' up his cook camp and fireplaces."

Liam nodded yes enthusiastically and took off towards the chuckwagon at a brisk trot.

The men scrambled to unsaddle their horses and turn them over to the wranglers. Sean tore out a piece of paper from the back of the small diary he carried in his saddlebags. He then dug out a stub of a pencil and the lists of names of his hired hands. He sat down on the ground in the shade of a small pine tree. Leo sat down beside him. Sean drew what appeared to be a pie cut into thin slices. Then he labeled the wedges with the directions on the compass and the men's names.

While they ate supper, Sean assigned the men their search areas for the following morning. "Ya can always orient yerselves by checking the tongue of the chuckwagon as it will be pointin' due north every mornin'."

The Cookie carried the drive's compass to keep track of the route using the rough maps and journals from previous drives.

After supper, the men retrieved their bedrolls and shaving kits from the single axle pup wagon pulled behind the chuckwagon. They spread out and found their sleeping areas away from the cook fires. Leo chose a place under a big gnarly Pinyon pine tree. "See, Sean, the dry pine needles will soften the ground for our bed."

As the sun lowered over the distant purple mountains to their west, Sean pulled out his guitar. He began playing a popular bawdy song about finding the ideal place to hunt the elusive black-haired hare. The sassy verses told how a pretty lass helped the handsome hunter find it nesting between her legs. One of the younger men yelled, "Yippee. Some hoedown music. Let's go!"

Tho men ran to fetch their instruments and returned with a mouth harp, two harmonicas, and the always popular banjo. Charlie, one of the permanent ranch hands, played the fiddle exceptionally well. He also called steps in a carrying voice, making him popular at the local barn dances. He tuned the steel strings on his old violin with a loud flourish. "All right, men and boys. Everyone grab yerselves a partner, now, and form up in squares of four couples. Let's get this shindig started!"

One young cowpoke grabbed the rough hand of the cowboy next to him and ran over in front of Charlie. "Yeehaw!"

Charlie set the beat with Ross, who played a mean banjo. "Honors right and honors left."

The men dancing lead bowed to their partners on their right, then their partners returned the bow.

"All join hands and circle to the left."

The couples strutted around in a clockwise direction, stepping high in time to the music. Before they made it halfway around the circle, Charlie called out, "Break and swing and promenade back!"

They all dropped their hands. Each lead took their partner's left hand in his right then wrapped his left arm around his partner's waist. When they both faced the same direction, they promenaded smartly back around the circle, counterclockwise.

Charlie and Ross had the music well in hand, so Sean put away his guitar and grabbed Leo's arm. They ran over to a three-team square and leapt right in. When Liam saw Sean stop playing, he took off running, hoping to rope him into a dance. But when he saw Sean grab Leo's bicep, he stopped short, angry he had missed his chance. He stood with his fists on his hips, glaring daggers at Leo's happy face. Gibson, a farm boy Liam knew from Idaho Falls, walked up and held out his hand. "Care fer a spin?"

Liam decided to make the best of it and nodded yes. Gibson grabbed his arm above his elbow. Together they promenaded over to join another square, stepping in time with the music, laughing at the antics of the men. Everyone forgot the late hour, dancing and spinning, playing their instruments, or at least clapping their hands while they watched. Thomas carried over a corrugated zinc washboard and sat down on a log. Using a spoon handle, he added a rhythmic, percussive beat to the dance music. The tempo sped up. So did the dancing. Charlie hollered, "Right hands crossed, and how do ya do? Back with the left, and how are yew?"

117

As soon as the dancers followed his directions, he called out, "OK, now. Are ya ready fer another simple step?"

Leo heard men answering all around him. "Yessirree!" "Let 'er rip!" "Yahoo!"

"All jump up and never come down. Swing your honey around and around till the hollow of your foot makes a hole in the ground. And promenade, boys, promenade!"

After a breathless half an hour, Charlie called a break and ordered the men to change partners. Liam took that as his big chance. He ran over and skidded to a stop in front of Sean. He looked pleadingly into Sean's eyes. "Will ya dance with me, Boss McKay? Will ya, please?"

Both a little irritated and a little amused by Liam's anxious begging, Sean gave in. "Why sure, Liam. Why not."

Leo glared furiously as Liam claimed Sean and turned to the square. Tommy Boy invited Leo to dance. They both hummed the well-known melody of *Red River Valley* as they followed Charlie's calls. Leo's Irish temper soared higher and higher when he observed Liam leaning into Sean's arms whenever he could. Leo vowed to cut in at the end of the first song and end the farce. He paid close attention as they drew near the end of the song. As soon as Ross strummed the final chord, Leo rushed over and cut in on Sean and Liam. Liam glared defiantly, but Leo ignored him. He grabbed both of Sean's hands and dragged him over to a different square, determined Liam would never get his grubby hands on his wonderful Sean again.

After a rousingly fast rendition of *Turkey in the Straw*, the musicians began flagging, as did several dancers. The next song contained a series of difficult calls and promenades, danced to the demanding lyrics of *Bird in the Cage*. Charlie ended the song with his own ad-libbed words. "Yew know where and I don't care. Take your honey to a nice soft chair."

The dance ended with a long strum on the banjo.

The men all applauded the musicians' efforts. Charlie and Ross wiped their foreheads with their shirt sleeves as several men walked by and thanked them for a good time. "Great hootenanny, guys."

Thomas had turned his washboard over to a young cowhand with good rhythm earlier in the evening. He limped up carrying tin cups filled with cold creek water and offered them to Charlie and Ross.

Leo chuckled when he remembered missing a step and throwing off the other couples. He had blushed beet red, so embarrassed at tripping up in front of Sean like a dumb young kid.

Even though the temperature had dropped into the mid-fifties, Leo dripped with sweat. "Bow howdy, Sean. This here stag dance sure is a lot more fun than tame ol' barn dances with all the womenfolk. It's a lot more fun!"

Sean squeezed Leo's shoulder as he tugged him along towards their bedrolls. They heard calls of "Good night" and "Don't let the bedbugs bite" as everyone settled in for the night. Leo noticed some took off by themselves, and others spread their bedrolls close to friends. Finally, Leo only heard crickets and a night breeze soughing in the pine needles overhead.

Three of the men who had hammed it up, hooting and hollering all during the dancing, sauntered off into the trees at the edge of the base camp. Leo noticed but didn't say anything.

Leo and Sean spread their blankets side by side. Sean sat down crossed-legged. "Too bad Charlie's not goin' on the drive with us, isn't it? He surely plays a mean jig."

Leo nodded yes, still smiling as he pulled off his boots and placed them beside the blankets. Then he took a quick look around to see if the night concealed them enough to enjoy a little private fun. He couldn't see anyone else except those close to the fire. He yanked off his pants, rolled them up, and tucked them under his pillow. His heart sped up in anticipation.

Leo unbuttoned Sean's long johns and helped him out of his clothes. The boys rolled into each other's arms, feeling each other's strong, sweaty backs and damp butt cracks with their rough, callused hands. Leo slowly licked his way down Sean's chest, enjoying the salty hair and firm stomach until he reached his goal. With the prize claimed in his watering mouth, he lin-

gered and lingered, enjoying every taste and smell of his wonderful hero until Sean exploded blissfully. Sean's ejaculation thrilled
Leo so much he erupted at the same time.

Sean and Leo fell asleep, sticking to each other, cuddled under scratchy wool blankets on top of an old patchwork quilt. The
night around them cooled down into the mid-forties, hinting at the
fall weather on its way up the mountains.

Chapter 9: Cowboy Arts

The crew ate a hearty breakfast standing around the chuck-wagon. After everyone finished, Sean sent his men out to round up the cattle within their designated wedge-shaped territories. Sean and Leo carried their saddles and canteens over to the wrangler. Tommy Boy, the wrangler, found a spry black mare for Leo's first day on the job. Naturally, Sean requested Brown Sugar. Sean nodded his thanks then turned to Leo. "Come on, pardner. Our area to search is up the hill, there, to the northeast. Mount up, and let's ride!"

They took off at a business-like canter. Leo appreciated the smooth ride of the young black mare and patted her neck approvingly.

As they rode higher up into the hills, Sean told Leo about the cattle living in the mountain desert. "Ol' man Henderson and his father started breedin' cattle to be resistant to the desert climate forty years ago, now. He's been mixing his breeds, tryin' to find the best combination of traits, doncha know. He brought in Texas Longhorns fer their ability to survive on minimum fodder and water. But they're ornery and skinny, and their meat is tough. Then, he introduced Herefords, which have good meat and do nearly as good in the wild as they do domesticated. Mind, they're not like milk cows going tamely to the barn every morning and evening, believe me! They're still wild cattle, and doncha forget it! Then he bought sturdy Spanish Corrientes. They do well up here in the high desert. Their meat's lean but still good fer eatin'. They bring a good return on a minimum of pasturage."

They rode around an outcropping of pinyon trees and scrub oaks, startling a group of five Longhorns. Sean pulled in his reins, gesturing for Leo to back away. "Leo, these here Longhorns're mean and skittish. Stay back aways and watch quietly. I'll use a minimum of motion in me lasso so as not to spook 'em. Watch yerself, now. These cattle're so mean they can fight off cougars and bears, so don't let 'em get close to ya."

121

Sean directed Leo to pull around behind him with a flick of his wrist.

Using only his heels to direct Brown Sugar, Sean slowly walked towards the small herd of five skinny cattle rooting for foliage beneath a knotted old spruce tree. He measured out his rope and gave it a quick spin to set the loop spinning. With a quick flick of his wrist, he tossed it over the bull's thirty-inch long left horn. With a jerk, he closed the loop around the bull's chin, taking him under control. Brown Sugar, trained from years on the trail with Sean in Texas and Arizona, immediately backed up to keep tension on the rope. The bull snorted and tossed his head angrily, trying to dislodge the rope. Sean gently nudged Brown Sugar with his heels to walk backwards, pulling the resisting thousand-pound beast. At first, the big skinny, black and tan bull spread its front hooves and dug in. Then it yielded with a snort and took a step forward.

As Sean dragged the bull from the shrubs, the cows and yearling heifer turned from their grazing to watch. They slowly followed, stopping every few steps to check the ground for fodder. The sun beat down strong and hot with not a cloud in the sky. With a nod of his head, Sean indicated for Leo to head back to camp. The little parade slowly wound its way down the gently sloping hillside, meandering around sparse scrub oaks blocking their direct route.

As they drew nearer to the base camp, they saw several cattle already in the corral, including calves and a couple of unbranded yearlings. Sean pulled his handkerchief up over his nose as they approached the dust stirred up by the restless cattle. Leo soon followed suit.

The iron man had his fire well stoked, heating two Lazy H brands. Leo recognized the Henderson brand, a simple, unadorned H on its side, making it 'lazy' in brand parlance. As they led their Longhorns towards the corral, two drovers ran over and let down the two logs barring the gate. Sean led them through without stopping. The cowhands quickly replaced the logs so none of the wild cattle could escape.

Once inside the corral, Sean released his lasso, letting the bull go free. They rode over by the fence to have a look around. The wrangler who also served as the round-up's ketch hand walked into the corral and efficiently lassoed a healthy reddish-brown Hereford calf with a dirty white face. He dragged the calf, complaining and resisting, over to the iron man. Soon, the unpleasant pungent smell of burning hair from the round-up's first branding wafted over the men.

The cowboys knew they were in business.

Two by two, the cowpunchers brought in their cattle and secured them in the corral. Then they rushed over to the chuck-wagon for coffee and a quick bite of dinner eaten on the run. They often stopped at the wrangler's to change mounts before heading back out. Even Sean had to let Brown Sugar rest every other trip into the wild. Tommy Boy knew his horses well and made good matches with the men.

By the third day, the herd grew so large they had eaten everything inside the corral. Sean and Leo rode in from their afternoon search, driving seven black and brown Corrientes to the fenced enclosure. Sean climbed up on the fence and raised his arm high in a big cowboy wave used to communicate over long distances out on the prairie. "Hey, Tommy Boy, come here a minute, will ya?"

Tommy Boy leapt on his favorite sorrel mare and galloped quickly across the corral. He touched the brim of his hat politely. "Yessir, boss? What can I be doin' fer ya?"

Sean pointed at the bare dirt and the trampled mud that used to be a small stream to water the livestock. "I think we need to get the herd organized, Tommy Boy. After yer sure all the stock's branded all legal like, I want ya to take a small notch off the left ear of each one. Keep the notches in a bag so I can count 'em up at the end of the rodeo. Otherwise, I'll have to count the hooves and divide by four."

Leo looked up and grinned.

Sean pointed to a swale leading southeast from the camp. "Once ya got the beeves processed, send 'em down that gully where they can range fer food and water. We don't want 'em to lose weight while we finish the rodeo, doncha know."

Tommy Boy turned towards the gate and nodded his head. "Understood, boss. Gotcha!" He kicked his spirited reddish-brown mount with his spurs and tore off to organize the herd.

Sean ordered a small posse of men to herd the cattle out for grazing. He set watches with the men, rotating between watching the herd, riding out to find more strays, and enjoying a little down-time in the camp.

The rodeo's fifth day started blustery and windy. Clouds piled up, threatening storms, but the clouds blew away towards the east without dropping any rain. Sean and Leo both pulled on Levi jackets to use as windbreakers. They rode out to the eastern edge of their search area until they came across a small pocket of Herefords. Leo happily followed Sean, as always. They shouted and waved their hats in the air to start the fourteen heavy brown and white cattle lumbering towards the corral.

Leo pointed at a young summer-born calf. "Sean, that there summer calf doesn't look like it's growin' right, does it?"

Sean shook his head. "Its mother probably couldn't find enough nourishment fer her milk, so he didn't get fed right when he was first born. Obviously, he can't make a seven-hundred-mile trip through the wilderness. Poor little thing would be the first beast to fall prey to coyotes. Hey! I know! I'm tired of eatin' venison. Let's give this little guy to Cookie, and we'll have ourselves a feast tonight."

Leo swung his horse around to stop a heifer from wandering aside. "Sounds good. I could go fer some tender veal fer a change."

They drove their small herd into camp, just in time for their noonday dinner. "Leo, lasso up that summer calf and take it over to Cookie. If ya see Mick or Slim, tell 'em to give Thomas a hand butcherin' the calf. Ask Thomas to do us up a right nice feast fer tonight. Okay?"

Leo roped the calf and pulled it towards the chuckwagon. "Will do, Sean."

That evening, after Thomas called the men to supper, Sean and Leo stood in line wondering what Cookie had done with the veal. Liam saw Sean heading for the chuckwagon and rushed over to get in line right behind him. Sean and Leo picked up their utensils, waiting their turn. Thomas proudly served each man a big ladle of slow-cooked veal stew from a big Dutch oven on the wagon's tailgate. He topped off the stew with a suet and flour dumpling, scooped out of a smaller Dutch oven.

Leo lifted up his tin plate and took a deep whiff. "Oh, Cookie, this smells right heavenly!"

Liam stood next to Sean, trying to strike up a conversation. When Leo turned away, he bumped into Liam, spilling most of his stew to the ground with a plop. Leo scowled, glaring daggers at Liam's sunburnt freckled face. Liam looked back innocently with a vapid smile on his face. Leo stepped up, angry, ready to call him out. Sean grabbed his arm and turned him back to Thomas. "Cookie, give this growin' lad a bit more of yer fine stew, if ya would, please."

Sean let go of Leo's arm, muttering under his breath, "Let it go, Leo. Just let it go."

Leo sat down beside Sean on a fallen tree trunk. "Doggone it, Sean, that danged Liam tripped me up on purpose. I've seen how he's jealous of me fer bein' yer sidekick. I've seen how he's always bringin' ya coffee and smilin' at ya, tryin' to get yer attention. The little weasel! It's not proper fer 'im to be watchin' ya all the time with 'is big ol' eyes starin' at ya, neither."

While Leo sat beside Sean eating his veal stew, he daydreamed about teaching Liam a lesson. Then he made plans.

As the hands began waking up the next day, a sharp kick to his thigh woke up Leo with a start. Liam stood glaring down at him, fists balled at his sides, angry as a stirred-up hornet's nest. His carroty hair stuck up at all angles, all glopped together with ants crawling over his head.

"Why, whatever's the matter, Liam?"

Leo darted a quick look over at Sean. Sean sat up in a hurry.

"Ya know what's the matter, ya gol-danged varmint!"

Liam pulled back and kicked Leo's leg again with all his might.

"Ow! That hurt!" Leo scrambled out of his blankets and pulled on his pants as quickly as he could. Liam gave Leo a hard shove, knocking him off his feet. Leo landed on top of Sean with a big humph! Sean angrily scrambled away from the incipient brawl, shoving Leo off his legs.

"That does it!" Leo jumped up and head-butted Liam. He grabbed Liam around his hips and tackled him onto the bare ground with a hard plop.

"Hey, now. Stop that!" Sean dove into the fray wearing only his BVD long johns. "No fightin' among the crew!" He grabbed Leo's right arm and Liam's left arm and shook them both until their teeth rattled. "Stop it! No fightin'!"

The men over by the camp's cookfire turned to look in their direction.

Sean gave Liam a hard shove towards the chuckwagon. Liam shuffled away with his fists balled up, swearing under his breath, kicking angrily at rocks in his path. A large twig stuck out of the back of his hair like an Indian feather. When Liam walked out of hearing, Sean turned on Leo and grabbed his arms with both hands. Staring angrily, he demanded, "Ok, Leo. What'd ya do to that kid? And what in tarnation happened to his hair?"

Leo glared back defiantly for a long count, then lowered his head. He had never seen Sean angry with him and discovered he didn't like the feeling at all. "Tweren't nothin', Sean. I just sorta accidental-like found a leak of pine tree sap drippin' on a little stick. And I sorta picked more up with that little branch. And then it kinda got smeared all over Liam's hair. And his pillowcase. In the dark of night. Somehow."

Leo couldn't hold it in any longer. He burst out laughing as he remembered the thrill of taking his revenge on Liam.

"It's not funny, Leo!"

Sean frowned even as his lips quivered, forcing himself not to laugh. Liam's hair *had* looked mighty peculiar. "Now get dressed, and let's go get some coffee. And I expect ya to apologize to Liam like a man before ya eat yer breakfast."

126

Still grinning, Leo meekly looked down at the ground. "Yes, Sean."

Liam complained to Thomas that the creek water didn't wash out the pine gum. Thomas shrugged sympathetically. "Well, I don't have nothin' in the chuckwagon that'll clean it, neither."

Liam shoved his hands in his pocket and turned to walk away. Thomas limped to the side of the chuckwagon and opened a small drawer. He pulled out a pair of steel hand-operated hair clippers and called Liam back. Smirking, he handed Liam the clippers. "Probably best to cut off yer hair afore puttin' on yer hat."

Liam dashed out of sight of the cowboys and cut his hair down to the scalp. Since he didn't have the advantage of a mirror or a helping hand, he ended up with a sorry jagged haircut. When Leo saw it while eating his noonday dinner, he pointed and laughed, infuriating Liam all over again.

As the off-duty cowhands sat around chewing the fat that evening, Hank stood up. The oldest drover in the company, he considered himself a real ladies' man. The men knew him to be quite scandalous in his affairs. He even had two divorces under his belt, while most of them didn't even have one marriage to their name. Hank coughed to get attention and raised his right arm like a preacher emphasizing a point.

Sean leaned over to Leo. "Watch out, Leo. Hank's as full of wind as a bull in a ripe cornfield."

Hank pointed his right finger around at some of the younger cowboys. "Seein' all of ya new kiddies, some who haven't even lost all their baby teeth yet, reminds me of the day I met a youngster name of Bobby. He was lookin' to get hired by Ol' Man Henderson back at the ranch. That kid swore on a Bible all he ever wanted was to be a cowboy. Well, Ol' Man Henderson, being a kindly man if he gets up on the right side of the bed that particular morning, decided to hire 'im and give 'im a chance. 'Come along, young Bobby, and I'll show ya 'bout the place,' the ol' man said.

"Henderson took 'im over here and over there, pointin' out the various work equipment around the barns and sheds. He picked up a well-worked length of rope and said to young Bobby, "This here's a lariat. We use it to catch the cows.""

"Young Bobby nodded his head as he carefully examined the lariat. He tried to look all experienced and knowledgeable-like. Then he looked up innocently at Ol' Man Henderson and asked, "Whaddaya use fer bait?""

The boys sitting around the fire burst out laughing, guffawing as they repeated the punch line, "Whaddaya ya use fer bait?"

After a pause for the laughter to die down, Hank continued. "Well, let me tell ya! Ol' Man Henderson about fell down fer laughin'! Thought he was gonna bust a gut!"

Sean leaned into Leo, still chuckling. "Didn't I tell ya? That guy gives 'imself calluses from pattin' his own back with his cleverness in tellin' stories."

Hank raised both hands high for the lads to quiet down. "That reminds me of the time I was sittin' around the lobby of a fine hotel down Texas way. A cowboy and his pretty new bride, who proudly clasped his elbow with both of her hands so as not to let 'im get away, walked up to the desk clerk. 'My good man,' the cowboy said as important as he could manage, 'we just got ourselves hitched this mornin', and we'd like to get ourselves a room.'

"'Certainly, sir. Congratulations!' said the clerk with a little bow. Lookin' at the cowboy, the clerk leaned in and asked, 'Would y'all like the bridal then?'

"'Naw, but thanks anyway," said the cowboy. 'I reckon I'll just hold her by the ears till she gets the hang of it."

Laughing along with the rest of the men and boys, Sean pulled Leo up to his feet. They took off for bed as the others settled in for a long spell of tall tales and impossible boasts, passing the time around the campfire.

In the pre-dawn dark a few hours later, Leo woke up feeling something crawling over his face. He reached up to brush it away. His fingers came away sticky with molasses. Sitting up in a hurry, he looked down. Thick molasses covered his pillow. "Why... that... no... good..."

Sean woke up. "What is it now, Leo?"

When he saw the condition of Leo's hair and pillowcase, Sean burst out laughing. "Turn about's fair play, doncha always say?"

"It's not funny!"

Sean laughed and snorted. Leo pouted, planning the next stage of his vendetta, determined not to be outdone by his archenemy. Sean finally stopped laughing. "Grow up, Leo. Yer pert near fifteen, and it's time ya started actin' like a grown man, not a spoiled little brat!"

Later that day, Leo and Sean sat on a fallen log eating dinner by the chuckwagon. Leo's old felt hat flew off his head, followed by tepid water poured over his hair. When he licked his lips, he tasted salt in the water. "Liam!"

Grinning a feral grin, Leo growled deep in his throat. He calmly set his enameled tin plate down on the ground before he jumped around and fell into a crouch facing Liam. Liam pointed at Leo's drenched head and shirt and laughed. "That'll teach ya to put salt in my canteen, ya little sneak!"

Leo lurched towards Liam, but Liam spun and took off at a dead run. Leo gave chase but couldn't get near enough to tackle him. Liam ran into the center of the remuda, sending the horses milling about nervously, pulling against their rope corral. Leo gave up the chase.

That evening, at the end of a long hot day in the saddle, Leo turned his horse over to Tommy Boy. "This here mare may look pretty, but she rides real rough. I'm all battered and bruised from the past three hours. Please don't give 'er to me again."

Leo slowly dismounted the yellow mare and rubbed his posterior. He stretched to the left with a moan, then to the right with an even louder moan. He slowly leaned over forward, clenching his teeth.

Every day saw more sore muscles, bruises and scrapes as the men rode through the scrublands, chasing after wild cattle.

That night, under cover of dark, Leo managed to tie Liam's legs together outside his bedroll with a thin leather strap. The entire camp heard Liam yelling and cursing first thing in the morning. Liam struggled to crawl over to retrieve his knife and cut the thong. The buckaroos whooped and hollered, teasing Liam for being such a sound sleeper. Liam ground his teeth, swearing he would have revenge.

The following morning, Leo woke up to find a smelly fresh cow pie under his blankets. It wouldn't have been so bad if he hadn't rolled over on it during the night, smearing the stinky goop's moist center all over his underwear and blankets. For the rest of the day, the cowboys held their noses and laughed whenever he walked by. Leo hated Liam more by the minute.

A few days later, Sean stood up after the hands finished eating supper. He looked around the camp. Some of the buckaroos sat on logs. Others relaxed on blankets playing cards. Some sat on the ground Indian style with their plates on their laps.

"Men, tomorrow those hands not goin' on the cattle trail can head back to the ranch, with thanks fer a job well done. The rest of us will turn the herd southeast towards Soda Springs and start this here drive. We've rounded up pert near two thousand head, and it's time to hit the trail."

All the men cheered.

Charlie's cheerful voice called out, "Since this is me last night with this here company, how's about I call us some dances in celebration? Anybody interested?"

The cowboys perked up at his invitation. In a group, they rushed to the squirrel can by the chuckwagon to scrape off any remaining food before they dunked their enameled tin plates in the wreck pan to be washed.

Ross ran to get his banjo from the pup wagon. Charlie yelled to be heard over the commotion. "Since this here's another stag dance, I'll walk around and count ya off. One, two, one, two, and so forth. If yer a two, then get yerself heifer-branded by tyin' yer neckerchief on yer left arm. This way we'll know yer assumin' the female part and will follow."

Some of the twos ended up older or taller or homelier than some of the ones. This resulted in some very odd couples and lots of joking and ribbing. Young Leo ended up with Franklin, a big-boned older cowhand with a bushy beard, bald head, and a pot-belly so big Leo couldn't see his belt buckle.

Leo grinned as he grabbed Franklin's hand and bowed. "May I have this dance, pretty miss?"

Franklin faked a curtsy while simpering in a falsetto voice, "Why yes, kind sir."

Everyone guffawed and pointed.

Charlie stomped his foot four times to set the beat. "Grab yer partner and do-si-do."

Leo tried leading Franklin. But Franklin weighed at least twice as much and didn't know how to follow. It turned out he couldn't even lead properly. Instead of Leo spinning Franklin around, Franklin spun Leo. They couldn't stop laughing as they messed up the dance steps something horrible. By the time the song ended, Leo wanted a partner who could actually dance. Naturally, he sought out his handsome Sean. Leo wouldn't have minded dancing with some of the other men, but the very idea of Sean dancing with Liam made him see red. He just knew Liam would try to seduce Sean away if he didn't claim Sean first.

The men worked up a sweat, dancing like crazy. Sean sent some of the older men out to relieve the herd's night guard, allowing everyone a turn at dancing. He let the party go on until the musicians dropped.

After the dance, nearly everyone off duty meandered over into the cold creek bed to wash up and clean their clothes for the drive. While cleaning up, several cowboys couldn't help themselves. They tripped or dunked their neighbors, accompanied by shouts and rowdy laughter.

Sean and Leo took advantage of the nighttime wash-up to scrub each other and wash each other's hair. Shivering, they hiked over to their bedrolls carrying their damp clothes. Between the cold creek water and the cooling breeze, they had goosebumps by the time they rushed under their blankets. Once wrapped in each other's arms, they managed to warm up just fine.

As Sean began drifting off, he heard a plaintive voice from the creek bed. "Leo! Where the blazes did ya put me clothes? Dagnabit, Leo!"

Sean's eyes popped open. Leo sat up, looked around, then lay back down and spooned Sean's warm back, gloating. The men still awake chuckled. More than one man thanked the almighty for keeping him out of the sights of those two feuding pranksters.

After an early breakfast, several ranch hands rode away for the homestead, herding seventeen young calves ahead of them. Newborn calves couldn't make the long drive. Sean and Leo had counted 1,847 ear tags taken from the cattle making the journey. Sean reported the size of the herd in a short letter. As he shook hands goodbye, he asked Charlie to give the letter to Mr. Henderson.

The cowboys packed up their bedrolls and stacked them in the pup wagon. Thomas co-opted a couple of the hands to top off the water barrel built into the side of the chuckwagon. Then he carefully stowed his portable supplies. Thomas had to head out ahead of the herd and find the next stop along the trail. He needed to have a hot meal waiting when the men and herd arrived at high noon.

The men spontaneously gathered around the low campfire and helped douse the fire by peeing on it. Leo enjoyed ogling the cowboys as they joked and carried on. One cowboy shoved Leo's shoulder, causing him to splatter Liam's boots – accidentally on purpose. Despite their best efforts, they didn't completely douse the fire. Leo and a couple of others grabbed pails and carried water from the creek to drown the coals. With the land so dry at the end of the summer, they couldn't leave a fire smoldering behind them.

Liam ignored them as he washed off his boots in the shallow creek, scowling yet again.

Leo heard Sean shouting orders. Sean sent men to ride point at the head of the herd. He ordered others to ride drag at the foot of the convoy. Then he set most of the hands riding swing at the shoulders or flank at the hips of the long, strung-out trail. Leo heard the three men ordered to ride drag complaining they didn't want to start the trip eating dust all day long. Sean heard them and yelled, "Shut yer damn traps. Everyone's gonna take turns ridin' drag, so don't stand there bellowin' like a new-made steer!"

All the hands fell into place.

Sean stood up in his stirrups and yelled, "Move 'em out!"

Today Leo rode a spirited gelding with patterns similar to a pinto. He trotted up to join Sean riding swing at the front right of

132

the herd. Leo grinned over at Sean. Sean smiled back with a wink. The sun cast a tiny shadow in the dimple of Sean's happy lopsided smile.

Chapter 10: On the Drive

For the next few days, everyone accustomed themselves to their new routines. The wild cattle didn't like to be pushed and pulled along. They resisted, especially at the beginning. The livestock typically spent their days meandering around, following their noses for what little fodder they could find in the open desert. On the trail, they instinctively set out to do more of the same. But the cowboys earned their keep. They forced the cattle into traveling in the direction Sean set.

The herd strung out along a two-mile trail, averaging only ten miles a day. They could have gone faster, but Old Man Henderson didn't want them to lose weight. Beef sells by the pound.

Leo's assignments had him riding different points of the herd with a variety of partners during the long fall days. He became acquainted with most of the men. Sean refrained from assigning Leo and Liam to ride together, to both boys' relief.

The exhausting schedule of droving beeves began at three in the morning for Cookie Thomas. First, he stirred up the cookfire and set a twenty-cup coffee pot to boiling. Then he pinched a sourdough starter out of the covered wood crock in the chuckwagon and mixed up a huge batch of biscuits. Cowpunchers called biscuits hot rocks, even though Thomas's were light and flakey. This early on the drive, Cookie still had plenty of fresh eggs packed in straw. He cooked up a big batch of scrambled hen fruit and fried up plenty of chuckwagon chicken, otherwise known as bacon, to fuel the hungry men for their day's work.

Sean started the morning drive half an hour after daybreak. The drovers didn't have much time to pee, eat breakfast, and saddle up.

Leo leaned up against the chuckwagon, eating off a white enameled plate held in his left hand. He forked in another mouthful of eggs and took a bite of fresh hot biscuit. "Boy howdy, Thomas. I sure thought I was all broken in to ridin' long days, but I swear the days're longer out here on the trail. Yep. A lot longer."

"I know what ya mean, Leo."

Thomas didn't stop packing up the chuckwagon. He had to clean up and ride ahead to their noon stopping point. "I don't have to stand night watch over the herd, but I still have plenty to keep me busy durin' the day, startin' in the wee hours of the early mornin'."

Leo scraped off his plate and dumped it in the washtub full of soapy water. "Well, I'll see ya at dinner, Thomas."

"Yep."

Thomas turned his attention to hurrying the slowpokes along so he could hit the trail. "See ya."

Leo tossed the last of his coffee onto the fire as he rushed over to the horses. "What bronc ya got fer me today, Tommy Boy?"

Sean had ordered Leo to relieve the early morning watch and help organize the herd. The sun slowly warmed the cool air. Leo pulled off his Levi jacket and hung it on the saddle's pommel. He kicked his mount into a trot towards the rear left side of the trail, where he would ride flank. He instinctively looked around until he found Sean. Only then did he feel entirely at ease.

The second evening on the trail, Sean rode up to find Leo sitting on his horse, looking back along the path they had just traveled. Sean brought his spirited stallion to a stop alongside Leo. Leo glanced over and nodded. Sean sensed Leo had something troubling him. "What're ya doin', me boyo?

"I don't know. Just thinkin'."

"About what, pardner?"

"About mom and dad and all my family back in Wapello. We're a long ways away, now, aren't we, Sean?"

"Yes, we are, me boyo. And gettin' further away every moment. What's the matter, Leo? Ya feelin' a little homesick, maybe?

"Guess so. Must be. I kinda feel sad all of a sudden, not knowin' when I'll see my folks again. Other than travelin' around the fences of the ranch, I've never been away from my family before. It gives me an odd empty kinda feelin', doncha know."

Sean reached out a gloved hand, squeezed Leo's arm, then patted his shoulder. "I still feel homesick ever once in a while, meself, Leo. Just remember ya have me now. I'll be yer family. Okay, pardner?"

Leo turned his sad face and looked Sean in the eye. "Guess yer my only family, now, Sean. But ya know what? Even though I'm a bit sad and homesick now, I'm mighty glad I could come with ya and not have to stay home with the little kids, missing ya."

"I'm mighty glad, too, me boyo. Mighty glad."

Drawing Leo's shoulder towards him, Sean pulled Leo into a brief one-arm hug. Then he turned his big stallion away to check on the rest of the men. "See ya at supper, Leo."

"So long."

By the time Sean took out his guitar and began serenading the camp after supper, Leo's homesickness had vanished. His usual cheerful smile lit up his face. When Leo saw Liam walking towards them, bringing Sean a cup of coffee, he realized he had been too tired by the end of the day on the trail to even think about him. Apparently, Liam felt the same way. Liam set the coffee down by Sean without interrupting the song. Completely ignoring Leo, Liam sauntered leisurely back to the campfire.

Riding long hours in the saddle under a relentless sun left all the men exhausted at the end of the day. Their backs and knees ached from constantly compensating for the horse's movements and the rise and fall of the land. Many of the drovers and wranglers experienced painful saddle sores where their pant seams rubbed them raw between the legs. Since Cookie only had Vaseline to treat their abrasions, he liberally dosed out petroleum jelly to all and sundry.

Those who rode downwind from the herd ended up with gummy red eyes and runny noses despite using their bandanas as dust masks. The men's exhaustion made for quiet evenings around the camp that first week on the trail. A few men sat or lay on blankets close to the fire and played cards. Occasionally they heard a clink or clank from the chuckwagon as Thomas cleaned up after supper, preparing to start all over again first thing in the morning.

Sean packed his guitar in its case and stored it in the pup wagon for transportation. He returned, carrying his and Leo's bedrolls and shaving kits. They meandered off to scout out a private place to spread their blankets. Sean intentionally moved them further away than usual from the other men. He wanted to relax and make love with Leo without worrying about the hands overhearing their moans. After they climbed into bed together, Sean wrapped his arms and legs around Leo in a passionate embrace. They both wore long johns against the cool evening as they lounged on their joined bedrolls.

In a soft intimate voice, Sean's lips brushed Leo's ear. "Leo, me boyo, I want ya to always remember, whenever ya ever feel sad or lonely again, that I love ya more than anyone in me whole life. I'll always be here for ya, pardner. I love ya more than words can say."

Sean had never before expressed those thrilling terms of affection out loud. Leo's heart swelled to overflowing when he heard those magical words, words he had longed to hear from the day they first met. He squeezed Sean more tightly. "I love ya, too, my handsome, wonderful Sean. I love ya, too, so, so much."

Sean rolled over until he stretched out full length on top of Leo. Kissing passionately, Sean rocked his hips against Leo's growing erection. Leo's hands roamed everywhere, delighting in the feel of Sean's lean muscles beneath thin cotton. Soon he wanted to feel Sean's bare skin. He unbuttoned Sean's long johns and thrust his hands under the fabric. He caressed Sean's back and fondled the hairy cleavage of his butt. Sean sat on Leo's crotch and slowly unbuttoned Leo's long johns. They shed their underclothes and rolled into each other, delighting in the touch of smooth flesh against hard muscles.

Sean turned himself around on top of Leo, facing his crotch. Then he slowly, tantalizingly drew Leo's hard manhood into his mouth. Leo pushed his face up off the quilts until he could smell and lick Sean's musky hairy balls. Then he licked up Sean's erection and pulled the moist head into his salivating mouth. They languidly sucked and licked and groaned and writhed, their hands caressing everywhere in passion and pleasure. Eventually, they worked their way to a crashing, moaning conclusion.

Afterward, they rolled apart and lay side by side with Leo's leg thrown over Sean's. Sean reached out and pulled Leo over until his head rested on the pillow of Sean's chest with his shoulder tucked under Sean's armpit. Leo felt content, loved, and happy. He smiled as he remembered their mutual bliss, their connectedness, their selfless sharing. His heart swelled with feelings of love for his wonderful Sean.

The sweat of their exertions dried quickly in the cool desert air. Sean pulled their blankets up over their entwined bodies. Leo leaned and gave Sean a tender kiss goodnight. Sean gave Leo a last warm hug before he drifted off to a peaceful sleep.

In the distance, Leo heard one of the cowpunchers singing. The night watch always sang to the herd to keep them calm. *Whoopee ti yi yo, git along, little doggies, it's your misfortune, and none of my own. Whoopee ti yi yo, git along, little doggies, for you know Wyoming will be your new home.*

Leo felt entirely at home that night, even though they slept under the starry sky within shouting distance of nearly two thousand head of cows. A thin new moon cast a pale light on the clouds scuttling easterly overhead. Leo drifted asleep at peace with the world, thinking he wanted to note this day in his journal, the day Sean first uttered those beautiful words, I love you.

As soon as he woke up, Leo dressed as fast as possible. He dug his unused blank book out of his saddlebags, then sat on a boulder and sharpened a new pencil with his pocket knife. He opened to the first blank page as he contemplated what to write. With a deep breath, he set pencil to paper. *I, Leonard Andrew Hayes, was born on the 17th of January 1896, but my life really began on the day I first met Sean the first week of August of this year, 1910. Last night Sean confirmed what I had hoped and dreamed of since that first day we met when he told me that he loved me. Today I am a man, no longer a child. I am loved.*

Ten days after the drive began, Sean ordered the drovers to turn more southerly. They had nearly reached Soda Springs, a small town where springs of naturally carbonated hot water gushed out of the ground. Before whites settled this land, the Sho-shone Indians had considered the healing waters holy.

Thomas advised Sean that his journals and maps warned about rustlers from the far-flung ranches around Soda Springs. He warned Sean to be wary of strangers. Sean ordered his men to be vigilant about anyone trying to cut out cattle from their brand. He ordered his men to arm themselves and carry live ammunition for the first time on the trail.

A little before mid-afternoon, Sean spotted six men on horse-back galloping towards the head of the drive. Sean dashed off to intercept them. When Leo saw Sean's horse running full out, he took off to lend his support. The guards at the head and the shoul-ders of the herd closed up to block the intruders.

Sean pulled ahead of the line of meandering cattle and stopped Brown Sugar. He stood up in his stirrups and held up his right hand in an imperative order for the riders to stop. The six strangers pulled up directly in front of him, their horses winded and restless. The men pulled on their reins, trying to control their mounts and hold them in place.

"State yer business, strangers. What is the meanin' of this?"

An older heavier man, dressed like a cowboy or working rancher, stood up in his saddle and shouted loud enough for eve-ryone to hear. "We are a legally deputized posse sent out to in-vestigate reports of poaching of our local cattle. We hereby accuse you of stealing our brands and mixing them in with your herd."

Leo pulled up beside Sean, a deep frown of concern on his face. Sean shook his head. "I am Sean Michael McKay. The only brand in this herd is the Lazy H brand and no other. If yer missing local cattle, then ya must look elsewhere."

"I will have to inspect your herd to ascertain the truth of the matter. And heaven help you if you are cattle thieves."

Sean didn't trust these men. He emphatically pointed back towards Soda Springs. "I do not give ya permission to cut out any of our cattle fer inspection, so be on yer way back the way ya came!"

The middle-aged leader, who still hadn't given his name, leapt off his horse. He pulled out his six-shooter and aimed it directly at Sean. Sunlight reflected off the revolver's shiny gray barrel. His posse dismounted and pointed their pistols. Sean found himself staring at six handguns aimed directly at him.

Leo reluctantly pulled out his old hand-me-down Colt .44. He held it nervously, uneasy at the idea of shooting at men.

Momentarily stunned by the quickly changing dynamics of the encounter, Sean struggled to think of a way out of this predicament without resorting to gunplay.

Sean hadn't heard Mick and Slim pull up behind him during the brief shouting match. Mick glanced at Slim, then nodded towards the leader of the so-called posse. They both nodded. Mick pointed down with his left hand, out of sight of the strangers, and counted one, two, three with his fingers. Both men fired. Bam! Bam! The cattle jumped at the loud noise but didn't run away.

The leader and the man to his left fell to the ground, writhing in pain. Sean's men pulled up closer around him with their weapons drawn and ready. Still standing tall in his stirrups, Sean shouted, "Take yer wounded and retreat before we open fire."

Sean fired his pistol directly in front of the closest rustler's boots. When the thief saw how close the bullet came, he jumped back and raised his pistol to point at Sean. When he saw ten drovers aiming at him, he slowly lowered his arm and dropped his gun to the ground. The other three interlopers also dropped their weapons.

Sean gestured for his men to lower their arms. "Take yer wounded and leave before more blood is spilled. Go now!"

The four locals leapt into action. They dashed up to tend their wounded. The spokesman for the posse had taken a shot to his right shoulder. Blood dripped below his left hand pressed against the wound. His face contorted in a grimace of agony. His men couldn't find an exit wound on his back. They knew they had to transport him to a doctor to remove the bullet as fast as possible. One of the men yanked off his neckerchief and wadded it up for the leader to hold over his wound. Two men helped him mount his horse. He sat his saddle unsteadily.

The other fallen man had a wound in his left bicep, the arm that had held his pistol. The bullet had passed clean through the muscle without breaking bones. One of the strangers removed the wounded man's bandana and tied it around the entry and exit wounds.

The six men mounted their horses and rode away in two tight groups of three riders. The unwounded men held out their arms to help the wounded remain upright in their saddles. Because of the injured, they moved at a slow trot.

Leo sidled up closer to Sean. He holstered his heavy old revolver then shook out his hand to relax it from gripping so tightly. He found himself still trembling from nerves. His voice quivered when he broke the silence. "They weren't really a sheriff's posse, were they, Sean?"

"Nope. I surely don't think so. I think it was all just a ruse to get close to the cattle and cut out some dollars on the hoof. I think they were just clever rustlers, but cattle thieves, all the same."

Sean glanced over at Slim and Mick and waved them to pull in closer. Sean doffed his big Stetson hat and nodded at them. "That was fast thinkin', men. Things were lookin' pretty grim there fer a minute. I surely do appreciate yer fine marksmanship. Thank ya kindly."

Slim nodded back. "If ya run into a rattlesnake, ya don't wait till it bites ya before ya shoots it dead. I reckoned the same applied to rustlers pointin' guns, too."

"Quite right, Slim. Quite right."

Sean sat back down on his saddle in relief, shaken by how badly things could have gone once the guns came into play. He forced himself to focus back on moving the cattle. Shaking his head, he pulled off his hat and wiped the nervous sweat off his brow with his shirtsleeve. He looked around at his men talking excitedly about their close call and sat up straighter. "All right, men. Get that herd organized and on its way pronto! Look at those longhorns drifting away from the body over there. Now let's move this herd away from these rustlers and not give 'em a chance to try again."

That evening when they pulled up to Thomas at the night camp, Leo hustled over to tell him the exciting news of the rustlers and gunplay. Thomas shook his head in amazement. "I told everyone this morning, didn't I? I warned Sean this area was notorious fer rustlers. Sure do wish I could've been there and seen it, though."

The next day the herd crossed dual ruts ground deeply into the gently rolling hills. Sean pulled up next to Leo, sitting on his horse, looking puzzled at the deep parallel furrows in the ground. Sean answered the unasked question. "Yer lookin' at part of the old Oregon Trail. The iron-bound wheels of thousands of covered wagons takin' pioneers and settlers and gold hunters out West made those ruts. Fer years, these roads flowed with train after train of wagons and hand carts. Now that we're civilized and have railroads, no one rides the trails anymore."

Leo looked left and right, observing how the lines dwindled to a point in the distance. "Wow. And the road's still visible after so many years."

The next day, Sean directed Leo to ride right shoulder with Gibson Halloway, a hometown friend of Liam's. Leo raised his eyebrows in surprise but didn't say anything. He had, of course, spoken to Gibson over the past weeks, but they hadn't actually become acquainted. The day turned clear with cool breezes blowing from west to east warmed by a bright fall sun. Leo trotted over to take up his position on the herd and met up with Gibson. They both nodded and began their slow ride, keeping pace with the foraging cattle.

Gibson spoke up first. "So, Leo, did you and my buddy, Liam, shake hands and make up? I haven't seen you fighting and pulling pranks on each other lately."

Leo glanced over bashfully and shook his head. "Nope. Just too busy and tired at the end of the day fer much playin' around. Besides, Sean doesn't like it none, and I don't want to get on his bad side."

Gibson nodded, smirking. They rode in silence for a while. "So, Gibson, where d'ya know Liam from anyway?"

"Liam and I met in High School back in Idaho Falls, although until this drive, we never really spoke or got to know each other. We hardly had any classes together. He's not a Mormon or an athlete, so our paths didn't cross much. We both graduated this past spring, and I, for one, am sure glad to be out of school. The only bad thing about not going to school is that I don't get to see my lovely Sue Lynn every day."

Leo heard an overtone of sadness in Gibson's voice. "Who's Sue Lynn? She yer girlfriend?"

Gibson sighed, smiling at the same time. "Yep. We knew each other from school for years, and I always found her attractive. But she grew tall early. When I was a sophomore and started growing up, I suddenly found that I could look her in the eyes. We were the same height. One spring day towards the end of the school year, I spotted her walking home ahead of me. I rushed up and asked if I could walk with her. She just smiled and nodded yes. And I felt so happy. From that day on, I passed by her parent's home and carried her books on the way to school. We had lots of time to get acquainted. The more I got to know her, the more I came to care for her."

A bull turned away from the trail in his grazing. Several head of cattle followed. Leo and Gibson interrupted their conversation while they rode over and drove them back into the body of the herd. With the dust blowing away from them, they easily resumed their conversation. Leo found himself interested in Gibson's story. "So ya started walkin' out with 'er regular like?"

"Oh, yeah. I couldn't wait to see Sue Lynn every day. We did everything we could to spend more time together. I took her to all the school and church events and socials. When summer vacation started, she asked me to attend church with her. We always sat behind her family, holding hands. It was a wonderful time. Before long, her mother began inviting me to join them for Sunday dinner. I got to spend the afternoon with her playing croquet or badminton or just sitting in their gazebo back by the apple orchard until we went to Sacrament Meeting. We found more and more that we had in common and began falling in love. The next two years were heaven. We managed to see each other every day

143

during our Junior and Senior years. I miss her so much, Leo. You just can't imagine. We've not been apart like this before. She's all I can think about, even out here riding the trail."

Leo found himself smiling sadly. *Boy, how would I feel if I had to be away from Sean for weeks on end? I think my heart would break from loneliness and worrying if he's all right.* "It must be real tough, Gibson, to love someone so much and have to be separated fer so long. So why did ya leave and come on this cattle drive, then?"

"Well, Leo. My lovely Sue Lynn and I made plans to get married. While I haven't yet proposed and made it official like, for us, it's all settled. But we need some seed money if we are to head out on our own. I know my family would let us live with them on the farm, but we want a place of our own. So, we decided to sacrifice a few months to raise some cash. Then when I get back, we'll get married and start our own homestead.

"We were out riding one Saturday afternoon not long ago and found some raw acreage on federal land that has a little artesian spring. We decided that as soon as we're married, we're going to homestead it. With the enlarged Homestead Act that passed last year, we can get a grant for three-hundred twenty acres now just so long as we build a home on it. The Act also requires we make improvements and plant trees and farm it for five years. The filing fee is only eighteen dollars. But as you might imagine, that's only the beginning of the costs of setting up housekeeping together."

"Gee, Gibson, that sounds like a real dream. A real nice goal. I can't imagine goin' off to live with the love of my life like that. Wow. I envy ya."

"Yep. I can't wait. My dad said he would help what he could with raising up a little two-room house to get us started. And Sister Wadsworth, Sue Lynn's mom, said she would ask all the ladies of the Relief Society to help out furnishing our starter home as she calls it. It will be only the basics, but we'll have so much work to do, it won't matter. Of course, we'll still have to buy livestock and equipment and seed. But both our families said they would pitch in to help. Oh, Leo, it's all I can think about as I ride herd on these here dang smelly cows all the livelong day. I'm so in love. I miss her so much."

"Well, Gibson, I'm a little jealous but real happy fer ya at the same time. I wish ya all the luck in the world in makin' yer dreams come true."

"Why, thanks, Leo. That's mighty neighborly of you."

After their dinner break, Leo and Gibson returned to their assigned position. Leo picked up their conversation. "So tell me, Gibson, what's Sue Lynn like?"

A big smile broke out on Gibson's sunburned face. His eyes lit up. "Oh, I hope I can someday introduce you to her, Leo, so you can see for yourself. She's the loveliest girl I've ever known. She has fair skin, blond hair, and pale, pale blue eyes from her Danish mom. And she's real smart like Mr. Wadsworth. He was educated back in England before he immigrated in the eighteen-eighties. She cooks like a dream, sews, paints in watercolors, and has the nicest reading voice. She loves to read. When we're by ourselves, she's always reading to me. She's going to be the best wife and mother in the world. We both want to have lots of children. As soon as we're married in the Temple, we're going to start our family at the same time as we start our little homestead. Oh, Leo, you'll have to meet her to understand what I'm talking about. I dream about her day and night."

"Wow, I think ya got it bad there, Gibson!"

"No, Leo. I've got it good. Real good. Other than missing her like the dickens, I'm the luckiest man alive. Now watch out, there goes that ornery old bull, again, taking off on his own."

That evening as Sean and Leo spread their bedrolls away from the camp, Leo told Sean about Gibson falling in love with a girl named Sue Lynn. "He's really been bit by the ol' love bug bad. Must be horny as a goat, daydreamin' all the day long about his girl, but sleepin' all the night long by 'imself. Poor guy."

Sean leaned over and pushed Leo against the quilts, nuzzling his whiskers against Leo's sensitive neck. "Well, we don't have to sleep by ourselves, now, do we?"

Chuckling, Leo reached through Sean's long johns and grabbed a handful of Sean's warm privates. "No, we don't. We're so lucky."

They stroked each other, feeling each other's loose hairy balls and occasionally reaching a finger back to gently stroke each other's backsides. By silent mutual agreement, they threw off their underclothes and crawled beneath their quilts.

Leo snuggled his way down under the hand-quilted blankets and wedged himself in the wide V of Sean's hairy legs. Leo began sensuously licking up and down Sean's already hard cock. Leo's mouth watered. His warm saliva drooled down until it began coating Sean's hairy balls. Leo took his time, giving Sean all the pleasure he could. Before long, Sean's leg muscles strained in ecstasy. Leo's left hand rubbed Sean's dangling balls, smoothing his saliva over them, pulling them away from Sean's writhing groin. Leo's right hand smoothed his precum over the swollen head of his own erection. He moved more and more slowly on Sean and himself until they erupted with muted cries of joy and rapture.

After several long shuddering breaths, Sean reached down and pulled Leo up to lie full length over him. Sean turned Leo's face to his and kissed him, licking his own musky slickness from Leo's lips and tongue. Leo hummed wordlessly, completely happy.

After they caught their breath, Leo began thinking about Gibson's dream of setting up his own home with Sue Lynn. Leo gazed at Sean's closed eyes as he fantasized. "Wouldn't it be nice if someday we could settle down with a place of our own, Sean? Instead of traipsing all over the land? Do ya think maybe that could be fer us one day?"

"I don't know, me boyo. But the life of the cowboy is disappearing right before our very eyes, doncha know. There aren't many big herds movin' anymore because the whole land is gettin' chopped up with fences and obstructions. Besides, the railways're spreadin' out all over, makin' it easy to move beeves to market without long drives. So, who knows? Maybe a permanent home will be fer us someday in the future. It's worth thinkin' on, I suppose. But, like I've told ya before, Leo. From the time I was knee-high to a grasshopper, all I ever wanted was to ride the cattle trails and be a cowboy. So, fer the time bein', and while we still can, let's ride herds fer a while more before makin' plans to settle down. Is that okay, me boyo?"

"Sure, Sean. Whatever ya say."

Thomas and Sean led the herd in a meandering path along natural waterways into a shallow valley leading towards Montpelier. Arid blue-gray mountains rose around them to the east and to the west. They traveled close to water and camped among trees, a pleasant change from riding through the arid desert.

Their route kept them three miles west of Montpelier to avoid its outlying ranches. At midday, Sean called a halt to give the drovers a rest. Thomas served the hands dinner. After he ate, Sean sought out Thomas. "Cookie, I think we should take advantage of bein' so close to a big railroad town and go in to replenish our supplies."

Thomas nodded his agreement. He began reviewing his supplies and making a mental list of the provisions he needed to buy. "I think I'll need the pup wagon to carry everything. Would ya please have yer men unload it? I'll detach it from the chuckwagon and hook up two mules to take into town."

Thomas unlocked a small compartment in the wagon's side and took out enough cash to go shopping.

When Gibson saw Tommy Boy hitching up two mules to the pup wagon, he jogged over to Sean. "Hey, there, boss. Are you sending Cookie into Montpelier this afternoon?"

Sean nodded affirmative then tilted his head in a question why Gibson asked.

"Listen, boss, would it be possible for me to ride along just this once? I want to send a telegram to my girl back in Idaho Falls, and this is the first place where there's a telegraph office. I just want her to know that I'm alive and well, and… and…" Gibson ducked his head, "that I'm still in love with her."

Sean smiled knowingly. "Why, sure, Gibson. Just make sure ya help Cookie with his load and make yerself useful. Draw some bullets from the store and be alert and ready fer anything that might come up."

Gibson broke out into a huge smile. "Gee, thanks, Boss. Thanks!"

Gibson jogged over to the remuda in a hurry to find a mount.

Sean also sent Slim and Mick riding guard duty in case Thomas encountered any trouble. Leo wished he could go with them, but Sean had to stay with the herd. Leo didn't want to leave Sean's side just to go sightseeing. Instead, he accompanied Sean as he inspected the restless cattle. Several men took advantage of the break by catching catnaps with their hats over their faces.

A few hours later, Thomas returned in plenty of time to make a special supper from his fresh supplies. They ate fried chicken with mashed potatoes and pan gravy that night, pleased not to be eating venison or rabbits or stringy wild turkeys.

As they sat around eating, the men shared what they remembered about Butch Cassidy's famous bank robbery fourteen years ago right here in Montpelier. Leo had already heard the stories of the notorious train robber and his Wild Bunch Gang. He listened avidly to the tales of Butch's sidekick, the Sundance Kid. Daydreaming, Leo wondered if they had shared a loving relationship or if they had just been partners in crime.

He remembered when his dad read them an article in the Pocatello Tribune during supper a while back. The report speculated that Butch and Sundance had escaped the Pinkertons by fleeing to Argentina. It suggested they ended up in Bolivia, where they were reportedly killed in a shootout in 1908. But their deaths were never confirmed.

Piece by piece, the cowboys shared what they knew of Butch Cassidy's story. They told how Butch's parents had to leave England to escape persecution for their polygamist Mormon faith, so he grew up in southern Utah. Butch's parents named him Robert Leroy Parker. The oldest of thirteen children, Butch left home in his early teens. He became friends with his teacher, Mike Cassidy. Later Butch worked as a butcher, where he picked up his nickname. He combined his nickname with his mentor's name and came up with the moniker of Butch Cassidy.

The Pocatello Tribune reported how Mike Cassidy had worked on a dairy farm before turning horse thief and cattle rustler. The Tribune said Mike taught Butch the thief trade that became his life's career. Leo fantasized about how Butch Cassidy and the Sundance Kid might have ridden these same paths and might have made passionate love right here in this valley. That night Leo entertained himself, pretending to be the Sundance Kid to Sean's thrillingly dangerous Butch Cassidy.

Two weeks after they began the drive, the weary cowboys drew near Bear Lake. They drove the strung-out herd along the west coast of the thirty-mile-long lake. A ridge of mountains thrust up along the east side of the lake. The land along the west coast provided a flatter trail before it rose gradually into foothills. The cowpokes enjoyed riding through this green strip of valley free of dust.

That afternoon Leo rode right shoulder with Hank, the oldest of the men. Hank just wouldn't stop talking. It drove Leo to distraction. Hank told story after joke after lie and exaggeration, if not about his personal sexual prowess, then he told hand-me-down tales.

The cattle stopped at a low-lying patch of ground covered with green grasses watered from below. The surrounding grasses had dried out and turned gold or gray at the end of the summer. As Leo and Hank sat waiting for the cattle to crop down the patch of green weeds, Hank crossed his right leg up over his saddle horn. "One day, I was out ridin' with muh buddy, and we comed upon a Injun lying on the ground on his stomach. He had his ear to the ground like he was listenin' at somethin'. Muh pardner told me, 'He's listenin' to the ground and can hear things fer miles in every direction.' Just then, the Injun looked up and said, 'Covered wagon. Two mile away. Have two horses, one brown, one white. Man, woman, child, traveling goods in wagon.' Muh friend said, "Amazin'! That Injun knows how far away they are, how many horses, their color, and who and what's in the wagon! Isn't that just amazin'!' Just then the Injun looked up and said, 'Ran over me about half hour ago.'"

Leo moaned and kicked his horse in the flank to move away from Hank. Shaking his head in helpless exasperation, he trotted on down the herd.

Nights found them camping and fishing near the lake or on one of the streams that fed the natural freshwater lake. Cavorting and frolicking in the water became the recreation of choice after supper and sometimes before, work schedules permitting. Sean and Leo enjoyed plenty of time in the bright, turquoise blue water, a pleasant change from the muddy brown lakes they usually encountered.

Leo and Thomas waded into the lake one afternoon wearing nothing but vests. They had pinned lures to the vests and carried worms in the pockets. It didn't take them long to catch a large carp, a few small native white fish called Ciscos, and several native cutthroat trout. Thomas particularly liked trout. After a while, their shivering from the icy cold water drove them ashore, their man parts shriveled and barely visible.

One evening, as the last hint of the sunset faded to the west, Sean led Leo down to the lake. Leo spotted Liam already naked, wrestling in the shallow cold water with Gibson. Gibson had become Liam's regular partner at dancing and card games in the evening.

Leo grabbed Sean's hand and pulled him in the opposite direction. They came upon a natural ramp leading down to the shallow waters. Willows, poplars, and an occasional pine tree sheltered the grove. The dry fall grasses and bright yellow goldenrod gave way to greener, taller grasses along the rocky shoreline.

The boys left their clothes on a low bush at the edge of the beach. Stepping gingerly over the rocks leading to the sandy shore, they approached the gently lapping water. Leo dropped his towel and bar of soap on the dry sand and ran into the icy cold lake water. Sean followed and tackled Leo with a flying leap. They splashed into the icy water, laughing all the way.

After a quick soap and rinse, they shivered their way back to their clothes and dried off as quickly as they could. The setting sun took with it what little warmth remained in the air. The temperatures plummeted down to near fifty degrees. Sean took extra care that evening to find a private area for their bedrolls. Since they were so clean from their swim in the lake, he wanted to treat Leo to a tongue bath on all his most private and sensitive areas. He rushed to get them out of their long johns and under the covers to warm up.

An hour of pleasure later, both men consumed the other's love offerings at the end of a sensual sixty-nine. Sean turned around to lay side by side, then leaned over and kissed Leo. They shared their slippery tastes with each other, humming with delight as they hugged each other tight. Leo fell asleep with his head on Sean's shoulder, happy to be with his handsome lover, enjoying Sean's reddish blond chest hair tickling his cheek.

Their route south took them into the Utah side of Bear Lake. When they reached the southern end of the beautiful blue lake, Thomas guided the herd southeast again. They passed just north of Laketown, an old Mormon settlement, where Thomas stopped to purchase supplies. Their next brush with civilization would not be until three or four days later when they would cut across the southwest corner of Wyoming on their way to Colorado.

After supper that night, the drovers piled more wood on their cookfire. Their fire soared, sending sparks drifting off in the evening breeze. Hank led off the night's entertainment with a bawdy story ending with, "Must think her ass is a gold mine since everyone's a diggin' at it!"

A quiet young man named Georgie had a clear tenor voice. Hank's story reminded him of a rowdy song. He stood up to get everyone's attention, then began singing,

My love has a gun that has gone to the bad,
Which makes poor old Jimmy feel pretty damn sad;
For the gun, it shoots high and the gun it shoots low,
And it wobbles about like a bucking bronco.
Lie still, ye young bastard. Don't bother me so.
Your father's off bucking another bronco.

My love had a gun that was dirty and long
But he wore it to visit the lady gone wrong

151

Though once it was strong and it shot straight and true
Now it wobbles and buckles and it's red, white and blue.
Lie still, ye young bastard. Don't bother me so.
Your father's off bucking another bronco.

Someone whose voice Leo didn't recognize whooped and hollered out, "I know just what that's like. It now takes me all night just to do what I used to do all night!"

Sean shook his head, muttering, "Oh, lord."

A couple of the rowdier men began singing the tale of *One-Eyed Reilly*. Sean pulled Leo up by his hand. "That song has more verses than a sailor's drinking song, and each verse is worse than the one before, doncha know. I think we could find ourselves something a little more entertainin' and upliftin' to occupy our time. Shall we?"

Leo grinned his agreement. They headed over to the pup wagon to retrieve their bedrolls, anxious to begin their preferred nocturnal activities.

The land changed to a high plateau, riddled with small meandering streams of water. Only a few trees here and there broke the monotony of sagebrush, dry wild oats, and flowerless sego lilies. Desolate mountain ridges marked the edges of their distant horizons all around.

A couple of days south of Laketown, dawn brightened the sky, revealing great thunderclouds in the west above the high mountain peaks. Sean ordered the men to carry their oiled water slickers in case it rained.

Sure enough, the clouds burst open in a deluge. The cowboys found themselves forging through mud as they kept the herd on the move. The rain continued unabated when they reached the noon camp. Thomas had rigged a canvas tarp by the chuckwagon for the men to sit under while they ate. Leo ducked under and shook the rain off his hat. Unfortunately, the wind kept changing direction, blowing the smoke from the cook fire into the open tent. The wet cowboys had a choice of eating dry or eating with smoke in their faces.

Leo spent a miserable afternoon in the gusty wind and spotty rain showers. They set up camp at the usual time of half an hour before sunset. Storm clouds poured in from the West, darkening the sky fast and early.

When Sean saw lightning, he became concerned. He called his hands to gather round. "Men, the livestock don't care fer lightenin' and thunder, doncha know. So tonight, I want everyone to sleep fully clothed, ready to react at a moment's notice."

Sean nodded his head to the west. "If that there lightning storm passes this way, there's a chance fer a night stampede, and that's the worst kind there is, ridin' in the dark. I want every man jack ridin' nightguard to sing or whistle to calm the herd."

Sean looked out at the level land around the herd. "Remember, men. If we have to mill the herd, turn 'em clockwise. Get 'em all movin' in a circle. Otherwise, we'll be tracking down the runaway strays fer days."

The men frowned. Nobody liked the idea of a hard ride in the rain at night with wild cattle running full out in a panic.

Around the time the miserable cowboys settled down in their makeshift tents and damp bedrolls, the lightning storm drew nearer. Thunder grew louder and louder. The men lay awake, counting the seconds from the lightning strike until the thunder reached them. The intervals grew shorter as the storm crawled closer.

For several moments the storm went silent and dark. Everyone hoped it had blown over. Then a tremendous light flashed close by the camp. Lightning struck a tall pine tree, lighting it on fire with a shocking whoosh! At the same time, a tremendous sizzle and boom cracked out, startling the men and the cattle. The skittish Texas Longhorns took off running away from the burning tree, bellowing in alarm.

The men jumped out of their bedrolls, pulled on their boots, and dashed over to the remuda. Tommy Boy had ordered them to leave their saddles on their mounts when they returned their horses before supper. Quickly cinching up the loose saddles, they mounted up. Sean waved his hat in the air, yelling, "Quick, now! Mill the herd to the right, clockwise. Mill 'em right!"

Other hands picked up his call as they rode towards the panicking herd.

The cowhands rode in dread towards the huge herd, scattering in all directions to escape the shockingly bright thirty-foot-tall flames of the burning pine tree. The storm sent waves of rain driving across the ground with more lightning strikes and more appallingly loud claps of thunder. The cowboys heard the air sizzle at the close strikes immediately before they heard the thunder. The noise of hard cattle hooves striking the damp ground sounded like an echo of thunder.

When Leo drew up alongside the panicking longhorns, he heard their horns knocking against each other with a sound like dozens of castanets clicking in a wild dance. Leo took off his sodden hat and waved it at the running cattle, trying to turn the lead bulls. But they ignored him. Not knowing what else to do, he pulled out his Colt 45 and fired a shot into the air. The longhorns turned to rush away from the new noise, moving to the right as Leo had intended. He rode alongside them to make sure they continued turning.

The scattered herd began milling back in on itself.

Leo slowed his horse's frantic run as the cattle began settling down. His horse caught a foot in a hidden burrow and stumbled. Leo went flying head over heels. He landed on his head and shoulders on a low pile of rocks. The fall knocked him out. He lay sprawled over burrows of rock chucks. His horse ran around in circles, still excited by the milling herd and noise.

In the light from a lightning strike, Sean noticed a riderless horse and rushed over to investigate. He caught the restless horse's reins, then rode around, leaning down, anxiously trying to find a fallen cowboy in the dark. When Leo's horse darted in closer, Sean recognized his saddle. Fear shot through him with a jolt of adrenaline. He screamed, "Leo! Where are ya, Leo?"

Frantic, Sean traced backward as best as he could estimate based on the direction the herd had been traveling.

A multiple-branched lightning strike lit the area enough for him to spot Leo lying on his back on a jumble of loose rocks. Sean rushed over, leapt off his horse, and crashed to his knees beside him. "Leo? What happened? Are ya alive? Oh, damnation! Are ya alive, Leo?"

He leaned over anxiously and inspected Leo for wounds. Sean pulled off his right glove and placed his hand under Leo's shirt. To his relief, he felt Leo's heart beating and his lungs expanding and contracting. "Thank God he's still alive."

Fearing Leo could be concussed or have broken bones, he refrained from moving him. He shouted at a cowboy riding nearby in the dark, "Leo's down and hurt. Run fetch Thomas and some dry firewood and come back quick as ya can!"

Slim waved his hand in acknowledgment and rode away as fast as he could spur on his horse.

Fifteen minutes later, Thomas and Slim rode up at a run. Thomas carried a lit kerosene lantern. Slim pulled along a mule laden with firewood in a canvas sling. Thomas handed Sean the lantern, then untied the chuckwagon's modest first aid kit from the back of his saddle. Slim laid a small fire beside the pile of rocks. Rock chucks scampered out of their burrows and ran away, chattering in anger at the intrusion.

Sean held the lantern over Leo, searching anxiously for blood or bruises. *Leo, me love, doncha dare up and die on me. Ya gotta live and get better. I'll be here with ya, doncha worry!* He knelt in the mud. "Stay with me, Leo. Please wake up. Say something! Tell me what's the matter with ya? Where are ya hurt?"

Thomas knelt beside Sean and inspected Leo up close. Thomas noticed moisture glittering more darkly than the falling rain. He grabbed Sean's hand and pulled the lantern closer. They both saw blood. Thomas pointed at Slim. "Fetch a wound dressing from the medicine kit and bring it here with a roll of gauze. Quick now!"

Thomas gently lifted Leo's head and turned it, exposing a bleeding gash. They could see a lump already swelling from crashing on the rocks. Thomas slowly lowered Leo's head to the ground. "He's knocked 'imself clean out from the fall and took a blow to his head. Head wounds bleed a lot, but I don't think loss of blood is why he's unconscious."

155

Slim handed him a large bandage. Thomas gently covered the egg-sized swelling, then wrapped gauze around Leo's head to hold it in place.

Sean sat back on his heels, concerned that Leo remained unconscious for so long. Thomas stood up, shaking his head. "I don't think we should be moving Leo until he comes to and can tell us if there's something else wrong, too. He might have broken bones we can't see."

Sean nodded his agreement. He rose to his feet and walked over to his mount, wishing it were his trusty Brown Sugar. He turned back to Thomas. "Stay here with 'im, if ya please, Thomas. I'll go fetch our bedrolls and a small tent, then come back and set up camp here."

Sean dashed away towards the distant cookfire, shouting orders to the men to double the night guards as he rode.

An hour later, Thomas and Slim helped Sean erect a small three-person tent next to the fire. Sean spread a heavy quilt over Leo's wet clothes, then spread their ground tarp over the quilt to keep Leo dry. He held Leo's hat over his head, anxiously waiting for him to wake up and open his eyes.

Thomas looked on with a frown. "I do not like that he's out for so long, Sean. I think we should try to rouse him."

Sean nodded his agreement. Thomas found the small green bottle of smelling salts in the first aid kit. He pulled out the cork stopper and waved it under Leo's nose. The irritating fumes of spirits of ammonia triggered Leo's inhalation reflex. Leo gasped. His eyes fluttered open. "Wha... what? What happened?"

Leo moaned, then closed his eyes again. Sean grabbed his hand and held on like a drowning man looking for a hand up into the rescue boat. "Ya took a fall, me boyo, and knocked yerself clean out. Does it hurt much?"

Leo moaned. "Oooohhh, my head!"

When he moved his head experimentally, the bandage pushed against the lump, and he moaned again more loudly. Thomas felt Leo's face to sense his temperature and noticed Leo shivering. Leo muttered, "What happened? Where am I? Where's Sean?"

Sean leaned over to tenderly stroke his face. "Here I am, me boyo. Here I am right by yer side. Stay with us now, pardner. Here, look at me! Can ya focus yer eyes, Leo?"

Sean and Thomas tried to determine if Leo had a concussion, which they knew could be serious. But, neither knew what to do for it other than cold compresses, which they didn't have. Thomas thought if the swelling didn't start to go down by first light, he would have to improvise.

Leo wriggled under the tarp. "What happened? Oh, my head hurts!"

Sean patted Leo's shoulder. "Looks like yer horse took a spill, and ya landed pretty much on yer head, so far as we can tell. Doncha remember?"

Leo began shaking his head, but the slightest movement made him nauseous. He groaned as his stomach settled. "Last I remember was the stampede startin' to mill and slow down a touch. Oh, my achin' head!"

Thomas reached out. "Leo? Do ya hurt anyplace besides yer head?"

Leo experimentally moved his arms. He winced as his right shoulder screamed in protest. "Yep. It seems I landed on my shoulder, and it's smartin' somethin' fierce. Ooohh!"

Sean peered anxiously into Leo's face. "Anythin' else, pardner?"

Leo moved his legs. When nothing else hurt, he held his bruised right shoulder and moved his hips. Leo took several quick breaths in a row when his shoulder shot pain down his arm and across the top of his back. "Nope, just my shoulder and my noggin. Everythin' else seems to be workin'."

Sean motioned to Thomas to lend him a hand. "Let's get ya moved into the tent, then. It'll be more comfortable out of the rain and in yer bed. Come along now. We'll help."

They gently lifted Leo to his feet. Leo managed the four short steps to the tent. When he bent over to crawl inside, the movement hurt his shoulder. He laid down with a sigh of relief, then turned his head to the side to keep pressure off the swelling. "Thanks, Sean. Thanks, Thomas."

Thomas mixed a teaspoon of aspirin powder and water in a tin cup, then ducked into the tent and held it out to Leo. "Here, Leo. Drink this. It'll help the pain some. Try not to move around too much, and try to get some sleep if ya can. I'll be back with breakfast after first light."

"Thanks, Thomas. So long."

Sean walked Thomas over to his horse. "Thomas, we won't be movin' out in the morning. Please pass the word along to rotate the guards but don't break camp. We'll take a day off and see how the patient is recoverin' before makin' any decisions."

"Not a problem, Sean. I think that's probably fer the best, too. I'll pass the word along."

"Thanks, Thomas."

Thomas and Slim rode away, dragging the pack mule behind them. Sean crawled into the small A-frame tent. He snuggled himself down along Leo's left side, then wrapped his arm around Leo to comfort him and gentle him. "Sleep a little, Leo, if ya can. Rest and get yer strength back. I'm here. I'll be right here with ya, me boyo. Fer now and fer always."

Sighing as the aspirin and Sean's gentleness gave him a little relief, Leo relaxed and drifted off to sleep. Sean stayed awake, alert to any changes in Leo's condition, nervous and concerned. *Ya gotta get better, Leo. Ya gotta live. Ya just gotta!*

Chapter 11: Trail's End

The brightly dawning sun revealed the last of the storm system pulling away to the east. Already, the thirsty desert dust had absorbed all the rain. Tiny yellow flowers burst open from spindly gray-green stalks growing low to the ground. Sean awoke with a start. He anxiously leaned up on his elbow and peered into Leo's face. He gently laid his hand on Leo's uninjured left shoulder. "Are ya awake yet, Leo?"

Leo opened his eyes then squinched them closed eyes with a scowl. "Yeah. Tarnation, Sean! What on earth happened?"

"Ya don't remember last night?"

"Last night? No. What?"

"Do ya remember the stampede after lightning set a pine tree to burnin'?"

"Oh... yeah... I do, sorta. But, where am I? Why does my head hurt so bad?"

"Well, I'll tell ya again, pardner. Yer horse took a spill, and ya landed on yer head and right shoulder. Ya have a really big goose egg on the back of yer skull, doncha know."

"Oh."

"Ya ready to try gettin' up? Ya need to pee?"

"Yeah. I think maybe I do."

Sean placed a hand behind Leo's left shoulder and eased him up to a sitting position. Leo wobbled a little, instinctively reaching out his right hand to steady himself. A stabbing, sharp pain shot down his arm and across his back. "Ouch!"

"Easy does it, me boyo. Easy now."

Sean put his arm around Leo's waist and slowly pulled him up to his knees. "Can ya walk on yer knees to get out of the tent?"

Leo nodded yes. Swaying, he leaned over against Sean. "Oh! I'm a bit dizzy, Sean."

"Well, no wonder, seein' as how ya got yerself concussed but good last night."

Sean helped Leo crawl out of the low tent. Then he helped Leo stand up. Leo grabbed Sean's shoulder with his left hand for support. They slowly made their way past the fire, now reduced to a wisp of smoke from dying embers. Sean assisted Leo's one-handed fumbles with the buttons of his jeans. After Leo peed, Sean buttoned up his fly.

"I think I need to sit down fer a bit, Sean."

"Sure thing, me boyo."

Sean eased Leo down to sit Indian-style beside the fire. He picked up a twig and poked at the remains of the fire, stoking it back to life. Then he added a few larger damp branches. Sean walked back to the tent and picked up his canteen. He took off the lid and handed it to Leo.

Leo groaned as he leaned his forehead on his left hand. "I sure don't remember takin' a spill last night."

Sean pointed to the rock chucks' nest right beside them. "Well, I'm afraid ya did, pardner. I found ya last night, laying all sprawled out over that little pile o' rocks over there. Ya gave me quite the scare, too. In the dark, I couldn't tell if ya was dead or alive. It nearly gave me a heart attack. Scared me plumb to death to see ya layin' there, not movin'."

"I sure don't remember."

"Well, maybe it'll come to ya. Look, there's Thomas bringin' us some breakfast."

Thomas rode up and fairly jumped off his horse. "How ya feeling this morning, Leo?"

"My head hurts, and my shoulder hurts, and I'm a bit dizzy, and I don't remember fallin' last night."

"That's natural, Leo. Don't let it bother ya none. I brought ya another powder of aspirin and a bite of breakfast."

After Leo drank down the powdered aspirin stirred in water, he took a bite of a fresh sourdough biscuit. He chewed it slowly, then shook his head and handed it to Sean. "I can't eat anythin' right now. Sorry, Thomas."

"No need to be sorry, Leo. Yer doing real good just bein' up and about. Here, let me tie yer right arm in a sling so's ya don't jostle yer shoulder so much. That aspirin should kick in soon, too. I'm just glad ya aren't hurt more seriously."

Sean retrieved their bedrolls from the tent. He shook them off, rolled them up, and tied them. Thomas stepped over to help him take down and fold up the little tent. When they finished, Sean put his hand on Leo's left shoulder and gave it a gentle squeeze. "Think yer up to makin' the trip over to the camp?"

"Well, I can try."

Sean and Thomas saddled up the horses and tied the tent and bedrolls behind the saddles. Sean picked up Leo's damp hat and brushed it off. "I don't think yer hat's gonna fit ya just now, seein' as how ya have such a big goose egg on yer noggin. Why don't I carry it for ya?"

They helped Leo struggle up into the saddle without using his right arm. Sean saw how Leo gripped the saddle horn with his left hand to steady himself. "Maybe I should lead yer bronc, so ya can just concentrate on keepin' yer saddle. All right, me boyo?"

"All right."

Sean and Thomas guided their horses at a slow walk with Leo in the middle. They reached the camp five minutes later. They helped Leo dismount, then walked him over and sat him down under the tarp at the side of the chuckwagon. Leo leaned against the big rear wheel, sitting upright in the shade. Several of the hands wandered by to say good morning and to inquire how he was feeling. Thomas had told them about Leo's accident while they ate breakfast. They all felt relieved to see him alive this morning.

Sean set Leo's canteen close beside him. "Here, me boyo. Sip some water a bit. Maybe it'll start to settle yer stomach. Will ya be all right here while I go check on the herd?"

Leo tried to smile but didn't quite manage it. "Sure. Yer the boss, and ya got yer duties. Just let me sit here a spell. I'll be just fine."

"Sure ya will, me boyo. I'll be back to check on ya in an hour or so."

Leo leaned back on his left shoulder. He turned his head to the left and rested it against the wagon wheel. He closed his eyes and took deep long breaths, willing his stomach to stop churning.

Around noontime, the smell of cooking woke Leo up from a catnap. He felt a little better... and hungry. He used his left arm to pull himself to his feet, then glanced around at the camp until he found Sean over by the remuda talking to Tommy Boy. It made him feel better just knowing where to find Sean.

He took a step closer to Thomas. "That smells good, Cookie. Listen. I know yer real busy just now, but could I get some more aspirin, please. This headache just won't quit."

"Sure thing, Leo. Glad to see ya on yer feet."

Thomas quickly stirred the powder in a tin cup of water. "Here ya go, Leo. Relax a spell. I'll be servin' dinner in just a few minutes. Think ya might be able to eat something, now?"

"Well, my stomach's rumblin', so I think I'm gonna try."

"Good to hear. Ya must be on the mend then."

Sean strode up, smiling at seeing Leo on his feet. Sean walked right up and stared Leo in the eye. He winked then looked him over closely. "How ya doin' there, pardner?"

"Better, I think. I've still gotta bloomin' headache and a sore shoulder, but I'm not so dizzy now."

"Great! That means yer on the road to recovery."

Thomas banged a wooden spoon on a pot lid. "Dinner's ready. Come and get it!"

Sean and Leo sat under the tarp attached to the chuckwagon while they ate. Sean told Leo that Tommy Boy would take advantage of the day off to inspect the shoes on the horses.

Before Leo finished eating, Tommy Boy walked over and dumped his dishes in the wreck pan for washing. He waved Randy, one of his wranglers, to come help him. He opened a cupboard in the side of the wagon, pulled out a small heavy anvil, and handed it off to Randy. He handed a hammer and a pair of tongs to another cowboy. Then he pulled out a long file, a heavy case of blank horseshoes, and a smaller box of horseshoe nails and handed them off to other men. He carried the small bellows and a bag of coal himself.

Sean spread out Leo's bedroll by the chuckwagon. Leo curled up on his left side and promptly fell asleep. Tommy Boy and his three assistants spent the afternoon checking all the horses and making repairs.

That night the hands took advantage of all the deadfall around the camp and built a larger bonfire than usual. After supper, they began bragging and telling tall tales. Hank Tillison couldn't help but try to upstage everyone else. Slim told the boys an unlikely story of bedding down two Mexican senoritas at the same time while riding herd along the Rio Grande down in Texas. Hank stood up and held his hands up for silence. "I knew me a Mexicana maid once down in San Antone. Pretty little thing. Very lively in bed, too. Well, one day, she asked the lady of the house fer a raise. The housewife was real put out. She put her hands on her hips and shook her head. 'Now, Maria, why do ya want a pay increase, anyway?'"

Hank did his best to imitate a Mexican girl's accented English. "'Well, Senyora, there are tree reasons why I deserve more money. The first eez that I iron better than jew.'

"The insulted housewife demanded, 'Who said ya iron better than me?'

"'Jor huzban. He say so. So there!'

"Getting red in the face, the lady of the house said, 'Oh, yeah?'

"Maria answered back, sassy as ever, 'And the second reason eez that I am better cook than jew!'

"'Nonsense!' The housewife shouted. 'Who said ya cooked better than me?'

"Maria pointed a finger at her mistress and said, 'Jor hozbun did!'

"'Oh, he did, did he?'

"Maria nodded her head as she glared daggers at her mistress. Then, pointing her finger again at her lady, Maria shouted, 'And the third reason is that I am better at being sexy in the bed than jew!'

"Oh, boy! The lady of the house got really boiling at such an insult and demanded through gritted teeth, 'And did my husband say that, as well?'

"Maria hesitated and then said, 'No, Senyora. The foreman did!'

"The housewife stared hard at Maria then finally gave up. 'So how much of a raise do you want?'"

The cowboys burst into laughter. Hank grinned, nodding around at everyone lounging around the fire. He took a bow and then sat down.

Not to be outdone by old man Tillison's gift of gab, Tommy Boy stood up and began pacing back and forth in front of the fire. "I was in a bar down in El Paso last year when I saw this lady walk in. She spotted a cowboy with his feet propped up on a table with the biggest feet she ever had seen. I heard the lady, who weren't no lady, obviously, ask the cowboy if it's true what they say about men with big feet. The cowboy grinned and said, 'Sure is, little lady. Why doncha come on up to my room and let me prove it to ya?'

"The woman wanted to find out the truth of the matter for herself, so she spent the night with 'im. The next morning, she handed the cowboy a fifty-dollar bill. The cowboy blushed and said, "Why, thank ya, ma'am. Ah'm real flattered. Ain't nobody ever paid me fer me services in bed afore."

"The woman told the cowboy, 'Don't be flattered. Just take the money and buy yerself some boots that fit!'"

The men chuckled. Sean pulled Leo up from his bedroll by the chuckwagon. "Let's move away from this rowdy crowd, whaddaya say? Time to get us some shuteye."

Sean carried their bedrolls far enough away from the campfire they could find a little peace and quiet. Leo followed, staggering a little, still wobbly on his feet.

At daybreak, Sean and Thomas decided Leo should ride shotgun on the chuckwagon. Leo didn't want to be separated from Sean but knew it made sense. Between a bad headache and a painful right shoulder, riding a horse could be difficult and uncomfortable.

It took a couple of days for Leo's healthy young body to reduce the swelling on the back of his head. His badly bruised shoulder remained sore for several more days. Eventually, he resumed his duties, glad to be back to work.

164

Sean and his crew drove the cattle for seven more days, following shallow valleys surrounded by arid hills. Only a couple of the valleys had water. Their path led them southerly and easterly. On the eighth day, they crossed the unmarked border into Wyoming.

They stopped that evening several miles west of Evanston. The Union Pacific Railroad had built a huge machine shop and roundhouse in Evanston to repair and refuel their cross-country locomotives. The area around Evanston had plenty of wood and water when the railroad arrived forty years earlier. They had chopped down all forests for fuel since then. Young trees grew around the town now. Fortunately, they had discovered coal a few miles north in Almy. With coal, Evanston remained an important fuel depot for the increasingly busy traffic crossing the country.

Thomas took the pup wagon into town and replenished their coffers. He returned with a healthy young porker. The cowboys would feast on fresh ham for a couple of days.

Early the following morning, Leo ate fried ham and mustard on a sourdough biscuit. As he washed it down with black coffee, he couldn't remember the day of the week. "Cookie? What is today?"

"Whaddaya mean, Leo?"

"Ya know. The day of the week and the date."

"Oh. Well, let me see now. Today is Wednesday the fifth of October."

"Oh. Thanks. Doin' the same thing day after day, the days all kinda run in together. I can't tell the difference between a Sunday or a Friday. They're all the same."

"I know what ya mean, Leo. It does get a bit boring after a while, don't it?

That night, Sean and Leo lay on their bedrolls after a passionate bout of lovemaking, gazing at the waxing crescent moon. Sean sat up. "Ya know what, Leo? I'm in the mood fer some music."

Sean pulled on his boots and walked over to the pup wagon for his guitar. He returned and sat on a tree stump while he tuned the guitar. Then he began picking out the melody of *Streets of Laredo,* a sweet yet sad song with a lyrical melody. As his fingers warmed up, Sean added the base note with two strums of his fingers across the chord, setting the three-quarters time of the waltz. When the verse started over, he sang the lyrics of the sad cowboy song for Leo.

He finished the last stanza. "For we loved our comrade, so brave, young and handsome. We all loved our comrade, although he'd done wrong."

Leo walked over and sat down by Sean, nudging him with his hip so they could share the tree stump. He put his arm over Sean's shoulders and hugged him. "That was beautiful, Sean. Thanks."

Sean hummed the last phrase of the song again, then carefully set the guitar aside. Leo leaned over to rest his head on Sean's shoulder. "Ya know what, Sean?"

"What, me boyo?"

Leo pointed at the guitar leaning against the tree roots. "Ya never did finish telling me the story of how ya ended up with Jackson's guitar. Back when we were riding the fences on the Sugar Company Farm, ya told me about Jackson bein' yer first love, but ya never finished the story."

"Oh, Leo. It brings back such sad thoughts I really don't like to go there. But, I guess there's no harm in tellin' ya. I think I might o' tol' ya that Jackson was the handsomest man I'd ever seen, didn't I?"

"That ya did, Sean. Ya described 'im real good, as I recall. Tall, dark, and handsome, I believe ya said."

"That he was, Leo. And talented. Jackson could sing like an angel. Pure delight it was to hear 'im. And he had a head fer the lyrics. He always knew all the words to the entire song. It used to make me so jealous. Back then, I was, let me see, about fifteen goin' onto sixteen. And Jackson was an old man fer still ridin' the trails, bein' about thirty-five or so."

Leo nuzzled Sean's neck. "Um-hm."

"Well, I was madly in love with 'im, even if 'e was an old man. I thought the sun rose and set on 'im. It took me a few weeks before I got 'im to start takin' me serious. Then, after the first night that 'e let me sleep with 'im, I woulda done anythin' fer 'im. He took me in hand and showed me the ropes of how to make love.

166

Not the little boy stuff I'd played around doin' with me friends, but the real passionate stuff of acheivin' real ecstasy. And boy, was he talented in bed, too!"

Sean gave Leo a little jab with his elbow. They both chuckled softly.

"So, anyways, the drive came to an end in Kansas City. It was the biggest city I'd ever seen. Jackson and some of the other hands took me into town. We stayed in rooms over a saloon. We caroused all the day long and just had a good ol' time, glad not to be eatin' dust. The next night, in walked this dude, all spiffed up with the fanciest tooled boots ya ever did see. A right handsome gent, and clearly a man with money to burn. Turns out 'e was a big rancher there in Kansas City and recently widowed. He was about the same age as Jackson, I do believe."

"Well, that night, before the drinks got too long and the cowboys too rowdy, Jackson brought down his guitar and sang some songs fer the men. The rancher invited Jackson over to his table fer a drink when Jackson finished singin'. They struck up a conversation that went late into the night. I reached the point where I was plumb knackered out and wanted to go to bed. But Jackson ignored me hints and told me to go on up. He said he'd come up later. So I did."

"The next day went pretty much the same. The rancher showed up a lot earlier, though, and he was wearin' even fancier clothes and boots. Jackson went over and sat with 'im just like the night before, and they talked the day away over some hands of cards. I was feelin' more than a little jealous at bein' left out, but there were lots of me friends around from the drive, and we just shot the breeze, sittin' around laughin' and jokin' all the day long."

Sean leaned forward and rested his elbows on his knees, cradling his chin in his hands. "Jackson didn't come up to bed that night. Next mornin' when I asked 'im where he'd been, he avoided tellin' me. I was feelin' a bit scared and real jealous about me handsome lover, but I didn't know what I could do. I thought 'e loved me back. That afternoon, as soon as the rancher came in the saloon, Jackson immediately went over and sat next to 'im,

167

ignorin' me completely. I got more concerned and more depressed as the day went on. Late that night, I just lay in bed, wide awake, wonderin' and worryin' where Jackson was, feelin' sick inside, like me stomach was droppin' into a pit."

Leo squeezed Sean's shoulders affectionately.

"I must've fallen asleep, eventually, 'cause when I woke up, I saw that all of Jackson's gear was gone except fer his black guitar case. He left it leanin' against the wall by the door. He pinned a note against the wall by the neck of the guitar case. I went over and read it. It said only goodbye. Keep practicing. He signed it with his initial, J.

"Well, I panicked that Jackson'd left me. I threw on me clothes and rushed down the stairs, frantic to find 'im. The guys from the trail were sittin' around gabbin' as usual. Well, when Danny saw me, 'e beckoned me over to 'is table. He tol' me that Jackson had taken off with the rich rancher dude and that they'd already boarded a train headin' East. He said he had overheard 'em talkin' about takin' a trip to Europe last night. Jackson was just gone, just like that!"

Sean snapped his fingers with a flick of his wrist. "Just like that! Well, I was so hurt, Leo. I couldn't believe that Jackson had only used me body to satisfy his lusts and hadn't felt none of the deep affections that I felt for him. I got real depressed. I didn't know what to do. He treated me real bad, knowin' that I was so in love with 'im. Then 'e runs off with someone who bribed 'im with his money and fancy clothes and got 'im to leave me and go off traipsin' the world with 'im. I got left behind fer a taste of the easy life."

Sean coughed uncomfortably, then sat up and snuggled up to Leo. "I'm afraid I spent days just stayin' in me little room above the saloon, drinkin' rotgut whiskey till I couldn't stand the smell of meself nor the room. I just felt so lost, so empty and abandoned. I felt discarded like a worn-out ol' shoe. Then I reached a point that I got angry – but really, really angry – and I cursed Jackson and damned 'im to hell and back. Finally, me anger just turned to ice inside of me heart. I swore I would never fall in love with anyone else ever again. I just couldn't leave meself open fer such bad hurtin' again.

"Well. I finally cleaned meself up. I headed out with some of the hands and traveled down to the Star Ranch, down in Texas."

Sean gave Leo a big hug, then pulled away and looked Leo in his eyes. "Those feelin's of ice inside me didn't begin to melt until I met yew, Leo me love. Now that we've met, me heart has thawed, and I've come alive again. I'm really very happy, now, doncha know."

"I am too, Sean. I love ya so much."

"I love ya, too, me boyo."

Days of boredom, discomfort, and exhaustion turned into week after week of following the same miserable routine. Only Sean seemed to enjoy the journey. They rode their horses, droving the meandering herd of cattle along a tried and true trail, their un-exciting, predictable routine broken only by an occasional late-night dance. They drove through rain and wind, scorching sun, and chilly nights. Practically every day, one or more cowpunch-ers walked or limped over to the chuckwagon, asking Thomas to do what he could about their sprains, bruises, scratches, and abra-sions.

The cowboys ate their meals and told their stories around the campfires at night. After a while, they had shared all their good stories, so they retold the old ones with even more outrageous ex-aggerations than the first time.

They herded the cattle cross country. They cut across a north-eastern corner of Utah and then continued on to Grand Junction, Colorado. From there, they struck a more southerly course. Fi-nally, after seventy-three long exhausting days, they pulled up to Henderson's sprawling winter pasturage in the mountains ten miles northwest of Durango.

At breakfast that morning, Cookie told Sean they should ar-rive at the Lazy H sometime around midday. All the men perked up when they heard the good news. Sean had to yell to be heard over the excited babble of men making plans to get drunk, visit whorehouses, find a hotel with a bath, or head for home. After

Sean quieted down the men, he ordered them to move out for their final five-mile trek. Leo and Sean rode point together that sunny, cool morning, leading the men and cattle south.

Leo spotted a big gate in the distance and pointed it out to Sean. Its size made it stand out like an ink drawing against the barren hills and blue sky. Leo's pulse quickened at the thought of reaching the end of the long drive. Three thirty-foot-long trunks of thin lodgepole pines formed the gate to Henderson's winter spread. Henderson had planted two on either side of the barely graded dirt path and lashed the third across the top. A giant, rusted iron rendition of the Lazy H brand hung by chains from the top of the gate, swinging gently in the dry breeze.

A heavy older man rode towards them on a big brown Hano-verian with a flowing black tail. Taller than the usual horse, it carried the overweight man with a healthy athleticism, its muscles flowing attractively beneath its hide. The rider pulled up to Sean smiling a big smile. "Hey, boys. I'm Ricky, ol' man Henderson's foreman here about. Your Cookie told me you should be along right about now."

He looked over the two young men before him, then pointed at Brown Sugar. "I'll bet anything you're Sean, the trail boss for this here drive."

Sean smiled and nodded. "And ya would be winnin' that bet, Mister Ricky."

Sean turned and pointed at Leo. "This is me sidekick, Leo."

Ricky turned his big horse around and pointed up the drive. "Follow me, boys. I'll show you to the reducing corral where we'll count and inspect the herd for delivery."

Ricky laughed as though he had told a hilarious joke. "Follow me, boys."

Sean and Leo followed Ricky at their usual plodding speed. They rode under the big gate even though it didn't have fences to its left or right. During the ride, Sean reported on the drive and the condition of the cattle. Ricky had all kinds of questions about trouble from locoweed, botflies, and other ailments. He asked how many cattle they had slaughtered to feed the men. Sean answered, "Only a couple of stragglers that were slowin' us down and four calves that couldn't keep up."

Ricky laughed. "Well, that's real good, Sean. I hate hearing about feeding the men with dollars on the hoof. You did real good!"

"Oh, but we lost a couple of slowpokes to wolves, and a couple more died of natural causes."

"Still, Sean. That's not too bad at all."

About an hour and a half later, they neared a large, low clapboard house built of raw sawn pine. It nestled in a clump of mature trees the Hendersons had planted decades ago. A split rail fence began in front of the house, angling back to an enormous barn. Another split rail fence began two hundred yards to their left and ran back to the unpainted barn.

Sean pointed at the two unconnected fences. "That yer reducin' corral, Ricky? Never saw one quite like that before."

Ricky chuckled. His bearded face split into another big grin. "Yes, sir. Ol' man Henderson got tired of fighting the cows to get them corralled up, so he invented it. It works right good, too. You'll see. Of course, it helps that we have no shortage of land to spread it out on."

As they rode past the house, they spotted Thomas by the chuckwagon at the back of the low building. Thomas stood talking to an older cattleman, the Cookie for the ranch hands.

The funnel-shaped fences converged on a series of corrals that spread out behind the barn. A complex arrangement of gates stood at the juncture of the fences. Ricky nudged his big horse over to the right side of the gate. "Follow me, boys. I'll show you how we sort and count your herd so I can give you a receipt."

The split rail fence changed at the gates to a six-foot-tall post and beam fence. The three men dismounted and tied their reins to the tall fence.

Belying his obesity, Ricky quickly climbed the fence like a ladder. He swung his beefy behind over the top rail and sat down. The big heals of his worn cowboy boots latched behind the second rail to secure his seat. "Come on up, boys, and take a seat."

Sean and Leo grinned at each other as they scrambled up to watch the sorting.

Ricky waved over some of his hired cowhands to man the gates. He pulled a small pad of paper out of his shirt pocket. Then he dug back in for the stub of pencil he had put there that morning. As the cattle plodded by, the overweight foreman directed the gatekeepers to sort them. He sent those ready for market through the first gate. He sent skinny cattle through the second gate. They needed time to fatten up. The cattle he wanted to inspect for disease went through the third gate to the smallest corral. He sent young bulls through the fourth gate, which led directly to the barn. They needed to be gelded so they would fatten up.

It took two dusty hours to count and sort the herd. The hands rotated back to the ranch house for their noonday meal. Sean, Leo, and Ricky stayed up on the fence, counting the herd. Finally, the drag riders herded the slowest cows through the gates.

Ricky wrote out a receipt for 1,836 head of cattle and handed it to Sean with a flourish. As soon as they finished, Ricky nimbly climbed down the fence. "My stomach's so empty I can pert near feel my spine meeting up to my belly button."

Ricky laughed at his joke as he untied his tall Hanoverian. "Follow me, boys, and I'll buy ya dinner at the best restaurant this side of Durango."

Still laughing, Ricky kicked his horse into a gallop, heading to the ranch house. Sean and Leo, hungry from their missed dinner, scampered to catch up.

The three men tied up their horses at the rail beside the back door of the large low building. The Hendersons had built the house of rough sawn pine boards. It stood unpainted, grayed and splintery from the sun and weather. Ricky held open the door and waved them in with a big grin exposing his missing teeth. They stamped their boots on the small back porch, then ducked their heads as they entered the low door.

They entered a dining room with a kitchen at the other end. Ricky led them to a table close to the wood-burning stove. "I'm starving here, Cookie. Where's my vittles? I'm perishing here!"

Leo took it all in. The place looked more like a bunkhouse than a home with a wife and children.

The old cook began dishing up plates. "All right. All right. Hold yer horses."

Ricky put away more food than Sean and Leo combined, even though they were hungry and ate up a storm. Ricky asked Sean how many head of cattle he had when he started the drive. Sean leaned back in his chair. "We started out with one thousand eight hundred forty-seven head."

Ricky laughed as though Sean had told a joke. "Why, I think that might be a record, only loosin' eleven head in over seven hundred miles of hard cross-country travel. Congratulations, Sean!"

Sean nodded and smiled, his mouth full of spicy bean and beef chili. He knew many of his hands felt anxious to return home, so he rushed through his late dinner. The ranch's cook cleared away their plates and brought them coffee. Sean went out to his saddlebags and retrieved his small notebook. The notebook held the folded-up list of hands Alex Henderson had prepared before the round-up.

Sean checked his notes carefully then looked over at Ricky. "Well, sir, me men have earned eighty-four days of pay. Ten at the round-up, seventy-three fer the drove, and one fer delivery here."

Ricky nodded amicably with a smile. He stood up, lumbered into the ranch office, and removed a lockbox from a floor safe. He carried in the heavy box and set it on the table. He dug a set of keys out of his pants pocket and unlocked the box.

Sean nodded at Leo. "Listen, me boyo, how about ya go tell the men to come in fer their pay. And tell 'em I said no horseplay nor rough housin', neither."

Leo jumped up, excited about his first payday. "Sure, Sean. I'll be right back."

Leo ran out the door, yelling at the top of his voice, "Hey, everyone! Come on in fer yer pay. And Sean said no horseplay!"

At that news, the men ran in, pushing and shoving and laughing boisterously. Leo held the door open as he watched the men form up in a loose line. Liam and Gibson shoved their way to the front. *Dang it all! I wanted to be the first in line.* Thomas arrived last and held the door for Leo.

Inside, Ricky counted out the pay and gave it to Sean. Sean carefully checked the amount and then entered the payment next to each man's name. They required each man to sign the ranch register and Sean's list before receiving their pay. Sean shook hands with each man and thanked them for a job well done.

The cowboys and wranglers received the standard one dollar per day. Thomas, the Cookie, and Tommy Boy, the head wrangler, received a buck fifty per day. Sean, as trail boss, earned a whopping two dollars a day.

Leo's smile wouldn't stop. He carefully counted his eighty-four dollar pay then gleefully stuffed it in his pocket. He had never had that much money before. He couldn't wait to spend it. He and Sean had discussed how he needed to buy a horse so he could ride with Sean. When Ricky and Sean finished up with Thomas, Leo sat down next to Ricky. "Mister Ricky? Mister Henderson told me that if I found a horse I liked, I could buy 'er. And, well, ya see, I need a horse. There's a lively black mare I've been ridin' a lot over the past few weeks. And, well, sir, I'd like to buy her off ya if I can."

Ricky chuckled and nodded. "And just how much are you willing to offer for this lively black mare, Leo?"

Leo looked at Sean, then focused back on Ricky's grinning face. "Well, I was hopin' to buy 'er for forty dollars." *Half of my first pay is an awful lotta money!*

The smile on Ricky's face slipped as he shook his head no. "Leo, my boy, I'm no horse trader, but even I know a good riding horse fetches at least a hundred bucks."

After fifteen minutes of nervous haggling, they shook hands. Leo bought his first horse for only seventy-two dollars and fifty cents. He reluctantly counted out the money. *Dang it all! This only leaves me with eleven and a half dollars. Oh, well. At least I have a horse and some money in my pocket now. That's more than I had before the drive.*

Both Sean and Ricky knew the horse would bring a hundred or more at auction, but they were happy to help the boy get a start in life. Ricky knew Alex Henderson would approve if he were there.

Sean watched Ricky and Leo shake hands after Ricky wrote him out a bill of sale. He clapped Leo on the back in congratulations. "A cowboy ain't much good without a good cow horse, now, is he?"

Sean and Leo went directly to the pup wagon to retrieve their personal effects. Liam and Gibson jogged over to them, each leading a borrowed horse already saddled and loaded with their bedrolls and gear. Gibson smiled from ear to ear. "Liam and I are going into Durango and taking the train back to Blackfoot. I just wanted to say thanks and goodbye."

Leo gave Gibson a big wink. "Can't wait to rush home to the welcomin' arms of sweet Sue Lynn, eh?"

"That's right, Leo. I can't wait to see her again. I'm so in love with her."

"Well, good luck with yer marriage and new homestead and all. Maybe I'll look ya up if I'm ever up Idaho Falls way."

"I wish you would look me up so you could meet Sue Lynn. Then you would understand why I'm in such an all-fire hurry to get home to her."

They shook hands all around. Even Leo and Liam shook hands once quickly. Liam mumbled, "Well, so long, then."

Leo looked away with a slight frown. "Yep, so long."

Leo picked up his saddlebags and headed directly to Tommy Boy to claim his horse. Tommy Boy had just turned over the remuda to the ranch's assistant manager, Ricky Junior. Young Junior had already grown every bit as large and heavy as his father.

Leo proudly held out his bill of sale and asked for the black mare Tommy Boy had given him to ride so many times. Tommy Boy nodded. "Good choice, Leo. Good price, too. Congratulations."

Tommy Boy cut out the mare and ceremoniously turned her over to Leo. Leo shook Tommy Boy's hand. "Thanks! Thanks a lot. See ya later, Tommy Boy."

Sean and Leo saddled up, tied their belongings behind their saddles, and took off at a trot towards Durango. They both looked forward to a hot bath, sleeping in a real bed, and enjoying a few days without responsibilities.

Ricky had recommended the Strater Hotel in the big city of nearly five thousand people. They found the prominent four-story red-brick Victorian hotel without any trouble. The fancy hotel had public rooms, restaurants, a pharmacy, a saloon, and ninety-three guestrooms. Leo's eyes bugged out as they rode towards the front door on Main Avenue. "Wow! That's the biggest buildin' I ever saw."

They checked their horses in the stables behind the main building and then walked into the spacious wood-paneled and wallpapered entrance. Leo nudged Sean with his elbow. "Wow! This is the fanciest place I ever did see."

Sean asked the desk clerk for a simple room with a bathtub. Leo gaped around at the tables scattered around the lobby. Elegantly dressed ladies sat at the tables playing euchre and laughing with high twittering laughs. The clerk offered Sean several options, including rooms with grand pianos. Sean settled for a small fourth-floor room in the back with a big bathtub.

A skinny teenage bellhop helped carry their saddlebags and bedrolls up the grand staircase to the fourth floor. He opened the door and bowed them in. Leo looked around in awe at the fine English wallpaper and a small wood-burning heat stove. "Wow!"

Leo's eyes grew bigger when the bellboy showed them the washstand with a white chamber pot hidden in its base. He explained the morning maids would empty it for them. The bellhop then pointed out their fine hotel had a centrally located three-story privy just down the hall. Sean tipped the boy a nickel. He left, closing the door behind him. Leo pulled Sean into a big hug. "Wow. This is the fanciest place I've ever seen in my whole entire life. I never imagined somethin' so nice. Wow!"

Sean asked Leo to unpack their saddlebags and stow their bedrolls in the wardrobe while he went back down to the front desk to order hot water for a bath. Shortly after Sean returned, he answered a knock at the door. Four liveried young men carried in eight covered pails of steaming hot water. They poured seven buckets of hot water into the enameled cast iron bathtub set in a small alcove. They left the eighth bucket on the little stove to stay warm for rinsing at the end of the bath. A maid in a starched gray dress and floor-length white apron delivered a stack of four white towels, four washcloths, and a paper-wrapped bar of store-bought Ivory Soap "that floats."

"Wow. That's real service, isn't it, Sean? Hot water just fer the askin'!"

Sean and Leo took their time bathing. They shaved, even though Leo didn't really need to, before changing into fresh clothes. Finally, they strolled down to the fancy restaurant for supper. Gleaming gas chandeliers and wall sconces adorned the wood-paneled and wallpapered room. Tall candles lit each cloth-covered table. China and silverware adorned the tables, along with a rose in a small crystal vase. Leo looked around, his eyes wide with amazement at the luxury and beauty of the room. "Wow, Sean. This place is somethin' else, ain't it?"

Sean gave Leo a weary look. "Yea. Wow. Ain't it, though."

As they ate a big steak dinner, they reviewed their options now that the drive had ended. They finally decided to continue their trip south to the Star Ranch outside Dallas, where Sean knew they would find work. They toasted their past and future success with a porcelain china cup of weak coffee at the end of their meal.

They stopped off at the lively Diamond Belle Saloon just off the lobby on their way up to bed. They savored a glass of port, Leo's first, served by scantily dressed dance hall girls. They enjoyed the honky-tonk piano player's lively music before Sean called it a night.

After a few more days of leisure, they headed southwest. They took their time traveling, camping out along the trail, and sharing blankets every night. They finally arrived at the Star Ranch five weeks later, rested and ready to go back to work.

Greenwich Village
December 26, 2010

Josh woke up, contented to lounge in bed with Art. With a bitterly cold wind blowing outside, they didn't want to venture out for Sunday brunch. Instead, they relaxed in Art's condo, sipping gourmet coffee generously laced with Bailey's Irish Crème.

Art asked if Josh wanted to tell more about Grandpa Leo's life. Josh snuggled up under Art's hairy armpit. "Leo and Sean worked as cowboys down in Texas and Arizona for four years. But during that short time, the ranchers stopped driving their cattle to the railheads. Two reasons. First, increasing numbers of settlers claimed homesteads and put up fences, making it increasingly difficult to find unobstructed cross-country trails. And second, by this time, railways were crisscrossing America. They could now get cattle to a railhead without big drives."

Josh looked up at Art's manly two-day stubble and kissed his chin. "Just to put the time into perspective, Art, think about what else happened between nineteen ten and nineteen fourteen, four historically significant years of great changes in all walks of life."

Josh held up a finger in emphasis. "The outbreak of The War to End All Wars brought about the biggest changes. Back then, World War One didn't have a number, even after it spread to engulf the entire civilized world."

"Sir Roger Casement became a hero for cleaning up horrendous abuses of slaves in the Congo and Peru. Then England stripped him of his knighthood. They hung him in 1916 for being a homosexual and an Irish Nationalist."

"During this period, a hundred and forty-six young immigrant girls died in the Triangle Shirtwaist Company sweatshop when it caught fire in New York City. The calamity led to reforms in building codes and child labor laws across the nation."

Art picked up Josh's hand and held it on his bare leg. Josh smiled up at him. "The Titanic sank on April the fifteen, nineteen-hundred and twelve, killing one-thousand five-hundred twenty-two men, women, and children from all walks of life, rich and poor. People around the world spoke of little else but that great

178

tragedy for weeks afterward. The people of the United States elected Woodrow Wilson as President. Zippers became popular. Momentous times. Momentous events."

"The Panama Canal opened to shipping. The Ford Motor Company introduced the moving assembly line. Horseless carriages not only became affordable and popular, but they also became known as cars. New words entered the vocabulary like car parks, airports, airmail, babe, birth control, cartoon, and sex object. All this happened in those last four years while Grandpa Leo and Sean worked as cowboys on the trail."

"And last, but not least, the Boy Scouts of America began. It happened three years after General Robert Baden-Powell, a fifty-year-old English bachelor, founded the organization for boys in England. Chapters sprang up across the States.

"So, now, let's get back to Grandpa Leo's mother, Lizzie, still raising her children on the Utah Idaho Sugar Company Farm in Wapello, Idaho."

Chapter 12: Missing Years

The four years after Leo left home to work for Sean passed slowly for Lizzie. She taught herself how to walk on her twisted and poorly healed right ankle. She struggled with the inconvenience of crutches and then learned to use a cane. But even after she stopped using a cane, she still walked with a noticeable limp. Her unnatural gait caused pains in her left knee, hips, and lower back. Her ankle ached in the cold of winter and when it rained or snowed.

She continued attending the box socials and square dances, but only to listen to the music. She entertained herself by clapping and laughing with the dancers. She could no longer execute even the basic two-step. The popular new dance, the quickstep, fascinated her. She had just learned the foxtrot when she had her accident. She loved all the new music written for these dances but could only watch and listen. She missed square dancing more than she would admit to anyone.

Alma's business did not thrive during this time. The price of beef and sugar went down every year while the cost of everything else went up. The papers blamed the rising costs on wars in far-off Europe, China, and Japan.

Lizzie found herself worrying quite often about her oldest son, Leonard. She hadn't heard from him since he rode away that late fall morning in 1910 to work on a cattle drive. Many a night, she laid wide awake in bed, wondering what had become of him. Had Leo died on the cattle trail from an accident? Had he run away to seek his fortune? Did he pass away from sickness, all alone? Did he think of her as often as she thought of him? She had already lost one son in infancy and couldn't bear the idea of losing a second.

Why didn't Leo write? He knew how to write. It only costs a penny to post a penny postcard. Anyone could afford a penny postcard.

Chapter 13: Prodigal Son

Lizzie limped down the steps of Blackfoot's handsome stone train station, holding Alma's left arm. Her ankle had stiffened up from sitting for hours on the train. It also ached from the cold. They had just returned from an exhausting train trip to Farmington, Utah, to attend Alma's mother's funeral.

Their son Ralph had driven to the station to pick them up in their three-seat surrey pulled by two draft horses, a pair of large black Hamiltonians named Cash and Carry. After greetings and hugs, Ralph loaded their meager two pieces of old leather luggage next to his driver seat. He then lifted their small trunk onto the floor behind the second seat. Alma helped himself to a pinch of chewing tobacco before he climbed aboard.

Alma and Lizzie huddled together on the middle seat while Ralph drove them home to the farm. Since the October days had turned cold, they all wore hats, gloves, and coats with scarves tied up around their throats. Ralph hoped they made it home before sunset when temperatures would plummet to near freezing.

"Ya know, Ralph, yer grandmother was quite the lady. Why, when she was fourteen years old, back in eighteen forty-six, she drove a team of mules from Quincy, Illinois all the way to Winter Quarters, Nebraska."

Alma spat over the side of the surrey onto the road. "Um-hm."

"Yessiree, yer ol' grandma Elizabeth was quite the lady, Ralph. Her friends called her Ely fer short. They held her funeral at the Mormon Stake House in Farmington. Oh, and ya should've seen all the people that showed up. Ya would've thought she was a famous person or somethin'. And the feast of casserole dishes the Relief Society provided fer everyone after the funeral. Well, anyway, they told how Brigham Young 'imself asked Ely's parents to stay at Winter Quarters and raise a crop of corn to feed those who'd come along later. How's that for good planning? Huh? That Brigham Young was sure the organizer."

Alma spat again. "Um-hm."

Ralph glanced back at Lizzie and smiled distractedly. His thoughts replayed his conversation when he walked Maggie McFarland home after school. She seemed to like him as much as he liked her. But it worried him that she was also walking out with Jamie Davis. Jamie's father was the butcher and mayor. That darn Jamie even played baseball better than he did. Ralph wished Lizzie would stop talking so he could give the problem of Maggie the full attention it deserved. He decided he better say something. "Wow. Really?"

"Oh, yeah. Yer Grandma had the most interestin' life, Ralph. She was the first wife of Andrew Hayes, yer grandfather. He had three wives and twenty-three children. He died back in 1881 at the age of forty-nine. And the stories they told about his life! Why he was attacked by Injuns right here in Idaho, where Brigham Young had sent 'im and some others on a mission. They built Fort Lemhi and farmed the land. But then some ol' renegade Flathead Injuns from Montana swooped down on their Fort and killed his two brothers-in-law. They scalped 'em both, but they didn't scalp yer granddad, Ralph. And ya know why? It was 'cause his hair was cut too short. But they bashed his head in good with a toma-hawk, and speared 'im in the chest, and left 'im fer dead. And then ran off with all their livestock."

"Um-hm." Spit.

"Really? Wow."

"They told the story of how he'd entertain his grandkids by placin' an egg in the indentation in his head. He'd walk around, holding it balanced steady as a rock. Have ya ever heard the like? Oh, the stories I heard at the funeral! Alma was fourteen in Ireland during the Potato Famine of eighteen-forty-five. Over a million Irish souls starved plumb to death. Well, he survived, obviously, and at age seventeen, he became a sailor. He made three trans-Atlantic crossin's. Then he jumped ship in New York Harbor to escape punishment fer somethin' he didn't do. I've heard how brutal life was back then in the British Navy. So yer grandpa de-cided to head out to California fer the Gold Rush. But when he got to Salt Lake City, he met and married Ely. Can ya believe it?

And Brigham Young presided over their weddin' in the Endowment House on Temple Square. Brigham Young, himself! Yer very own grandparents, Ralph!"

"Wow. Really?"

Spit. "Um-hm."

Lizzie stopped talking while they jolted up and over the Union Pacific's Yellowstone Special railroad tracks, then down the other side onto a smoother stretch of the dirt road.

"Oh, the stories at the funeral, Ralph. Once yer Grandpa recovered from the Injun attack, yer grandpa was a gen-you-wine Pony Express rider! And ya know what? He had to ride with his left arm tied up in a sling, tied to his chest, due to the injuries from the Injun attack right up here in Salmon, Idaho. He died young, age forty-nine, back in eighteen-eighty-one. Sad. Three wives and twenty-six children. Can ya imagine that! Oh, what a life!"

Hawk, spit. "Um-hm."

Ralph turned around to look at his Mom. "Wow. And how many children did Grandma Ely have, Mom?"

"Oh, let's see now, she had twelve, and yer Dad here was their fifth child. Right, Dad? Do ya remember her visit, Ralph? Ya must've been just a toddler. The train line had just been completed. Grandma Ely wanted to take advantage of it and visit us. It was right after we moved into the stone house. Oh, the stories she told about all the famous people she knew. She personally knew Brigham Young, and John Taylor, and Wilford Woodruff, and Lorenzo Snow. They all became Presidents of the Mormon Church. She knew 'em because they ate meals in her parents' home when she was growin' up. Isn't that somethin'?"

"Really? Wow."

Spit. "Um-hm."

"Well, she will be missed. A part of our pioneer history died with her – as they said in her bee-you-tea-full eulogy at the funeral. I got her obituaries fer the family to read when we get home."

The hours of jostling on the train and then the surrey took their toll on Lizzie. She pulled her shawl up over her head and rested on Alma's shoulder for a cat nap.

An hour later, they arrived home at dusk. Myrtle had lit a lamp and built up a cheerful little fire in the parlor fireplace to welcome them home.

"Oh, daughter, how nice. Thanks fer settin' a fire and fixin' supper. Land o' Goshen, but a body's just plumb tuckered out from all this hustle and bustle of travelin' to Utah and back, all in a hurry. A body just needs a rest!"

Myrtle hugged Lizzie. "Here, Mom. Let me take yer coat. Please sit yerself down at the table and relax a spell."

"Oh. Thanks, daughter. Thanks. I'll sit just as soon as I'm back."

Lizzie scampered out to the convenience as fast as her twisted ankle would let her limp along. She chuckled at the surprised look on Myrtle's face. "Long ride from the station. Long ride."

Myrtle smiled knowingly.

Lizzie had no more taken her seat at the dining table than they heard a brisk, loud knock on the front door. Lizzie and Alma raised their eyebrows at each other in silent questions. They weren't expecting anyone. Alma reluctantly lumbered through the parlor and opened the door.

Lizzie and the children listened quietly to find out who had come calling this late.

"Well, I'll be! Lizzie, it's Leonard! It's Leo! Come in, boy, come in!"

Alma stepped aside and pulled Leo into the room, looking him up and down. Leo stood with his sweat-stained Stetson hat in his hands and a big smile on his suntanned face. "Howdy, Dad. How ya been?"

"Blazes, boy, it's been… it's been a good four years!"

Lizzie stood up in surprise. Her hand clutched her heart as she limped into the parlor. When she saw Leo, she burst into tears. Even as she smiled in relief, tears streamed down her face. She walked up and peered into his face. "Damnation, Leo. I thought ya was dead! Why didn't ya never write me?"

To her children's surprise, she began pounding Leo's chest with both fists. Crying and laughing in relief, she pounded some more.

184

Leo glanced sheepishly at his parents from under his ducked head. He never dreamed coming back home would create such a fuss. He hugged Lizzie to stop her hands. "Nope. I'm not dead, Mom. And neither is my sidekick, Sean, who ya might remember from years ago."

Leo pointed at the door where Sean stood politely, hat in hand, waiting for them to invite him in. He smiled his lopsided smile as he watched the dramatic family reunion.

Alma extended his hand in welcome. "Why, sure. I remember ya, Sean. Come on in and join us fer supper. We was just ready to sit down. And now it'll be a celebration supper fer the return of our prodigal son, here. Yessiree, the return of the prodigal son!"

Alma took Lizzie's arm and guided her into the dining room, beckoning the two young men to follow. Lizzie used her crocheted shawl like a hanky to wipe her eyes.

The kids jumped up and ran to hug Leo. They shook his hand and patted his back, all talking at the same time. "Leo! Leo!" "Where ya been all this time?" "What've ya been doin' fer so long? "How've ya been, Leo?" "Ya home fer good?"

Lizzie and Alma sat down at the head and foot of the long trestle table. Leo stood smiling, happy to see his brothers, sisters, and parents alive and healthy, still living at home. He didn't say a word.

Myrtle, a young lady now, strolled up and gave him a big hug. She immediately noticed he had grown taller over the past four years. He stood now a full-grown man of eighteen. Myrtle held Leo's arm and gestured to the benches at the table. "Now, have a seat and relax while I start serving supper. I'm really so glad to see ya, Leo. Ya just don't know!"

Young Honce, Leo's feisty eight-year-old little brother, pushed and elbowed his way in to sit between Sean and Leo. He smiled up at both of them, looking from side to side at Leo and then Sean. Things settled down around the table.

"Land o' Goshen!" Lizzie exclaimed, shaking her head in the sudden silence. "Oh, what a day this's been! We just now got back from yer Grandmother Elizabeth Tanner Hayes's funeral

185

down in Farmington, Utah, and here ya show up on the doorstep! What a day!"

Myrtle walked into the dining room carrying heavy bowls filled with steaming vegetables and mashed potatoes. Ralph walked in from parking the surrey in the carriage house and feeding the horses. He stopped short at the door when he saw Leo and Sean. "Leo? Oh my gosh! I don't believe my eyes! Leo!"

Ralph ran over. Leo stood up and stepped over the bench seat. They gave each other a big hug with lots of happy slaps on each other's backs. "Hey, Ralph. Good to see ya, little brother."

They stepped back and grinned at each other.

Myrtle turned to the kitchen. "Ralph, do me a favor and grab the platter of pork chops since yer up, would ya? And Honce, would ya please help by bringin' in the bowl with the hot sourdough rolls and pass 'em around to everyone? Okay?"

They all settled down and began eating. Sean gestured over at Myrtle with his fork. "Boy howdy, Myrtle, ya sure have learnt to cook good since ya helped me in the kitchen a few years back. Do ya remember?"

"Oh, yeah. I remember. Well, with Mom laid up in bed with her broken ankle fer three months, there was nothin' fer it but fer me to learn to cook. Mom kept me runnin' back and forth from the stove to her sickbed all the day long. She told me what to do step by step. I learned to bake pie crust by mixin' the dough right at Mom's bedside. Remember, Mom?"

Myrtle and Lizzie both nodded and shared a warm smile.

"Mom's always sayin' how necessity is the mother of invention. Well, in my case, Mother was the necessity of my cookin'!"

Myrtle chuckled, then scooped up a fork of mashed potatoes and gravy. She watched Leo and Sean while she ate. *My. My. My. But aren't they just two of the best lookin' men in the whole county? And Leo, he's all grown-up and a man, now. My. My. My.*

After everyone finished eating, Myrtle jumped up from the table. "Just a minute while I get the fresh peach cobbler out of the oven. We can relax over coffee and dessert while the two of ya tell us all yer tales of the past four years."

The other kids got busy clearing the table. Lizzie looked over at Leo. "Leo, ya will never know the grief I have felt in me mother's heart over the past few years because of yer absence and yer silence. I was sure ya was dead from some sickness or accident or somethin'."

Leo ducked his head, ashamed in retrospect for not writing. "Sorry, Mom."

Myrtle returned with a metal coffee pot and a ceramic jug of milk and placed them beside Lizzie. "Yeah, Mom. Remember when ya read in the paper last Spring about some bum they found dead over in Pocatello by the railway yards? And ya thought the description had to be Leo's?"

Myrtle put both fists on her hips and turned an angry glare at Leo. "Mom made me drive her in the surrey all the way to Pocatello and go in the morgue. The morgue where they keep dead bodies, mind you! It was awful. And I had to help her walk down the stairs to that horrible basement that was all cold and clammy. Oh, it was plumb awful. And it stunk down there, too. And Mom's a cryin' and a weepin'. Then the man in a white lab coat lifted the sheet off the corpse, and Mom saw a stranger, and then she *really* started a wailin'. Oh, it's not him. It's not my son! Then I had to drive her all the way back. We didn't get home till on towards midnight! Isn't that right, Mom?"

Myrtle turned back to the kitchen in an indignant huff. Lizzie looked sheepishly at Leo. "Well, it certainly sounded like ya in the description in the Blackfoot Optimist. And since I hadn't heard from ya fer so long, I was afraid ya might be dead."

Leo shook his head. "Well, thank heavens I wasn't!"

Sean grinned. "That's fer dang sure. Otherwise, I'd sure be in fer a big surprise!"

Everyone chuckled as they enjoyed Myrtle's peach cobbler, hot out of the oven, drizzled over with white sugar and heavy cream.

Chapter 14: Rose Corners

The following morning, Sean and Leo climbed down from their makeshift beds in the hayloft. They walked over to the yard's hand pump to wash up, shave, and brush their teeth. Leo shaved every day now, a morning ritual he shared with Sean. They carried their bath towels over their left shoulders, shaving kits in their right hands, and marched step in step like in the military. Then they stood at attention by the pump handle. They took turns holding the hand mirror while the other shaved. The kids picking strawberries in the garden saw their duo routine and got quite a kick out of it.

During breakfast, Leo spoke up during a break in their idle chatter. "Well, Mom, we're thinkin' of maybe settlin' down. Maybe we'll buy us a small spread and raise some cattle and breed some prime horses. Sean and me saved us up a little nest egg over the years of travelin' and workin'. We're thinkin' of bein' partners in a small stud farm operation. Whaddaya think, Dad?"

"Um-hm. Might work. Might work."

Lizzie perked up and gestured with her fork. "I heard that Widow Merriwell was wantin' to sell off all but five acres of her ol' homestead. It's a real nice spread. No irrigation, but they've got windmills fer some artesian well pumps."

"Where's her homestead, Mom?"

"Over at the intersection by Upper Presto, about a little less than an hour from here by carriage. About half an hour on horseback. It's back over towards Blackfoot. I could drive ya over and introduce ya. They're good people from way back, the Merriwells. Ya knew their kids at school, didn't ya?"

"I might've. Don't remember fer sure without seein' their faces."

Alma nodded thoughtfully. "Um-hm. Ol' Dick Merriwell died last year. Left Bertha alone with only three young daughters and 'er toothless ol' Dad from London to run the property. She don't like havin' hired hands on the place, what with her daughters and all, so she wants to sell off the pasturage and fields. I heard she wants to keep the house and barn and garden patch fer her family home."

Myrtle came in with a plate of hot buttermilk biscuits and passed them around. "Don't ya remember her, Leo? Muriel Anne Merriwell was just two years younger. But ya had classes with her. She speaks all elegant and educated like."

"Um, maybe. Pretty dainty little thing with long blond pigtails? Always reading a hardcover novel from her Dad's library at home? I think I remember, now."

Lizzie swallowed a bite of buttered biscuit. "Oh, I think ya will recognize them when ya see them, Leo. Don't ya remember their intersection at Rose Corners? It was four families of friends. Or was it relations by marriage or somethin'? I forget the whole story now. But they came out together in those big Conestoga wagons pulled by four oxen teams apiece and homesteaded. Oh, I guess it must've been around eighteen eighty or so. Back even before all the roads were built. They immigrated from London and came west. They got here before the canals were dug. They each took a corner and built their homes close together so it would be easy to have company. Their properties stretch out and away from the four corners."

"Ya know, I do seem to recall, now. There's lots of full growed cottonwood and poplar trees growin' at that intersection. And big rose gardens, too, if I remember the right place. And white picket fences, too. Boy! These biscuits're delicious, Myrtle. Really tasty!"

Myrtle nodded her thanks for the compliment. "Yep. That's the place. There's the Merriwells, the Murdochs, the Pattens, and the Gilberts. Ya remember Jeff Murdoch. He was one year ahead of ya in school and pitched baseball real good. And, of course, ya remember Josh and Mitch Patten. They looked like twins. They were two years ahead of ya in school and liked to play marbles all the time. They loved to ride and race horses, too."

"I might remember 'em. It's been a while, but it's startin' to come back to me, now."

Myrtle leaned over towards Sean and Leo with her eyes bulging out with pleasure at being the one to tell them such juicy news.

"What ya probably don't know is that one day last fall, Mitch Patten was drivin' one of those big heavy load wagons. Ya know, the kind that has the extra big wheels in the back. And the wheels're extra wide. Anyway, that wagon was filled to overflowin' with hay. And Mitch was drivin' it down the one-lane road over by their intersection. And this` Basque fellow, who hardly spoke English, was drivin' a load of somethin' else. I don't remember now what. Sorghum, I think. Anyway, he was goin' the other way, and they met in the middle. And neither one wanted to pull over so the other could pass. So they got down off their wagons and got into a fight. And that Basque fellow went and pulled a big huntin' knife on Mitch and stuck 'im in the guts. Pert near killed the poor guy! The Sherrif arrested the Basque. They tried him and sent him to the State Penitentiary fer attempted murder. Fer eight long years. It took poor Mitch near a year to heal and get back to normal. Isn't that somethin'?"

Leo grinned mockingly at Myrtle. "Boy, lots of stuff been goin' on around here since I left. Adventures and everythin'!"

Sean sat by Leo, listening to the conversation with a friendly lopsided grin on his face. Sean leaned over to look at Alma. "What did ya say the land was like at this farm that's fer sale?"

Alma put down his cup of chicory coffee with a clatter and looked at Sean. "Well, the four farms are on the side of a long gentle foothill. No irrigation, like Lizzie says, so they just dry farm some of their acreage. They use artesian wells with windmills fer their livestock pasturage fer the most part. Course, they got big kitchen gardens and well-established orchards. They've been cultivatin' their homesteads fer pert near two generations, now."

Sean placed his hand on Leo's shoulder. "Sounds close to perfect, doesn't it, pardner?"

"Do ya think we should go check it out?"

"Sounds almost too good to be true. Bet they're askin' an arm and a leg fer the land, though."

Sean turned back to Alma. "Do ya happen to know what they're askin'?"

Lizzie nodded her head. "I heard they're askin' three dollars a acre. That's a mite high fer these parts, but the land *is* all cleared."

Alma stirred a teaspoon of sugar in his coffee. "Yep. And they got several artesian wells already dug and plumbed with pumps with good sweet water. Why a couple of the pumps even have windmills on 'em, keepin' the cattle troughs full of water. Why doncha drive the boys over there this mornin', Lizzie, me girl, and let 'em look around fer themselves?"

"My idea, exactly, Dad."

Lizzie looked at the young men, all freshly shaved and cleaned up. "Shall we leave in a quarter-hour, then?"

Leo and Sean nodded their agreement with big smiles.

Lizzie turned to Ralph. "Son, please go hitch up Cash and Carry to the surrey. We're goin' fer a drive this mornin'."

Ralph scowled, irritated to be given extra chores before finishing breakfast. "In a minute, Mom."

Lizzie turned on him real fast. "If I wanted it done in a minute, Ralph, I would've waited a minute to ask ya!"

Ralph knew that tone of voice and gave up. "All right. All right. I'm goin'."

Ralph stepped over the bench with exaggerated reluctance as he grabbed another biscuit. He turned and walked slowly out through the kitchen, mumbling and grumbling to himself all the way.

Leo watched Ralph slouch away in his overalls, remembering back when Lizzie ordered him around like that. "Thanks, Mom."

Sean expertly drove the matched team of black Hamiltonians along the barely graded dirt county road, listening to Leo and Lizzie on the leather bench behind him. Sean enjoyed the warm sun and cool air. *A lovely day up here in Idaho. One could get used to livin' up here. Bit cool, though, after years in the heat of Texas and Arizona and New Mexico. It's a mite chilly up north here fer me.*

Lizzie pointed ahead with her gloved hand. "Oh! There it is up there."

Leo and Sean leaned forward, anxious to see the land for sale. They slowly drove towards two nicely painted clapboard houses surrounded by deep yards. Full-grown sixty-foot tall cottonwoods and tall columnar poplar trees shaded the grounds. Board fences neatly set the limits to the yards. The crisp whitewashed fences gleamed in bright contrast to the dark green of the pastures and gardens behind them.

To left and right behind the farmhouses stood the barns, out-houses, and sheds. Corrals of sturdy split wood topped with barbed wire extended out further behind the barns. Leo and Sean noticed three windmills, two on the left and one on the right. They had only seen windmill pumps twice before in their travels.

As they drew closer to the intersection, the other two farm-steads came into view on the other side of the first two. Lizzie pointed. "That there farm on the far right's the Richard Merriwell farm. It's the one fer sale."

Leo drew in his breath. His eyes opened wide with pleasure and delight. Just as he leaned forward to tap Sean on the shoulder, Lizzie caught his arm. "Ya remember I said the house and barns don't go with the land sale, right?"

Leo nodded, disappointed.

A few minutes later, Lizzie knocked on the front door of the nicely painted wood house. A mature woman answered the door and stepped out on the porch. After polite greetings, Lizzie intro-duced the boys to Bertha Merriwell. Lizzie then said her son might be interested in buying Bertha's land. Bertha replied in a cultivated voice, rich with a melodious British accent, "Well, let's go for a walkabout then, shall we, my friends? And I'll show you over my property."

As they turned to leave the wide front porch, a pretty girl walked out of the house. Bertha waved her closer. "Muriel Anne, this is Missus Hayes and her son, Leonard. And his partner, Mis-ter Sean McKay from Saint George. And this is my eldest daugh-ter, Miss Muriel Anne Merriwell."

Muriel Anne looked at everyone with a big smile. "Nice to make your acquaintances. But of course, I remember you, Leo, from school back when we were little kids. How have you been?"

192

"Hi, Muriel Anne. I remember ya, too."

Bertha led them across the side yard and past the barns and the big corral holding four Guernsey milk cows. A black and white border collie, obviously their household pet, ran up to check out the strangers. Muriel Anne stopped and petted him. "Good Scotty. Good Scotty."

Scotty's tail wagged a hundred miles an hour in pleasure at the attention. When Murial Anne stood up, the dog ran up to Sean and stuck his nose in his crotch for a good sniff. He then ran over and sniffed Leo's crotch. "Whoa there boy. That's a good boy."

Leo leaned over and let the collie smell the back of his hand. He then patted Scotty's head and scratched him behind his ears.

Murial Anne watched Leo petting her dog. *Golly, but Leo sure grew up to be a good-looking young man. I surely would like it if he were to stick around these parts for a while.* Muriel Anne daydreamed while Bertha explained about the land she wanted to sell. "And this is the original cabin that Dick's father, Bertrand Merriwell, built when they first homesteaded the land. They built it close to that little natural artesian spring over there. It still flows naturally out of the earth today. That's why the trees and orchards are so beautiful around the old cabin here. You see, it's never run completely dry."

Lizzie gazed around, admiring the mature trees in full leaf. "The trees are beautiful, aren't they? Oh, look! I just love cosmos!" Lizzie walked over to the far side of the garden, her limp hardly showing in her excitement. "Oh! I am so jealous, Missus Merriwell. I just love the pink of these Gloria cosmos. Oh! And look at these Crest Red cosmos. They are even taller than I am. Oh! Isn't it all too wonderful?"

Bertha had noticed the boys' crestfallen looks when they saw the dilapidated one-room log cabin. She feared she might lose the sale but decided to let them explore the old farmyard for themselves. Her British reserve held her back from being pushy.

Bertha turned and walked over to join Lizzie. "I love them, too, Missus Hayes. They are finally ready to be picked and dried in powdered borax for making winter arrangements."

Bertha pointed at big yellow flowers nodding over their heads behind the cosmos. "I'm particularly proud of my Gold Glows."

"Oh, Missus Merriwell. Are those giant Black-Eyed Susans, or sunflowers, or what? I've never seen flowers quite like those."

"No, no. They're called Golden Glow coneflowers. And they dry beautifully, too. If you would like, I'll pick you some to take home. You can dry them for your own winter floral arrangements."

"Oh, I would surely love that. I dry me little zinnias and marigolds and little wild yellow roses. But that's all I can raise. We don't have tree shade and moist ground over on the Utah Idaho Sugar Company Farm."

Bertha withdrew a practical little steel penknife from her long apron's pocket. She opened it and began cutting flowers, handing the stems to Lizzie. Lizzie's face beamed with pleasure at the bright yellow flowers.

Sean and Leo opened the crooked plank door to the log cabin. It screeched against the warped plank floor. Spider webs hung from rough, hand-hewn beams overhead. The stale smell of old wood and smoke permeated the closed-up little room. The cabin barely measured ten feet by fifteen feet. Leo took a step to enter, but Sean pulled him back. "Let's not bother, pardner. This obviously won't be a house fer livin' in, to be sure. Maybe a tool shed later on, but it's had too many years of sun and termites fer it to be a home fer people again."

Muriel Anne wanted to be helpful. She also wanted their attention focused on her. She stepped up with a big smile and bounced up on her toes. "Why the old barn isn't half bad, Leo. We've just used it for hay storage for the past few years. But it's still sound and secure from the elements."

Murial Anne took off, striding purposefully towards the large unpainted old barn. The barn's roof of split cedar shingles rose like a dark brownish-gray mountain ahead of them. Scotty jumped along enthusiastically, accompanying his mistress.

The young men chased after her, as she had hoped.

She unlatched the heavy bolt on the ten-foot-tall door and struggled to push it aside. She had trouble starting it on its rusted tracks. Sean reached over and took hold of the big wood handle. "Here. Let me, Miss Muriel Anne."

"Oh. Thank you, Mister McKay. It is heavy, and that's a fact."

Sean grunted as he pulled the door to the left. Leo leaned in to help. The large plank door hung from old rusted wheels that screeched in an iron track bolted onto the face of the barn. A single beam of sunlight from a cupola on the roof provided the only light. Muriel Anne rushed around, flinging open the wood shutters covering the unglazed windows. The light revealed an empty barn and lots of cobwebs. They smelled old dust, stale air, straw, manure, and dried cow urine. Leo glanced up at the large lantern-style cupola at the top center of the barn. It had open unglazed windows on all four sides.

Murial Anne flung open a board door. "Oh, and Mister McKay, you could use this tackle room as a temporary camp while you figure out what to do for permanent housing. See? It has a door directly to the outside where you could set up a cookstove and convenience. You could glaze its windows easily enough. And it's close to the barn's well, so you would have water close to hand. It would be a lot better than pitching a tent, wouldn't it, Mister McKay?"

Sean turned his charming lopsided smile and dimple on her and nodded his head politely. "Miss Muriel Anne, if we're to be friends and neighbors, please call me Sean."

Muriel Anne blushed. "Oh. I would like that... Sean."

Sean looked around, thinking of possibilities while he waited for Leo to share his thoughts.

Leo inspected the abandoned tack room. The one room appeared as wide as his parents' house but only ten feet deep. A person could ride a horse under its ten-foot ceiling. The Merriwells had built it with rough-sawn plank wood. Wooden dowels and rusted hand-forged nails littered the walls, holding all kinds of horse tack detritus and old tools.

Leo took a long deep breath. Dry, cool air entered his lungs. He smelled the subtle odor of age and clean dirt from the fields.

He identified lingering smells of livestock and dry hay stored in the hayloft above.

Leo glanced at Muriel Anne. He wished she would leave them alone. He wanted to stand close to Sean with their arms around each other's shoulders so they could discuss their future in private. Unfortunately, Muriel Anne didn't vanish at his wish. Leo turned to face Sean and smiled. "Sean, I feel somethin' here. I'm not sure what. Maybe I've had a little glimpse of the future. But I feel like we should try and make it happen. Make a life here. Build our stud farm here. We can always build a house. We have enough money in our savings bank account. We can have the breeder bulls and stud horses shipped up right away. That way, we could go to work and start earnin' money while we get everything else in order."

As he listened to Leo's evaluation and recommendation, Sean's smile grew bright and happy. Sean nodded thoughtfully. "I agree, pardner. I think we could make it work here."

Muriel Anne watched with delight, fantasizing about a future with a husband as handsome and fascinating as either of these men might be. On an impulse, she rushed over to the door leading to the outside, glanced back at Sean and Leo, and waved them over. "Wonderful! Let's go speak to Mother. Come on!"

The three left the barn, walking quickly back to the overgrown old gardens. They found Bertha and Lizzie happily tying up bundles of flowers for Lizzie to take home to dry. Both ladies held the bouquets upside down and shook them to remove all the little grasshoppers, caterpillars, aphids, and ants.

"Mother! The men have come to a decision, provided you can work out the financial details satisfactorily."

Bertha glanced at Lizzie, then back at the boys. "Oh, I say! Really now. Isn't that nice? Well, what say you join us for a spot of luncheon? We'll have a little chat and see what we can work out. Can you take the time, Missus Hayes?"

"I think we can, Missus Merriwell. And I thank ya kindly fer invitin' us."

Smiling, Lizzie handed each of the boys a bundle of flowers tied with a living rope of morning glory vine. The group strode off towards the main house. Scotty scampered about, herding them home, running happily here and there, head low to the ground as he worked.

Leo paused under a big old cottonwood tree. "What a difference grown trees make on the land. It just feels good and alive and protected. Doncha think so, Sean."

"I have to agree one always finds joy livin' beneath the changin' seasons of a tree's abundant leaves."

Leo gazed about with the proprietary air of an owner's pride. A red leaf, touched just the other night with the first light frost of the fall season, fell loose and floated gently down by their feet.

Sean and Leo placed the flowers on the back seat of the surrey. Bertha continued past the surrey to the house. She climbed the porch steps and stopped beside the door to the kitchen. "Please come in, everyone."

While they had been touring the property, an elderly man had come out to the porch. He sat in a rocking chair in the sun. He opened his eyes when Bertha called out but didn't stand up. Bertha introduced him as her eighty-nine-year-old father. She explained he had lived with them since before Muriel Anne's birth. Bertha spoke loudly to compensate for his partial deafness. "Father, this is Missus Hayes, her son Mister Leonard Hayes and Mister Hayes' partner Mister Sean McKay. And this is my father, Mister Nathaniel Morris Goodbody."

Mr. Goodbody looked up from the rocking chair and nodded at each one as Bertha introduced them. "How do you do. How do you do."

Sean and Leo stepped up to shake his hand. Leo noticed he had sunken cheeks, typical of a man who had lost all his teeth. The old man had wispy white hair, a thin beard, and bushy white eyebrows growing quite out of control.

As they turned towards the door, Mr. Goodbody held up a finger and stopped them. He gazed around at everyone and nodded sagely. A smile crinkled the chicken feet wrinkles at his eyes. "I say there. Eight-nine and three quarters. I'm not eighty-nine. I'm eighty-nine and three-quarters years old. When you get close to ninety going on to dead, the quarter years count, just like for a young child."

Everyone chuckled. Mr. Goodbody laboriously put his hands on the arms of the rocking chair and struggled to stand up. Leo stepped over to steady him, holding his elbow until he found his legs. "Here, sir. Let me help." Leo placed the old man's withered hand on his shoulder. "Lean on me, Mister Goodbody, and I'll walk ya into the house."

"Thank you, young man. Cheers. Just don't go too fast. I say, but my feet sometimes forget they need to go one in front of the other in order for me to move from one place to another."

Leo chuckled companionably as he slowly walked the shuffling old man into the kitchen.

Lizzie stood in Bertha's clean kitchen, holding her sunbonnet in her hands. "Are ya sure I can't help with somethin', Missus Merriwell? I don't feel comfortable sittin' down while there's work to do to put food on the table."

Bertha smiled. "Cheers. Thanks, Missus Hayes. But please have a seat and rest yourself a moment while I pour a cuppa tea. Do you take sugar or honey in your tea, Missus Hayes?"

"Why, honey would be right nice if ya have some handy. And please, me friends call me by me Christian name of Lizzie, short fer Elizabeth Ann."

"Why, I would be glad to call you my friend, Lizzie, but only if you will call me Bertha."

The ladies smiled warmly at each other as Lizzie accepted the cup and saucer from Bertha. *Oh, my. Look at how fine this china is. I've never seen anything so lovely.* Lizzie watched Bertha's retreating back. "Where did ya ever find some china like this, Bertha. It's the loveliest I've ever seen!"

"It came from my family's old shop in London that my cousins still own and keep. They think I've gone completely native, living here in the Wild West, but we try to keep a little culture alive. We send each other gifts from time to time and exchange letters at least once a month to keep in touch."

Lizzie shook her head in wonderment. "All the way from London, England. Land o' Goshen!"

Leo helped Mr. Goodbody to his chair and then sat down beside him. He gazed around the beautifully appointed room in awe at their gracious lifestyle. Bertha had furnished the parlor with fine varnished store-bought furniture. All the upholstery had needlepoint flowers embroidered on the seat and back cushions. *These people may be farmers and homesteaders, but they sure live like city slickers if ya ask me.*

Sean took a seat beside Mr. Goodbody. "And why would yer London relations get the impression ya might be livin' a crude and rustic existence, I might ask? Ya have a very fine home here, Missus Merriwell."

Sean had visited gracious homes in Salt Lake City and St. George, homes of prosperous merchants, bankers, and big cattle ranchers. But few had furnishings as tastefully European as this.

"Well, Mister McKay, it's because of those Shilling Shockers that are so popular in England."

"Shilling Shockers?"

"Dime novels, you know. Our American publishers are flooding the market in England with sordid tales of life in the Wild West. But in England, they cost a shilling, not a dime, so people call them Shilling Shockers. See? They sometimes call them Penny Dreadfuls. Dreadful because they are not fine literature and because they murder the King's English something dreadful. My family had read those lurid stories written by James Fenimore Cooper about frontiersmen fighting the noble savages. Now they think I wallow in poverty. They believe we run around barefoot on a dirt floor, raising chickens under the bed, and fighting off wolves and Indians at every turn. It's most horrible. But nothing I can do will overcome their prejudices and fearful notions."

Bertha laughed merrily, shaking her head hopelessly as she returned to the kitchen.

A moment later, they heard Bertha call out in a warbling voice, "Oh, Muriel Anne, dear. Won't you please come and chop up Grandpapa's food so that we can serve lunch?"

Muriel Anne didn't want to leave Leo and Sean's company, but she didn't want to appear childish, either. She heaved a big sigh and called out in a high musical voice, "Coming, Mother."

Leo leaned over to Sean and whispered, "They talk kinda funny, don't they?"

Sean smiled and winked, then softly imitated a British accent as best he could. "Euoh. I saeee. I deon't kneow. They ahh just Brrrritish, aftah all. All prrrrim and prrrrroper. Yew could take a lesson in diction here, old boy."

Leo laughed with a snort. *As if I could ever learn to talk like an English professor!* Lizzie gave them both the evil eye and nodded towards the kitchen with a frown.

The ringing of a silvery little bell called them to lunch. Leo helped Mr. Goodbody hobble into the dining room. Muriel Anne and her two little sisters, Jane Eve and Joslyn, carried in Bertha's simple luncheon. They served sliced cold roast chicken breast with Russian potato salad. The salad's red beets had bled into the mayonnaise, turning it pink.

As soon as they sat down, Sean turned to Bertha. "Ma'am, what might ya be askin' fer the acreage ya have fer sale?"

"Please, Mister McKay, let's not talk business over our meal. Won't you try one of these dill gherkins? I put them up myself with the kind help of Muriel Anne. She's just *so* talented in the kitchen. We raised the little cucumbers and the fresh dill ourselves, of course."

Sean picked one up between his thumb and forefinger. He hesitated. His eyebrows raised up in a question. He had never seen such a bumpy little deformed pickle before. He decided to be on his best behavior, so he raised his pinky finger all dainty-like and took a bite. His mouth puckered from the salt, vinegar, and dill. "Um. Delicious."

After everyone ate their fill, Bertha poured tea. They sat at ease around the table. Little Joslyn walked in carrying a plate piled high with sugar cookies in both hands. Her tongue poked out the side of her mouth in concentration as she struggled bravely not to spill them. Bertha took a nibble of a buttery cookie and leaned over to Sean. "Now. You were inquiring as to the sale price of my land, Mister McKay?"

Sean stopped moving with his hand halfway to his mouth, holding a cup of tea. "Yes, ma'am. Have ya figured out the askin' price yet, ma'am?"

"Why, of course, I have, Mister McKay. I consulted with our dear friends, the Murdochs, Pattens, and Gilberts. We all agreed the fair market value should be two dollars an acre for the dry farm and three dollars an acre for the pasture and gardens watered by windmill well pumps.

Leo held a hand under his chin to catch crumbs from his sugar cookie. "And just how much would that come to, in total, Missus Merriwell?"

"Well, by my calculations, which I think you will find are correct. I have sixteen acres with well water at three dollars an acre and a hundred thirty-nine acres of dry farm. That brings the total to three hundred twenty-six dollars. Plus, I'm charging a hundred dollars even for the buildings and three windmill pumps, which I believe is more than fair. That makes a grand total of four-hundred twenty-six dollars."

With a firm nod, Bertha took a big bite of her cookie.

Suddenly the delicious cold lunch didn't sit so well in Leo's stomach. He didn't see how they could afford that much. "Wow. That's a lotta money!"

Frowning in concern, Leo turned anxiously to Sean. Sean calmly nodded his head once. "Well, let's see now, pardner. We already bought the two breeder bulls and the three stallions to put to stud. We didn't plan on buildin' a house. But we have me inheritance which we never planned on usin'. And that should just about cover a new little cottage. So, then we'll need to buy some breedin' mares and cows, and we're in business. Right, me boyo?"

Frowning, Leo nodded yes.

"I don't see a problem, pardner. If we're careful, we'll still have a bit of reserve fer the proverbial rainy day, too, doncha know!"

Leo broke out in a smile. His shoulders slumped in relief. "Ya mean we can do it, Sean? Really?"

"Yep, pardner, we should just be able to carry it off if we watch every penny."

They smiled at each other, thrilled at the possibility of making their dream come true.

Muriel Anne smiled dreamily, lost in a fantasy of falling in love with one or both of these handsome fellows. She imagined them fighting a romantic duel over who would win her hand in marriage as she sighed happily.

Bertha sat back, hoping her and her three daughters' future would be more secure.

Lizzie also smiled, proud of her son's business savvy. She would be delighted to have Leo living close by so she could see him regularly.

Leo stood up, full of boyish enthusiasm, eager to go to work. "Let's go pack up and move into the barn!"

Sean waved him to sit back down. "Whoa there, pardner. We've gotta pay Misses Merriwell and sign the deed before we own the land, doncha know."

Leo sat down heavily. "Oh! I hadn't thought of that."

Bertha saw Leo's disappointment. "I say there. I have an idea. What do you say we shake hands on the deal? Then you can move in while we attend to the formalities. Will that do, Mister Hayes?"

"Oh. Yes. Thanks so much, ma'am! That would do nicely, indeed!"

"My good friend's son, Josh Patten, who lives across the corner, has had two years of law school at the University of Utah. I'm sure he can draw up the transfer of deed in no time." Bertha narrowed her eyes at Sean, wondering if he really had that much money. "And just *how* did you plan on paying the four-hundred twenty-six dollars, Mister McKay?"

"Why, Missus Merriwell, fer the past four years, Leo and I worked the cattle trails. We broke horses whenever we could, fer a buck each. We lived real frugal like because we had a dream. We wanted to settle down and raise livestock on a small operation. So we saved pert near every copper penny that came our way. And we put it all in the savings bank to earn interest, doncha know.

Right now, we have those savings on deposit at the First National Bank of Utah in Salt Lake City."

Both Lizzie and Bertha nodded approvingly. The way these young men had made a plan and worked to make it a reality impressed Bertha. It reminded her of her late husband.

Sean took a sip of tea. "So, we can write ya a check, or we can wire the bank to transfer the money to yer bank if that's what ya prefer. Either way's fine with us."

Leo happily nodded his agreement. "Either way."

"Cheers. Your check draft on your savings account will be good enough for me, Mister McKay."

Bertha stood up and held out her hand. "It's a deal, then?"

Sean stood up and shook her hand three times. "Yes, ma'am. We have ourselves a deal."

Bertha turned to Leo. "We have a deal?"

Leo's grin grew so big his face could hardly contain his happiness. "Oh, yes, ma'am. It's a deal. Thanks, ma'am. Thanks very much."

Leo pumped her hand until she had to step back to pull her hand out of his grip. She chuckled at his bubbling excitement.

Leo leaned down and held his hand out to help Lizzie stand up. "Let's go, Mom. We gotta get packed up. Ya don't mind if we rush off, now, do ya?"

Lizzie laughed her silent laugh. She shook her head in apology to Bertha. "Okay then, it's off we go. And thanks very much fer the mighty fine luncheon, Bertha. And fer makin' me boy so happy with yer land deal."

"No, no. I should be thanking you, Lizzie, my friend, for bringing me such fine young men to buy my dearly departed husband's homestead. So I thank you!"

Leo helped Lizzie climb into the middle bench of the surrey, then took the reins. "Giddup! Giddup!"

Leo drove Cash and Carry at a brisk trot all the way home to the Utah Idaho Sugar Company Farm. Bouquets of pink and yellow flowers bounced around on the third bench. It's a wonder none fell off.

Chapter 15: Bungalow

A month after they shook hands with Bertha, Leo and Sean woke up on their new horsehair mattress. Leo stretched and blinked as he gazed around their one-room camp in the tackle room of their recently purchased barn. Sean closed his eyes again. "Hey, me boyo, today's Sunday. Besides, it turned cold last night. Well, it is the first day of November, after all. No need to rush."

Leo relaxed back down and snuggled up to Sean's warmth. *Ah, a chance to relax on our very own M & H Stud Ranch here in Upper Presto, Idaho.* Leo closed his eyes as he remembered the day they moved in. Sean had hung up his guns and holsters on a nail on the wall by the door. "I wouldn't mind if we lived the rest of our lives here, livin' in peace. Maybe I'd never have to strap on those guns again to defend us against any man or beast. Ah, wouldn't that be grand, pardner? Wouldn't that be grand?"

After a short nap, the boys woke up again. They slipped on their boots and Levi jackets and bustled outside. Leo set a coffee pot to boil on the used cookstove just outside their door. Sean dashed past the stove to their two-holer convenience, so new it still smelled like pine.

They sat outside in the cool morning air drinking their first cups of coffee, gazing at the foundation for their new house by the big cottonwood, just this side of the original log cabin. Masons had dug up their yard to install cesspools according to plans from Sears. They hadn't known that modern conveniences required such big underground leaching pools. A metal tower held a large wood barrel overhead. A new windmill pumped water up to the storage tank to supply water for their modern indoor plumbing.

They could hear their three stud bulls and newly purchased milk cows mooing from the other side of the big old barn. Their breeding stallions, purchased down south in Phoenix and Provo, cavorted in the pasture above the corrals. Leo and Sean expected their mail-order house to arrive, ready to assemble, in a week or so. They had already hired a traveling carpenter and his assistant to drive down from Idaho Falls to build the house. He traveled with a big horse-drawn wagon containing his entire woodworking shop. They would arrive in a week and set up a tent camp while they helped the young men construct their Sears bungalow.

Leo and Sean completed their morning milking and feeding chores then meandered back to the stove for breakfast. Sean stretched and yawned. "I'm plumb knackered out this mornin', pardner."

Leo slung his arm over Sean's shoulder. "Well, it's no wonder. We've both been burnin' the candle at both ends, goin' nonstop since that day we shook hands with Missus Bertha. I'm a bit tuckered out, myself."

"Maybe we could take it a bit easier today, what with it bein' Sunday and all. Whaddaya say?"

"I'm sayin' I would like that. Let's do it. Here, let me top off yer cup of coffee fer ya."

Sean sat down on the raw wood bench by the tack room door. He leaned back against the barn wall, stretched his legs out, and crossed his ankles. "Thanks very much, Leo. Since yer up, would ya mind terribly fetchin' me the Sears, Roebuck and Company's Book of Modern Homes and Buildin' Plans? I'm hankerin' fer a look at the house we ordered, again, doncha know."

"Why, Sean, yer gonna wear out that page if ya stare at it any more!" Chuckling, Leo stepped inside to retrieve the specialty catalog. They kept it on their raw pine dining table. "Here ya go."

Leo handed the heavy book to Sean with the page already open. They had studied and worried about which house design and budget would work best for them. They had read the descriptions and reviewed the floor plans until their eyes hurt from reading late at night by the light of a kerosene lantern.

They had finally decided on Modern Home No. 264P245. Sean read the advertisement aloud. "For seven-hundred and eighty-five dollars we will furnish all the materials to build this five-room Bungalow, consisting of Mill Work, Lumber, Lath, Shingles, Flooring, Ceiling, Finishing Lumber, Cabinets, Kitchen Cupboard (see plan and description below), and Medicine Case, Building Paper, Pipe, Gutter, Sash weights, Hardware and Painting Material. NO EXTRAS, as we guarantee enough material to build this bungalow according to our plans. By allowing a fair price for labor, cement, brick and plaster, which we do not furnish, this house can be built for about one-thousand seven-hundred fifty dollars including all material and labor."

Leo interrupted. "How much d'ya think we'll be savin' by doin' some of the work ourselves, Sean?"

"Got to save us at least two-hundred bucks, pardner. At least."

As Sean studied the rotogravure photograph in the catalog, he imagined it was already built on their property. His thoughts turned back to the day after they shook hands with Mrs. Merriwell. They had galloped into Blackfoot to post a penny postcard requesting the catalog of homes. Starting a week later, one of them had impatiently ridden into Blackfoot every day to see if the big book had arrived.

Leo looked over Sean's shoulder and mentally walked through the floor plan. *A porch on the south to shade the house in the summer. We will be able to sit on it in the lowering sun in the winter. Nice. Then, a parlor bigger than our tack room here. Sears calls it a living room. And it opens up into a dinin' room separated by two columns, all open and airy. Then a modern kitchen with plumbing to the sink and everythin'. Oh, boy! And two bedrooms separated by a bathroom with runnin' water to a sink, a one-holer water toilet, and a big ol' indoor washtub. Then stairs in the back goin' up to an attic and down to a cellar. And the basement even has a laundry space with windows in it. Gosh, but it's beautiful. And the basement has a coal heatin' plant fer the winter. Isn't that somethin'! It's a modern bungalow, all right!*

Leo squeezed Sean's shoulder as he recalled how they had enjoyed several lively discussions late into the night, endlessly debating the different plans and options.

They had combined their hard-earned savings with Sean's inheritance from his deceased grandmother to buy Modern Home No. 264P245. They had sent their check for $1.00 – to be applied against the total purchase price. In return, Sears, Roebuck and Company had sent them the full Bill of Materials and the blueprints. The plans had arrived two weeks ago, confirming the order. They had arranged for masons to come from Blackfoot for four days to dig the cellar, lay the cinderblock foundation, and lay in the cesspools and water tower for the indoor plumbing. The masons had just finished the day before.

Leo felt the chill penetrate his light jacket. "Hey. How about I heat up a bunch of hot water? We could take a long hot bath to start out the day?"

Sean's eyes lit up in anticipation and delight. "Why, Leo, that would be just grand, doncha know!"

"Just think, Sean. Oh. I can't hardly wait. But by Christmas time, we'll be able to go into our very own bathroom, turn a faucet, and get hot water out of the tank on the new heatin' plant. We'll be able to fill up a tub of water without pumpin' the water, carry it to the stove, wait fer it to heat, then lug it to the tub. Oh, I can't believe how nice and easy that's gonna be."

Sean put down the homes catalog. "Yep. We'll be livin' like kings, pardner. Like kings!"

The temptation of a hot bath overcame all other concerns and distractions. Sean picked up a big water pail and took off for the pump. "Here, I'll help ya get the water started on the stove."

Sean liked nothing better than to get cleaned up. He just felt better, all scrubbed up and smelling fresh from good lye soap. *Besides, I'm feelin' a bit frisky this mornin'. Maybe once we both get all soaped up, Leo will feel a bit frisky, too. This could end up bein' a really nice bath!*

Leo added more wood to the stove to heat their bathwater. Then he stoked up the new pot-belly stove in the tack room. After four years of hot winters in Arizona and Texas, they both felt the on-coming seasonal change more than they had expected. At least a dozen times a day, they complained how their blood must have thinned out down south in the heat.

They had debated putting a stove in the dry old barn. At the Blackfoot General Store, Johnny had explained they only needed to cut a three-foot square hole in the wood wall and install a sheet of tin. Then the smoke pipe from the little stove could safely exit through the center of the metal sheet without setting the barn on fire.

Half an hour later, Sean and Leo lugged in heavy pails of water to fill their galvanized steel washtub. They had purchased an oval-shaped rather than the usual round wash tubs so they could stretch out a bit.

After they filled the tub, they closed and latched the door. They hung their clothes neatly on the pegs they used for their wardrobe closet. Sean accepted Leo's gracious offer to go first. He sank slowly, savoring the hot water until he sat with his knees under his chin in the twelve-inch tall tub. Leo dug out the remains of a brick of Lizzie's homemade soap she had given them as a housewarming present. He grinned lecherously. "Hey, there, boy. Ya want me to wash yer back fer ya?"

Just then, a shadow crossed in front of the newly installed glass window above the dining table. They heard a high warbling voice sing out, "Oh, boys! Are you up yet? Where… are… you?"

Leo dashed over to hide against the wall by the window so Murial Ann couldn't see him naked. "Dang!" He scowled then shouted, "Hey, Muriel Anne, we're in the tack room takin' our weekly baths as we're takin' some time off from work this mornin'. How about ya come back later, okay?"

"Why, sure. You two need to take a break, and that's a fact. Listen, I was hoping to invite you gentlemen to go riding with me at midday and join me for a picnic luncheon. We could go up into the hills a bit and relax. What do you say?"

Sean quietly ordered Leo, "Tell her to come back at eleven after we finish our chores, and we'll go with her."

Leo shook his head, pouting in frustration. He wanted to enjoy a quiet day with Sean, not with their jabber-mouth nosy-body neighbor girl. But he did as Sean requested, as always.

Delighted with Leo's response, Muriel Anne sang out, "Oookaaay then. I'll see you two handsome gentlemen at eleven o'clock on the dot. Bye, now!"

She tapped her white stallion on its rear withers with her riding crop and trotted away.

Frowning, Leo shook his head. Then he saw the back of Sean's bare neck rising above his muscled shoulders. Leo rubbed the soap between his hands to start a lather. "Now, about that backwash, Sean."

After their first leisurely bath, they dried off and moved over to their new horsehair mattress from The Boise Mattress Factory. They took their time licking and kissing every possible part of each other's bodies. They made love until they soared to the clouds in rapture. Afterward, Leo used tepid water and a washcloth to clean Sean's crotch. "Dang, but that Muriel Anne's becomin' a pest, isn't she? I don't mind bein' all neighborly and friendly-like, but her droppin' by two and three times a day is too much. I want to live with y'all, not with her!"

"I know, pardner. But, have some patience. With us startin' construction on the house, we won't have time for her. She'll get bored with us ignorin' her, and she'll stop droppin' by all the time. You'll see. So, just be nice. After all, it's as plain as the day is long that she's got a big ol' crush on Mister Leonard Andrew Hayes Esquire, doncha know."

Sean grinned evilly at Leo, his lopsided grin mocking Leo's look of sheer horror at the very idea. Leo emphatically shook his head. "No! Don't say that. Yer wrong!"

"Why, sure enough, pardner. Why do ya think she comes ridin' by all the time?"

Leo grabbed Sean's balls and squeezed, punishing him for teasing. Sean swatted away Leo's wet hands. "Ouch! Stop that!"

Leo let go and stood up. He stared fiercely into Sean's dancing eyes. "Nope. I think it's the handsome Mister Sean Michael McKay Esquire who she's takin' a shinin' to. After all, yer the handsome one around here, not me!"

Sean reached out and grabbed Leo by the balls. "No. Yer the handsome one."

Leo laughed hysterically and made another lunge at Sean before dancing back out of range, "No. Yer the handsome one."

Sean jumped out of the tub and rushed at Leo. "No! Y'all are."

"No! Y'all are."

By the time they stopped laughing and mopped up the water, they barely had time to get dressed and pull a comb through their damp hair. They grabbed their hats and then scrambled out to saddle the horses. Sean took Brown Sugar, as usual, but Leo took another of the new horses. He wanted to try them all and see if he might want one for his regular saddle horse. Fortunately, he still enjoyed riding the black mare he had purchased from the Henderson ranch four years back.

At the stroke of eleven, Muriel Anne came trotting up the dirt path. She smiled when she saw her boys. She didn't have a clue her boys would be horrified to learn she thought of them as her boys. Leo saw she had a woven wood picnic basket tied on behind her saddle like a giant bedroll, padded with tartan lap blankets.

Murial Anne waved her white-gloved hand, urging them to hurry. "Mount up, boys. Let's ride!"

Her stallion spun around a full three-hundred sixty degrees, anxious to be off. The horse fought his bit while Muriel Anne waited for them. After Leo and Sean mounted up, she leaned over and gave her handsome white mount his reins. They took off like a shot up the path leading to the dry acreage at the top of the nearest low hill. Scotty barked excitedly as he accompanied them, anxious to start the day's work. The boys took off chasing her, just as she had secretly desired

They slowed to a walk as they neared the top of the hill. Muriel Anne led them to her favorite spot on a lava flow smoothed out over the eons by wind and rain. From that vantage point, they could see down to the Rose Corners intersection. They paused to admire the four – now five – homesteads spread out like a painting in miniature below them. Closer to the distant mountains on the other side of Rose Corner, the Craters of the Moon stretched for miles of lifeless black basaltic lava flows, like nothing of this world. The rough volcanic glass of the craters tore right through leather shoes and human feet. The Indians used to harvest the Craters of the Moon for raw material for arrowheads and obsidian knives, sharp enough to butcher a buffalo.

Muriel Anne spread the bright tartan blankets over the mostly flat rock. As she unpacked the picnic basket, she heard her mother's words of advice echoing in her ears. "The way to a man's heart is through his stomach, Muriel Anne, and don't ever think otherwise for a minute!"

She pulled out turnovers filled with spiced meats, then cold fried chicken. She lifted out a Kerr jar of chopped tomato and basil salad. She placed a quart Mason jar of pickled eggs on the picnic blanket. "You can take this home to eat later. The eggs and beets will stay fresh for up to a couple of weeks in this sauce. Just remember to keep the lid on tight."

She had baked a plum cake, still in its tin, with a sugary plum glaze on top for dessert.

The boys sat Indian-style like on the trail, wide-eyed with anticipation. Their mouths were watering by the time Muriel Anne had everything ready. Muriel Anne sat with her legs tucked under and to the side, side saddle-like, as she poured three tin cups full of sun tea.

Leo admired all the food. "By gosh, Muriel Anne, it's a feast, and that's fer sure. Did ya fix everythin' yerself?"

"Yes, kind sir. I love to cook and try new recipes from the ladies' magazines Mother subscribes to. Here, help yourself to my meat turnover to start with, won't you please?"

Leo picked one up with his fingers and took a big bite. "Um. Um. Good."

A minute later, Sean joined him. "Um. Um."

They finished the feast in short order. Sean lay flat on his back with his hat tucked up over his face for shade. "Not another bite. And it was all more delicious than the rest, doncha know. Thank ya kindly, Muriel Anne, but not another bite."

Muriel Anne tossed Scotty the scraps to reward him for sitting patiently and not begging. He snarfed down the food in a few big gulps with a muffled growl and snort.

Leo savored the last bite of sweet and tart plum cake as he stretched out on the blanket. His head came to rest on Sean's lean flat stomach like a pillow. He smiled while still chewing with his eyes closed. He swallowed with a gulp. "Not another bite fer me, neither, Muriel Anne. That was delicious!"

Leo plopped his ten-gallon hat over his face for shade from the noon-day sun.

Muriel Anne twittered a little laugh, pleased with the compliments. "Oh, thank you, kind sirs. You're both too kind in your praise of my humble culinary talents."

She sat contentedly watching her boys take a cat nap in the warm fall sun. She fanned away the gathering flies with shoo-fly flicks of her slim hands. Leo rubbed his stomach to demonstrate his appreciation of the food.

Muriel Anne smiled as she daydreamed about her boys. *Aren't they just the handsomest couple of cowboys a girl could ever want to know? One more handsome than the other. Isn't it nice to see them so friendly and comfortable with each other? So nice. Now, if only I could get one of them to fall in love with me. I could get our homestead back in the family, and I would be set for life. I would never have to worry my head about another thing. Either one would make a great husband.* She nibbled a bit more of the plum cake as she quietly repacked the big basket.

Muriel Anne heard a loud snort from beneath Leo's sweat-stained tan hat. She glanced up at him, surprised and amused.

It happened again.

Sean lifted his black Stetson hat off his face and looked at Muriel Anne. They both grinned broadly.

When it happened again, Sean and Muriel Anne stared wide-eyed at each other. They couldn't help themselves. They burst out chuckling. Sean's stomach bounced as he laughed, which woke up Leo. Leo uncovered his face and scowled. "What's goin' on? What's so funny?"

"Nothin', pardner. Just yer snorin' is all."

"I don't snore!"

"How do ya know, Leo? Ya never stay awake long enough to find out!"

Muriel Anne and Sean laughed boisterously, but Leo didn't find it amusing. He sat back up cross-legged, leaned his elbows on his knees, and pouted. Sean sat up, too. "Well, Muriel Anne, we thank ya kindly fer this most tasty picnic, but it's probably about time to be goin', doncha know."

"Yes. It *has* been nice, and that's a fact."

Muriel Anne stacked the noisy tin dishes into the hamper and closed the lid. When she leaned over to pick it up, Sean offered, "Here, Muriel Anne, let me get that."

"Oh, thank you, kind sir. It *is* heavy, and that's a fact."

Several days later, the proud owners of the M & H Stud Ranch stood with their arms leaning on the top rung of the fence of their horse corral watching their Arabian stallion breeding a neighbor's palomino mare. They heard someone ride up to their log cabin. Sean pointed at the joined horses. "Stay here, Leo, and supervise things. I'll go see what this rider wants."

Leo nodded distractedly, focused on the mating ritual before him. *Imagine privates that huge! Just imagine! It's nearly touchin' the ground. And it looks just like a human's, too!*

Sean walked briskly over towards the old log cabin. An elderly man in a lumpy blue uniform stopped at the log cabin. He knocked on the door and then peered in the window to see if anyone was home.

Sean strode up. "Mornin'! Ya won't find nobody at home there, mister, as no one lives in that old cabin, doncha know."

The man tipped his cap. "Good morning, sir. I'm from Western Union with a telegram for Mister Sean McKay. They said over at the Gilbert's house that I could find him here."

"Well, sir, yer in luck. I just happen to have the pleasure of bein' Sean McKay, meself."

"Nice to meet you, sir. Here is your telegram. Should I wait for an answer?"

"Well, now. Since I don't know who would be sendin' me a telegram, I don't know if there will be an answer. But please, come rest a spell and have a cup of coffee while I read it and see if it requires a reply."

Sean gestured towards the stove at the side of the barn. He carefully tore open the bright yellow envelope as he led the way to the stove. He saw the telegram came from the Shipping Master, Sears, Roebuck & Co., Chicago, Illinois. *Home on Yellowstone Special due Blackfoot 11 November Stop.*

"Well, Mister Western Union, I *will* be sending a telegram if ya don't mind waitin' a minute while I write it out."

"I can take it down for you, sir, if you prefer."

"No. No. Thanks all the same. But I can read and write, doncha know. Now, let's see, today is Friday the sixth. Right? Right! So Saturday, Sunday, Monday, Tuesday, Wednesday. Wednesday will be the eleventh. That means we'll need Mister Cummings here next Tuesday."

Sean handed the deliveryman a tin mug of overcooked black coffee. "Here ya go. Sit a spell while I write a message if ya would, please."

He ducked into the tack room to write a note. *Mr. Josiah Cummings, Carpenter, Elm Street, Idaho Falls, Idaho. Sears, Roebuck & Co. mail-order home will arrive on Wednesday the 11th in Blackfoot. Please be here on Tuesday to set up camp and be ready to receive the delivery and start work. Sincerely, Sean McKay, M & H Stud Ranch, Rose Corners, Upper Presto, Idaho.*

Sean read it over to check the spelling. When he handed it to the old man, the Western Union delivery man put on a pair of wire-framed glasses. He read it, then shook his head. "No, Mister McKay, sir. If you don't mind my sticking my nose into your business. This here telegram has too many words. You will pay far too much to send it. May I?"

He reached into his pocket and pulled out a stub of a pencil. He spoke out loud as he wrote a new message below Sean's. "Josiah Cummings, Elm Street, Idaho Falls. Home arrives 11th need you 10th stop. Sean McKay, Rose Corners, Upper Presto. There, sir. Now, that will only cost you ninety cents. The other way would cost you two whole dollars and sixty-five cents to send the exact same message across the wires. See what I mean?"

"Thank ya kindly, sir. Yer concise message will do just fine. And do I pay ya, now?"

The delivery man held out a gnarled, arthritic hand for the money. "Yes, sir. Ninety cents, please."

Sean pulled out his worn old leather billfold and withdrew a dollar bill. "Here ya go. And please keep the change fer yer courtesy and yer kind help."

214

"Thank you kindly, sir."

The old gentleman tipped his hat as he walked with a bowlegged strut back to his horse. Sean watched him ride away at a steady businesslike trot.

Well, it starts at last. Sean took off jogging towards the corral. "Leo! You'll never guess what *that* was."

Chapter 16: House Raising

As requested in Sean's telegram, their carpenter arrived on Tuesday the tenth. A boy sat beside him on the big wagon's bench seat. They introduced themselves as Josey and his apprentice, Abe.

After introductions, Sean showed them where to park their mobile tool shed and set up their camp. Josey and Abe pitched their big second-hand army tent. Then they dug a fire pit in front of the tent. They lined the fire pit with stones borrowed from the nearby garden's rock fence.

Sean gave them a deposit check against the agreed-upon price to assemble and plaster the Sears house. Sean and Leo hung around to get acquainted and help them settle in. They were thrilled to see the carpenter's elaborate, mobile tool shed open up like a Chinese puzzle box. They watched with big eyes as Josey and Abe pulled out wood boxes with rope handles and placed them on a level patch of ground by the foundation. They lined up the boxes precisely, leveling each one with care. Then they removed metal pins out of forged iron hinges holding one side of the wagon in place. They carried the wagon's side over and rested it on the boxes, creating a sturdy work table. They opened the wood boxes beneath the table, pulled out tools of all kinds, and arranged everything conveniently at hand.

Leo and Sean looked at each other and nodded in approval. They both liked things neat and orderly. Josey and Abe spent the rest of the cool fall day unpacking and organizing all their tools. Sean pointed at all the professional tools with a smile. "Most impressive, to be sure."

After breakfast, the four men stood around the workbench studying the seventy-five-page leather-bound instruction book. It outlined how to assemble the thirty thousand pieces of mail order home en route to them. They also reviewed the thick packet of blueprint drawings Sean had received a couple of weeks earlier. Sean looked at Josey with concern and suspicion when he read the boldface warning in the book's preface. **Do not take anyone's advice as to how this building should be assembled.**

216

At noon, two great Clydesdale horses lumbered up the county road, pulling a large freight wagon piled with lumber and crates of all sizes. The house had arrived at last.

Leo ran eagerly down to the road, waving the driver over to the dirt lane leading up to the construction site. He stood at the corner, pointing towards the foundation. The two giant draft horses and the tall freight wagon dwarfed Leo as they turned the corner. Even the wagoner appeared larger than life, burly and muscular. His big potbelly pushed open a massive leather vest.

The horses had feet the size of dinner plates, twice the size of a regular horse's feet. Their heads bobbed a good two and three feet over Leo's head. The big leather yokes and harnesses groaned as the giant Clydesdales leaned into them, pulling the heavy freight wagon by brute strength. One turned its white face and looked calmly at Leo as it plodded steadily past. Both geldings had long white hair covering their legs from the knees down, covering their big hoofs.

Leo turned in surprise when he saw another pair of Clydesdales and another wagon turn the corner at the intersection, heading towards him. He stayed to guide the second wagon to the site.

The lead wagoner pulled back on both reins putting his whole body into it. "Whoa, boys. Whoa, Spike. Whoa, Mac."

The driver stopped the wagon alongside the front of the foundation and used both arms to set its big brake lever. Then he hopped down off the high bench seat and shouted with a big rumbling voice that matched his appearance, "Hello, there, men! I be Wolfley of Wolfley Drayage. And where might I find Mister McKay? I've got a house to deliver to him!"

"Welcome!" Sean walked over and offered his hand. "I'm Sean McKay, and I'm mighty glad to be seein' ya this fine day, to be sure."

As they shook hands, Sean watched the second wagon turn into the lane, following the deep parallel ruts left by the first wagon. "Two wagons full, and all fer only me one house?"

Wolfley let out a big guffaw of a laugh. "Mister McKay! Hah! This here be only the fourth part of yore two railcar train delivery. It's gonna take us another *three trips* and another *three*

217

days to deliver everything in this here consignment from up Chicago way. It is, after all, a whole entire house, now ain't it? Hah!"

Wolfley clapped Sean hard on the back. Sean staggered from the blow, mentally and physically. He had no idea it required so much material to build a modern home. Sean joined the other five men unloading the wagons. Even with everyone working as a team, it took them most of the afternoon. Every time someone stopped to take a breather, Wolfley bellowed out, "Let's move right along, now, and get all this cartage smartly offboarded, men."

By the time they finished unloading both wagons, they all had aching backs, sore arms, bruised fingers, and broken fingernails. Leo moaned. "And we've got three more days of this before we can start construction? Oh, my aching back!"

By Friday, they had 'smartly off boarded' seven hundred fifty pounds of nails, twenty-two gallons of paint and varnish, and fifteen thousand shingles for the roof. And much more besides. Early Saturday morning, all the men of Rose Corners gathered around the foundation to lend a hand at house raising. They all placed themselves under Josey's orders.

Leo couldn't believe his eyes when his father drove up with Lizzie in the family surrey. Bob, Ralph, and Stanley rode in the back, ready to help. Lizzie kissed Leo on the cheek and then drove over to Bertha's. She and the women of Rose Corners had planned a pot luck dinner for the men's noon break. The men worked as teams nailing in all the floor joists. Then they framed and raised the first wall to a great cheer.

Murial Anne wanted to contribute to the work. She decided to help by preparing big dinners for the men doing the hard labor. The Sunday after work began, Muriel Anne arrived at noon with the first of many hot meals. Scotty accompanied her, barking happily. The men thanked her profusely.

Lizzie and Myrtle volunteered to cook supper for Sean and Leo, Josey and Abe. Every afternoon after school, Bob or Ralph drove Lizzie over. They delivered covered casseroles or Dutch ovens of meats and vegetables so the crews wouldn't have to cook after working all day.

Sean and Leo worked through each day, surrounded by friendly, helpful faces.

One cool fall evening after supper, the boys relaxed in their one-room home in the barn. Sean sat at the little pine table with the oil lantern turned up high, reading *The Saturday Evening Post*.

"Oh, Leo. What a world we're livin' in today. Everythin' ya read is about war. Germany declared war, not only on Russia but on France and Belgium. The British Empire declared war on Germany. Ya better watch out, or President Wilson is gonna drag us into war with all the rest of the crazy world!"

Leo looked up from the bed where he sat practicing chords on the guitar. "Nope. I don't think so. He's got better sense than that, doncha think?"

"I don't know, me boyo. The news from around the world ain't so good. Our own homeland of Ireland is sittin' on the very brink of civil war, again. And the Anglo-French forces're fightin' the Germans all over the place."

Sean closed the magazine and looked over at Leo. "Well, at least there's some good news. I just read how the Panama Canal is gonna open up the world to better trade and faster travel fer mail and passengers. That's good, wouldn't ya say?"

Sean turned down the lamp to the merest flame, then walked through the near dark to the bed. He snuggled up to Leo. "Put down that ol' guitar, pardner, and let's get some rest."

Sean reached through the un-buttoned front of Leo's long johns and grasped a handful of warm genitals. Leo chuckled. "Some rest? Is that what yer callin' it nowadays?"

Leo turned over and found himself a matching handful of pleasure, never too tired to make love.

The following morning, all four men worked up on the roof of the Sears bungalow. The structure began looking like a house.

Josey pointed at a small delivery van turning into the drive. "What's that? Another delivery?"

Sean and Leo walked carefully over to the ladder. The high heels of their worn boots made it treacherous walking the rooftop slopes. They backed down the sturdy ladder.

"Ah. It's me trunk from Saint George. Mom finally got me letter and shipped it up. Ain't that grand?"

With a burst of excitement, Sean bounded across the construction yard and signed for his souvenirs from his school days.

"Here, me boyo, grab a hold of that other handle, there, if ya please, and give me a hand. This here thing weighs a ton!"

They lugged the trunk to their tack room and placed it beside the small potbelly stove. "It's got all me favorite books and boyhood treasures, packed away neat and orderly like. I've just been waitin' fer the time to come when I had a home before sendin' fer it. Wait till I show ya me collection of favorite dime novels and all."

Sean resisted his impulse to open the trunk and rummage through his past. "Nope. We got ourselves a house to be raisin'. No time fer this now. But just wait till tonight, Leo! Just wait!"

That evening Sean showed Leo his history books. The trunk also held books on breeds of dogs and horses and cattle. Leo picked up Magner's three-inch-thick book with 1700 illustrations. "I never knew there was so much to know about horse and cow breedin', Sean. This here's a weighty book of knowledge and facts! Just feel how heavy it is!"

Sean handed Leo several well-worn paperback novels written by Horatio Alger with silk-screened paperboard covers. "Oh, these are some really great books. It'll give us somethin' worthwhile to do on a cold winter's night. I can't wait to read 'em with ya."

The young men knelt in front of the chest like an altar. Sean took the books out of Leo's hands and reverently stacked them back in the trunk. With tears standing in his eyes, he pulled Leo around until they faced each other, still on their knees. Sean reached for Leo's hands "Hey, Little Lion."

Leo smiled as he remembered earning that nickname four years back on a cattle drive. After the round-up, a big bully, easily twice Sean's size and weight, tried to pick a fight with Sean. Leo got his Irish dander up and rushed him like a mother lioness protecting her cubs. It took three men to pull Leo off the big lug. Leo was furious anyone would be disrespectful and mean to Sean. After the men saw Leo in action, they nicknamed him Leo the Lion. Sean called him his Little Lion after that. Years earlier, Sean had earned the nickname of Geetar Sean with guitar pronounced like the Spanish word guitarra.

Leo looked into Sean's eyes. "Yeah, Geetar?"

Sean put his arms around Leo. "This is like a dream come true. I've waited a long time fer this moment, Little Lion. Our future is secure in our new home. Me past is here in this trunk. Everything's comin' together beautifully. It makes me heart feel full of love and overflowin' with joy. Thanks, Little Lion. Thanks from the bottom of me heart. Now I have it all."

Leo returned Sean's hug. "I love ya, too, Sean. Ya know I do. Yer magic has rubbed off on me, and I'll never be the same again."

When they pulled back, they held onto each other's elbows and gazed deeply into each other's eyes. Tears of joy made their eyes glisten in the flickering yellow light of the oil lamp.

"My knees hurt." Leo struggled to his feet, breaking the spell. "How about ya read me a bedtime story, Geetar?"

Greenwich Village
End of December 2010

Since NYU did not have classes scheduled during the year-end holidays, Josh worked on his thesis at home. Art took several calls from clients who needed help fixing computer issues. Early that evening, they sat on Art's big white leather sectional sofa in the living room. They debated getting dressed and going out to the movies or staying in and watching pay-per-view on cable.

Josh stretched out on the sofa with his head pillowed on Art's lap. He playfully nuzzled and kissed Art's privates. "Huh-uh. It's too cold out. Let's stay in."

"Okay. What would you like to watch this evening?"

Art ran his hand over Josh's bare shoulder until it came to rest on Josh's chest. Art played with Josh's nipples, raising goose-bumps on his pale skin. Art leaned over and kissed Josh's erect nipple.

They forgot all about watching a movie.

After a couple of hours of sexual aerobics, they lounged around while they caught their breath. Josh snuggled up to Art. "Should we get back to Grandpa Leo's story? Their mail-order house is coming along nicely, and the ladies are planning Thanksgiving dinner."

Chapter 17: Fever

Two days later, they woke up to a chilling breeze blowing down off the snow-topped mountains to their west. All the trees had lost the last of their leaves days ago. They grabbed a cup of coffee and then hiked to the barn to milk the cows. An hour later, they ate a simple breakfast standing outside by the cookstove.

They discussed Bertha's invitation to Thanksgiving Dinner in three days. They both looked forward to their first day off since they took delivery of the house.

Sean chopped wood, making kindling for the cookstove and the potbelly stove in the tackle room. Leo pulled the covers over their bed and then gave the floor a quick once over. While sweeping the floor, he heard Lizzie's voice in his head. "If ya have yer floors clean, the dishes done, and the beds made, ya have a fairly clean house. Then ya can worry about other things, like sewin' and knittin' and gardenin'."

Leo heard the door open and stopped sweeping. Sean leaned against the door jamb, holding the long ax handle like a cane. His gloved hand shaded his eyes. Leo frowned. "What's the matter, Sean. Doncha feel good?"

"I don't know, pardner. I was doin' fine. Then all of a sudden, it was like lightning struck me in both eyes with a splittin' headache. And suddenly, I felt chilled and too weak to lift the ax. Ain't that somethin'?"

Leo leaned the broom against their little pine table. Then he took the ax and propped it against the wall. He pulled Sean into the room and closed the door. "Well, now, come take off yer boots and lay down a spell. I'm sure it'll pass. Maybe ya just took a chill. The wind is brisk and cold with the feel of new snow in the air this mornin'."

Sean shuffled over and sat on the bed, shaking his head. "I don't have time fer this. We have a house to raise. I have me chores to do."

Sean toed off his boots with a struggle then lay back on the bed. "Blazes, but I have too much to do to be nappin' in the middle of the mornin'."

Leo grabbed one of the extra wool blankets from the trunk at the foot of their bed. He shook it out and spread it over Sean. "Now, doncha fret none. The work will wait fer ya, sure as shootin'. It'll still be there when yer up to it. Doncha fret none. Just relax a spell. It'll pass."

Unfortunately, as the day went on, it didn't pass.

Every time Leo took a break from working construction on the new house, he ran in to check up on Sean. Each time, Sean looked a little worse. By evening, Sean was running a fever. Leo undressed him and helped him climb beneath the covers. Later, he brought in a bowl of lamb stew, but Sean didn't have an appetite. "Me throat hurts and me stomach hurts and me head hurts. Mus' be a cold or a flu or somethin'."

"I'm sure it's nothin' a good night's rest won't cure. Here, take two of these Bayer aspirin tablets. They should help bring down yer fever."

Leo helped Sean sit up to take the glass of water. "Golly geez, Sean, yer definitely runnin' a fever. There ya go, just lay down, now, and rest. It'll be gone by mornin'."

Leo pulled the quilt up under Sean's chin and rested his hand on Sean's feverish brow. Leo went out to do the evening milking. He asked young Abe to give him a hand. Otherwise, it would take him two hours to do it by himself. He fell into bed that night, exhausted from work and worry.

Leo woke up early. He stretched and looked over at Sean. Even in the pre-dawn light, he could see a slight sheen of sweat on Sean's face. *Gol dang. That's not good.* He placed his hand on Sean's brow, then sat up quickly, startled by how hot Sean felt to the touch. *Gol dang!*

Leo dressed to go to the barn for the morning milking. Before he opened the door, he glanced back at the bed. Shaking his head, he walked over to the bed, and gently shook Sean's shoulder to wake him up. "Hey, Sean. Good mornin' there, pardner."

Sean opened his eyes and looked at Leo. Leo smiled encouragingly. "I'm about to go out fer the mornin' chores, but I didn't want to leave ya to wake up by yerself, ya know. Um. Do ya need the chamber pot, or a drink of water, or maybe another buffered Bayer aspirin tablet or two before I go out?"

When Sean tried to answer, he discovered he had a sore throat. He coughed to clear his throat then clutched his stomach. The coughing caused a shooting pain like a bad cramp in his lower belly. He shook his head weakly. "I... I guess a drink of water would be good. But, oh, me stomach hurts real bad. Maybe water would ease me throat and me stomach."

Concerned, Leo poured a glass of water from the china pitcher on the chest of drawers. He held up Sean's feverish head so he could sip it. Sean didn't drink much before he shook his head and fell back against the pillow. He squinched his eyes closed. "I think maybe I'll just rest a spell, pardner. I'm sorry I'm not carryin' me weight, but I don't feel so good."

"Now, doncha worry none about that. Ya gotta fight yer fever and get better. That's the only thing ya gotta worry about. I'll take care of the chores. Just rest and get better."

Leo gently patted Sean's shoulder then smoothed the quilt up under his chin. Leo leaned over and gave Sean a tender kiss on the forehead. He did his chores by rote, worried about Sean.

At noon, Muriel Anne trotted up on Kensington with her usual bundle of goodies. Scotty barked a happy hello to everyone. He ran up and sniffed them, seeking attention. Muriel Anne called out melodically, "Hey there, Leo. Hi, Josey. Hi, Abe."

Muriel Anne looked around. "Where's Sean?"

"He's feelin' poorly, so he's restin'."

"Oh, no! What's the matter? He didn't hurt himself, did he?"

"I don't know fer sure, Muriel Anne, but I'm startin' to get worried. He's runnin' a real high fever, and he's weak, and he's complainin' about a sore throat. And that his stomach hurts 'im. I guess he's got the flu or somethin'."

"Oh, my! I'll go make him some chicken soup and come back to help you out with supper if that's all right with you."

"Oh, thank ya kindly, Muriel Anne. I'll take all the help I can get. Heaven knows I make a poor excuse fer a nursemaid. I can tonic horses and cattle with the best of 'em, but I don't know anything about treatin' human ailments."

"Here, have some cookies with your dinner. I'll be back around five with the soup. Good gracious me!"

With a flourish of her white leather glove, she waved goodbye and trotted back to her mother's home. Scotty followed, barking excitedly.

A little after five, Leo stood by the hot water reservoir to the right of the stove's fire chamber, washing up after a hard day. Muriel Anne drove up in a single-horse buggy with her mother. Scotty pranced alongside, herding the horse and carriage. Leo yanked up the top of his long johns, pulled on his Levi jacket, then hurried over and offered Bertha his hand.

Bertha lifted her long skirt with one hand and stepped down gracefully from the carriage. She smiled as she clasped Leo's hand. "Why, thank you, Leo. Cheers."

Muriel Anne hopped down on the other side. She leaned over the boot behind the seat and picked up the basket from their picnic lunch.

Bertha took Leo's elbow. "Now, let's have a look at the patient. What do you say?"

"Oh, thank ya kindly, Missus Merriwell. I can sure use all the help I can get. I've given 'im some buffered aspirin tablets, but they don't seem to be cuttin' the fever nor easin' his pains none. I'm startin' to get worried."

"Now, now. I'm sure it's just a little cold or a touch of the flu. Everyone catches something this time of year as the seasons change and winter comes in."

Leo held open the door to their tack-room home. "Please come in."

"Thank you."

Muriel Anne smiled sympathetically at Leo as she followed her mother. "Cheers."

Leo entered and then quietly closed the door.

Bertha perched on the edge of the bed and laid a cool hand on Sean's cheeks and forehead. "So, Sean. Have a touch of the fever now, do you? I say! Well, Muriel Anne brought you some delicious chicken soup and enriched black tea to help you get better. Now, that doesn't sound so bad, does it?"

Sean tried to smile, but his lopsided grin and charming dimple failed to appear. "Sorry, Missus Bertha, but I'm just not hungry. Me throat is like dry sand. And there's a lump of pain in me guts that hurts somethin' terrible, doncha know."

Bertha clucked her tongue sympathetically. She stood up, removed her neck scarf, and hung it on the back of a chair at the table. "I say, Leo. Would you mind bringing in a basin of warm water and a towel? Let's get the patient cleaned up and see if we can't get him to eat a little something."

"Yes, ma'am."

Muriel Anne took a tin cup out of the basket on the table. She filled it with dark tea from a mason jar, then set it on the potbelly stove to warm up.

Leo walked back in carrying a basin of hot water in both hands. He pulled the door closed behind him with a well-practiced catch of the heel of his boot. He placed the water on the table and then looked at Bertha with his eyebrows raised in a question. When he glanced down at Sean, his brow creased with a frown of worry. It hurt him to see Sean laying there with his eyes closed, breathing shallowly, panting softly.

Bertha nodded approvingly. "Come help me, Leo. Let's get the covers off and give Sean a little spit bath. It will help refresh his spirits."

"Oh, that it will, ma'am. Nothing Sean likes better than a good washup."

Leo sat down beside Sean and flipped back the quilt and sheet. "Oh, no! Look how soaked his underwear is from all his sweatin' from the fever. Here ya go, Sean. Let me hold ya up. That's it. Now, I'll just undo all the buttons, and we can take off yer BVD undershirt. Yep. Just like that. And now, just lean yerself back and close yer eyes while we give ya a nice little scrub up."

Leo moved Sean's arms around, helping Bertha move the soapy washcloth over and under every part of his torso, arms, and face. Muriel Anne silently handed Bertha a dry towel and then pulled a comb from her long skirt's pocket. She moved over behind Leo and began combing Sean's damp hair.

Sean opened his eyes momentarily before scrunching them closed again. "Sorry to be so much trouble, Missus Bertha."

"No trouble, Sean. No trouble at all."

Leo pointed with his chin at the chest of drawers they had picked up second-hand. "Muriel Anne, if ya don't mind, would ya please fetch us a clean top half of long johns from the top drawer?"

Muriel Anne handed Leo the undershirt. *Sean looks so weak. Like the fever burned him out just in one short day. Oh, I hope he will be all right. I'm just getting to know him. And look how gentle and caring Leo is with him. Everyone just loves Sean's feisty Irish ways and his bright, cheerful eyes. I do hope he'll mend soon. And that's a fact!*

Bertha straightened the undershirt as she asked Muriel Anne to bring the tin cup of warm tea. "Here, try taking little sips of this, Sean. It's full of honey and chamomile and Darjeeling tea from India. It will help soothe the stomach and give your body something to use for energy."

Bertha handed the cup to Leo. Leo held it up to Sean's lips, murmuring as though speaking to a baby, "Here ya go. Take a little sip now. That's it. And another. Um-hm."

Bertha stood up. "Daughter, let's warm up your chicken soup and see if we can't entice him to eat something. He needs to keep up his strength, even if he doesn't feel well."

"Yes, Mother."

The two women walked out into the dark evening. Muriel Anne carefully placed the quart jar of soup on the warm side of the stove, away from the hot spot. "Mother, what's wrong with him? He looks just terrible. And why did he become so weak so quickly?"

"It may be too early to tell, but I'm afraid it might be serious. I think we should send one of the Murdoch or Patten boys to ride in for the doctor first thing in the morning."

Muriel Anne gasped. Her hand flew up to cover her mouth. "So, you don't think it's really just the flu or a cold then, do you, mother?"

"No. I'm afraid it might be a short fever or a long fever. Typhus or typhoid. Now listen carefully, daughter. As a precaution, I want you to wash your hands twice with soap and hot water. And I don't want you to touch him anymore until we find out if he's contagious."

Muriel Anne stared at her right hand as if it belonged to someone else. She turned her stricken eyes to her mother. "But I only combed his hair. I only combed his hair!"

"That's all right, Muriel Anne, dear. No harm done. Just take precautions, please. That's all I'm saying. Just take precautions. I've seen this sort of thing before, and it needs serious precautions."

"Yes, Mother."

Sean and Leo had a very bad night that night. Sean tossed and turned, too restless to sleep, too feverish and sweaty to hold or cuddle. Neither man found any rest or comfort from sharing their bed that long winter's night. Several times during the night, Sean's cramps woke him up. He complained of feeling cold. Leo gently tucked a spare quilt over him up to his neck, then watched, concerned, until Sean drifted off to sleep again.

Shortly past noon the next day, Dr. Parrish arrived from Blackfoot. Jeff Murdoch rode alongside on his favorite sorrel mare, Sitsdown. Moments later, Bertha and Muriel Anne arrived and joined the conference at the stove. Leo handed out cups of hot coffee to warm everyone's fingers. They heard the sound of hammering from inside the new house. Since everyone ignored Scotty's energetic attempts to gain their attention, he ran off to find Abe for a game of fetch.

Dr. Parrish listened to the symptoms and then took charge. "Let's see the patient, then. Um, Mister Hayes, if you would be so good as to lead the way."

"Yes, sir. Right inside the tackle room of the barn, Doctor."

Dr. Parrish carried in his two medical bags and set them on the table. The others followed, but the doctor turned back and held up his hand. "Thank you, but, um, I don't need any help. If you will please wait outside, I'll only be a moment."

Bertha frowned, then turned and shooed Muriel Anne and Jeff out ahead of her.

"Now, son, let me just slip this thermometer under your tongue to take your temperature. Although we don't, um, need it to see that you are, um, running a fever. That's for sure."

Sean winced at the bitter bite of rubbing alcohol on the thermometer. The doctor picked up Sean's clammy fever hot hand and counted his pulse. Then he pulled his leather stethoscope out of his tool bag. He leaned over and unbuttoned Sean's long johns so he could move the metal listening bell over Sean's heart and lungs.

"Your throat hurt, son?"

Sean nodded yes.

"You have a pain in your stomach?"

Sean nodded yes. He nodded up at Leo to explain since he couldn't talk with the glass thermometer in his mouth. Leo pointed at Sean's lower stomach. "He's been complainin' more about down in his guts rather than up in his stomach, Doctor."

"Um. When was the last time you had a bowel movement, son?"

Leo answered for him. "Not since the mornin' of the day before yesterday, sir. I've offered 'im the chamber pot several times, but he hasn't needed it fer anythin' yet."

"So, a little, um, constipation, perhaps. And with all the sweat from the fever, there's not much liquid left to expel through the, um, more usual routes. Now, let's see what the thermometer tells us. Um-hm. Well. That's not good."

Leo looked up in alarm and stared. Dr. Parrish stood shaking his head. "Just over a hundred and three. That means his body is fighting a really big infection. Um-hm. That's for certain. Um-hm. A really big infection."

230

The Doctor stared into the distance, his eyes unfocused, thinking for a moment. "How long have you boys been settled here, Mister Hayes?"

"We got to Wapello about six weeks ago. We've lived here over a month now, buildin' the new Sears house."

"Hm. And before that, where were you?"

"Before that, we were ridin' up from Texas. First, we went over to Arizona, then up to St. George, then Salt Lake City, and then on to the Utah Idaho Sugar Company Farm that my Dad runs."

"Um-hm. And when you were traveling, did you cook for yourselves in camp, or did you stay with friends and in hotels?"

Sean and Leo exchanged a puzzled look. Sean managed to croak out, "A bit of everythin' Doc, doncha know. When we could, we availed ourselves of the hospitality of the road. Sometimes we splurged and stayed in a hotel, like in Salt Lake City."

Sean's voice gave out, so Leo took over. "In Salt Lake, we ate at a couple of different public restaurants. But most of the time, we camped out along the road and cooked fer ourselves. Why d'ya ask that, Doctor Parrish?"

"Well, boys. Chances are you were exposed to typhoid fever. Maybe typhoid pneumonia. We can't be sure for a few days. But, chances are you were infected on the road by eating contaminated food. Um-hm. The incubation period can take weeks. That would place you boys out on the road, eating with strangers from time to time, where you were most likely exposed. Now, I don't want you to get all excited, but I think it would be best if we um quarantined your barn here. Just as a safety measure. Now, who all have you touched since you came down with the fever, Sean?"

Sean glanced over at Leo, stricken with fear he might have exposed Leo to a deadly contagious disease. Everyone knew typhoid fever was a mortal sickness. They had all heard and read the sensational newspaper stories about Typhoid Mary back in New York City a few years back.

Leo's voice quivered with nerves. "Well, sir. There was me, of course, livin' here and all. And, let's see. Besides me, there was only Muriel Anne and Missus Merriwell. They dropped by last night with some soup for Sean. They helped me bathe 'im and feed 'im. That's all, I think."

"Um-hm. Well, let me call them in then. You'll all need to hear this."

Frowning, Dr. Parrish walked over and opened the door. He beckoned the ladies to come in, then held up his hand to stop Jeff from joining them. Leo walked over and sat down on the mattress by Sean's head. He picked up Sean's feverish hand and held it on his knee.

'Um, ladies and gentlemen, I'm afraid I am going to have to, um, officially quarantine this barn as a preventative measure. I fear that perhaps Sean has been infected with, um, yes, typhoid."

Bertha and Muriel Anne exchanged concerned glances. Bertha nodded. *I was afraid of that. I was afraid that might be the problem.*

Muriel Anne shook her head in denial. *But I only combed his hair. I only combed his hair.*

Bertha pulled Muriel Anne's shoulders into a hug. "How can we help, Doctor Parrish?"

"Thank you. Now, you only can catch typhoid by eating or drinking food infected by a carrier who didn't wash their hands after going to the toilet. Scientists established that without question in ninety-eight during the Spanish American War. More than twenty-five hundred men died of disease in camp during the war, while only a few hundred died from fighting. It's my guess that Sean was infected on the road before he got here. So, Sean is not to share food or drink with anyone. Also, and this gets important, you can get infected by close contact with the fever. So, if you have to touch him, you must wash your hands with plenty of hot soap and water after *each* and *every* contact. If you don't have to touch him, um, then don't. And under no circumstances are you to touch any of his fecal matter. Do you understand?"

Leo looked up with stricken eyes. "Uh, his what matter, Doctor Parrish?"

"Fecal matter, Mister Hayes. That's scientific lingo for bowel movements. Stool. Poop. Under no circumstances are you to touch anything that comes out of Sean's bowels. Now, do you

232

understand? When he has bowel movements, use store-bought toilet paper, not catalog pages. Then clean him up with a wet rag. But don't touch anything directly with your skin. Then wash your hands, like I said. And boil the rag for a good fifteen minutes to disinfect it. Do you understand?"

They all nodded, dumbfounded at the seriousness of the doctor's orders.

"Now, I'm sure you've all read in the papers about Typhoid Mary back in New York. Over three thousand souls took sick there in ought-six. She darn near caused an epidemic all by herself, simply because she did not take precautions. But *you* will, or you will answer to *me*!"

Dr. Parrish gave them a stern glare and shook his finger at each of them. "Since the three of you are already exposed, it will be up to you to provide the nursing care. If it turns out to be the flu or a bout of food poisoning, he will start to mend soon. But if, as I fear, he's contracted the typhoid pneumonia, he'll have bad headaches and suffer from a high fever. He'll be weak. He'll have abdominal pain, just like he's already complaining about. He'll either get very, um, constipated, or get really bad diarrhea, or both."

The doctor pointed his finger at Sean's mid-section. "If Sean develops a red rash in the second week, we'll know for sure it's the typhoid. And the quarantine will be in place until the disease runs its course."

Bertha shook her head sorrowfully. "Oh, my, that doesn't sound good at all, does it? What do we have to look forward to, Doctor? And what can we do to help?"

"Well, like I was saying, if Sean develops flat red spots on his lower chest or upper abdomen a week to ten days from now, it will confirm my diagnosis. The rash will go away after a couple of days."

Leo made himself a mental note to start a diary to track the progress of the sickness and symptoms.

Sean braced himself to croak out, "Then what, Doc?"

"Then you may, um, enter the second stage, during which many patients become very ill indeed. Your fever will remain high. Most people lose a lot of weight during this phase. For some, their abdomens become extremely distended and, um, painful."

Sean scowled. "Ugh. Sorry, I asked." His fever made it hard for him to focus. "And when will I start feelin' better, Doc? I've got work to do."

"Well, son, I'm sorry, but by the third week, things can get really tough. After three weeks of fever, most patients can only lay in bed in what's called the typhoid state. Some might become delirious from the fever by that point. By the fourth week, the fever will very gradually begin to decrease. Maybe in another week or two, you will be over it."

Leo looked at Bertha and Muriel Anne like a trapped rat seeking an escape route. "That's a month and a half of Sean being sick, Doc! Can that be right? Six whole weeks?"

Leo stuffed his fist into his mouth to keep from choking out his grief. Bertha stepped over and put her arm around his shoulders. "I say. We'll be here to help you, Leo. You won't have to go through this on your own. I'm sure Sean will be fine. We will just have to help him live through it. He will get better, won't he, Doctor? Won't he?"

"Um. Well. Two out of three people who develop the fever survive and return to their normal lives. That's pretty good odds. Um-hm. Two out of three."

Muriel Anne gasped when she realized it also meant one out of three did not survive. But then she felt ashamed for interrupting. Her heart went out to Sean and Leo. She looked over at Leo holding Sean's hand. He grasped it tightly, like a drowning man holding onto a lifesaver. Sean clutched back just as tightly, equally scared.

Bertha walked over and plopped down on a chair by the table. Muriel Anne joined her. They instinctively reached out and held each other's hands for reassurance.

Dr. Parrish packed his tool bag and opened his medicine bag. "There's really not much we can do now except let the sickness run its course and keep Mister McKay as comfortable as possible. Lots of strained soups, meat broths, barley water, enriched tea, and water. Keep him from getting dehydrated. Cold damp compresses on the forehead. Sponge baths when his temperature flares. It sometimes helps after the sponge baths to rub the spine gently. Have a blanket on hand if he starts shivering from a fever chill. Keep his feet warm. And don't touch anything that, um, comes out of his bowels. That's the most contagious part! Get a good bedpan and some store-bought toilet paper. And you will find it helpful to buy paper drinking straws. They'll help him drink when he's weak. Give him an aspirin tablet every four hours. It might help reduce the fever. That's about all we can do other than wait and pray. Mister Hayes is young and strong. His body will fight hard to throw off the fever."

Dr. Parrish picked up his bags and turned for the door.

Leo reluctantly let go of Sean's hand. He stood up and opened the door for the doctor. Dr. Parrish stepped over to the hot water spigot on the reservoir of the wood-burning stove. Taking his own advice, he washed his hands carefully with soap and hot water. Leo walked up to the doctor. "Thanks so much fer comin' this mornin', Doctor Parrish. How much do we owe ya fer the house call?"

"Three dollars, please, Mister Hayes. Now, don't go getting yourself in a panic, young man. Stay positive. Go about your life and live it as best you can while your friend fights his, um, private battle. Ah, thank you for the cash in hand. Much obliged. I'll drop in every time I make the rounds here about to see how he's doing. Try not to let the worry get you down. So long, now. Remember the quarantine!"

Leo took a deep breath and held it, trying to figure out how Sean's sickness would complicate their lives and routines. He tried to plan what he would need to do. He looked up to the skies seeking inspiration, shaking his head helplessly. He wanted to reject the past two days entirely.

Jeff Murdoch walked over to ask how he could help, but Leo stopped him with a raised hand. "Sorry, Jeff. But we're under quarantine right now. Sean might have the typhoid fever. So please don't touch me or come into the tack room for any reason."

"Good grief, Leo! I'm really sorry to hear that. Will Sean be okay?"

"We can only wait and see. The doctor said that two out of three survive and return to live normal lives. So we can only wait and pray."

Jeff cautiously backed up two steps. *Boy, no matter how often you hear of people getting sick, it's a shocker when it happens to someone you know.*

"Jeff, I hate to impose on ya more since ya already lost yer entire mornin' fetchin' the doctor, but would ya mind terribly tellin' my Mom what's going on here? I'm gonna need some help. I'm wonderin' if maybe Bob and Ralph might come and stay to lend a hand."

"Certainly, Leo. That makes a lot of sense. Good thinking. Of course, I'll be happy to ride over and deliver your message for ya. And anytime ya need anything, just ask. We'll all do everything we can to help. That's what friends and neighbors are for, after all."

"Thanks, Jeff. I'm mighty beholdin' to ya fer all yer help. Thanks."

Leo waved as Jeff mounted Sitsdown and rode towards Lizzie's home. Leo walked back into the tack room, worrying about what to do. He fervently wished Sean felt better so they could talk everything through, like usual, and make plans together.

When Lizzie arrived, Leo warned her off from hugging. "Sorry, Mom, but Doctor Parrish said we're under strict quarantine."

Leo brought his mother up to date with Sean's condition. They discussed having Bob and Ralph help out while Leo nursed Sean. Leo gave Lizzie money to buy the supplies Dr. Parrish had recommended. Lizzie took it on herself to buy a sheepskin for Sean to sleep on so he wouldn't develop bedsores from lying in bed for days on end. She had learned about using a sheepskin from her prolonged bed rest after her accident.

By the next day, Thanksgiving Day, Bertha had coordinated with Mrs. Murdoch, Mrs. Patten, Mrs. Gilbert, and Lizzie to take turns cooking meals for Sean and Leo.

The boys regretted missing Thanksgiving Dinner with the Merriwell family. Muriel Anne brought Leo a plate brimming with turkey and all the usual trimmings. She also brought Sean a pleasantly seasoned soup of mashed root vegetables.

That night, Leo fed Sean the soup. Sean only ate a couple of spoonfuls before he turned his head away. Leo helped Sean sip a little barley water. Then he carefully and tenderly gave Sean a sponge bath. Tears stood in his eyes, blurring his vision from time to time as he lovingly dried Sean and combed his hair. "Here, now, my love. Let's get ya turned over on yer stomach. I'll try some of that rubbin' of yer spine like the good doctor recommended."

Sean moaned from a cramp in his abdomen when Leo turned him over. Leo winced when he heard Sean's whimper. "Sorry, Sean. Just close yer eyes and relax. Let me see if maybe I can rub out some of yer pain."

After a few minutes, Sean sighed. "Oh, that does feel good, me boyo. Ahhh."

All of Sean's joints ached from the fever. Leo patiently massaged each joint of his fingers. Sean forced himself to speak. It came out nearly a whisper. "Leo, me boyo. Yer gonna have to keep goin', no matter what. Build the house. Build a life. No matter what."

"I know, Sean, my love. Don't worry yerself none. I already have my little brothers, Bob and Ralph, campin' out in the new house. They'll help with the chores and the buildin' and runnin' errands and all. We'll manage all right. Doncha fret none."

"And, Leo," Sean coughed, then winced from a shooting pain in his guts. "Would ya please ask Josh Patten to come over and see me? I need to get a will written all legal-like on paper."

"Ya don't need no will, Sean. Ya just need to rest and get yer health and strength back."

"Leo, I'm gonna put me affairs in order proper-like with or without yer help. It's fer yer own good, too, because I love ya, ya dumb kid. Now, don't argue. I'm far too weak. Just bring Josh over as soon as ya can before me fever gets worse, and I maybe can't think clearly. Okay, me boyo?"

Leo gently messaged Sean's neck and the base of his skull, willing him to relax and heal and live. "Okay, Sean. I'll do whatever ya ask, just like I always do. Don't get yerself all worked up. Take it easy now, boss. I'll do what ya ask."

When Muriel Anne arrived with lunch, Leo asked her to sit with Sean. He walked over to the Patten farmstead and knocked on their front door. Leo asked Josh to help them with more legal paperwork. Josh slipped on his jacket and grabbed his silver-plated fountain pen and a pad of paper. "I would be glad to offer whatever help I can, Leo. Lead the way, my friend."

Leo stopped at the door to the tack room. "Please remember that we're under quarantine, Josh. Please don't touch anythin', okay?"

"I understand the dangers of infectious disease, Leo. But thank you for reminding me."

"All right, then. Please come in."

Leo opened the door and waved Josh over to sit at the table. Muriel Anne moved the oil lamp to the side, clearing space for Josh's pad of paper. She stood up to leave, but Sean croaked out hoarsely, "No. Don't go. Please wait a spell if ya can, Muriel Anne. I'm gonna need a witness to me last will and testament, doncha know."

"Well, of course I can stay if you need me, Sean. Hello, Josh, it's nice to see you again. How's Mitch and your parents?"

"They're all doing fine, Muriel Anne. Here, please sit down. This might take a few minutes."

Leo pulled one of the white kitchen chairs over beside Sean and sat down. Josh held out a chair for Muriel Ann and then took the chair opposite her. He hung his hat off the back of the vacant chair but didn't remove his coat and gloves. He opened the notebook and uncapped his fountain pen. "Now, Sean, what may I do for you this afternoon?"

Sean answered softly but clearly, "Thanks fer comin', Josh. I need a written will if ya please. Can ya write it out fer me all legal like and bindin'?"

Josh believed in doing things properly and approved of Sean making plans for a future only God could foresee. "Of course. I would be pleased to write down your wishes. And what do you want to say in your will, Sean?"

"I want to leave one-hundred dollars to me Mom down in Saint George, Utah."

"Yes. Got it. And...?"

"Then I want to leave everythin' else, if and when I die, to Leonard Andrew Hayes, me partner in this Ranch and co-owner of everythin' I have."

Leo leaned over with his elbows on his knees and lowered his head to his fists. He closed his eyes, unable to bear the thought of losing Sean.

Josh wrote for a moment. "Very good. Easy enough. Anything else?"

"Nope. Just what ya need to make it all legal and bindin'."

"And who do you designate to be the executor of your estate?"

Sean glanced over at Leo, sitting beside him. "I'm not sure I know what that means, Josh, legal-wise."

"You need to say who you want to represent your wishes and see that they are carried out."

"Oh. Um. Would ya mind doin' that fer me, Josh?"

Josh hesitated a moment, then nodded his head. "I don't see why not. I would be honored, in fact. Just rest a moment now while I get this written down and copied in triplicate."

Josh bent over the table and wrote steadily and carefully. Restless, Muriel Anne stood up and retrieved the tin cup of tea off the edge of the potbellied stove. She took it over and handed it to Leo. Leo nodded his thanks. He then tested its temperature and blew on it. "Here, Sean. Have a sip of tea. The honey will ease yer throat from all the talkin'. That's the way, now. That's good. No more? Okay. Just rest a minute till Josh has the papers ready to sign."

Leo handed the cup back to Muriel Anne.

They listened to the soft scratching of the fountain pen's steel nib on paper.

Josh finished writing and sat up. "There, now. I believe everything is in order. I just need Sean to sign the original. Then the three of us will sign as witnesses of his signature, and all will be correct and legal."

Muriel Anne stood up and took the paper from Josh. She reached for his pen and then remembered the quarantine. She opened the top drawer of the boys' unpainted chest of drawers for Sean's fountain pen. She grabbed a book from the open trunk for a hard writing surface and carried everything over to Leo.

Leo nodded his thanks and leaned over the bed. "Here ya go, Sean. Do ya need to sit up, or can ya do it layin' down like that?

Sean swallowed hard, licked his lips, and opened his eyes. "Hold it up so I can read it, pardner. There. Thanks."

Sean read silently, relieved he had secured Leo's future in case the worst happened. "Help me sit up, please. I can't sign with the pen upside-down, doncha know. Ugh. Ouch. Okay. Thanks. Now, hand me the pen, please."

Leo uncapped the old pen, gave it to Sean, then held the will against the book. Sean signed on the line drawn above his printed name. His arm dropped wearily to the quilt. Sean sighed in relief. "Thanks, everyone. Thanks, Josh. Now I can rest easy no matter what."

A small blot of ink bled into the quilt before Muriel Anne removed the pen from Sean's hand. She capped it and returned it to the drawer.

Leo took the will over to Josh. Josh checked the signature, then turned the page to face Leo. "Leo, go ahead and sign your name as a witness above where I printed it. Then Muriel Anne can sign as the second witness. I'll sign as the will's author and executor. Good. I've marked these two copies as true copies of the original. I'll keep the original in my father's safe."

After Muriel Anne and Josh signed, Josh folded one copy in fourths and held it out to Leo. "Here, Leo. Put this in a safe place for when and if it is needed. As executor, I will keep the original. Muriel Anne, if you would be so good as to keep the second copy of the will in a safe place, that would be greatly appreciated."

"Of course. I'll put it with Mother's important papers under lock and key."

Leo took the copy of the will and stood up. "Josh. Thank ya kindly fer comin' and helpin' us out again. I would shake yer hand goodbye, but that's not a good idea."

He walked over and opened the door. "Thanks again, Josh."

"You are welcome, Leo, my friend. So long, now, Sean. I sincerely hope you get well soon. Bye-bye, Muriel Anne."

Leo closed the door and sat down by Sean. Sean had already fallen to sleep, worn out by the anxiety of making his will. Leo absently waved goodbye to Muriel Anne as she left.

Leo sat reading the will, a testament of Sean's love for him written down in undeniable black and white.

Greenwich Village
End of December 2010

Art sat up straighter, interrupting Josh's narrative. He shook his head with a sigh. "Aren't we lucky that typhoid fever and other serious illnesses no longer ravage us fragile humans? It's hard to imagine living with such a serious illness and not being able to do anything about it."

Josh took Art's hand and squeezed it. "I know."

Art picked up the iPad on his big glass coffee table, touched the google icon, then typed in typhoid treatment.

"Hm. Antibiotic therapy seems to clear it right up these days, with prompt treatment. Good god, but that must have been rough on your eighteen-year-old Grandpa Leo. Can you imagine? And for it to go on for weeks. What a strain, mentally and emotionally."

"Yep. We're lucky to be alive today, enjoying the miracles of technology and science. I don't know where people found the strength to live through all their trials and tribulations. Back then, a simple carriage accident could leave you crippled for life. The flu ravaged the population as it spread in waves across the country, time and time again. Now, I've got to warn you, Art. Grandpa Leo's story takes off into some pretty strange territory right about now. It all started…"

Chapter 18: Handfasting

Muriel Anne brought the workmen their lunch the following day, pleased to be making an important contribution to their work. Today she brought generous turkey sandwiches on freshly baked sourdough bread. The men expressed their sincere appreciation and thanks most vociferously.

Muriel Anne walked back to the tack room with Leo. Before Leo shrugged off his jacket, she stopped him with a hand on his arm. "If you would like to take a break, I would be pleased to sit a spell with Sean. You could take a break and enjoy some fresh air and sunshine. Go for a ride or something. I can take care of him for an hour or two and with pleasure."

"Oh, thanks, but…"

"Yeah, Leo," Sean grunted hoarsely. "Let me see a pretty face fer a change instead of yer sad puss. And besides, I'm dyin' fer a detailed report on the progress on the new house. How's about ya go do an inspection tour and report back here?"

Sean did his best to grin his most charming smile but didn't quite make it.

Leo shrugged. "Okay. Ya talked me into it. I'll go fer a walk-about and check out the construction job site. I'll see ya later."

Muriel Anne waved as Leo pulled the door closed behind him.

Muriel Ann poured Sean half a glass of fresh-pressed apple cider. She grabbed a paper straw and sat down in Leo's chair by the bed. She offered the cider with a smile. Sean nodded, then wrapped his calloused hand around her cool thin hand to hold the glass closer.

After a couple of sips, Sean let go of Muriel Anne's hand. "Muriel Anne. Ya know that I like ya, doncha?"

"Well, I guess I do, Sean. And I hope you know that I really care about you and Leo, too."

"Good. I'm glad. Ya know once yer exposed to typhoid fever ya either get it or not, right?"

"I do believe that's right, Sean. But, don't worry. I'm young and strong, and I don't believe I will catch the fever. I've been washing up like the stern doctor ordered."

"I've been doin' a lotta thinking, Muriel Anne. I do nothin' but lie here worryin' about what might happen and about what I might do to make things better fer Leo if I should die."

"Oh, such morbid thoughts, Sean. You needn't worry about such things. You're going to be well and strong in no time."

Sean shook his head and closed his eyes. "I hope so, but remember what Doctor Parrish said. One out of three dies from typhoid pneumonia, Muriel Anne. So I've gotta think and plan as best I can fer dire contingencies, although I hope I won't need 'em."

"Well, that's mighty honorable of you. But Leo's a grown man of eighteen. He can take care of himself."

"I know. But I don't want 'im to be alone. I love 'im, and that's the plain honest truth. It hurts me to think of Leo here on our ranch with no one to share his life and only memories of our short time together to keep 'im company on a cold winter's night."

Muriel Anne frowned and gazed directly at Sean's handsome face. He lay peacefully with his eyes closed, his fingers interlaced over his chest on top of the quilt.

"Just what is it you're trying to say, Sean?"

"I'm sayin' plain as I can, my dear friend, that I want to set things up so that he'll not be alone if I die."

Muriel Anne glared, mystified. She sat up when she read between the lines. "Are you saying... that maybe you might want me to... to marry him if something happens to you?"

"I'm sayin' maybe that's part of what I've been thinkin' about. And now I'm gonna ask ya a big favor. And I'm gonna ask ya to think on it before answerin'. Think carefully because, fer me, it's a matter o' life and death."

Muriel Ann scowled, not sure she heard and understood his fiercely whispered words. She leaned in closer. "Very well, Sean. I'll consider what you say before I answer."

Sean prayed for strength to debate his proposal with her. "All right, then. This is me plan, Muriel Anne. I want ya to marry me Irish style in a proper handfastin' only totally in secret."

Muriel Anne gasped, nearly choking as her eyes went wide in shock at the idea. She sat up straight.

Sean turned his head to look her directly in the eye. "And that's not all. I want ya to have me baby so some part of me will live on should I die. So Leo will have a bit of me to remember me love and affection... and me life. Should I die."

"Oh."

Muriel Anne's head pulled back. She frowned. *Surely I misunderstood. Surely he didn't just say...* "You want to marry me in secret? And you want me bear you a child for Leo in secret? Is that what I'm hearing? Is that what you said?"

Sean gazed at Muriel Anne in a silent plea for understanding. "That's the essence of the plan, me dear, sweet friend."

"Why… why… I've never heard of such a thing before. I can't believe you are… seriously…"

She shook her head as she tried to absorb his words. *Wait now, Muriel Anne. Wait a minute. Haven't you been wanting this all along? To marry one of these nice boys? And bear their children? And build a life together with one of the best-looking cowboys in the state? This might just be a way to secure your own future. And if he dies, and I have his baby, then I might be able to marry Leo and have my family farmstead back. I would have it all. Think, Muriel Anne. Think carefully. Take your time. If you are honest with yourself, you're already a little in love with both of them. You daydream about this all the time. And that's a fact.*

Sean closed his eyes, content to let her think while he rested. *If only me gut didn't hurt so bad. If only I could smile and try to win her over with smooth talk and flattery. But, since I'm layin' here sick as a dog, I've just gotta focus me thoughts and make it happen. Somehow. Please, Lord.*

"Sean."

"Yeah."

"It's totally an insane idea. It would never work. My mother would kill me. The neighbors would shun me. And what if Leo didn't want to marry me? And what if you live and you decide you don't want me? What of our secret marriage then? No. No. It's a crazy idea. I'm sure that your heart is in the right place, and you have good intentions. But no, this is just a delusion of your feverish mind. It's totally crazy!"

Sean rallied enough to order in a louder whisper. "Muriel Anne! Look at me. If this disease runs its course, I will be deathly sick in just a week or so. I don't have time to woo ya or try and sweet talk ya into helpin' me. But I've gotta do it. I've thought it all through. Please just listen a while and let me try and explain."

Muriel Anne observed the pain of concern and fever on Sean's face. She had always enjoyed watching his handsome face whenever she could in the past. She loved his bright, intelligent eyes and the sweet dimple in his left cheek. His expressive, appealingly lopsided smile had charmed her from the day they met. She nodded slowly, once. "I'm listening, Sean. Take your time. Don't wear yourself out."

"Trouble is, I don't have any time!"

Sean reached out and took her slim smooth hand in his rough, fevered hand. He held her hand softly. His eyes pleaded that she listen and understand and agree to what he needed. "Yer ancestors were Scottish and English, have I got that right?"

"That's right, Sean. My mother's family is from London. My father's family came from Glasgow, up on the west coast of Scotland."

"Then ya may have heard the stories about our common Celtic ancestors' marriage custom called handfastin'. Have ya?"

"Yes, of course. All the novels and plays of the old country are full of the romances and intrigues and adventures of handfasting."

Sean nodded. "If ya tie a string around two people's hands. And if ya say that one takes the other as husband or wife. And if ya make a contract like custom requires. And if ya sleep together to consummate the marriage. Then... the two... are... married!"

"Well, now. I know that was the custom from ancient times, but I don't think it's lawful nowadays. Although I *have* heard that people still get handfasted on May Day back in the old country."

"That's right. The church wanted to perform all the marriages, so they ordered a change a long time ago. But the tradition and validity of handfastin' still carry down to the present day modern world."

"Mm. Well." *That's right, in the romance stories, they got married for a year and a day. Then they decided, after that, if they wanted to renew for life or go their separate ways. And, now that he mentions it, they always made an agreement before the ceremony. A written contract. Hmm. There might be a way. Oh, but Mother would kill me. She would just kill me for even thinking about it. But, I'm going on to seventeen. Mother was married and pregnant and lost a baby before she turned eighteen. It's time I took whatever steps are necessary to secure a future for myself. I no longer have a father to provide my living and look out for my interests. I was raised with the Murdoch and Patten boys. They are all nice boys, but they aren't going to be husband material for me. So I better think this through. Sean and Leo have property and prospects. They are hard-working and honest. And they are both blessed with good looks, and...* "What's that part about a contract, again?"

"Based on what I've read, I seem to recall that the couple had to arrange in advance fer disposition of property and fer the rearin' and carin' of any children resultin' from the marriage. And that's what I propose we do. To handfast by contract, but fer a month and a day because we don't have time fer the usual year and a day."

Sean stopped to catch his breath, worried his strength wouldn't hold out until he convinced her.

"A month and a day. I see. Then, if you live... and I have not conceived a child, then what, Sean? Do we go our separate ways?"

"Probably, but we can also decide that when the time comes."

"And if you live and I am pregnant, then what?

"Then I would do the honorable thing and marry ya before God and yer family. And before the pregnancy becomes noticeable and the gossip mongers could start talkin'."

247

"Um-hm. I see. Very good. But if I am pregnant and you… you… um, pass away? Where does that leave me? It leaves me out in the cold, is where! With a bastard fatherless child. With my future in ruins. With my family despising me for being a stupid, foolish girl."

"No! Listen, Muriel Anne. I'll write a letter fer Leo. I'll tell 'im how we secretly made a baby as a love offerin' from the both of us. I'll ask 'im to marry ya and make an honest woman out of ya and raise me baby as 'is own."

How could we keep it all a secret? Oh, Mother would just kill me. She would just kill me. Can I trust them? Both of them? "And you think Leo would marry me just because you ask him to?"

Sean croaked out with firm authority, "Yes!"

"How can you be so sure? How can I be sure?" *How can I know absolutely positively that they would take care of me? How can I dare take such a risk?*

A warmth entered Sean's voice as he whispered, "Haven't ya ever noticed how he loves me? How he does whatever I ask? How he follows me about like a happy puppy? With somethin' this important, he wouldn't even hesitate to accept me gift and raise me child, a part of me, as his own. Ya *can* rest assured, Muriel Anne. I guarantee it!"

When Sean asked if she hadn't ever noticed how Leo loved him, it suddenly became clear. *Stupid girl! You've been blind. You've been fantasizing about one or both of them falling in love with you. You should've seen it before. Their affectionate ways together. Their easy smiles and winks. The way they share everything. They share everything… including this bed. Oh, you've been stupid and blind and foolish. Silly girl! You've read the stories about Oscar Wilde and his three trials, how he died destitute in Paris. You've read about others of his ilk, too. Did you think it only happened among the aristocracy of Europe? Stupid girl. Stupid. Stupid. Stupid.*

She sat there, shaking her head as she lost her cherished fantasies of a romance with one or both of them. How many times had she fantasized about them having an early morning duel over the right to her hand in marriage? She had fantasized about them since she first saw them talking to her mother the day they bought the family land. "You're in love with Leo, aren't you, Sean?" *This is why you are doing this, isn't it, Sean?*

Sean felt uncomfortable at her new tone of voice, but he knew he had to be honest for this to work. "Yes, Muriel Anne. I love Leo with all me heart."

"And Leo loves you back, doesn't he, Sean?"

"Yes."

"And you are partners."

"In everythin', Muriel Anne."

"And you share everything."

"Everythin'. Equally."

"Including… including your bed."

Sean smiled. Even sick, he felt warmed and renewed when he remembered their days and nights of sharing everything for more than four years. He quietly and happily answered, "Yes."

"I see. Well. I've got to think. Goodbye."

Muriel Anne leapt to her feet, grabbed her coat and hat off the wall, and slammed the door behind her – before Sean could even call out.

Oh, what've I done now? What've I done now? Oh, Leo, I was only tryin' to provide fer ya in the best way I could think of doin', doncha know. Oh, Leo. Oh, Muriel Anne. My dear, dear Leo. Oh, help me, Heavenly Father. Help me, dear Lord Jesus in heaven.

Exhausted from his efforts and the stress of worry, Sean slipped into a fitful, feverish sleep. He didn't even wake up when Leo went in to check on him. Leo had seen Muriel Anne ride away at a gallop with her unbuttoned coat flapping behind her in the breeze. Scotty had followed her, barking loudly. Leo felt disappointed when he found Sean sound asleep. He had such a good progress report to give him.

Around 11:30 on the day after Sean's secret proposal, Leo finished reading them a chapter of their current paperback book, *The Emerald City of Oz.* They had already enjoyed the first five

Oz novels before Sean took sick. Leo noticed Sean had drifted off to sleep. He decided to check on the construction progress.

Before Leo entered the new house, he caught sight of Muriel Anne riding down the hill from the back pastures. She flew like the wind on her big white stallion. Her ponytail streamed behind her like blond ribbons in the air. She wore her steel gray riding habit buttoned up against the cold. She pulled up in a flurry of dust.

"Muriel Anne! This is a surprise. Yer here early today, aren't ya? It's not even noontime."

Muriel Anne rode her spirited stallion over by the barn and tied his reins to the top rung of the corral. She walked briskly over to meet Leo, who had turned back. "Good morning, Leo. And isn't it a fine morning! How is dear Sean doing?"

To Leo's surprise, Muriel Anne grasped both of his shoulders in her gloved hands, hugged him, then kissed his cheek. Her eyes glistened bright and happy. Her cheeks glowed from the chilly air and the wind from riding. She stood close, holding his shoulders lightly, and looked him in the eye. "And how are you doing, Leo? I know how much you are concerned with Sean's health. I know how his illness has thrust so many extra duties and responsibilities on your shoulders. How are you holding up, really?"

Leo stepped back unconsciously to reclaim his personal space. He smiled gratefully. "Why I'm a little tired, but I'm all right, Muriel Anne. Nothin' I can't handle. I'm just worried about Sean and anxious fer 'im to get well, that's all."

Scotty ran up, hoping to be petted, his tail wagging excitedly. Leo absentmindedly reached down and scratched his ears while he watched Muriel Anne's face.

"Well, I think you are doing a perfectly wonderful job, Leo. You are not only keeping your operation going, but you are supervising the construction while giving such tender loving care to Sean in his sad hour of need. I think it really shows a lot of character, Leo. And I want you to know that both you and Sean have my complete admiration and support."

"Why, uh, thanks, Muriel Anne. That's very nice of ya to say."

"In fact, Mister Hayes, I talked it over with my good Mother yesterday evening at supper. I would like to propose myself as the morning nursemaid to sit with dear sick Sean. I could feed him his breakfast and lunch. Maybe read to him, if he wants. I figure if I tend him in the morning, you could take care of your work on the ranch and the new house. Then, you could rest in the afternoon while you tend Sean. Mother agreed to prepare dinners for everyone if I help her in the afternoons, which works fine for me. What do you say, Leo? Will you accept my help from daybreak until noon?"

Leo shook his head, pleasantly surprised but a bit bewildered. It sounded good to him. Chores demanded someone to tend to them, or they just piled up, nagging him. His little brothers, Bob and Ralph, had taken up some of the slack. That left everything else begging. Leo smiled warmly at Muriel Anne. "That sounds like an awfully good idea, Muriel Anne. Heaven only knows I can use all the help I can get. But it's such an imposition, I hate to ask it of ya."

Muriel Anne laughed brightly. "But, Leo, you're not asking me. I offered it freely out of friendship and affection and with best wishes for you both."

"In that case, I accept. And gladly, too."

Muriel Anne leaned in and hugged Leo again. "I'll start this afternoon if you would like, and then come back tomorrow morning at first light. Oh, look. There comes Mother. And she's riding rather than driving. You hardly ever see her ride anymore. She used to go riding almost every day for an hour or so before Father passed away."

Muriel Anne skipped over to where Bertha stopped next to Kensington. She untied the picnic basket from the back of Bertha's saddle. Bertha dismounted and nodded at Muriel Anne. "Did you have a nice ride, daughter?"

"Oh, yes, Mother. Thank you for letting me take the time. I feel so much better about things."

"Yes, Muriel Anne, I can see that. This morning you left the house in a cloud. And that cloud is now gone. I'm glad for you, daughter."

They hugged, tenderly and briefly. Bertha gestured towards the picnic basket. They picked it up by its handles and carried it in the back door of the new house. They worked together to unpack dinner for the workmen. Muriel Anne picked up the jar of enriched peppermint tea and the jar of chicken broth. She and Bertha hoped the beverages would soothe Sean's symptoms while giving him some nourishment. She took them over to the barn to serve Sean his midday meal.

Muriel Anne knocked briskly and then entered the tackle room hospital. She called out brightly in her lilting English accent, "Good morning, Sean! And how are we feeling on this bright and glorious day? Hm? Are you ready for a little light luncheon? We must keep up our strength, you know. We never know what the day might bring!"

She twittered a light laugh as she set the jars on the stove to re-heat. She hung up her bowler hat and riding habit on the wooden pegs by the door.

Sean struggled to wake up. He had been napping when she burst into the quiet room like a clap of thunder, startling him with her boisterous energy. He felt such relief to see her. He hoped her upbeat mood indicated a positive response to his proposal.

Muriel Anne poured a glass of tea, grabbed a straw, and held it out to him. "Here, Sean. Have a sip of tea. Maybe the peppermint will soothe your stomach and give you a little energy to deal with my questions this afternoon. Here. I'll hold the glass. That's good. Take your time. Good."

Muriel Anne wiped his chin with the flannel towel hanging by his head on the wood headboard. Sean weakly smiled his thanks. He patted the seat of Leo's chair by his bedside. "Please have a seat, Murial Anne," he whispered to conserve his voice. "Have ya been thinkin' on me proposal? Have ya made a decision?"

Murial Anne sat down with a smile. She impulsively picked up his hot hand and held it loosely, palm up on her knee between both of her chilled slender hands. Her thoughts had been flying about wildly since yesterday. She focused and took a deep breath. "Well, Sean. I was in a bit of a state after you startled me with your outlandish and totally improper proposal, I must say. I rode home all in a dither."

Sean turned his head so he could watch her face. Muriel Anne closed her eyes, unaware of his scrutiny. She remembered galloping home, agitated and confused. She ran up the stairs to her room, slammed the door shut, and threw herself on her bed. About an hour later, Jane Eve knocked timidly on the door. "Mother said to call you to come down to supper, Muriel Anne. Did you hear me?"

Muriel Anne stood in front of her mirror and wiped her eyes. She retied the ribbon holding her blond ponytail and smoothed down the wisps of hair that had escaped the ribbon. She smiled at herself for practice, then walked downstairs, outwardly composed.

Muriel Anne opened her eyes and saw Sean watching her. "During supper last night, I spoke with Mother about you and Leo. Of course, I hid the reason. I didn't even hint at your terribly indecent proposal. I told her I thought you were two very nice young men of good character, honest, trustworthy, and hard-working. Mother agreed. She thinks the world of both of you. She admires and respects you both for being so enterprising and focused on your goals. Mother's parents raised her in a very organized home in London. She admires those traits when she sees them in others."

Sean smiled and closed his eyes, relieved at the direction the conversation was going. He had spent a restless night fearing her reaction.

"I told Mother, and truthfully so, that I felt attracted to both of you. I told her I had developed strong feelings of friendship with you both. Mother said she was happy for us. She wished us to enjoy our friendship for many years to come. Well, I went to my bed feeling somewhat better. I still felt worried, especially about keeping everything a secret, and maybe bearing a child. I'm still a bit worried about all the, you know, the intimacy required to, uh, you know, to conceive a child. I am still a… a virgin, unschooled in any of the arts of lovemaking. Although, since I grew up on a farm, I have learned about the basic process of procreation from watching the livestock breeding."

Embarrassed, Muriel Anne broke off giggling. She glanced over at Sean. Her heart fluttered as she studied his handsome face. He lay relaxed with his eyes closed. His gentle smile barely hinted at the expressive lopsided grin she had found so adorable before he became sick.

She leaned her shoulders against the chair back, relaxing a little. "I kept waking up during the night. One time filled with hope and excitement. The next time filled with fear and doubts. By the time I got up this morning, I was really, but really, confused. I told Mother I needed to go for a long ride to sort some things out in my head. She gave me a hard look and then said to go ahead. So I took off on my stalwart Kensington. I galloped all around the four farmsteads of Rose Corners. My thoughts tumbled about as I remembered the past and thought about the present. I kept trying to envision the future."

Muriel Anne paused when she felt her heart beating quickly in fear or excitement. Sometimes, she couldn't quite tell the difference. She pulled her left hand out from under Sean's and grasped his fingers loosely in her right hand. She rested her left hand over her heart to calm her fears and excitement.

Sean sensed her struggles. "And did ya manage to find that inspiration and perspective ya sought on yer ride, Muriel Anne?"

She nodded her head. A subtle smile of relief eased the tension on her face. Her cheeks glowed from the morning in the sun and wind. "Yes, Sean. I believe I did. I hope I don't live to regret it. But if we can make a contract that covers every possibility to our mutual satisfaction, I am willing to marry you. And try to conceive a child with you – either for Leo and me or for you and me. Oh! I can't believe I actually said that! Mother would just kill me!" She paused and looked Sean in the eye. "But, I think it's the best thing we can do under the circumstances."

Sean squeezed her hand again in thanks. "Aye, me darlin' girl, it's all any of us can do with our mortal existences. What else can we do but struggle to find our way and build our lives as best we can? And no one can do it fer us, neither. Nor can they tell us the way, though society does try. I'm both delighted and relieved,

Muriel Anne. I know ya won't regret it no matter what happens. And we'll take good care to guarantee you won't."

Muriel Anne squeezed his hand in return before placing it back on his chest above the blankets. She walked over to the rustic chest of drawers where Sean kept a box of writing paper beside his old tarnished silver fountain pen. "I told Leo I would sit with you this afternoon so he could attend to the ranch and construction of your new home. This will give us an opportunity to work out the details of the contract. Would you like a sip of chicken broth first? I see a wisp of steam rising up from the jar on the stove, so it should be nice and hot."

She pulled one of her riding gloves from the belt of her black riding jodhpurs and used it to protect her fingers from the hot jar. She poured some of the steaming broth into a glass. She grabbed the straw used earlier in the tea and sat down by Sean. "Here. This will give you the energy to stay alert and replenish your fluids at the same time."

For the next hour and three-quarters, they discussed possible scenarios and how they would handle each if it happened. Leo only interrupted once. They pretended Muriel Anne had been reading aloud. Muriel Anne scribbled her notes furiously, intent on capturing each agreement in its original words and meanings. Sean struggled to whisper loud enough for her to hear him from the table. It still hurt his throat to talk out loud. In the end, they had a contract to which they could both agree. Muriel Anne also had a secret letter for Leo from Sean, which she could keep to use if she needed it. Muriel Anne crumpled up the three pieces of paper from the drafts and notes with a big sigh and then methodically pushed them into the stove. She watched them burn to a crisp before she dared look away. *You better believe we're going to keep this a secret from everyone. Mother would just kill me on the spot. Oh, Mother would just kill me!*

Sean spoke out loud, hoping he projected a little warmth into his coarse voice. "So, Miss Merriwell, will you marry me, now, in the ancient and traditional ceremony of handfastin'?"

Muriel Anne turned and gazed down at Sean. She smiled weakly and nodded twice. "Yes, Mister McKay, I will."

Muriel Anne reached up and untied the long white ribbon securing her ponytail and then shook out her long hair. She walked over slowly and sat down on Leo's chair. Sean placed his right hand in her lap again, palm up. Muriel Anne placed her right wrist over his, palm down. Using only her left hand, she wrapped the ribbon around their wrists, then tied a simple loose knot. With one end of the ribbon in her fingers, she ceremoniously handed Sean the other.

Sean turned onto his side. His face pinched from a flare of pain in his lower abdomen. He gazed at Muriel Anne with hope and with relief. He coughed to clear his rough, sore throat. "With this, I take ya, Muriel Anne Merriwell, as me married wife fer a month and a day or until death do us part."

With her voice throbbing with emotion, Muriel Anne quietly vowed, "And with this, I take you, Sean Michael McKay, as my married husband for a month and a day or until death do us part."

They both gently pulled on the ribbon as they tied the knot, binding them together, sealing their fates as one in the old tradition. Their wrists tied together, Muriel Anne leaned over and gave Sean a brief but tender kiss on his chapped, feverish lips. "Aren't there supposed to be lots of flowers, a bridal gown, and bride's maids? A feast and laughter and dancing? I think we got short-changed here, husband."

"No, wife, we've secured the future as best we can, plantin' seeds rather than pickin' flowers. The rest will all come in good time, doncha know. Rest happy that we've done a good deed here today, to be sure, me darlin', darlin' wife."

Muriel Anne sat back down, quietly holding Sean's feverish work-toughened hand. She unconsciously massaged his calloused fingers as she took a long look around her, memorizing the barn chapel of her wedding ceremony. The light streamed in through the new glass window. The pair of doves that lived on the barn roof cooed peacefully to each other. The dry wood in the small stove crackled and popped merrily. She treasured up in her mind the handfasting ceremony and the exchange of vows, her first marriage, so she would never forget it.

She slowly untied the knot, then wound the ribbon around her finger and tucked it into a pocket.

Leo came in from the fields. He stomped his boots to knock off the dirt and manure then entered their tack room home. He found Muriel Anne and Sean sitting quietly with contented, easy smiles on their faces. Muriel Anne held Sean's fingers loosely interlaced on the knee of her riding jodhpurs – her de facto wedding gown.

Chapter 19: A Gift

The day after their handfasting, Muriel Anne walked to the barn early. Scotty kept her company. She left Kensington unsaddled so he could run free in the pasture. She wore a long free-flowing beige skirt below a fitted white cotton blouse. The blouse sported billowing sleeves in the latest fashion with a touch of lace and ribbons at the throat and wrists. A wide tan leather belt cinched in her narrow waist. A simple long tan dust coat kept her warm on the walk. Her breath puffed out visibly before her in the cold November air as she strode along the path between her home and the old barn. She had tied up her hair in a pink ribbon.

The night before, Muriel Anne had carefully wound her wider white handfasting ribbon around her forefinger into a ring of silk. Then, using a short scrap of a narrow lavender ribbon, she tied the white ribbon so it wouldn't unwind. She then knelt in front of her cedar hope chest at the foot of her brass bed and opened the lid. With reverence and solemnity, she tucked the ribbon down in the very bottom right corner, where she would treasure it forever.

She carried a jar of Darjeeling tea enriched with honey, cream, and cinnamon. She hoped it would give them both the bravery and energy to complete their wedding ceremony this morning. She felt a tremor of fear, a jittery attack of nerves and excitement. For the marriage to be lawful, both by the old traditional ways and current modern laws, they had to have sexual relations to consummate it. She also knew they had to make love in order for her to conceive Sean's love child. She had bathed languidly and carefully after supper, applying oils and flowery perfumes to prepare for this morning. She felt jittery with nerves. She would never be a virgin again, even if circumstances developed where she might want to be for another man at another time. But, she told herself she had to risk it in the hope of securing a future with good prospects.

Muriel Anne knocked on the tack room door more boldly than she felt. She turned and looked out at the tent camp and construction site. The men and boys stood around drinking coffee as they planned their morning's labors. The rising sun did nothing to take the winter chill out of the air. Leo called out, "Come in."

Muriel Anne opened the plank wood door and stepped into her wedding bedchamber. Her heart pounded with fear and anxiety. She called out as cheerfully as she could, "Good morning. Good morning, Leo. Good morning, Sean. My, but it's a beautiful brisk, clear day this morning. Beautiful as can be, for this time of year."

Leo looked over to the door as she hung up her dust coat and hat. He smiled, warmed by her apparent cheerfulness. "Well, yer certainly in good form this morning, Muriel Anne. And it's welcome ya are to this day's nursin' duties. Sean's already had a bite of breakfast and is resting easy, considerin' his fever. So, if yer ready to assume the nursin', I'll go tend to my chores and see ya both at noontime."

Leo patted Sean's shoulder and squeezed it affectionately. He pulled on his Levi jacket and gloves, then plopped on his big hat. He nodded thanks to Muriel Anne as he strode out the door, his cowboy boot heels clomping loudly on the plank floor.

In the silence of the small warm room, Muriel Anne heard the wood fire crackling in the potbelly stove. She suddenly felt shy, like a little girl. Excitement and nerves blended, blurring into one intense emotion. She felt her heart in her throat.

She carried over two glasses of tea, one with a straw. "Here you go, Sean. I'll be joining you this morning for a warming spot of tea. I brewed it extra strong to give us both the bravery and strength to do the gentle deeds that await us."

Muriel Anne blushed, not used to being forward about such matters. She knew she had to take matters into her own hands since Sean lay bedridden, weakened by fever. "How are you feeling today, Sean?"

Sean pushed himself up higher in the bed so he could drink the tea. "I'm feeling about the same, Muriel Anne. The fever and the aches are plaguin' me body, but me mind is greatly relieved by our formal handfastin' ceremony. How are you… wife?"

Muriel Anne glanced over, startled, then giggled. "I guess I am your wife, aren't I… husband?"

"Yes, ma'am. Yer me handfasted bride. And I couldn't be happier, doncha know."

They sat lost in their thoughts, sipping the tea. They both knew what they needed to do, yet they both felt shy about taking the first step.

Finally, Sean broke the silence with a gentle cough to clear his throat. "In order fer there to be a baby, there are certain, uh, requirements that must be met, doncha know, before a man and a woman can conceive. Ya know what I'm talkin' about, doncha, Muriel Anne?"

She answered with a nod. She picked up Sean's hand from on top of the quilt. The fever didn't seem as high this morning, which she took as an omen that things would go well. "I know about these things from observing nature and from things girls talk about. Mother taught me female precautions as I grew up. But... I don't know from personal experience."

Sean frowned. "If I weren't so weak from the fever, I could be more active. I could give ya pleasure, maybe even that ecstasy that is the joy of married life. But I'm afraid I won't have the strength to do much more than lie here and let ya do all the work. I can coach ya. It's not complicated. The body seems to know what to do by instinct. I only hope the fever doesn't keep me down if ya know what I mean. Certain biological steps *are* required to sire a child, doncha know."

Muriel Anne felt herself blushing, not only from embarrassment but from a naively childish anticipation of making love fueled by romance novels.

"Muriel Anne, yer gonna need to lower the britches of me BVD's to make me privates available fer the work at hand, doncha know."

Quietly, Muriel Anne murmured, "I know, Sean. And that's why I decided not to wear any pantaloons under my skirts this morning. I was afraid that, what with the other men outside liable to come in and interrupt us, we wouldn't dare to get undressed for our intimacy like most married people do in their wedding bed, or at least, so I've read. So I just... ah... made myself more available."

260

She blushed again, her face and neck hot. She was also warm from walking all this way without any undergarments. Her imagination also warmed her, fantasizing about losing her virginity and engaging in sexual intercourse. She had seen males coupling with females in the pasture and barnyard many times over the years.

"Don't be shy or embarrassed, Muriel Anne. We're just doin' what the body finds natural, even if people have lots of differing ideas about propriety and modesty and such. Please put the latch on the door, and let's give this a try while we're still both fresh and rested and able."

Excited despite herself, Muriel Anne locked the door and scurried back to the bed. She lowered the quilt and sheet then folded the bedding neatly over Sean's ankles and feet. She unbuttoned the small white buttons at the waist and flies of Sean's BVD bottoms with trembling hands. Firmly but slowly, she dragged them below his knees.

Muriel Anne's first look at a grown man's privates pleased her immensely. Instinctively, she reached out and gently caressed him into hardness. As she felt herself growing moist between her legs, she knew what she needed to do.

As gently as possible, out of consideration for Sean's painful abdomen, she climbed up on the mattress and knelt over Sean's knees. A little ashamed at her forwardness and wantonness, she studiously avoided looking Sean in the eye as she caressed him to hardness and gently cuddled his hairy bollocks. She delighted in the way they felt, so cuddly, so warm and soft in her hand. Then, closing her eyes, she moved forward. She held Sean upright in her right hand and held up her skirts in her left. Crawling up over his hips, she lowered herself slowly. She experienced a moment of discomfort, hesitated, then slid down his shaft. Finally, his masculinity filled her where only her dreams had been before.

Sean kept his eyes closed, imagining Leo sitting above him. His body began the automatic age-old pelvic movements. Muriel Anne's body instinctively took over. She matched him, slowly, sensually, move for move.

While Sean lay there, his thoughts drifted. He found himself marveling how not even illness could completely dampen the need to procreate, the urge to make love. *Oh, Heavenly Father, let me sick body not betray me now. Let me seed shoot forth and make a baby fer Leo and fer me.*

Her eyes tightly closed, Muriel Anne explored each new sensation, enjoying Sean's masculine strength and hard virility. She moved up and up again, gently pulling his seed up into her womb. She found herself praying silently. *Yes. Yes. Let me be fertile. Let this labor of love produce a child for Sean. For me. For Leo. For us. Yes. Yes. Yes.*

Even though she enjoyed the physical closeness, she did not achieve a climax during the consummation of their wedding vows. After Sean feverishly released his seed, she gradually slowed down, not wishing to impose on his weakened body. She waited until he shrank and naturally withdrew from within her. Her breathing returned to normal.

Muriel Anne carefully stepped off the bed. Then she leaned over and straightened Sean's undergarments and bedding. She stood up tall and took a deep breath. Smiling, gently shaking her head in wonderment, she smoothed out her skirt and tucked in her blouse. Then she sat down in the chair by the bed, a bit overcome yet thoroughly content and satisfied.

Sean lay still. Even though worn out, he watched Muriel Anne out of the corner of his eye. He couldn't help the weary smile on his face, relieved he had delivered, happy they had taken the first step together on this particular secret journey.

Muriel Anne sat with her legs crossed. She instinctively wanted to hold in any possible future between her legs, up in her womb. She gently fanned her face with her hand as she considered how she had enjoyed her first experience despite suffering two nights of nerves and doubts.

'You know, Sean, it's about two weeks since my period, if you don't mind my discussing such intimate female details. From all the old wives' tales, that's when a girl is most likely to conceive. Of course, you realize it seldom happens that the first time results in a baby. That usually only happens, from all I've heard, when a girl *doesn't* want to conceive."

Sean closed his eyes serenely. "Um-hm."

"Not to be immodest, husband, but what I'm saying is that we should keep trying for as long as you are able to increase our chances of conception."

"That makes sense, Muriel Anne. I know about the mechanics of breedin', leastwise fer cattle and horses. It often requires more than once to take."

They sat quietly for a few minutes. Sean smiled. A shadow of his typical roguish grin showed through his weariness. "Muriel Anne? I'm sorry I didn't have the energy to make it pleasurable fer ya. Yer first time should've been special, tender, unforgettable. I wish I could've helped ya find yer pleasure in the act of makin' love. That's the way it's supposed to be."

"I'm doing just fine, Sean. Don't fret yourself none at all. It was surprisingly good. I found it natural and fulfilling, even if it wasn't all that passionate. I think it's a miracle you could rise to the occasion at all, given you've been flat on your back for the past few days. Don't worry, Sean. I'm fine."

When Leo came in around noon, he found Sean sound asleep. Muriel Anne sat by the window reading one of their old paperback dime novels. "Did everythin' go all right, this mornin', Muriel Anne?"

"Oh, yes, Leo. Sean is an ideal patient. We talked a bit. Then I read to him before he drifted off into a nap. Shall I come back tomorrow morning, then? Was it helpful for you to have some time away from the sickbed?"

"Yes. Thanks, Muriel Anne. It was mighty helpful. If ya don't mind, I'd appreciate it if ya came back again tomorrow. Yer a godsend, and that's fer sure. If ya don't mind then, I'll be watchin' fer ya about the same time tomorrow mornin'? And thanks, again, fer everythin' you've been doin' to help us out. You've been just the dearest friend a body could ever hope to have."

Muriel Anne smiled as she pulled on her long dust coat. *You may never know just how good a friend I've been, Leonard Hayes. But I hope you will be as pleased as I am if and when you do find out.* She gave Leo a brief kiss on the cheek with a quick hug on her way out the door. She turned and waved from the open door. "Bye, now. So long, you boys!"

For the next six mornings, Sean and Muriel Anne repeated their private wedding dance. A couple of times, Muriel Anne floated off to the clouds during their simple lovemaking. Once, to their mutual disappointment, Sean couldn't achieve a climax due to a spike in his fever. They worked together diligently, determined to make a baby no matter what obstacles they had to overcome – the fever be damned.

Leo spent those six afternoons and evenings reading to Sean. After Sean fell asleep, Leo usually practiced the guitar. He also worried. He worried a lot. Every evening during the sponge bath, both boys remembered all the beautiful times they had shared, the joy of their physical intimacies, of making love over the years. Every evening ended in renewed declarations of love with tearful sobs and tight hugs, as tight as Sean's tender abdomen permitted. His stomach swelled a bit more each day from constipation and nasty infection.

While Leo tenderly bathed Sean's privates, he attempted to stimulate him and give him a little pleasure. When nothing developed, Leo wrote it off to the depredations of the fever and aches. He had no way of knowing Sean had already spent his passion earlier in the morning.

Leo tried to keep himself busy during the mornings while Muriel Anne tended Sean. He buried himself in the myriad duties required to run the ranch and build the house. Bob and Ralph had freed him from the usual morning and evening milking chores. Josey and Abe worked diligently, determined to keep to the schedule to finish the house even without Sean's help. They planned on returning to their homes in Idaho Falls by Christmas Eve at the latest. Each night they worked a little later. Each morning they began a little earlier, burning lots of lamp oil.

Leo found it hard to wake up in the morning. He subconsciously sought to remain in the oblivion of sleep. In his dreams, Sean had his health. He smiled and laughed as charmingly as ever. Leo didn't want to face the fact of Sean suffering from typhoid.

He did everything he could to avoid thinking about the seriousness of Sean's severe illness.

Several times Leo had to run out to the convenience or grab the chamber pot when his bowels turned liquid from fear and nerves. Each time it happened, he feared he had caught typhoid fever, which increased his anxiety. More than once while working, Leo found himself nauseated and light-headed. He had to run to the convenience, where he fell to his knees and vomited explosively. His body rejected their frightening circumstances and uncertain futures.

Despite worrying about contracting typhoid from Sean, Leo never became ill. He hadn't become infected during their travels on the road when Sean caught the fever. He didn't catch it from tending to Sean despite their close contact.

Leo remembered Dr. Parrish's stern warnings. He scrubbed his hands with hot water and soap after every time he touched Sean. He also washed his hands again before eating, which probably saved him.

Monday the seventh of December, one week after consummating their secret marriage, Muriel Anne arrived with her enriched tea and enthusiastic loins. Sean could barely rouse himself to consciousness. A bitter, chill wind howled around the barn, finding cracks and crevices through which it whistled, intruding into the bare little tack room. Leo stoked up the potbellied stove to where the iron glowed a dull red in the dim light of the overcast day.

As soon as Muriel Anne hung up her coat, Leo beckoned her to join him by Sean's bed. Leo raised the sweat-dampened sheet and quilt, then lifted the top of Sean's BVD long johns. He pointed at the newly developed red blotches spreading up over Sean's swollen stomach into his hairy chest. Muriel Anne gasped in alarm. They both noticed Sean's belly appeared more swollen. The skin looked stretched and tender, pulsing with a hint of blue veins just beneath the surface. Sean opened his eyes to acknowledge them, but they fluttered closed as a wave of pain wracked his feverish body with a shudder.

Leo shook his head mournfully. Tears flooded his eyes and dripped down his cheeks. "This confirms it, Muriel Anne. Sean has definitely come down with the typhoid pneumonia. Oh, I'm afraid we're in fer some bad times over the next few weeks before things start gettin' better."

Muriel Anne leaned in close to examine the rosy blotches on Sean's lean, hairy torso. She rested her right hand on Sean's feverish brow then grabbed Leo's hand. "Don't you boys worry. We're all here to help you in any way we can. I love you both so much."

Muriel Anne tenderly kissed Sean's forehead. When she stood up, she kissed Leo's cheek and then enfolded him in a tender hug. Since her voice failed her, she tried to communicate her sympathy and support without words. Leo hugged her back as he looked down at his beloved Sean. Leo's eyes filled with fear, overflowing with tears as he faced a bleak, hard future.

Muriel Anne also shed a silent tear. *Well, that's that, then. Either we made a baby, or we didn't. From what Doctor Parrish said, Sean will have a couple of really bad weeks now while we wait and see if I have my period on time or not. We will have to watch the typhoid ravish Sean's body even more before he starts healing. Then, we'll know which fork of the road we'll be traveling. Oh, I hope we made a baby in time! I hope Sean pulls through! Oh, great God in heaven, give us all strength!*

Leo straightened Sean's underwear and bedclothes, gently tucked him in, then gave Sean's feverish brow a soft, loving kiss.

Greenwich Village
End of December 2010

Yawning, Josh glanced at his iPhone to check the time. "Well. No wonder I'm tired, Art. It's coming on to one A.M. We've got to stop for the night."

Art stood up and stretched. "Yeah. Time for bed. Still. What a story! So, do you think your great-great-grandfather Sean was bisexual? I don't think I could hook up with a girl, even with the good intentions of making a baby. How about you?"

"I don't know, Art. I've never been interested in playing with girls, so I've never tried it. But, I don't think I would enjoy it. Could I perform the sex act to get a girl pregnant? Possibly. I'm not sure I could reverse the roles in my head, imagining she was a hot man. I would rather use artificial insemination."

They chuckled.

Art walked over to turn down the bed while Josh visited the bathroom. When Josh came in, he snuggled up against Art's warmth. "You know, people didn't think in terms of gay or straight back then. The words hadn't even been invented yet. The term homosexual first appeared in writing in eighteen seventy. It wasn't incorporated into the Bible until nineteen forty-six. Terms before then described practices and activities, not identities or groups of people. I think male sexuality included everything, the whole spectrum, and it was more a matter of liking or preferring one aspect of male sexuality over another.

Josh yawned. "I suppose, without the blinders of our modern definitions of what we are and what we do and what is appropriate, Sean could have had sex outside of his preferred activities without giving it much thought. Of course, sodomy was against the law back then. If you chose to go that route, you had to hide yourself and your activities under all circumstances. What do you think, Art?"

Josh waited for an answer. He received it when he heard Art softly snoring.

Chapter 20: Love Lost

Sean's condition deteriorated rapidly that next day. He couldn't eat. He didn't rouse to full consciousness.

Wednesday evening, during the loving sponge bath, Leo noticed the rash had begun fading. Sean's stomach had become so distended Leo feared turning him over to massage his back.

Sean scared Leo that night with the first of many delusional dreams. Sean jerked about, talking out loud, his voice distorted from hoarseness. He woke Leo up hours before sunrise on Thursday morning, croaking out in his rasping, dry voice, "Wake up, me boyo, we've gotta go milk the cows."

Leo reluctantly climbed out of bed in the cold uninsulated barn room. He turned up the oil lamp so he could check on Sean. Sean lay moving his head side to side, denying something only he could see or hear. Sean's eyes were partly open but un-seeing, with no sign of intelligence or awareness behind them.

Leo leaned over and patted Sean's shoulder. "No, Sean, my love. We don't have to go milk the cows. We can sleep in this mornin'. My two little brothers are doin' the chores fer us today. Go on back to sleep now. Don't fret none. Go back to sleep, Sean, my love."

Leo pulled the blankets up and tucked Sean's arms beneath the sheets to keep them warm. Sean settled down a little bit and seemed to rest easier.

But, from then on, Sean either lay in a stupor or struggled against unseen demons and delusions. He never again said anything coherent.

Leo and Muriel Anne faithfully took turns sitting by his side, ready to respond to whatever he might need during those long cold winter days of Thursday, Friday, and Saturday. Leo left Sean's side only to chop wood in the morning when Muriel Anne first arrived. He found he craved relief in physical activity. Plus, he needed wood for the potbellied stove so he could keep the sick room warm.

The neighbor ladies and Lizzie took turns delivering suppers. They placed the casseroles, covered roasting pans, or covered Dutch ovens on the outdoor wood stove. Each evening Leo stood at the open door and thanked them.

After Sean entered the typhoid state, Muriel Anne spent the entire day with Leo. Since Sean couldn't speak or respond intelligibly, she wanted Leo to have some human companionship. In the evenings, she pulled on her coat and gloves and brought in their supper. They both stopped to wash their hands before eating. Muriel Anne ate with Leo to keep him company. Then she cleaned up and washed her hands again before going home to her Mother's to sleep.

Sunday morning, Leo saw blue blood vessels pulsing beneath the thinly stretched skin of Sean's distended stomach. It alarmed him how big the stomach had swollen since yesterday. It looked like it threatened to explode from pressure within. It made Leo's stomach hurt just looking at it. He could no longer button the undershirt over Sean's stomach. He also had to leave Sean's underpants unbuttoned.

Leo didn't go out to chop wood that morning, afraid to leave Sean's side for even a moment. Sean had lain in the stuporous typhoid state, hardly moving, for five full days now. It had taken a severe emotional toll on Leo. Sean's unconsciousness drained Leo's spirits and energy. He sat holding Sean's hand, willing Sean to take strength from him, to grow stronger and survive.

Muriel arrived that morning. Leo invited her to inspect Sean's distended belly. She shook her head as she lifted the bed covers and saw his swollen stomach. She didn't like the sour smell wafting up from Sean's unwashed body. *That's what I'm going to look like soon, my belly swollen in pregnancy bearing a bit of Sean into posterity. But I'm afraid Sean's belly is carrying the seeds of death with this unnatural swelling, with this horrible typhoid fever. I only hope to high heavens we were able to plant the seeds of his life in my loins before he slipped away, and we couldn't try again. Get well, secret husband. Please survive this. Please live for us all.*

Muriel Anne pulled the sheet and quilt back over Sean with a heavy heart. It pained her to see him in such distress. She straightened the bedding, then tenderly pushed his unruly hair back off his forehead and tucked the sides behind his ears. She looked up at Leo. "He's going to need a haircut soon. When he's back on the road to recovery."

Leo sat in silence by the sickbed. He patiently dribbled honeyed water from a spoon over Sean's parched lips, willing him to swallow and absorb its moisture and energy. The visible signs of Sean's dehydration worried him. He saw the muscles on Sean's handsome face and body clearly etched beneath his fevered parchment-thin pale skin. Since he stopped eating, Sean had lost so much weight his ribs poked out like fingers above his swollen abdomen.

Suddenly, Sean's face turned a bluish powdery white. His eyes flew open. His heart began pounding and pounding. Seeing the frantic heartbeats in the pulsing blood vessels at Sean's temples, Leo caught his breath in a gasp. "Muriel Anne! Somethin's wrong!"

Muriel Anne jumped up from the table by the window where she had been reading, knocking over her chair. She leapt across the few feet to the bedside. She arrived as Sean jerked upright in a spasm, convulsing with pain.

A silent cry of agony contorted his face. In a gasp, he choked out the words, "Little Lion."

Sean fell back against his pillow and let out his breath, his last breath.

He lay still.

He didn't move.

He didn't breathe.

His charming smile and roguish wink disappeared as his facial muscles relaxed in death.

A single tear dripped down to his pillow from his left eye.

Muriel Anne's hand covered her mouth as she leaned over, desperately seeking a sign of life.

Leo sat frozen on the bedside chair, the glass of sugar water in his left hand, a tin teaspoon in his right. He slowly stood up and leaned over, thoughtlessly tipping the sugar water out onto the unvarnished floorboards. "What's that, Muriel Anne?"

Leo pointed with the spoon at a blackish-red stain spreading slowly up the sheets, wicking up along Sean's sweaty white long johns. "What's that? Is that blood? What's going on? Sean! Sean!"

Leo whipped the quilts aside, exposing a pool of blood and khaki green diarrhea. The nauseous fluids began settling around Sean's hips, between his unmoving legs. The gore slowly absorbed up into the porous fabrics of his underwear, staining the cotton sheets. "Oh, no. No. No. No!"

Leo grabbed Sean's shoulders and shook them. "Don't die, Sean. Yer supposed to start gettin' better, now, any day now! Ya gotta live, Sean. Ya can't die!"

Leo's legs gave out. He dropped heavily to his knees on the floor and instinctively threw his arms protectively over Sean's still body. "Don't die. Don't leave me here all alone. Oh, Sean. Sean!"

His shock and sorrow barked out of him in one loud, harsh wail. "Ooooh!"

The sound of his voice hurt Muriel Anne so much she would remember it for the rest of her life. Then Leo sobbed and sobbed, helplessly, desperately.

Muriel Anne stepped back and bowed her head to her hands, weeping with Leo. Watching Sean cross over from her secret handfasted husband to a lifeless corpse had shocked her senseless. She fell to her knees. She couldn't stop crying, sorry for Sean, sorry for Leo, sorry for herself, and sorry for her unborn baby. Sean's baby. Now fatherless. An orphan before birth.

Neither heard the quiet knock at the quarantined door. Josey had been pouring a cup of coffee at the stove when he heard their cries and tears. He scrambled over to find out what had happened. He remembered the quarantine in time to stop outside the closed door. He reached a trembling hand for the door handle, hesitated, then knocked. When they didn't answer, he knew Sean had died. It broke his heart not to rush in and offer his support.

Josey jogged over to the new house, shouting for Ralph. When Ralph poked his head out the door, Josey pointed at the barn. "Hop on yer horse. Don't waste time saddlin' up. Just race over to Missus Merriwell's house and tell 'er Sean just passed away. Ask 'er to come quick as possible. Hurry now. Ride like the devil was on yer tail!"

Their hopes for Sean's recovery dashed by the shocking news, Abe and Bob stood listlessly by the cookstove. They didn't know what to do, so they simply stood silently, hats in their hands, holding an informal wake in the cold. Their thoughts turned to their lost friend.

Bertha rode up on Ralph's horse. Ralph led the horse at a full-out panicked run. Bertha's coat flopped open behind her. She had forgotten, in the shock of the news, to put on a hat or gloves. Panting breathlessly, Ralph led the mare up to the tackle room door and helped her dismount. Bertha noticed the somber faces by the cookstove and nodded. Straightening her coat, Bertha took a deep breath and entered the tragic tack room. She closed the door behind her as she took in the heartbreaking scene. Leo knelt prostrate over Sean's corpse. She glanced at the ugly evidence of Sean's massive intestinal hemorrhage, a black stain from his waist down, then averted her eyes in horror. Muriel Anne knelt, crying, bowed down in her sorrow and loss, her hands over her face.

Bertha wanted to give in to her own tears of sorrow. Her heart and breath caught in her breast. However, seeing things that needed her attention, she told herself to be brave. She determined she would cry her tears of sadness later at a more opportune time.

Bertha knelt down beside Muriel Anne and pulled her into a warm embrace. Muriel Anne turned and hugged back. "Mother... he died... just like that! Ooooh..."

"There, there, daughter, I know it's a shock and a loss. Let it all out. Go ahead and cry. Cry, my darling daughter. It will cleanse your soul and make you strong for what comes next."

Leo had nearly sobbed himself to exhaustion, clutching Sean's dead chest in his arms. Now he whimpered wordlessly with each of his slow gasping breaths like a dog beaten by a cruel master. Leo desperately pressed his ear tight to Sean's breast, struggling hopelessly to hear a heartbeat.

As Muriel Anne calmed down, Bertha guided her over to sit in one of the chairs at the table. Muriel Anne folded her arms on the raw pine tabletop. Bowed down by grief, she laid her head down over her arms.

Bertha stepped over to Leo collapsed over Sean. She reached down and gently tugged him away from Sean's still remains. Leo looked up at her with stricken eyes and burst into tears again. She cradled his head against her motherly bosom and patted his back. Not knowing what else she could do, she tenderly muttered those meaningless phrases one hopes might offer comfort. "There, there. It will be okay. It will be all right. Let it all out. Let it out. There, there."

After Leo relaxed against her and his shoulders stopped shaking with his sobs, she helped him to his feet. She steadied him as he stumbled over and sat down at the table opposite Muriel Anne. He sat there, dumbfounded, in shock, his eyes glazed and unseeing. Leo found himself reeling with his overwhelming loss, unable to say goodbye – or even consider saying goodbye.

Bertha straightened up and pulled her shoulders back, steeling herself for the unpleasant duties facing her. Already the carnage slaughterhouse smells of death and blood had turned intolerable in the warm closed-up room. Bertha forced herself to think through the steps required to clean the body and dress it. Then she realized they needed a coffin. Nobody had done anything about a coffin. They had all expected strong, vibrant, and virile Sean to survive and recover.

Bertha sadly walked over to the door and opened it. She propped it open with one of Sean's dirty black cowboy boots. She wanted to let in fresh air to sweep out the stench of blood and diarrhea. Bertha took in the unhappy faces of Josey, Abe, Ralph, and Bob standing outside the door. She nodded a wordless greeting and then took a deep breath. "Mister Cummings, we are going to need a coffin, if you please."

"Yes, ma'am. I can make a coffin, though it breaks me heart to have to do it."

"Thank you, Josey. Please do it now so we can lay out the body to rest for the night."

"Yes, ma'am."

Josey turned and placed his arm over the shoulder of young Abe. "Come along and give me a hand. We have some good pine boards stored on the other side of the house that will do just fine."

They walked away slowly, both reluctant to take up this next sad assignment.

Bertha turned to Bob and his younger brother Ralph. "Ralph, would you be so good as to ride to your mother's and tell Lizzie what has happened? Ask if she could drop by to help me make the funeral arrangements. Bob, would you please walk around and give the news to the Murdochs, Pattens, and Gilberts? They will know what to do while I stay here and help... clean up... things."

Ralph looked at his older brother for permission. Bob nodded for him to do as Bertha asked. Ralph then nodded to Bertha. "Yes, ma'am. I'll go carry the news to Mom. And I'll probably drive her back later."

"Thank you, Ralph."

Bob gulped as he clapped Ralph on his shoulder in farewell. He had never faced death before. He coughed, but his voice still trembled. "And I'll go around the intersection and spread the sad news."

"Yes. Thank you, Bob."

Bertha turned back to the tack room. Leo and Muriel Anne still sat at the table, leaning over their folded arms, weeping quietly. Leo couldn't come to grips with this horrible development. Bertha shook her head in sympathy as she remembered all the times she had mourned for lost ones over the years. *It never gets easier, either. When Dick died. When Mother passed away. When I lost my first two baby children. But, death is a part of life. Be strong. You've survived it before. You will survive it again. Now, to work.*

Bertha leaned over and gently closed Sean's eyes. *And now you, the bright boy with the enchanting smile, dazzling eyes, and quick wit. And now you.* She couldn't hold back the tear that trickled down her sad face. She had work to do, so she wouldn't let herself give in and cry outright. Leo and Muriel Anne had no choice but to weep to let go of Sean.

As Bertha stripped the quilts and top sheet off the bed, she began planning what needed to be done. *I'll have to put them in a washbasin of cold water so the bloodstains won't set in. Then I'll need to boil and disinfect them.* She walked over to the boys' rag bag by the inside door to the barn and pulled out everything absorbent she could find. With tears standing in her eyes, she tossed the rags onto the floor by the deathbed. Shaking her head, she walked out to the well. She filled a pail with water, then grabbed an empty bucket for the dirty rags. She forced herself to return to Sean's bedside. Despite the unpleasant smells, she leaned over the bed and began sopping up the blood and ugly evacuate from Sean's bowels.

When Leo noticed Bertha working by Sean, he reluctantly joined her. They worked together in silence, mopping up the worst of the foul liquid. They filled the empty pail to overflowing with saturated rags. Muriel Anne picked it up. "We better put these on the stove to boil."

Leo nodded. He stood up and followed her outside. He hoisted the big washtub onto the stove. They both lugged over heavy buckets of well-pump water. Leo pushed plenty of chopped wood into the fire chamber to build up the heat and then filled another two buckets of water from the hot water reservoir. Leo and Muriel Anne carried in the hot water and began washing Sean. Leo couldn't bear the thought of Sean lying in that smelly filth for a moment longer than he had to. *Sean would want to be clean, even if he weren't here to know it.* Leo leaned over and gently removed Sean's BVD long johns. *Let's get ya cleaned up, Sean, my love.*

An hour later, Ralph drove Lizzie, Alma, and all the family up to the house in their big black surrey. Jeff Murdoch walked up the road with Josh and Mitch Patten, carrying shovels. Their fathers, Bill and Zachariah, followed, carrying heavy pickaxes. Alma greeted them with a sober nod. "Bill. Zach. Boys."

Bill Murdoch offered, a touch of Irish brogue from the old country still tripping off his tongue, "We thought Master Leo could use a hand, ya know, in diggin' the grave. The ground's gonna be froze solid. A hard job of work it's gonna be to get down past the first few feet, doncha know."

Alma silently nodded his agreement and thanks.

Lizzie walked up to the huddle of men. "That's right neighborly of ya, gentlemen. I thank ya all on Leo's behalf."

They heard the sound of a hammer from the other side of the new house. Somehow they all knew why. They shivered as though the devil had walked over their graves and shook their heads, sadly. Lizzie frowned. "Let me go ask poor Leo where he wants the gravesite."

Lizzie turned to the barn. Zachariah Patten told the men, "Me dear Priscilla and Bill's lovely Faith are a cookin' up a storm. They'll be here just afore sundown with a supper fer ever' one."

Lizzie timidly knocked on the door to the tack room, afraid of the quarantine and fearful of the heavy emotions she would find within. Muriel Anne answered the door. "Oh! Missus Hayes. I'm so glad you came."

"How is me son doin', Miss Muriel Anne? Can I talk to 'im, please?"

Bertha walked over and placed her hands on Muriel Anne's shoulders. She nodded a greeting to Lizzie. "We're just about finished cleaning the body, Lizzie, my friend."

"Can I come in and help?"

"I'm sorry, but I'm afraid the quarantine needs to be strictly enforced, still."

"Of course. It's just I feel so helpless standin' around while there's work to be doin'."

"Once we get everything cleaned up and disinfected, then I think the quarantine will be over."

Leo heard his mother's voice. He didn't want to leave Sean, even on his death bed, but he needed to see his mom. He walked over to the door and peered out. Leo's haggard appearance shocked Lizzie. He had aged in the few days since she had last seen him. "Leo. How're ya doin', son?"

Leo couldn't help himself. He ran up and stopped in front of her. He carefully held his arms and hands out to his sides so he wouldn't get any of the contaminated gore close to her. "Sean's dead, Mom. There wasn't nothin' we could do to save 'im. He just passed. Just like that!"

Lizzie stepped up and hugged her tall son around his thin, strong chest, patting him on the back. She laid her head on his shoulder and softly murmured in his ear, "I'm so sorry, Leo, me boy. I'm so so sorry."

Lizzie took a step back so Leo could lower his arms. "Listen, son. The menfolk've come to dig the grave fer ya. Have ya thought where ya want it to be?"

"Oh, Mom! I haven't thought about nothin' like that. I thought he was gonna get better..." Leo stopped when his voice broke.

"I'm sorry, son. I know this isn't a good time. There's never a good time fer these sorts of things, doncha know. But please think now and tell me where ya want to bury yer friend. It's yer land and yer partner, so ya need to tell us where."

Leo sniffed as he struggled to control his welling emotions. After a moment, he managed to croak out, "Well, Mom. I think Sean would like to be put to rest beneath a tree. And near to runnin' water. He spent most of his life in the desert with no shade and little water. Could we find 'im a place over by the ol' homestead garden under the branches of the big ol' cottonwood? Maybe where the little natural spring could trickle down and keep 'im clean. He always liked to be clean and... freshly... washed."

Leo couldn't talk anymore. His thoughts flashed back over the years, remembering Sean alive and whole. It shook him to talk about Sean in the past tense. He raised his hands over his eyes and massaged his forehead, trying to stifle his tears from starting again.

"Of course, Leo. That's the perfect answer. I wish I could help ya out in there, son. But, the quarantine, ya know."

"I know, Mom. Thanks, anyway."

Leo turned and walked back into the tack room, his neck and back bent low under the weight of his sorrow.

Lizzie shook her head to see her oldest son so sad. "Is there anything I can do out here to help, Bertha?"

Bertha stood up from wiping the floor. "Seeing as how we have all these men working out in the cold, perhaps you could take charge of the stove and keep a hot pot of coffee on the ready."

"Of course, I can."

The two ladies smiled sadly at each other then turned to their duties.

Lizzie limped around the garden. Her broken ankle ached in the cold. The men followed her, carrying their tools. Lizzie finally found a spot at the edge of the cottonwood tree beside the garden. She pointed at an area below the little spring of frozen puddles. "Let's put the gravesite here, if ya please, gentlemen. And don't ferget the custom of puttin' the feet facin' the risin' sun in the east."

Bill Murdoch hefted his heavy pick ax off his shoulder with both hands. "All right, me hardy boyos, let's get through this frozen ground so we can dig the grave proper, doncha know."

His pick ax struck the frozen garden soil with a dull thud, barely making a dent. Scowling, he swung again and again.

In the tack room, Leo sadly finished Sean's final sponge bath. He had refused Muriel Anne and Bertha's offers to help. He knew in his heart he needed to do these last rites himself. He bathed Sean out of honor and respect for Sean's love and generous soul.

Muriel Anne and Bertha busied themselves carrying the soiled underwear and bed linens out to the stove to boil. Bertha added plenty of shaved soap. They both carried in pails of water from the last of the stove's reservoir. They mopped the floor and then washed down the bed frame, working silently around Leo.

When Leo finished drying Sean, Bertha walked over beside the small chest of drawers. "What suit of clothes should we bury Sean in, Leo?"

Leo glanced up and nodded sadly. "Why, Missus Bertha, I can't imagine him wantin' anythin' other than his black Levi jeans and his black cowboy boots and his black vest and hat. No sirree. We'll dress Sean just like he always liked to dress. And I think we should tie on his six-shooter and huntin' knife, too, in case he needs 'em. On the other side."

Leo choked up again and had to stop talking. He squeezed out the sponge and slowly wiped the soles of Sean's feet again, reluctant to bring the sad bath to its end.

Finally, Leo stood up and walked over to their chest of drawers. He pulled out long johns, a black cotton shirt folded neatly as only Sean would do, a black bandana with white piping, long black wool stockings, and folded black Levi jeans. Muriel Anne took each item in her arms as he pulled them out. Bertha retrieved the vest, gun, and gun belt off their hooks on the wall then picked up the worn black boots beside the outside door.

Wordlessly, with tears standing in their eyes, the three gently dressed Sean in his favorite familiar clothes. When they finished, Muriel Anne pulled a comb out of her pocket and looked at Leo for permission. After he nodded, she carefully combed Sean's reddish-blond hair. Then she kissed his brow.

They heard a knock at the door. Bertha walked over to answer it.

Leo and Muriel Anne stood gazing down at Sean, memorizing how he looked at the end. Still. Pale. Free of pain after so much suffering. Handsome even without the spark of life that lit up his eyes and smile so charmingly.

Leo heard Josey outside the open door. "The coffin's ready, Missus Bertha. Shall we bring it in?"

Bertha turned and studied the death parlor, carefully double-checking that they had scrubbed or removed everything contagious from the room. She nodded. "Yes. I believe the need for quarantine is over now. Please bring it in."

Solemnly, Josiah and Abel carried the simple pine box into the crowded tackle room. Bertha directed Robert and Ralph to use two chairs to hold the coffin. Once they had it set up, Josey softly asked Leo, "Can we help lift the... uh... Sean into the casket?"

Leo positioned himself at the head of the bed and waved his brothers and friends around the body. With a silent nod up of his chin, they leaned down and lifted Sean's corpse. They moved Sean over and gently lowered him inside the raw wood box. Leo walked over to the door and grabbed Sean's black ten-gallon hat off its hook. He then placed it over Sean's forehead like when he used to nap in the sun down in Texas. Bertha folded Sean's hands over his heart. She patted them before turning away, wiping a tear from her eye.

Leo ignored the others, not unkindly, but vacantly, abstractly. He instinctively slid the sickbed chair over beside the coffin. He sat down as though Sean were still alive and might need to call on him for a sip of water. Leo reached his arm over the edge of the coffin and rested his hand on Sean's shoulder in the familiar gesture of affection that had ruled their lives for more than four years.

Bertha thanked the men for their kind services. They left without a word. Muriel Anne sat down at the table at her wit's end, not knowing what to do. She felt adrift, lost, and hopeless. She only knew she didn't want to leave Sean and Leo at this time. Bertha put on her long dust coat and whispered to Muriel Anne, "I'm going to go home and get cleaned up now. I'll be back later with Jane Eve and Joslyn. If he's up to it, I'll bring papa Goodbody. I'll see you at supper time."

"So long, Mother."

After several hours of battle with the frozen garden and the small but very tough surface roots of the sprawling cottonwood tree, the men finally had the grave dug down the customary six feet. Scotty had worried around the group of men, puzzling at their strange activities. He eventually settled down to watch, sitting off to the side. The mound of frozen clods of earth grew to nearly twice the size of the hole. The men and boys put their coats back on and then headed over to the construction camp to clean up.

Back in the quiet barn, Muriel Anne pulled her chair up beside Leo and the coffin to keep Leo company. She softly held his hand in her own, just as she had held Sean's hand in this very room while he sold her on his handfasting and baby-making scheme.

Sean and Leo's friends and family arrived a few at a time to pay their last respects to Sean. Leo and Muriel Anne stood up to receive their words of condolences, their hugs of support and sympathy, then sat back down to wait for the next visitors.

280

Bertha leaned her head in the door and invited Leo and Muriel Anne to join everybody in the new house for supper. Muriel Anne stood up. Leo shook his head no. "I'm not hungry, Missus Bertha. Thanks all the same."

A few minutes later, Lizzie hobbled into the room carrying a plate of food. She sat down in Muriel Anne's vacated chair and kept Leo company while he tried to eat. The food had no taste for Leo. It gave him no satisfaction that cold, lonely evening.

Late that night, after everyone had departed, Leo dragged their new bed over alongside the coffin. Still fully dressed, he laid down to keep Sean company through the night. For hours he stared at the unlit ceiling, wondering how he could possibly live without Sean to show him the way and share life's moments.

The following day, Monday the fourteenth of December, the sun rose bright and clear. However, it shed little warmth in the high altitude of the foothills overlooking the eastern Idaho plain. Muriel Anne brought a hot breakfast for Leo. Leo groggily splashed his face with ice-cold water, struggling to wake up.

By previous arrangement, Leo's family and the neighbors from Rose Corners congregated in the empty living room of the new house at ten o'clock. Alma, Josiah, Robert, and Ralph respectfully knocked on the tack room door. Muriel Anne invited them in with a silent sweep of her hand. Alma led the way, holding his cowboy hat politely in his hands. Josiah followed, carrying the rough pine lid for the coffin. Ralph and Robert entered with hammers and nails. They both looked at the floor to avoid seeing a dead body.

Alma squeezed Leo's shoulder. "Leonard, son, may we close the coffin now?"

Leo knew it had to happen, but he didn't want to say goodbye yet. Choked up, he merely nodded yes.

"And may we have the honor of bein' the pallbearers this mornin', son?"

Josiah and Leo's brothers began placing the lid on the coffin. "Just a minute!"

The startled workers froze.

Leo lunged over and lifted Sean's hat off his face. He leaned over and gazed long and hard at Sean's still, dearly beloved face. No dimple or smile showed in death. Then Leo leaned in and lovingly, tenderly kissed him goodbye on his cold bluish lips. Leo stood up with tears brimming in his eyes again. He solemnly settled the hat back over Sean's face.

Muriel Anne came up and linked her elbow with Leo's. Leo gazed with tenderness and longing at his tall, lean cowboy, now laid low in death. Dressed in black, Sean looked like he had the first time Leo had seen him over four years ago on his father's farm. Leo made his private farewell in the silence of his distraught mind. *Goodbye, Sean. So long, my love. I hope we meet again if there really is life after death. I love ya, Sean. Goodbye, my love.*

Leo wordlessly waved at Josiah to close the casket. Leo bowed his head into both hands when Sean disappeared from view, shuddering with grief and more silent tears.

The solemn group of friends and family buried Sean that morning in frozen ground in the hibernating garden beneath the bare branches of a cottonwood tree. Sean's burial mound rose in an enormous hill above the buried coffin. The frozen clods of dirt refused to crumble and settle in to fill the hole. The grave would stay like that until the ground thawed. Lizzie and Bertha placed small bouquets of dried flowers tied with old ribbons at the head of the grave.

The quiet families of the Hayes, Merriwells, Murdochs, Pattens, and Gilberts stood silently around the grave dressed in their Sunday-go-to-Meeting clothes. The men held their hats in their hands. The little children hugged their mother's long skirts. Hannah Gilbert began singing in a soft clear soprano, *Abide with me; 'tis eventide.*

One by one, Priscilla, Faith, and Bertha joined in. Faith added a lovely peaceful harmony to the melody. Then Myrtle, Jane Eve, and Lizzie raised their voices in the impromptu choir. By the end, everyone joined in softly singing farewell to Sean. *Behold, 'tis eventide.*

Leo had never felt as alone as he did when he climbed into bed by himself that night. For the first time in over four years, he didn't have Sean sleeping beside him during the night. He cried softly as he remembered how their legs used to wind together affectionately. They used to hold each other as Leo slept on Sean's shoulder or chest, inhaling Sean's unique scent.

Leo hadn't slept alone since the first night they made love under a full moon while riding fences on his father's farm.

Chapter 21: From the Ashes

A bitter cold front moved in the Monday night after the funeral. The wind blew right through the slat board walls of the tack room and through the army tent shared by Josiah and Abel on the construction site. Leo woke at the first hint of pre-dawn light. When he opened his eyes, he remembered Sean's death and burial.

His heart dropped into his stomach.

Oh, Sean. How could ya leave me like that? We were gonna grow old together, breedin' prime horses and prize cattle. Now what? I'm alone and cold and scared, Sean. What am I gonna do now?

Leo heard Sean's voice answer in the depths of his mind. He imagined Sean's cheerfulness and the lilt from the old country he had learned at his mother's knee. *Well, now, me boyo. Ya must be gettin' up in the mornin' and gettin' yerself cleaned up all proper like and shaved, too. Then get on out and about the business of runnin' the ranch and raisin' the new house. Ya can't just lie in bed like an English Lord, takin' yer leisure, doncha know. Up and at 'em, me boyo!*

Smiling sadly, Leo threw back the covers and climbed out of bed. The cold hit him like a fist, stinging and hard. He pulled on his jeans, boots, and Levi jacket then fed more fuel into the pot-bellied stove as fast as he could. "Brrrr."

Leo slapped his arms with his hands. He plopped on his cold hat to help him warm up. *Might as well be out of the doors fer all the good this leaky ol' barn does in the wintertime!*

The stove began cutting the cold about the time the sun rose above the mountains. Leo made his bed, wondering who had changed the sheets and made the bed after he had washed and dressed Sean. He couldn't remember seeing anyone do it.

It surprised him to hear the familiar trotting clip-clop of Muriel Anne's big white stallion come up to the barn. Scotty barked at something then took off running. Leo hadn't expected her this morning. He didn't know if he wanted her company or not.

Muriel Anne knocked briskly on the door. "Yoo-hoo! Anybody home? Are you decent in there?"

Leo stepped over, opened the door, and pulled her in brusquely. "Quick. Don't let the heat out!"

Muriel Anne slid in. She pulled off her heavy wool scarf and placed a small cloth-wrapped bundle on the table. She shook out her ponytail and then smoothed down the fly-away hair that had escaped her ribbons. She gazed at Leo, trying to intuit how he felt today. He had been so withdrawn and unresponsive the day before. She stepped up, ducked her head to the side under his cowboy hat, and gave him a big hug and a warm kiss on his cheek.

They both sat down in their coats at the little table and smiled sadly at each other. Neither knew how to pick up and start living again with casual conversations, ordinary feelings, and routine activities. Muriel Anne untied the dish towel and spread it over the table, revealing a big ham and egg sandwich. The winter air had cooled the eggs on the ride from Muriel Anne's house, but they smelled delicious, anyway. They each picked up a quarter sandwich and took a bite.

Muriel Anne brushed the crumbs off her lap. "Well, now I feel fortified enough to brave the cold and brew a pot of coffee. I'm sure Abe and Josey will need a hot drink after sleeping outdoors in that blustery wind."

She lifted her wool scarf back over her head and tied it under her chin. "Boy, is it cold out there this morning!"

"Good idea, Muriel Anne. Thanks."

Leo pulled on his lambskin coat and went out to feed and stoke the cookfire. They stood downwind from the stove, trying to absorb any warmth the breeze might blow their way while they waited for the water to boil.

Leo held his hands out to the heat. "And just what are ya doin' over here this mornin', anyway, Muriel Anne? Ya should be sleepin' in late, all snuggled up in yer warm quilts, not traipsin' around in this harsh winter morning."

Muriel Anne pushed her hands deep into her long dust coat's pockets and laughed lightly, the first laugh in many long days. "I just didn't want you to be left all alone. And besides, I missed you. And Sean." *And besides, it's time for my period, and it hasn't come. So I want you to get used to me keeping you company because we may end up getting married, you foolish boy!*

Leo chuckled, shaking his head at her crazy notions. *Girls sure do silly things. Who can figure?*

They poured tin mugs of hot coffee and wrapped their gloved hands around them to warm their fingers. Leo headed over to the construction site. When they reached the woodpile, Leo handed his coffee to Muriel Anne. He stuffed a handful of kindling in his coat pocket then picked up a load of split logs. They felt warmer as soon as they closed the door of the new Sears bungalow. The tight windows and doors sealed the house from the winter wind. The new home also had insulation in the walls and ceilings, another modern improvement most homes lacked.

Leo knelt on the unvarnished new floor and laid his first fire in the decorative iron-lined firebox of the handsome brick fireplace. It didn't have its final wood trim or mantle, but it functioned. Leo reached up into the chimney and found the damper open from yesterday's potluck supper after the funeral. He didn't remember seeing a fire. He didn't remember the supper. Leo pulled out a book of safety matches and lit a match to the kindling beneath the logs. As soon as the fire flared up, they both backed up to enjoy its warmth. Leo looked around, thinking about what they still needed to do.

Josey and Abe ambled in, carrying mugs of coffee. They both wore fingerless work gloves and big wool scarves. They smiled rather timidly. Josey raised his cup of coffee as if making a toast. 'Ya know, Mister Leo, the heating system is all installed down in the cellar there. All we gotta do is fire 'er up. Shall we give 'er a try?"

Muriel Anne's eyes lit up. "Oh, can we? Please? My toes are so cold I can't even feel them anymore. Please?"

She grabbed Leo's elbow and pulled him through the kitchen to the cellar steps by the back door.

It took a while. First, Leo and Josey had to shovel the heavy coal from the coal chute into the fire chamber. They both worked up a sweat by the time they filled the furnace for the first time.

Leo had missed seeing the coal delivery last Friday afternoon while he tended to Sean. He barely remembered when the delivery man knocked at the door with black dust on his face and clothes. "Ya have yer coal delivery. Five bucks cash in hand, now, if ya please."

They carefully read the step-by-step directions stamped in a tin sign on the side of the big barrel of the Acme furnace. Josey sent Abe out for a fistful of kindling so they could start the fire.

They finally had everything ready. Josiah pulled a wood safety match out of his vest pocket and struck it on the side of the black cast iron fire chamber. Then he reached in and lit the kindling. They watched to make sure the fire took, then closed the heavy cast iron door and lowered its latch. A few minutes later, they felt a glimmer of heat as the soft coal took fire.

Leo gazed around in wonderment at the mechanical miracle of central heating. He traced the big tin pipes growing out of the top of the furnace like thick tree branches. The pipes ran overhead along the ceiling, ending in floor grates in each room. None of them had ever seen a house with a modern central heating system before. Leo visualized the heated air rising gently through those big funnels, going upstairs to warm his new Sears Bungalow.

Every day for the week after Sean's cold, bleak funeral, Muriel Anne and Scotty showed up at the crack of dawn to spend the day with Leo. She pitched in to help paint the inside of the house. She broke in the wonderful new cast iron coal range, cooking meals for the work crew.

On Tuesday, the twenty-second of December, Muriel Anne woke up in her childhood bed, rubbing her lower tummy. *I should have had my period a week or so ago.* A wave of dizziness passed over her. Suddenly she knew she was going to throw up.

Muriel Anne flipped out of bed onto her knees and pulled out the chamber pot. She barely had the presence of mind to pull her hair back and remove the lid before she spasmed and shuddered. Her body expressed her inner turmoils and tensions by ejecting what little sour fluid her stomach held. Her breath and vomit steamed white in the cold, dry winter air as she waited for her breathing to return to normal.

She wiped her lips with the back of her left hand as she struggled to her feet. She stepped over to her bedroom's chipped washbasin and pitcher. Though cold, the water hadn't frozen. Heat from her mother's cooking and heating stoves downstairs kept the house warmer than the blustery cold weather outside. She bathed her flushed, sweaty face with a flannel washcloth. She looked up into the washstand's mirror and blinked in surprise at the bloodshot eyes staring back at her. *I look just dreadful!* She poured a glass of water to rinse the sour taste from her mouth. She spat the first two mouthfuls of cold water into the chamber pot rather than the washbasin.

The cold wood floor stung her bare feet. Muriel Anne hopped into her rabbit fur-lined bedroom slippers. Shivering from the cold and nausea, she wrapped her quilted winter bathrobe around her shoulders. She pulled her hair back off her face and tied a wool scarf over her head before she fell back on her bed, wondering what had come over her.

Muriel Anne admired the crystal fern patterns of frost glittering on the bottom half of her bedroom window. The ice sparkled in prismatic rainbow colors in the early morning sun.

Then it dawned on her. She had just experienced – yes – morning sickness. Because she was pregnant. Her face flushed as she faced the fact that she bore Sean's love child without any doubt. Her left hand flew to the side of her face in alarm while her right hand slid down to cover her womb. She gently rubbed her flat lower belly. *Now, you silly girl, you just buck up there and do as you contracted to do in your handfasting agreement.* She knew the paragraph covering this possibility by heart. She had read it in secret, huddled in her blankets late at night, every night since she had written it in her own handwriting. Her thoughts drifted back to her secret wedding day just a few weeks, a funeral, and a lifetime earlier.

Muriel Anne softly recited the paragraph from memory. "And should a baby result from our marriage, and should Sean not survive the typhoid fever, then Muriel Anne will take Sean's letter to Leo. She will sit down in private with him to explain the hand-fasting and make him understand that it be Sean's fond wish that Leo take Muriel Anne in open marriage and rear Sean's child as his own to always keep Sean's love for Leo alive in the world in the figure of this unborn child."

Muriel Anne remembered the hope that gleamed and sparkled in Sean's eyes as they worked out the wording of this possibility, the whole purpose for their secret marriage. *But I'm not married anymore. My first secret husband lies in his cold grave. I must be brave, now, and somehow seduce Leo into proposing to me. Otherwise, our plans will come to naught, and my life will be ruined. So, buck up, girl! Get your head on straight. Get your job done as you agreed with poor deceased Sean.*

Muriel Anne went through her morning toilet slowly. She considered when, where, and how she would break the news to Leo, who suspected nothing. She recalled her mother's advice on how to win a man's heart and decided to start with a delicious breakfast.

Over in the tackle room of the cold barn, Leo struggled to wake up. His eyes blinked open, then drifted closed again as his mind and heart avoided the reality of another day without Sean's cheerful company. He turned over as a gust of wind rocked the old barn. A tiny wisp of straw, shaken loose from the hayloft overhead, fluttered down to the floor. He opened his eyes and watched it drifting in front of the window. It caught a flicker of light, looking for all the world like a firefly.

It reminded him of the first time he had seen fireflies three years ago at the end of June. He and Sean had complained about the weather, hot as Hades down in Texas. They had camped beside a creek. The gently rolling hills, covered in grass and occasional stretches of sagebrush, spread out in endless loneliness all around them. The sun finally dropped below the horizon after shining nearly horizontally to the ground for two hours. The boys could see sky below their horses' legs on these Texas prairies. Sean and Leo made camp then stripped down for a bath in the creek. It had turned fully dark by the time they waded out of the stream and headed back to the beacon of their small cook fire.

Leo remembered when they stepped up onto the stony, dark river bank. He had spotted a streak of light like a shooting star only close by, low to the ground. Then another and another. Leo stopped and grabbed Sean's damp arm. "What's that? Look! Did ya see that?"

Sean chuckled. "Yep, Little Lion, those're fireflies. Haven't ya ever seen fireflies before?"

"Nope. What're fireflies?"

As Leo reclined in his cold lonely bed, he recalled that magical warm nighttime walk. They had strolled back to the campfire holding hands, surrounded by streaking, blinking, darting little lights. Leo recalled how he felt like a giant striding among the stars of the night sky.

Later, sitting by the dying embers of their campfire, a firefly landed on Leo's bare leg. He reached out and coaxed it onto his forefinger. He raised his finger close and gazed with wonder at the tiny insect. "Look, Sean. Its tail blinks on and off. How does it do it?"

"I don't know, me boyo. It's a miracle of life, that's fer sure. A marvel and a miracle."

They had curled up together on their big bedroll of quilts over the usual canvas tarp. They fell asleep watching the bright stars overhead and the blinking of fireflies all around them in the silence of the night. A distant coyote's call bid them goodnight.

Leo sighed and opened his eyes. He wished he were down in the southern warmer states with Sean rather than alone in the cold winter of Idaho in December. He began rising out of bed but became depressed at the thought of another day without Sean. He fell back, thinking his heart would break. *I miss ya, Sean. I still love ya, Sean.*

Muriel Anne had no idea of the listless depression gnawing at Leo, leaving him enervated and uninspired in his lonely bed. She prepared herself to face the day and present her proposal to Leo, ready or not.

A short while later, Muriel Anne knocked briskly on the barn's tackle room door. Despite the nervous butterflies in her stomach, she sang out in her lilting English accent, "Good morning, Leo. Are you awake, or did you freeze to death during the night? Gooood mooorniiiing!"

Leo, barely dressed, not ready to face the day, opened the door and bowed her in. "Quick! Don't let the cold air in!"

Muriel Anne carried a pack of food tied up in one of her mother's clean dish towels. While Leo finished bundling up in layers of winter gear, she lifted her bundle to catch his attention. "I've got all the fixings for French toast and bacon in here. Let's get over to the warm house, and I'll fry it up all hot and smothered in butter. I even have a tin can of maple syrup from Vermont!"

"Oh. Good. I'm hungry enough to eat a horse. Must be from sleepin' in this ice-cold barn. Boy, I sure wish Sean and me were down... in..." Leo couldn't finish voicing his wish. He shrugged then pulled his hat down tight over his messy hair. "Let's run over to the new house, then. I've gotta stoke the furnace to start the day."

Muriel Anne had coffee ready when the four workmen came in the back door, noisily stomping their feet, blowing on their hands for warmth. Josey opened his neck scarf. "Hells bells! It must be close to zero degrees out there this mornin'. I woke up with icicles hangin' off me mustache from snorin'. Never knew sleepin' in a tent could be so gol danged cold!"

Muriel Anne forced herself to smile cheerfully despite her nervousness. "Well, here. Take a cup of coffee. It'll warm your hands as it starts to warm you up from the inside out."

Muriel Anne poured tin cups of coffee and handed them out.

Abe shifted the cup from one hand to the other. "Dang it all! How is it that the tin cup is hotter than the coffee is what I want to know!"

Chuckling, the men blew on their coffees to cool them enough to drink. Ralph glanced around the kitchen for his older brother. "Where's Leo, Muriel Anne?"

Then they heard the bang of a shovel hitting the edge of the furnace door below them. "He's down in the cellar building up the fire for the day. At least you boys will be warm as you finish the trims and painting."

"Yep. There's at least that. And we're almost done, by golly. I was so cold last night I had to get up and put on my boots and overcoat. After I crawled back under the quilts, I still lay there shiverin'. I sure don't know why we can't move our cots here into the house where it's at least above freezin'!"

Muriel Anne flipped the egg-soaked bread over to brown the other side in the cast iron skillet. "Why, I think that's a grand idea. Why should you poor boys suffer in the weather when you've built such a nice warm house? Help me talk to Leo, won't you? There's no reason in the world why he should still be camping out in that cold barn when he's got a fine new bedroom with central heating sitting here empty and unused."

She dished up the French toast and strips of bacon on enameled tin plates and passed them around. "Here, now, let me top off your breakfast with a little warm maple syrup."

Muriel Anne poured a generous splash of thick golden brown syrup over their steaming French toast. "I put a dash of cinnamon and nutmeg in the eggs, just like Mother does. It's delicious with the maple syrup."

Bob took a big bite of French toast. "Um! Muriel Anne, I could have this fer breakfast pert near every day and be plumb happy for it!"

Bob sat down at the little table and chairs they had brought over from the tackle room.

Leo clumped up the interior wood steps and went directly to the sink. He turned on the hot water faucet to wash off the clinging coal dust. "I don't think I'll ever get used to havin' hot water so easy."

Leo shook his head in pleased wonderment. His stomach growled when he smelled frying egg batter. He quickly dried his hands and grabbed a plate to join his friends and family in the warm kitchen.

When they finished eating, they sat around the small table, sipping the last of their coffee. Muriel Anne jumped up and began clearing the plates. "I say, Leo. You have a nice warm house here, all snug and tight. Maybe it's about time you moved in here and left that drafty old barn behind. You've got a beautiful empty bedroom just waiting for you."

Leo brightened up at the idea of a warm bedroom. But then he remembered his dream of moving into their first real home together with Sean. That dream would never happen now. His easy smile wilted to a sad frown. He shook his head. "Nope. Muriel Anne, I'm just not ready. Not yet, anyway."

Muriel Anne stepped over and laid her hand on his shoulder. "Well, now. Maybe it *is* time for you to move on with your life."

Leo pulled away from her hand and stood up. "Not yet. I'm just not ready. Not yet."

Josey tried helping Muriel Anne's cause. "We could all pitch in and get ya moved into this here nice new warm house in just a few minutes, Leo, me boy."

Leo thrust his plate and fork into the sink with a clatter. "Thanks, but I'm just not ready yet."

Leo stood staring out the window over the sink with a sad frown. "I'm just not ready yet."

Josey knew when not to push. He turned and clapped Abel on the back. "Let's get to work, Abe, or we'll never make it home fer Christmas!"

With a clatter of chairs, the workmen left the kitchen to begin their day's scheduled work.

Muriel Anne picked up the coffee pot and went over to the table. "Leo, my friend. I say. Come sit with me a spell, won't you? Here, have a little more coffee and relax a minute."

She topped off his empty cup on the table and pulled out a chair for him. He sat down with a shrug and wrapped both hands around the tin cup, enjoying the warmth.

Muriel Anne closed the freshly varnished door to the dining room to block out the noise of the work. "There. That's better."

Rather than start washing the dishes, she patted her skirt pocket beneath her apron. She needed to reassure herself she had Sean's letter. Satisfied, she poured herself a cup of coffee and sat down beside Leo. She did her best to exude calm and warmth despite her inner turmoils and nervousness. She placed her hand over Leo's. "Sean really truly loved you, Leo. You know that, don't you?"

Leo looked over at her, not quite sure what to say. He looked up and saw kindness in her eyes. "Yep. I know." He paused. "I'm just surprised that y'all knew."

Muriel Anne squeezed his hand gently then let go. She picked up her coffee cup in both hands and leaned back in her chair. "Oh, yes, Leo. Sean and I had many a long conversation during those long bleak days when I nursed him. He shared many things with me. He told me of his dreams of building a life with you, his trusted and beloved partner. He shared his fears he might not survive the typhoid."

Muriel Anne glanced away from Leo. Her eyes took on a distant, far-away look. "Sometimes, I think maybe he had a premonition. The way he talked and planned."

Leo shook his head, puzzled.

"Leo, dear. I hope you know that I loved Sean, too. And that I love you, too. Before Sean took ill, I wanted nothing more than to have you as dear friends and neighbors for many years to come. I really took a liking to both of you. I admired each of you a lot."

Not knowing how to respond, Leo only nodded. He lifted up his cup of coffee, blew on it, then took a sip.

Muriel Anne looked intently at Leo, trying to catch his eyes. Tilting her head, she leaned in. "Leo, Sean asked a big favor of me. A favor he hoped would please you. A favor he hoped would perpetuate his love for you, even should he not be here."

Leo frowned. Puzzled, he shook his head.

Muriel Anne reached for his hand again. She gently pried his fingers from around the coffee cup and held his hand tenderly in hers. "Leo, my friend. Sean proposed I join him in marriage through a handfasting with a contract in the old ways to assure any eventuality that might happen."

"What!?"

Leo pulled his hand away and pushed his chair back.

"Listen, Leo. Sean did it so that we could try and make a love child, a baby of his for you to raise and always remember the special love he had for you."

Leo jerked to his feet in surprise. "What!?"

"Please be still a minute. Let me tell you all about it. Please sit down, Leo. It was a beautiful gift, a gift of love for you and only for you. Sean did it right after he wrote his will. He began feeling more poorly every hour, and he *so* didn't want to leave you. He especially didn't want to leave you alone. So he proposed a plan. And even though it scandalized me, I eventually went along with his wishes."

Speaking quickly but softly, Muriel Anne related the whole story. She explained about a month and a day, about the contract, about tying the knot, about their secret love-making. She fearfully watched Leo's face as she spoke, praying nobody would interrupt them. She felt concerned as she watched emotions race across Leo's clear pale complexion as she told the story. Surprise. Dismay. Puzzlement. Shock. Bewilderment.

"He just didn't want you to be alone if he didn't make it. He didn't want to leave you. He wanted you to know that he wasn't abandoning you like he had been abandoned. He said you would know what that meant. He said it was too personal to share with me, even though I was his wife. This baby was his final love offering, Leo. Can you understand that? His final ongoing expression of his undying love for you."

Leo sat dumbfounded with his mouth hanging open, shaking his head back and forth in denial, unable to take it in.

Muriel Anne gently took his hand again, hoping to communicate support and affection. Leo stopped shaking his head. He focused his eyes on their hands entwined on the tabletop. "Sean wanted me to marry ya? Is that what yer tryin' to tell me, Muriel Anne? No! I don't believe it. He couldn't. He wouldn't. He knew that's not in my nature nor my desires. He knew me better than that."

The sun peeked out from behind a cloud, its hard bright light highlighting the lines of tension in both their faces. Leo shook his head in denial. Muriel Anne nodded her head yes. Disappointed, she realized she lacked the charms and ability to ensnare Leo's affections on her own, despite her attraction to him. She reached into her deep skirt pocket with a sigh and withdrew Sean's secret letter. She handed it to him without a word. The sealed envelope had no writing on it.

His eyes stricken with grief and dismay, Leo tore the side off the envelope and tipped out the letter. As he unfolded it, he saw at a glance that Sean hadn't written it. But then Leo saw the signature. He recognized Sean's signature at the bottom of the page. *I love you, even from beyond the grave, Sean Michael McKay.*

Leo felt lost again, alone and confused, like a young kid instead of a grown-up eighteen-year-old man. His mind and emotions couldn't process Muriel's story. His lips began trembling. Through tear blurred eyes, he read Sean's simple letter. *If Muriel Anne has given you this letter, then it means that I did not survive the typhoid fever. It also means she is carrying my child, the child we worked hard and lovingly to create for you so you can have a part of me to take with you into your future. Please accept my gift and marry Muriel Anne. Please raise my child as your own so that he or she can have an honorable name and a loving home. We did this for you out of our mutual love and respect for each other but mostly for you.* Then, in Sean's slanted, shaky handwriting, Leo read the closure. *I love you, even from beyond the grave, Sean Michael McKay.*

Leo re-folded the letter carefully with tears streaming down both cheeks. He bowed his head over his arms and sobbed.

Muriel Anne began crying with him. She wept from sorrow and nerves. Her heart went out to Leo as he worked through his loss and grief all over again.

Bob needed a drink of water. He pushed open the kitchen door. But when he saw Leo and Muriel Anne crying, he silently backed up and closed the door. He knew why they were crying.

When Leo's grief finally relinquished its hold over him, he took several deep breaths. He sat up, wiped his eyes and cheeks with the palms of his hands, then rubbed them on his blue jeans. Finally, he looked at Muriel Anne. She daintily dabbed her tears away, using her long blousy sleeves as handkerchiefs. She met his look with a timid quivering smile. "Muriel Anne, is it true? Is it true what he said in the letter? Are ya carryin' Sean's seed... his... his baby?"

Muriel Anne didn't trust her voice, so she merely nodded yes.

Leo hesitated. He couldn't believe Sean had made love with a girl, any girl. He suddenly wondered if Muriel Anne might be trying to foster off someone else's child as Sean's. "How do I know…" Leo hesitated when he remembered Sean's letter. "Nope. I guess I do know. Well. That's that, then."

Leo leapt to his feet and held both hands up to his head.

Startled, Muriel Anne also stood up.

Leo squeezed his head between his hands like a vise trying to contain his thoughts. He couldn't focus. His thoughts darted all over the place like birds let loose from a cage. He struggled to make sense of Sean's letter. "Well. That's that, then."

Muriel Anne sat back down, clutching her folded hands between her breasts. She waited. *It took you time to agree to Sean's wild proposal. Be patient. You can trust Leo to do the right thing. Just give him time. Sean promised me Leo would accept his letter. And I believe him.*

Leo walked over to the sink. He looked back out the window for the second time that morning. His thoughts roiled. Long purple shadows from bare overhead tree limbs made a watercolor sketch over the frozen ground around the construction site. It took several minutes of hard thinking before Leo gradually accepted what Sean had asked of him. He finally grasped what Sean wanted if this eventuality should come to pass. And it had.

By force of will, Leo shunted aside his fears and doubts. He squared back his shoulders and took a deep breath. Leo strode over and knelt on one knee in front of Muriel Anne, just like in the romance novels he had read with Sean.

Leo gazed up at Muriel Anne's tear-streaked face. "Muriel Anne Merriwell, will ya please marry me and be my wife?"

Nearly faint with relief and giddy with joy, Muriel Anne leaned over and wrapped her arms around Leo's neck. She gave him a kiss, then whispered in his ear, "Yes, Leonard Hayes. I will marry you."

Leo and Muriel Anne stood up and hugged, tentatively but affectionately, as they shared the spirit of Sean's plan between them. Leo felt as if Sean were there, sharing the moment with them.

Both Leo's and Muriel Anne's lives changed irrevocably in that brief embrace.

After a few moments, Leo released Muriel Anne from their first real hug. Still a bit bewildered, he chuckled helplessly. "What in tarnation are we supposed to do now, do ya suppose?"

Muriel Anne twittered a little laugh of relief. Her hand covered her mouth. "Well, I suppose we should tell Mother of our engagement. She can advise us on how to make the announcements and plans. She's good at organizing things like that. You'll see."

Muriel Anne followed Leo into the living room. Leo picked up Muriel Anne's coat off the trestle workbench where she had tossed it just an hour earlier. "What are you doing, Leo?"

Leo held her coat for her. "If yer already expectin', we have no time to waste. So, let's get the ball rollin'."

They both laughed, giddy from the speed of change in their lives.

On the brisk cold walk to Bertha's house, Muriel Anne let herself exult over how well her plans had worked out. *Things are going really, really well for you, just as you planned with Sean. If you're really, really careful, you'll get it all. You'll marry a handsome husband with good prospects. You'll get your family land back. You'll bear a beautiful child. Everything! You'll get it all. But, be careful, girl. Don't let on to anyone that you planned this. Mother can't ever know about Sean's handfasting. Oh! You're going to get it all! You'll be set for life. You won't have to worry any longer about a husband, or where to live, or where your money will come from. All that work and all those nervous secrets are finally paying off.*

Chapter 22: Wedding Plans

Leo woke up in the dark pre-dawn of the morning after asking for Muriel Anne's hand in marriage. He stretched his hands above his head, then quickly shoved them back under the quilts. The wood in the little potbelly stove had burned down, leaving the room freezing cold. His sheered lambskin overcoat lay heavy but warm over his feet. He had even worn two pairs of thick wool stockings to bed. *Oh, Sean, I still miss ya so, so much. Why didn't we stay down south together where it's warm?*

Overcome with lethargy and depression, Leo lay in bed thinking back on all the craziness the day before.

Bertha had been thrilled to death at the "children's" announcement of their engagement. She had burst into a dervish swirl of activity and organization. "Now, children, what date have you set for the ceremony?"

Leo and Muriel Anne stopped and looked blankly at each other. They hadn't discussed a date. With Bertha watching, they could hardly discuss the urgency of getting married before the pregnancy began to show.

Leo raised his forefinger dramatically. Muriel Anne and Bertha gave him their immediate attention. "I know. Let's get hitched on New Year's Day and start the new year off right, doncha know. Whaddaya say, Muriel Anne?"

Muriel Anne squealed in relief and excitement. "Oh, I think that would be just perfect!" Her smile wilted. "Oh! Unless. Mother, would that be too soon after Sean's funeral to be seemly?"

"Oh, pshaw, daughter. It's not as though you were married to Sean and needed to wait a respectable time before remarrying. I think the first day of the New Year is perfect. Most propitious. It's just that it doesn't leave me any time to make all the preparations."

Muriel Anne and Leo looked at each other guiltily. Blushing, Muriel Anne turned away so her mother wouldn't see her rosy cheeks. *Oh, Mother, if only you knew. You would just kill me. I know it. My first husband dead and buried only eight days, and now I'm arranging to be remarried in only another ten days. Oh, Mother, please forgive me. Sean, I'm trying.* Muriel Anne took a deep breath. *Just take it easy, girl. Don't reveal anything, now or ever. Be careful. Be very, very careful, and everything will be yours. A good life. Everything.*

Bertha interrupted the sudden silence. "I say, but we are going to have to write *everyone*, just everyone. And should we… now let me think. Should we invite that lovely new Reverend Loughton to officiate? He's so young and handsome. No, no. We should invite Bishop Lighthall to come and preside over the wedding. Oh, but he would have to travel all the way down from Boise. Oh, but we don't have enough time for him to get my letter, write back his acceptance, and travel in time for a wedding on the first. January first is just a week from Saturday, even if he is free. Oh, my! So much to do. No time to do it. So much to do!"

They spent the rest of the day happily, frantically, endlessly busy making plans.

Leo lay in bed, relishing the warmth of his blankets, musing on all of yesterday's developments. Bertha had dashed into her bedroom and retrieved her wedding gown from her cedar hope chest, where she had stored it for over two decades. When she carefully unwrapped the tissue paper, dried rose petals fell on the table. Bertha had called out to Jane Eve to run and fetch Faith Murdoch. "She's so handy with the needle, Muriel Anne. We have to get started altering the gown for the wedding immediately!"

Her mind spinning, Bertha sat down at her writing desk. She began jotting down a list of people to invite, crossing out names as fast as she wrote them. "I'm afraid we must keep the wedding party small. We will have to arrange accommodations and meals for anyone traveling any distance. And since it will be the holidays, all the children and grandchildren will be back at Rose Corners. The homes of the Murdochs, Pattens, and Gilberts will already be full. Oh, so many details! So much to think about! It's just too, too thrilling!"

Finally, Leo couldn't put it off any longer. He hopped out of bed and yanked on his overcoat over his long johns. He rushed across the icy floor and shoved wood into the stove, bouncing from foot to foot to keep them from pressing on the icy floor. As soon as he closed the stove's door, he raced to pull on his pants, boots, and hat. He removed the overcoat and pulled on a long-sleeved, plaid wool shirt. He quickly buttoned up his rawhide leather vest over it. *I know, Sean. I know. I haven't shaved fer two days. But, it's yer fault fer bringin' me to this freezin' cold land. I can't help it if it's too dang cold fer washin' up in the mornin'.* Leo felt guilty. He knew Sean would have heated water for a shave despite the cold.

Leo stood next to the potbellied stove, shivering, soaking up its warmth. He gazed around at the little tackle room in the dim light of a gray winter's dawn. *Guess I should move into the new house. It's only logical, after all. But, it just doesn't matter to me if I can't share it with ya, Sean. And that's a fact.*

That Wednesday developed into another day of major changes in Leo's life. Josey and Abe began gathering their tools and packing the carpentry wagon for the trip home. They packed up their camp, leaving only the cots and tent for their last night. They wanted to take off the next morning, Christmas Eve, as early as possible.

Ralph and Bob moved their folding travel cots out of Josiah's tent into the tackle room. They placed the cots close to the pot-belly stove. They hung their simple change of clothes on nails in the wall. Ralph & Bob both liked it a lot, better than their open porch at home. Their saddles and saddle blankets made a sofa for them beneath the window. They looked forward to a night with heat. They laid in a big store of chopped wood for the stove.

Over breakfast, Leo hesitantly proposed taking up residence in the empty house. Muriel Anne enthusiastically took charge. She organized her mother and little sisters to help with a thorough sweep-up, mop-up, and dust-up. She then ordered Ralph and Bob to fetch all of Leo's furniture and personal articles from the tackle room so she could arrange them in the new house.

All the while, Muriel Anne's mind whirled faster than a race of horses. She mentally listed all the things the house would need to become her new home after her marriage. *A hall tree for hats and umbrellas by the front door. A parlor set of sofa and chairs, tables and lamps. Curtains – well, just everywhere. Rugs for the floors, again, everywhere. Flowers for the window sills. A real dining table. Not that little old pine thing. Something nice. Mahogany with varnish and brass trims on lion claw feet.* Her list went on and on until she finally despaired. She began worrying about how much money Leo had and how much he would let her spend fixing up the house. She knew he had a frugal turn of mind. But, most importantly, they simply had to have some proper English wallpapers. "These plain white walls just simply will not do!"

Bertha suggested that Muriel Anne bring some of her extra clothes hangers for the new closets. While at her mother's home, Muriel Anne grabbed a small dried flower arrangement, hoping to bring some cheer into the empty new house.

By the end of the day, they had moved in all of Leo's portable belongings. Muriel Anne despaired at how the house still looked unoccupied and inhospitable.

Leo found it all quite grand. He knew Sean would have loved it. The new Sears bungalow had turned out just exactly as they had dreamed. Even though happy with the results, Leo felt lonely as he walked through his new home without Sean to share their dream come true.

At the end of the exhausting day, Muriel Anne walked through the clean, sparse house. Scotty stayed close at her side. She began having doubts about moving out of her mother's comfortably appointed home into this empty unwelcoming house. The new house smelled strongly of plaster, varnish, and paint. The new house lacked all the creature comforts, except for the central heating system and modern plumbing.

Bertha took her cleaning supplies into the kitchen and stored them away for Leo and Muriel Anne. As she walked through the empty home, she envisioned it filled to overflowing with grandchildren and laughter. She couldn't have been more pleased.

Leo crawled into bed by himself. The quiet kept him awake. His homesickness for Sean had him tossing and turning, unable to find a position that would let him sleep. Christmas Eve dawned freezing cold but still no snow. Leo reluctantly forced himself to get up and wash his face in the new water closet. He pulled his fingers through his unruly hair, trying to make himself presentable. He stood looking at the big white iron bathtub. He couldn't bring himself to try it out, not just yet. He had daydreamed about their first time together in the tub for so long. But without Sean, he didn't feel right using it.

The sounds of a horse-drawn wagon stopping at his front door roused him from his melancholy thoughts. He pulled on his sheepskin overcoat, grabbed his hat, and stepped out on the porch to say his farewells.

Josiah stepped down from the wagon seat and walked up the steps to the porch with a sad smile on his face. "Good morning, Leo. I hope we didn't wake ya up too early, but we have a long ride ahead of us."

"Nope, Josey. I was up already. Ya all packed up?"

"Well, I surely do hope so. If we left anythin' behind, please save it fer us."

Leo chuckled. He found it hard to imagine how someone with Josiah's fanaticism for detail might actually forget a tool. "Of course, I will."

His chuckle faded to a frown. A crease appeared between his eyebrows. He held out his hand to Josey. "Mister Cummings, sir, if my wonderful Sean were here, he would join me in tellin' ya what a great job ya did and how much we appreciate it."

Josey pulled off his worn right glove. They shook hands long and hard. "Thanks, Josey. Thanks a lot."

"Yer very welcome, Mister Hayes. It's been our pleasure to help raise this nice new house fer ya."

Leo handed Josiah the check he had written out earlier that morning. "Oh, here's the balance of yer contract, Josey."

Josey read it over to be sure it was all correct. "Thanks, Leo, me friend."

Leo called out louder to Abel, sitting shotgun on the wagon seat with a blanket wrapped over his shoulders. "And thanks to y'all, too, Abe. Take care of yerself, now."

"Bye."

"Bye."

The carpenters drove off. Steam flared from their horses' nostrils as they pulled the heavily laden carpenter's wagon over bumpy frozen ground. As they turned at the intersection, they both leaned over the sides of the wagon and gave a final wave. Leo sadly waved back from his new porch, where he stood by himself in the cold, dim pre-dawn light.

The day after Christmas, he woke up alone. He didn't feel like getting up. For one thing, he had a splitting headache from drinking too much wine at Bertha's big Christmas supper the night before. He remembered passing the day singing Christmas carols, listening to an abundance of twittering female laughter, and over-eating. He had stuffed himself on roasted goose, baked sweet potatoes, puddings, and pies. Everyone took turns toasting his and Muriel Anne's upcoming nuptials, just one week away. Leo rarely drank and then only a little. He certainly wasn't used to having a hangover. He sat up, his head spinning, and fell back down. He moaned out loud and pulled the blankets back up over his head.

Muriel Anne arrived before Leo had struggled into the bathroom to wash his face. She knocked briskly on the front door and bustled in. "Yoohoo! I'm here, Leo! I'm going to put on some coffee while you get dressed. I say, if you are feeling anything like I felt this morning, you are going to need lots and lots of coffee this morning."

She carefully filled the new stovetop percolator Bertha had given Leo for Christmas. "It's both a Christmas gift, my dear boy, and an early wedding gift. No more boiling coffee like a cowboy out on the plains. This is the civilized way to brew coffee."

Leo answered Muriel Anne with a groan and a moan. He pushed himself up and pulled on his pants before staggering clumsily into the bathroom.

Three cups of coffee later, he answered a knock on the door. "Good morning, mother Bertha. Please come in."

Bertha walked right in and took charge, happily organizing every detail for the rapidly approaching wedding. First, she requested that Leo and Muriel Anne take a spare bed and mattress from her attic and set it up in Leo's second bedroom. "It's for the lovely new Reverend Loughton. There's just no other place to put him in all of Rose Corners. So much to do! So much to do!"

While up in her mother's cramped attic, Muriel Anne did a little raiding. She looked over everything in storage up there with a proprietary eye, looking for things she could use to make her new and future home more attractive and livable. She started by sending Leo down with a plain wood headboard. She found a small chest of drawers to put beside the guest bed. Then she absconded with two old overstuffed chairs for the living room.

"Leo, dear, when should we start planning how to finish the house and make it our home?"

"Huh?"

Leo stopped at the landing and rested the heavy headboard on the floor, careful not to nick Bertha's wallpaper or neatly painted trims. "What did ya say, Muriel Anne?"

She stepped over to the door and glared down at Leo with her hands on her hips. "I was just wondering when you might want to begin thinking about finishing up the house."

"Why, Muriel Anne, we already finished the house. What on earth are ya talkin' about?"

"Oh, you know. Things like wallpapers and furniture and rugs. Those sort of things."

"Well, I don't know, Muriel Anne. Doesn't that cost lots and lots of money? I never lived in a house with wallpapers and all that sorta stuff. I'm just a cowboy, Muriel Anne. I don't need none of that fancy stuff."

Leo picked up the headboard, thinking they had finished the conversation. Little did he know that Muriel Anne hadn't even begun.

He made it nearly to the first floor when Muriel Anne caught up with him. She carried a pile of old bed linens and a ceramic flower pot for one of the window sills. "Oh, but wouldn't it be nice to have a lovely parlor set in the living room so we could relax in the evening and enjoy the fire? And we simply must have a proper dining table and dining chairs so we can entertain."

"Entertain? Fer land sakes, Muriel Anne! What are ya carryin' on about? I'm a horse and cattle breeder, not a bloomin'

305

politician or preacher. Who're we gonna be entertainin', yer Mom?"

Leo set down the heavy headboard at the bottom of the stairs, thinking he could sure use Sean's help. "I've gotta get the stud ranch producin' a steady income. I don't have time nor money to spend on frippery. And I have to watch the money, Muriel Anne. Like Sean always said. Once ya spend it, ya don't have it."

Muriel Anne gazed around at her mother's two decades of tasteful furnishings and accessories. She dreamed of decorating her new home but decided she would have to make do in the meantime.

Bertha talked to her friends at the other three corners of the intersection, Hannah, Faith, and Priscilla. They each invited Muriel Anne to raid their attics and cellars, preparing for the wedding. Piece by piece, she added a small area rug and faded curtains to the bedroom. Faith gave her a wedding gift of a plant stand with a lush Boston Fern for the dining room. Muriel Anne found a couple more upholstered chairs for the living room and a smoke-darkened oil painting for over the fireplace. She found all sorts of cooking utensils and tools for her new kitchen. So what if they were a bit dinged or bent? They would do until she could afford to buy new modern pieces.

Every day Muriel Anne took pains to spend time with Leo. She instinctively sensed his depression. She went out of her way to be bright and cheerful, sometimes to the point of grating on his nerves. She did everything she could think of to get him to like her, unknowingly becoming quite the seductress. She constantly stood close to him, caressing his arm or back or neck, holding his hand, and leaning up to kiss him on the cheek. She gave him long warm hugs of greeting and farewell.

Muriel Anne found Leo very handsome. She looked forward to exploring those sensual delights Sean had described during her first wedding. She positively glowed every time she saw her tall, strong cowboy. She couldn't wait to become his wife and have her family property back to secure her future.

Leo tried to reciprocate and respond, though his heart wasn't in it. He never pulled away, but then he never reached out for her,

306

either. He missed Sean's warm intimacy with his appealing masculine scent of clean sweat with a hint of wood smoke. Leo missed the freshness of Sean's baking soda toothpaste and lye soap. He found Muriel Anne's perfumes, oils, and toilet waters too cloying and floral. Whenever Muriel Anne leaned in to kiss him, her breath always smelled a bit of milk. When it smelled of buttermilk or yogurt, he found it off-putting. It made him irritable, but he didn't know what he could do about it.

The days before the wedding sped by in a blur of chores, supper parties at the neighbors, and endlessly decorating the house. Muriel Anne's scavenger hunts dragged more and more things into their formerly empty house.

Naturally, Muriel Anne had to try out each item in every possible location at least twice before making up her mind. She wore Leo out.

Chapter 23: Bachelor Party

Leo roused himself before dawn on Wednesday morning, the thirtieth of December, and jogged over to Bertha's barn through the freezing wintry air. Bertha had offered her single horse carriage to take to the train station. He needed to pick up the popular new Anglican priest from Pocatello's Trinity Episcopal Church. The Reverend had accepted Bertha's telegraphed invitation to officiate at their wedding. Leo pulled Bertha's heavy bearskin lap blanket over his legs. With a snap of the reins, he took off for the Blackfoot train station, nearly two hours away. The cold ate through his gloves. He traded off driving with one hand and holding the other beneath the lap blanket to warm it up.

Leo reined in at the Union Pacific Depot in Blackfoot around half-past eight just as the sun rose over the hazy purple mountains. He tied Bertha's horse to an iron ring on one of the hitching posts. He marched past several other carriages, horses, and two new horseless carriages as he rushed into the waiting room.

The handsome eighteen-year-old building still looked new. Square cut sandstone blocks held up a broad, overhanging roof. A passenger's lounge and ticket area occupied a third of the generous station. The railroad used two-thirds of the building for freight, offices, and crew quarters.

Leo rushed up to the waiting room's large potbellied stove to warm up from the drive. He stomped his feet a couple of times to start his blood moving. He smiled apologetically at the others waiting with him. Everyone huddled up to the stove, holding out their hands to capture the warmth. A big clock with Roman numerals above the ticket window showed 8:41. The train wasn't due in until 9:10. After he warmed up, Leo walked over to the little food and magazine counter along the far wall. He ended up purchasing a mug of hot chocolate and a Danish roll on waxed paper for a late breakfast.

Leo heard the rumbling of the massive steam locomotive as it slowly and majestically pulled into the station. He joined the small group of people heading out to meet the train. They all checked their buttons and scarves then pulled their gloves back on before pushing through the heavy double doors onto the frozen platform.

Leo recognized the priest by his white Roman collar, black overcoat, and new black bowler hat. He strode up and held out his hand. "Might ya be the Reverend Loughton of Pocatello?"

The young priest smiled then answered in a cultured, educated British accent, "I am he, sir. And might you be Mister Leonard Hayes, the lucky husband-to-be?"

Leo winced as he reached out to take one of the priest's big leather travel bags. *Oh, y'all will get along just fine with Bertha and Muriel Anne with yer fine speech and hoity-toity high-falutin' ways. What a dandy, all spiffed up just to travel on the train. And in this weather! Bet he's a real soft poof, just like those city folk Sean and me met back in Salt Lake City. Look at 'im, his nose up in the air, lookin' down on us who don't have much education and have to work with our hands fer a livin'!*

The handsome young priest touched the brim of his hat with a nod. "I'll follow you, Mister Hayes. Lead on, if you please."

Reverend Laughton studied Leo's robust figure as they walked to the carriage. *At last, a real cowboy, just like in the books. Just like Bishop Lighthall said I would meet if I accepted a call to serve in Idaho. Oh, yes. I'll let you lead me anywhere you want, Cowboy Hayes.* The Englishman's eyes grew large with delight. He suddenly found himself full of energy, looking forward to the long cold ride to the distant farmstead with this tall young cowboy.

Leo secured the luggage in the buggy's boot. The city slicker stood watching Leo, clutching his long black coat closed at the neck against the cold breeze. Leo pointed at the buggy's seat. "Well, climb aboard, Reverend, sir. The sooner we get started, the sooner we'll get out of this here cold spell."

Leo checked the horse's lead lines and harness cinches then climbed up to sit next to the priest. He saw the Englishman sitting with his gloved hands between his knees and his shoulders hunched so his upturned coat collar could warm his ears. "Here,

Reverend Loughton, sir. Ya might find a little warmth from this here bearskin lap blanket. It is a might chill out this mornin'!"

Leo dragged the heavy brown fur over both their laps. He then pulled on the reins for the horse to back them up into the street. "Giddup, Brownie. Let's head fer home."

Leo bounced the reins on the horse's back. They took off at a steady gallop. A few minutes later, as they bounced along over Blackfoot's frozen roads, Reverend Loughton shivered. "A might chill, you say, my good man? That's an understatement if ever I heard one. I say, but it never gets this cold in merry old England, let me tell you! Mind, it gets cold and damp in the winter, but never so cold it sucks the warmth from your very blood like this! Brrrr!"

"Well, Reverend Laughton, sir, just sit yerself back and relax. I'll get ya to Missus Merriwell's warm hospitality just as soon as young Brownie can take us."

Leo clucked at the horse and shook the reins. They accelerated to a faster trot. He stole a quick look at the priest. *Good looking man. Nice strong chin. Maybe just a little older than Sean was when he...*

"Mister Hayes, a title becomes a heavy thing to bear so early in the morning, especially when heard too often. My name, if you please, is Wenford Loughton. Wen to my friends. And no jokes, please. I know Wen sounds like when. Believe me. I've heard all the jokes about my name over the years at boarding school."

The Reverend chuckled as a shiver went through him. "I say, Mister Hayes. If it's not too forward and un-British, couldn't we be friends and drop all the reverends and the sirs?"

"I always prefer to be friends with a man. And I'll be pleased to call ya Wen but only if ya call me Leo."

"Very good, Leo. My pleasure. I say, is it always this bloody cold in Blackfoot?"

"Nope. Summers get right hot. It's the dry desert and the high altitude combined, I suspect. We have all four seasons at their strongest, but spring and fall get short-changed. The summer heat and winter cold get more than their fair share of time, doncha know."

310

After a few minutes of quiet, they left the small-town streets and entered the country road to Upper Presto. "Leo, if I'm not being too forward, it seems that I hear a bit of an Irish brogue in your speech. Do you hail from Ireland?"

"Me? No. Though I think my grandparents were Irish before they immigrated in the mid-eighteen hundreds. But, ya see, my partner and sidekick fer the past four or five years was a right character. He spoke just like a leprechaun, to be sure. And he was as charmin' and witty and lively as one, too."

Really? A charming sidekick for the past five years? "Well, I guess you just picked up some of his speech by osmosis, then."

"By... what-osis?"

"Just from rubbing together for so long. I guess his accent just rubbed off on you, you know." *And I wouldn't mind rubbing off on you for four or five years, myself.* Wenford gazed over at Leo's handsome youthful profile, admiring the dashing young man with his worn cowboy hat that curled down in front and back but curled up at the sides. Leo missed the careful examination as he kept his eyes on the road ahead. "I look forward to meeting your charming leprechaun partner, Leo. Will he be at the wedding?"

"Nope."

"Oh, no? I'm sorry. I thought if he were such a good friend for so long, he might be your best man or something."

"He can't, Wen." Leo peeked over at the priest shivering next to him, his clothes much too thin to wear out in this weather. "He died of the typhoid fever just two weeks ago Sunday."

He hadn't been able to mention Sean before this without a catch in his voice, although he couldn't keep his tragic loss and sorrow out of his tone of voice. "Yep. And I miss 'im somethin' terrible. A happy and good part of my life died with 'im, doncha know. And I think of his joyful ways pert near every hour of every day. Yep. My Sean took real sick and didn't survive it, leavin' me all alone."

"But. I'm sorry. Don't you love Miss Muriel Anne? You are not quite *all* alone, it would seem to me."

Wenford liked hearing that Leo had a close cowboy friend. It fit in with his idyllic daydream about cowpunchers, loyal to each other through thick and thin, traveling together from one rowdy adventure to another.

"Well, sir. Wen, rather. There's all kinds of love in this here world. All kinds. And there's all kinds of loneliness, too."

"Hm. Wiser words were never spoken, my friend."

A big shudder ran through Wenford's entire body with such force Leo felt it through the seat.

"Here, now. Ya mustn't take a chill. Ya gotta be healthy the day after tomorrow, or all our plans will be spoilt."

Leo reached behind the seat and hauled out an old Scottish tartan travel rug. He put one end over his left shoulder and took the reins in his left hand. He flipped the heavy wool blanket over Wenford's shoulders and pulled him in tight against his side. "Here. Snuggle up under this. And tuck it in around yerself. Pull that bear hide up till ya get good and wrapped up like a cocoon. It'll warm ya up soon."

Leo didn't withdraw his right arm around Wenford's shoulder to their mutual pleasure, even through all the layers of clothing.

Wenford turned and looked again at Leo's young face, so close to his. He shivered again. Unthinkingly, he reached out his hand under the blanket and squeezed Leo's thigh. "I say, that's mighty cricket of you, Leo. I'm afraid I am freezing clear to death here. You're a lifesaver, to be sure. Sorry to be so much trouble."

Leo just squeezed Wenford's shoulder in a manly, friendly fashion. He flicked the reins, urging the horse to trot a little faster. "Hang in there, Wen. Brownie'll get ya to Missus Bertha's nice warm house before ya know it."

Wenford gradually warmed up. His shivering eased off, though his toes and fingers remained chilled through. He occasionally stole glances at Leo. He noted his strong long neck, firm, clean-shaven jaw, and clear eyes. "I say, Leo, my friend. Are you a cowboy? Didn't Missus Merriwell write to me that you were a cattleman and a horseman?"

"Well, now. I guess ya could call me a cowboy, one of the last of a dyin' breed of men. I went on my first cattle drive when

I was, oh, fourteen or so. Sean was boss of the fall round-up and drive. He taught me all about bein' a man, ridin', huntin', ropin', and brandin'. He taught me about breedin' cattle and breedin' horses. He was my hero, my leader, and my dear friend."

"How old are you now, Leo, if I may be so bold as to ask?"

"Why, I guess I'll be nineteen, on, uh, the seventeenth of next month, in January."

Leo glanced over at Wen, sitting all hunched up under his bowler hat and cuddled up under Leo's arm. "And how old might y'all be, Wen?"

"I just turned twenty-nine, Leo. Pocatello is my first ministry since I graduated from Wycliffe Hall at Oxford."

"Well, just how did ya become a priest, anyway, Wen?"

"Oh, I say, that's a long story. Are you sure you want to hear? It's not nearly as interesting as learning the manly arts of driving cattle and breaking horses."

"Wen, we've got pert near an hour's drive left. Besides, I would enjoy hearin' about life in faraway England. My fiancé's family hails from London Town. They talk real fine and educated. But I've never traveled further east than Kansas City. Nope, I've never even seen the ocean. So, yeah, I would like to hear about yer growin' up and yer adventures crossin' the ocean and crossin' the states to get where ya are now. I mean, did ya ever in yer wildest dreams imagine freezin' on a long ride in Idaho State just to marry a cowboy to his intended?"

"Well, now that you mention it, Leo, it does seem rather strange that a young man of good family from the peaceful, civilized countryside of England would end up under the arm of a cowboy. I never dreamed I would be trying not to freeze to death in the far Wild West reaches of Idaho, of all places!"

Wen chuckled as he faced Leo. His good humor returned along with his warmth. He squeezed Leo's thigh again with a friendly nudge. He couldn't help but notice Leo's strong lean leg muscles. *A real cowboy! And he looks it, every inch. A real man. I bet he rides his horses really hard. Just feel those strong legs!*

Wen faced forward again, sighing happily. "So, where do I start? Well, now. I was born to good Anglican parents of English descent. My father was a professor of English Literature. My mother was a political activist working for women's rights. So I enjoyed a very progressive and liberal home life. I was a naughty boy, dallying about, not serious about anything. Somehow I managed to make it through preparatory school. Then I began reading English Literature at Oxford, following in my father's footsteps as it were. But really, I mostly played football. What you Yanks call soccer. I spent my days hanging out in the pub with my mates, getting into as much mischief as I could, just having a lark.

"Then, my parents took a holiday to Minorca. That's a small island in the Mediterranean Sea just south of Spain, in case you haven't heard of it. My parents had gone there to take the sun for a winter holiday. They finished their restful two weeks and embarked to return home. They were traveling on the French ship, *General Chanzy*. It wrecked shortly after leaving port four years ago on February the ninth. I'll never forget that date. My parents were among the two hundred or so who did not survive the wreck. I received a telegram at Oxford on February tenth... and... well... it sent me into a spiral of depression and guilt, truth be told."

Leo pulled Wenford into his side more firmly in a gentle hug of sympathy. "I'm sorry to hear about yer parents, Wen. I can identify with how ya must have felt."

"Yes. Well. I felt quite lost, to be sure. I didn't know why God took them, leaving me all alone. Even though my parents left me pretty well off, I felt that my life was useless. I was tired of being a playboy and a ne'er-do-well, wasting my time with frivolities and sensualities. I went for many a long walk and did lots of hard thinking during that time after their funerals. One gray and rainy day, as is typical in winter in Oxford, I ended up wandering along aimlessly, meandering all around the historic old colleges. I ended up in leafless University Parks by the banks of the River Cherwell. I looked up at Wycliffe Hall in the distance. Wycliffe Hall is a theological college for the Church of England. I went in to look around and get out of the weather. A very nice gentleman, the Reverend Graham Duff, who later became the Bishop of Liverpool, struck up a conversation with me, and... well... over a bit of time, I felt a call to the ministry. A few days after that, I began

314

reading the three-year honours course to become a Bachelor of Theology. I devoted myself to finding ways to minister Christ's love to the faithful."

"Gee. That's interestin', Wen. I guess ya studied the Bible a lot, then, huh?"

"Oh, to be sure. Plus, I had classes in preparing sermons, preaching, and voice training. I studied courses in evangelism and apologetics, philosophy, and history. It was all quite wonderful. I experienced a spiritual change from my wonton days as a trouble maker."

"Sorry, Wen. But I can't see ya as a trouble maker. Ya look so respectable and mature."

"Well, take my word for it, young man. Before my call to the ministry, I played the field in every way I could. And with every-one I could. Most shamelessly."

"But that still doesn't explain how ya made it from England all the way here to Idaho."

"Ah, yes. Well, in my senior year – um, about two years ago, now, we had a visitor at the Hall. Reverend Middleton S. Lighthall and his newlywed wife, Margaret, were on their honeymoon, vis-iting cathedrals and seminaries in the south of England. We struck up a conversation. He came across as such a robust man, so strong and full of brotherly love. He told me about all the adventures one might have in taking a call to minister to the wilds of Idaho. He was the field secretary to the Bishop of Idaho, over in Boise, at the time. He wooed me with his romantic stories of the stalwart cowboy, the noble savage, the daring miner, and the brave pioneer farmers. He told me about how they were taming the land and building a secure future for themselves and their families. I was fascinated. Enchanted really. And he knew it."

Leo took his arm from behind Wenford to shift hands for the reins. He thrust his frozen left hand between his legs beneath the bearskin lap blanket to warm his fingers.

Wenford noted the problem. He took off his gloves beneath the blanket, tucked them between his legs, and reached for Leo's ice-cold hand. "Here, Leo. Let me return the favor."

Wen pulled off Leo's glove and gently massaged his icy hand between his warm hands. Leo looked over sharply at Wenford and frowned in surprise. Then he shrugged. His hand began tingling painfully as circulation returned. Wenford massaged his hand more briskly. "Here. We'll get your hand warmed up right smartly. That's the ticket. It feels nearly frozen. Here, try opening your fingers a bit more."

"Gee. Thanks, Wen."

Leo looked back at the road. He found it strange that Wenford could be so easily intimate and physical, actually touching hands with a stranger. *These odd English ways! These over-educated gents sure have queer ways about 'em, that's fer sure!*

"So, to continue my story. Middleton became Bishop last year. He wrote and offered me a position at Trinity Episcopal Church. His letter told me the Pocatello congregation had built a new church about sixteen years ago. Have you seen it? It's on North Arthur Avenue and Lander Street in Pocatello, on the good side of the tracks, of course. He promised I would rise to the challenge and find it rewarding work. And, to be sure, he was right."

Wenford stopped massaging Leo's cool hand and let it rest warmly in his hands. Wen's thoughts turned back to his fantasies from when he was a young boy. He had read every book he could get his hands on about adventures in the Wild West. He loved reading about the camaraderie of cowboys working hard together and playing hard together, friends against the world come what may. He hoped Leo would become his cowboy friend. A special friend. He hadn't had a special friend since he left off playing with his soccer chums and entered the seminary. Leo's hand felt so strong in his. He felt the calluses on Leo's palm and fingers. He pictured all the hard outdoor man's work it took to make them.

He suddenly realized he shouldn't be so forward. He pulled his hands away and reached for his gloves.

As they neared Rose Corners, Leo pulled on his glove. He waved at Muriel Anne, who had been watching for their arrival from the frosty parlor window of Bertha's home. Scotty ran down to the road, barking frantically until he recognized the buggy and Leo. Then he trotted alongside the single carriage to herd them in

316

the right direction. Leo drove up to his house. "This here is my new Sears house, Wen. Muriel Anne's mother arranged fer ya to spend the nights with me, over here in my spare bedroom. I hope that's all right."

"Oh, to be sure. Delighted. Absolutely."

Wenford couldn't have been happier with the arrangements. He hoped he would get to spend plenty of time with Leo. He wanted to get to know his new cowboy friend a lot better. *My Lord, maybe I'll even get to see him stripped down to his bare essentials when he goes to bed at night. That would be a dream come true.*

They each grabbed a heavy valise. Leo opened the front door and invited Wenford in. Leo took great pride in showing Wenford the modern bathroom with running water between the two bedrooms. Wenford stood in the open doorway. "Oh, splendid! Palatial. What a superb water closet. Who would have expected this out in the wilderness of eastern Idaho? And with central heating, no less. Oh, splendid!"

After Wenford unpacked his bags, Leo drove them to Bertha's for a light luncheon.

Bertha had invited Lizzie to join them. Lizzie shared Bertha's excitement about the first marriage of one of their children. Leo made introductions all around. Bertha invited everyone to find a seat at the table. After everyone sat down, she beamed at Wenford. "Reverend, would you do us the honor of saying grace this lovely day?"

Used to such requests, he nodded, folded his hands before him on the tabletop, and bowed his head. "Bless us, O Lord, for these thy gifts which we are about to receive from thy bounty. And bless us to thy loving service. Through Jesus Christ our Lord. Amen."

Leo heard the others around the table softly repeat, "Amen." He had watched the ritual with open eyes, not used to the formality of saying a blessing on the food before eating it.

"Thank you, Reverend. All right, everyone, please help yourselves!"

Bertha served a pleasant, leisurely meal to the satisfaction and appreciation of everyone at the table.

They retired to Bertha's parlor and spoke quietly, getting acquainted. Muriel Anne held Leo's hand as Wenford watched jealously. As mid-afternoon approached, Bertha excused herself to prepare an afternoon's low tea to lubricate conversation and be sociable.

A quarter of an hour later, Bertha proudly wheeled in a serving cart with a pot of freshly brewed oolong tea. It also held plates of freshly baked scones and pretty little cut glass bowls of lemon curd, clotted Devonshire cream, and her own strawberry fruit preserve. Everyone oohed and aahed as they helped themselves to the bountiful spread. Muriel Anne prepared a scone for Leo, showing him how to dab a generous spoonful of thick clotted cream on the scone and then top it with a dab of strawberry preserve. Leo's eyes lit up as he took a bite. He smiled his thanks at Muriel Anne and Bertha as he chewed, savoring the treat with great pleasure.

Wenford positively beamed. "I say, but this is most civilized and gracious of you, Missus Merriwell. And you have lemon curd, too!"

Wenford hadn't had a scone with his favorite thick lemony cream since he left the ship to New York Harbor nearly a year ago. He didn't even try Bertha's strawberry preserve.

Bertha handed her toothless eighty-nine-year-old father a scone on a linen napkin. "So tell me, please, Reverend. How do you find your ministry at Trinity Episcopal Church?"

"Oh, it has been such a challenge and such a trial, Missus Merriwell. You just don't know. When I arrived, the vicarage was a disgrace. I had to rent lodgings in a house down the street, which, I must say, weren't a whole lot better. But you know the history of Pocatello, don't you? How the Shoshone Indians sold the land along and between the railway lines to the Union Pacific Railroad? Then the railroad built the original town, with only the cheapest of materials, between the switching lines. Soon the town overgrew the permitted land. The whites occupied the lawful land. All the Italians, Mexicans, Chinese, and criminals built over on the wrong side of the tracks, usurping land that wasn't rightfully permitted. And let me tell you, they didn't build any solid buildings over there, either. What a disgrace! So shoddy."

Wenford looked over at Leo as he took a sip of lukewarm tea. Leo's glazed eyes and bored expression disappointed him. He eagerly wished for Leo's attention and approval. Bertha and Lizzie clucked sympathetically.

Wenford sat up straight to get Leo's attention. "So I went right to work, grabbing the bull by the horns, so to speak. Hardly anyone attended Sunday School or sang in the choir. I saw young people, from both sides of the tracks and all denominations, running around wild and loose all day long. They played games of violence, like cowboys and Indians, or horse thieves and sheriff posses, with mock battles, shootouts, and hangings – and sometimes not so mock. Every day the rough games hurt some child or other."

Wenford placed his cup in its saucer, leaned forward, and focused on Leo. "So, to promote a spirit of friendliness among the teenage ragamuffins, I formed a Christian Endeavor Society to which young people from any denomination could belong. It became so popular we had to move from the Vestry into the main chapel. I canvassed the parish and rallied support for a boys' choir. I invited every boy with any form of good voice to join. Now we have a choir of thirty-five boys of all ages. Oh, and they are a good-looking group, once you get them cleaned up and standing together in a friendly assemblage."

Leo perked up. Wenford winked, pleased to have his attention at last. "I found an excellent vocal teacher and an organist and began rehearsals. We pay the boys one dollar a month, provided they don't miss any practices or performances. Well, boys being boys, we naturally have hardly ever had to pay any of them."

He paused as everyone chuckled knowingly. "Yes, Bishop Lighthall was most pleased when he heard their angelic voices singing during service when he visited last month. He saw that our little Mason & Hamlin reed organ could not hold up to the volume of so many lusty young voices, so he promised to help us buy a new pipe organ. Isn't that splendid?"

319

"Oh, yes, indeed," Bertha agreed enthusiastically. "Splendid, indeed. How I wish we were close enough to attend services more than once or twice a year. Why, Muriel Anne, can you imagine how perfectly wonderful it would have been to hold your wedding in the lovely Trinity Church with a fine boys' choir singing praises during the services. Oh, just imagine!"

Muriel Anne squeezed Leo's hand. They smiled at each other. "Yes, mother. It would be grand, wouldn't it, and that's a fact. But, Leo's new parlor will be chapel enough for me. And Hannah Gilbert's lovely singing voice will be more than enough choir for me. I am content, mother. Really, I am."

"Why, of course, you are, my dear. And with the handsome young Reverend Loughton to read the ceremony, your wedding will be just lovely. Won't it, Reverend?"

Wenford beamed at Leo. "I'll do everything I can to make the day memorable and beautiful for both of you lovely young people. Everything I can."

Lizzie stood up to leave. "It's time fer me to be on me way. Otherwise, I won't make it home before dark."

Lizzie shook hands with Wenford and welcomed him again to Upper Presto. As she limped out, she wished she hadn't left her cane in the buggy.

After a leisurely supper, Wenford and Leo rushed back to the new Sears house. They strode faster and faster as the biting cold penetrated deeper and deeper through their coats until they fairly burst into the parlor, laughing and shouting at the stinging pain of the frigid air. "Oh, I say! Just feel how nice and warm in here!"

Leo quickly slammed closed the front door behind them. Once inside, Leo lit the kerosene lamp. A soft, warm yellow light spread a friendly welcome through the parlor. Leo turned to Wenford with a big grin. He imitated Bertha's sing-song British accent as best he could. "Please do come in, most Reverend Wenford Loughton, sir. Oh, please let me take your fine overcoat, kind sir."

"Oh, please! That dear Missus Merriwell almost wore out my name and modest title with her endless formalities and courtesies. Why, by the end of supper this evening, I felt quite a hundred and ten years old with the weight of responsibilities she heaped on my simple little title. After all, I'm only a cleric of the Church with a Bachelor of Theology degree. It's not like I've even got a doctorate or anything."

Leo chuckled as he lit a wood match to the already laid-out firewood in the new fireplace. "Well, y'all are just the most important fellow Missus Bertha has had the pleasure of entertainin' fer years, and my, my, my, but wasn't she in her best form tonight! Lah de dah! Oh! The handsome young Reverend this. And the handsome young Reverend that."

Wenford walked up and stood beside Leo as they gazed down into the fire. He put his hand on Leo's shoulder and gave it a friendly squeeze. "Now, you just stop it right there. I've had quite enough of that for one night, sir. Can't we please get back to being friends, like in the buggy on the way here from the train depot? Just plain Leo and Wen, traveling companions and brothers under the skin?"

"Brothers under the skin, eh?"

Leo looked at Wenford with a wink then sank into one of the four mismatched upholstered chairs in front of the fireplace. Wenford stepped over to the chair beside Leo's and sat down with a sigh. He stuck his legs out towards the hearth and contentedly crossed his hands over his chest. They sat in silence for several minutes, nearly hypnotized by the flickering light of the crackling hardwood fire. Wenford sighed. "Ah, this is the ticket. No endless female chitter-chatter."

"Um-hm."

"If you wouldn't mind, Leo, my friend, I would so enjoy taking advantage of your new indoor facilities by taking a soak in a tub of hot water. I haven't had a real bath in a real tub for months. And I haven't felt warm since I rolled out of bed this morning."

Leo didn't respond. He wanted to say no. He had looked forward to sharing the bathtub with Sean for so long he still hadn't used it. Reluctantly, he gave in. "Sure. Make yerself to home, Wen. Help yerself. I'll light a candle. We can leave it burnin' as a night light since yer in a strange house fer the first time. Or, would ya prefer a lamp?"

"No, no, a soft candle would be just the ticket. I can unwind and warm up at the same time from this long cold day. Ah, a real bath in a real tub. I can't wait!"

Wenford sprang to his feet, loosened his tie, and began unbuttoning his vest.

Leo placed a lit candle on the back of the sink. The mirror on the medicine cabinet reflected and doubled its light in the small white-tiled room. He knelt down by the tub and turned on the spigots. After the first rusty gush of water ran clear, he picked up the rubber stopper and plugged the drain. He stood watching the tub fill for the first time. After wanting to share the tub with Sean for so long, he felt odd sharing it with a man he had just met. It saddened him. "Let me get some extra towels fer ya."

Leo turned and looked at the door expecting to see Wenford. Then he heard hangers jingling on the wood rod in the guest room. He went to his bedroom and removed four towels from the used chest of drawers. He placed them on the floor beneath the small window between the tub and the toilet. He turned around and found Wenford standing in the bathroom doorway wearing only his one-piece wool long johns. Wenford's neatly parted hair stood messed up from pulling off his shirt.

Wenford struck a pose. He leaned against the door jamb, crossed his arms over his chest, and cocked one ankle over the other. He smiled as he watched Leo look him over from top to bottom. He returned Leo's appraising looks. *My Lord, what a tall, lean, handsome cowboy I've lassoed here. I wonder if I can get him to rope me and saddle me and break me in tonight? How I've dreamed of this since I was just a little tyke, reading penny dreadful after penny dreadful about American cowboys in the old Wild West.*

Wenford seductively unbuttoned the front of his BVD long johns. Intentionally blocking the door, he slowly slipped off the shoulders and then pulled his arms out of the long tight sleeves, one at a time. He hoped Leo found him as attractive as he found Leo. He knew all the hours on the football pitch with his chums had left him trim and lean. He hoped Leo found his muscular hairy chest pleasing. He religiously did fifty push-ups, fifty squat-thrusts, and one-hundred sit-ups every morning to keep in trim when away from the rigors of the soccer pitch. With the top of his long johns hanging low over his lean hips, barely covering his privates, he took a step into the small room and leaned over the bathtub. "How's the water temperature? I see quite a bit of steam. It's not *too* hot, is it?"

Leo swallowed hard. He had trouble tearing his eyes away from Wenford's tight torso. Leo leaned over and tested the water with his hand. He shook off the water. "It's perfect. Just hot enough, fer me at least. Go ahead. Climb in."

Leo leaned back against the wall between the porcelain toilet and the cast iron tub and thrust out his hips to avoid stepping on the towels on the floor. He eagerly watched Wenford push down his underwear and slowly peel them off his muscular, athletic legs. Wenford finally stood in the candlelight as nature made him. Wenford gazed at Leo as he stood up. He tossed his long johns out the door into the hall between the bedrooms. He glanced down at the steaming water and stepped into the tub. "Ah. Ah. Just right, indeed, my cowboy friend."

Wenford leaned over and grasped the sides of the tub. He slowly lowered himself into the water, savoring the hot water as it rose over his legs and torso. "Ah. Just perfect. The decadence and civilizing influence of the Roman baths cannot be underrated or underpraised."

Wenford leaned back and closed his eyes to a slit, pretending he had shut them all the way. "I say. Perhaps you could turn off the water, now, Leo. We don't want it overflowing, do we?"

He surreptitiously watched Leo lean over and turn off the water. He took great delight seeing Leo's eyes rake over his body, widening in pleasure at what he saw. Wenford's pulse quickened. "I say, Leo. I hate to be so selfish as to keep this lovely hot water all to myself. This tub is certainly big enough for two. Won't you please join me? It's absolutely delicious! Why I think this is the first time my toes have been warm since I left my flat this morning in Pocatello and ran for the train station."

Conflicting emotions gave Leo pause. He still loved Sean. He remained loyal and devoted to Sean. Yet this pleasingly athletic body laid out before him invited him to dalliance. A hot spike of desire fought a cold fear of losing his love for Sean. In all the five years past, he had never exchanged intimacies with another man besides Sean, despite the occasional flirtation. He recalled visiting Salt Lake City with Sean, where they met several young fellows who liked to flirt. The boys flitted from man to man like a butterfly, trying to taste the nectar of every flower. But that went against the nature of his relationship with his handsome, sweet Sean. He could almost hear Sean's voice, as though Sean spoke to him from beyond the veil. Leo's mind supplied what he knew Sean would say if he were here. *Now, me boyo, ya know ya gotta live yer life the best ya can. Take advantage of rare opportunities that may come yer way, doncha know. It won't make any difference to me. It won't alter me love fer ya in the slightest, me boyo. So go fer it, pardner! Grasp the brass ring whenever it comes yer way.*

With a wistfully sad smile, Leo slowly undressed in the flickering light of the candle. He sensed Wenford watching his every move. The only sound came from Wenford's hands splashing hot water over his chest and shoulders. *I love ya, Sean. Ya know I do. But, I've been so lonely fer the touch of a man's body fer weeks now, ever since ya took sick. I miss ya so much, Sean. Muriel Anne's soft ways just don't compensate fer yer loss, doncha know. I love ya, Sean. I miss ya.*

Leo stepped over to the tub with a frown creasing his brow. He stepped in between Wenford's feet, his back to the faucet, and slowly sank between Wenford's spread knees. Leo felt quite exposed as Wenford stared with delight at his body slipping into the water. He didn't know he personified Wenford's dream cowboy miraculously made flesh, a daydream vision of masculine beauty and Western virtues come to life.

Wenford's breath caught in a gasp as Leo sat down between his feet. Leo pushed his long legs up and over Wenford's until he reclined wide open to Wenford's lustful gaze.

They both took great pleasure in their languid bath and sensual caresses as they became better acquainted. After the bath, they dried off and retired to Leo's horsehair mattress without speaking a word. Later, when the older and wiser Wenford entered Leo, Leo closed his eyes and imagined Sean had returned to fill him up with his love and strength.

Wenford, on the other hand, kept his eyes wide open while they made love. He wanted to see the handsome young cowboy on all fours below him, lit by the flickering light of the parlor fireplace entering the open bedroom door. He fantasized they were riding together as cowboy sidekicks, sharing adventures and their bodies by the light of a bonfire lit to keep the wolves at bay.

Soon, they slept soundly, wrapped in each other's arms. They woke up happy and content when the first cock crowed. "Ya know, Wen ol' buddy, Miss Muriel Anne has a most annoyin' habit of walkin' in all unannounced of a mornin'. She always brings over breakfast and makes coffee while I shave and wash up."

Wenford bolted upright in the bed with a look of horror on his face. "Oh, I say! It just wouldn't do for her to find me here in bed with the groom. No. No. No."

Wenford leapt out of bed and fairly ran to the guest bedroom. He only slowed down enough to pick up his long johns and yank them on. He didn't stop to straighten the seams on his arms and legs, fearful he might hear the front door open at any moment.

When decently covered, he glanced back at Leo, lying propped up on his elbows grinning. Wenford smiled back, a little ashamed at his reaction. He winked. Without saying anything, he crawled into the bed in the guest room to make sure it looked like he had slept there.

Sure enough, about half an hour later, Muriel Anne arrived to make breakfast for her fiancé and her mother's cherished parish priest. Both young men pretended to wake up from sound sleeps, grunting and groaning and yawning. Leo held a quilt over his nakedness as he closed the hall door to the parlor. "Good morning, Muriel Anne. I thought it might be too cold fer ya to come over this mornin'. Ain't it freezin' out?"

"Oh, yes. But I simply added more layers and a scarf across my face. I couldn't pass up the opportunity of spending some private time with you two good-looking men without my dear mother dominating the conversation." She twittered a bright, happy laugh. "I'll have breakfast ready about the time it'll take you two to bathe and shave. Don't hurry. I'll need a good half an hour to stoke the oven and whip up the buttermilk biscuits and bake them to a golden turn."

"Golly, Muriel Anne. That sounds great. We'll be out in a minute."

The two men met at the door to the bathroom, Wenford in his BVD underwear and Leo wrapped in a blanket. Leo dropped the quilt to the floor and put his arms around Wenford for a silent hug and a quick kiss on the neck. Wenford clasped Leo with rib-crushing strength and enthusiasm. Leo leaned close to Wenford's ear. "Let's go shave and grab some breakfast. Sorry, but any other fun will have to wait until after the rehearsal supper tonight!"

"That's all right, my fine-looking baby-faced cowboy. I'm just happy to get to know you and spend some time with you before you become a happily married man and put all your childish passions behind you."

Leo goosed him hard to punish him for teasing. Wenford yelped, jumped back, and clapped his hand over his mouth to stifle the sound of his laughter.

Leo took the first turn at the toilet and the sink. Wenford luxuriated in another hot soapy bath, only solo this time.

They enjoyed a quiet breakfast with Muriel Anne, relaxing and getting to know each other better. They only had an hour before they expected the neighbors to drop by to prepare Leo's house for the wedding rehearsal and supper.

Bertha arrived around eleven, clearly the general in charge of her newly conscripted army of helpers. She imperiously directed moving the borrowed chairs into the parlor and dining room from the buggies and wagons outside. She showed them where to set up a long plank table on wood trestles and a separate narrow table along the wall to hold the buffet. Bob and Ralph carried a small folding table over from Bertha's house to set up by the front door for the wedding gifts.

Wenford watched all the hustle and bustle of setting up for the reception and grinned at Leo. "You know what they say, don't you, cowboy? It's an old Irish proverb. Marry a mountain girl, and you marry the whole mountain."

A little later, the neighbor ladies began arriving. They brought in plates of sandwiches for their noonday dinners and large covered pans to warm up for the big supper after the wedding rehearsal. Bertha set Muriel Anne to work stoking the coal fire in the new cast iron stove in the kitchen.

Soon, Lizzie showed up with her entire brood huddled beneath blankets in the family surrey. Little eight-year-old Honce ran over and latched on to big brother Leo's leg. He wanted Leo to pick him up. He didn't like all the strangers, noise, and confusion of converting the house into a wedding chapel and banquet hall.

By four o'clock, all the menfolk had arrived. Everyone settled in for the rehearsal, which went off without a hitch. Leo, unexpectedly nervous, stood in front of all his neighbors and family. He felt their eyes on him as they watched every little thing he did. Lizzie and Bertha burst into tears at the end of the exchange of vows right on cue, as if it were the actual wedding.

Everyone enjoyed a pleasant rehearsal supper. They ate until hardly anything remained to be set aside as leftovers.

The ladies worked as a team and washed the dishes. The men enjoyed cigarettes, cigars, and small glasses of port from David Gilbert's wine cellar. By seven o'clock, everyone began retrieving their wraps from piles on the beds. They took their leave with promises to return at noon the next day. As they trickled out the door in family groups, everyone shouted, 'Happy New Year!'

Josh and Mitch lit off a string of firecrackers. The noise scared everyone's horses but received a big cheer from Lizzie and Alma's younger kids. As they pulled away, Leo heard his younger brothers and sisters squabbling over lap blankets.

Muriel Anne kissed Leo goodbye. She stopped at the door and shook her finger at him. "Remember, I can't see you tomorrow before the wedding, or it'll bring bad luck. So make your own breakfast. Mother and I will come in the back door and I'll put on my gown in the kitchen. You must be finished and out of there before I arrive. Can you remember, Leo, dear? Okay, then. Happy New Year. See you tomorrow. I love you, honey, and that's a fact."

Leo tried to put a brave face on it, despite feeling a distinct lack of affection. Since he knew Muriel Anne expected him to respond, he called out, "I love ya, too, Muriel Anne. Happy New Year!"

Wenford waved as she closed the door behind her. "Happy New Year, Miss Muriel Anne."

Finally, silence descended on Leo and Sean's dream home. Leo and Wenford sat down, gratefully, at the long table filling the center of the room. Wenford removed the detachable white linen collar from his black clergy shirt and then poured them each a small glass of port. They sat and sipped the rich red wine in companionable silence.

The small black mantle clock over the fireplace struck midnight with twelve soft metallic dings. The two exhausted men, mellowed from good food and wine, retired to Leo's bed.

Anxious to resume their frolics from the night before, they didn't take time for another bath. Wenford rushed to undress and hang up his clothes. Leo pulled the top sheet and quilts to the floor at the foot of the bed. Leo turned the lamp's flame down low and stretched out on the mattress. He slowly massaged his cock while waiting for Wenford.

Wenford stopped in his tracks when he saw Leo splayed out, ready for him. His eyes lit up. "Oh, cowboy!"

Wenford didn't waste any time. He placed his small travel tube of Vaseline beside the lamp on the nightstand. Then he jumped on the bed, drew Leo's turgid member into his mouth, and began humming for joy. He turned his body until his erection waived in Leo's face. After he had Leo's cock thoroughly slicked up, he licked down to Leo's balls, lavishing his attention on them, delighting in their hairy softness. He pulled one testicle into his mouth, massaged it with his tongue, then shifted his attention to the other. He tried to draw both into his mouth at the same time, but they were too big. He gave up trying, happy nonetheless.

After Wenford had Leo's balls slicked up, he moved lower. The spice of Leo's perspiration in his hairy ass crack acted like an aphrodisiac to Wenford. Wenford aggressively pushed his face closer to lick and taste Leo with a passionate fervor.

When Wenford's tongue caressed between Leo's clenching behind, Leo raised his head to lick Wenford's drooling cock, then up to his dangling balls. They both moaned as they gave and received pleasure in each other's crotches.

When Wenford felt Leo relax, he sat up and reached for the tube of Vaseline. Leo looked up, puzzled. Wenford waved the small tube in Leo's face. "The perfect pecker slicker-upper."

Leo chuckled, then reached out and massaged Wenford's saliva-slick erection. Wenford knelt on the bed and crawled up between Leo's legs. His thighs nudged Leo's long hairy legs aside.

Wenford opened the tube and squeezed the petroleum jelly onto his palm. Leo raised his hips off the blankets and shoved a pillow under his butt. He wanted to make himself available for whatever pleased this handsome, passionate lover.

Content that he had prepared Leo for a smooth and enjoyable penetration, Wenford pushed his cock between Leo's clenching buttocks. When he found the target, he pushed in slowly. Leo took deep breaths as he received Wenford's domineering manhood. Finally, Wenford's pubic hairs smashed against Leo's oil-slick butt. Wenford gave in to his lust. He leaned forward and kissed Leo passionately. As he sucked Leo's tongue into his mouth, he pulled Leo's head closer. They kissed madly, writhing together sensuously, as they worked their way to a crashing conclusion.

Wenford nudged Leo awake after only a couple of hours of sleep. He stimulated Leo enough to return the favor by giving Wenford the ride of his life.

After Leo exploded in Wenford, he closed his eyes and basked in the afterglow. He liked knowing he could enjoy sex with someone other than Sean. He liked sex with Wenford nearly as much as he had with Sean. For the first time, he acknowledged his attraction to all men and their masculine bodies. It struck him like an epiphany. His eyes sprung wide open.

He lay there, content and happy, thinking about finding a new friend both in and out of bed. *Hm. So why am I gettin' married to a girl, then? Oh, yeah. Sean's wishes. But, he must've known that making love with females isn't in my nature. Sean must have known.*

Chapter 24: Consummation

The next morning, the wedding ceremony came off without a hitch. Muriel Anne glowed radiantly in her mother's old-fashioned wedding gown of creamy white satin with a yoke of lace. Bertha had forced several paperwhite narcissus bulbs for Christmas. She used them to make a coronet for Muriel Anne to wear over her veil. Their pungently sweet perfume wafted in waves through the warm room.

Muriel Anne's father had passed on. Her grandfather could barely walk. So she had invited Leo's father to walk her up the aisle. Hannah sang to start the service. Alma escorted Muriel Anne from the kitchen door to her place beside Leo to give away the bride. When Muriel Anne entered, she smiled warmly at her friends and family.

Leo and Muriel Anne stood in the dining room facing the kitchen wall. Everyone sitting in the dining room and parlor could see them during the ceremony. Wenford faced the congregation with his back to the kitchen. Leo stood self-consciously with his back to his family and neighbors. Muriel Anne stood at his right hand. Little Honce stood close by as their ring bearer with his blond hair combed neatly for a change. Hannah concluded the opening song.

Reverend Wenford Loughton began reading from The Book of Common Prayer. "Dearly beloved, we are gathered together here in the sight of God, and in the face of this company, to join together this man and this woman in holy matrimony."

Wenford took his time, allowing everyone to savor the romantic ceremony. Leo and Muriel Anne responded at the appropriate places, just as they had rehearsed the afternoon before.

"With this ring, I thee wed."

"I will."

Reverend Loughton signaled for everyone to rise and recite the Lord's Prayer. After everyone sat down, he followed by reading the matrimonial blessing.

He placed Muriel Anne's right hand in Leo's right hand for the handfasting. "Those whom God hath joined together let no man put asunder."

Wenford directed the young couple to kneel in front of him. "I pronounce that they are man and wife, in the name of the Father, and of the Son, and of the Holy Ghost, amen."

Wenford then concluded with the blessing, "…bless, preserve, and keep you."

Leo and Muriel Anne kissed to cheers and happy jeers from their assembled friends, neighbors and families. Lizzie and Bertha, along with most of the women in the room, used their lace-edged hankies to blot their tears as they smiled on approvingly.

After Leo kissed the bride, everyone organized themselves into a reception line. They all wanted to congratulate the newlyweds with kisses, hugs, and wishes for a long and fruitful union.

The ladies bustled off to the kitchen to finalize preparations for their reception luncheon. The youngsters formed a line to use the bathroom almost immediately. Everyone wanted to try Leo's modern indoor plumbing. They loved pulling the chain handle dangling from the wood water tank hanging high up on the wall. Indoor plumbing became the biggest attraction of the day – second only to the wedding cake.

The wedding party toasted the bride and groom with champagne from David's cellar. Then they toasted with homemade elderberry wine from Bertha's cellar. The time drew near for Ralph to drive Wenford to the Blackfoot train station. Before he had to leave, Bertha and Faith carefully carried in the three-tiered wedding cake. Everyone admired its rich white frosting topped with miniature pink sugar roses. Muriel Anne and Leo cut the cake to polite applause. Bertha served everyone a small slice.

The reception officially drew to its end.

Wenford approached the newlyweds, still sitting at the head of the table. They stood up and thanked him for performing their wedding ceremony. Wenford hugged them both. With a wink at Leo, he invited them to visit him at Trinity Church in Pocatello whenever they could. In return, they extended him an invitation to drop by if he were ever in their area. They all hugged each other, again, in parting.

Leo and Muriel Anne received lots of advice and teasing, some tasteful and some not, about what to do on their marriage night. Then everyone happily returned to their homes, leaving the newlyweds alone.

Exhausted from too much rich food and wine, Leo and Muriel Anne fell into the overstuffed chairs in the living room. Muriel Anne reached across and took Leo's hand. They sat quietly, side by side, staring into the bright, warm fire. "So, husband."

"So, wife."

"We did what Sean wanted, husband, exactly the way he asked, and that's a fact."

Leo turned to his new wife. A brief sadness passed over his face. Then he smiled and shrugged. "Yep. We surely did, wife."

After a moment's rest, Muriel Anne poured them each a cup of over-cooked coffee. She sweetened it with a splash of brandy, one of their wedding gifts, and took the drinks into the parlor. "Would you like a little coffee, husband?"

Leo opened his eyes. "Sure 'nough, wife. Thanks."

They sipped in silence. Muriel Anne gathered her nerves. Excitement built within her as she anticipated her second wedding bed.

Leo sipped his coffee, wishing he could just go to bed and sleep. He had been up most of the night before while Wenford coached him in variations of the art of making love. He could seriously use some shut-eye. But, Muriel Anne wouldn't let Leo deny her full marital rights a second time.

After they finished their coffees, Muriel Anne stood up, reached out her hand, and pulled Leo to his feet. She linked her arm in his and turned towards the bedroom. "Shall we freshen up a bit with a bath before we retire to our wedding bed, husband?"

"Sure 'nough, wife."

Since they both felt shy undressing in front of a member of the opposite sex, they quickly wrapped up in their bathrobes. Leo pulled on his Christmas present from Lizzie and Alma, a new plaid flannel bathrobe. Muriel Anne snuggled into her comfortable old pink satin bathrobe.

Muriel Anne wrapped her hair in a white Turkish towel and then gingerly stepped into the tub of hot water. Leo polished his teeth at the sink. He glanced briefly at Muriel Anne as she quickly soaped and rinsed. She stood up and tied a towel across her breasts and torso. Leo hopped into the tub. He efficiently took care of business with a washcloth in one hand and a brick of homemade soap in the other.

Leo walked into the bedroom with a towel around his waist and his bathrobe over his arm. He found Muriel Anne sitting demurely on the bed with the covers turned down, brushing her hair. She smiled somewhat wistfully at Leo. Her smile turned into one of delight as she boldly watched Leo toss his towel on the chair and walk toward her. As she watched her handsome cowboy head towards her, a blush gave her breasts and cheeks a rosy glow.

Muriel Anne set aside the hairbrush, then turned down the flame in the lamp. She stood up and allowed her towel to drop. She felt as brazen as the first time she had exposed herself to Sean, four weeks and a lifetime ago.

Leo flopped down on the bed, all gangly and loose, and gazed up at Muriel Anne in all her feminine splendor.

Based on her limited experience with Sean, Muriel Anne took the initiative and crawled up over Leo's long slim body. She leaned down and gave him a lingering kiss. Her long blond hair crackled with static electricity in the dry winter air as it cascaded over Leo's neck and shoulders.

Since she didn't feel much of a response from his privates, she knew what she needed to do. She kissed her way down his throat and across his brown nipples. She licked at his tight lean stomach, lingering a moment to tickle his indented navel with her tongue. Then she sat on his thighs. Gazing into his eyes, she eagerly reached out with both hands to arouse him – just as she had learned to stimulate Sean.

Young and healthy, the animal side of Leo reacted to her erotic caresses. In response, he reached up and stroked her arms, shoulders, and neck while she fondled him to a full erection. *How soft she is, where I'm used to hard muscles.*

Leo ran his thumbs over her nipples, amazed at how large and firm they grew under his touch. *She's round where I'm used to flat and flat where I am used to round.* He let his rough, callused hands roam down her torso. He grasped her narrow waist. His fingers almost touched. He slid his hands down to her broader hips. *She's wide where I'm used to slender.*

His eyes fell, at last, on her pubic region, covered with soft dark blond hair. *She's in where I'm used to out and empty where I'm used to findin' a handful of joy. I know it's supposed to be natural this way. I understand this is what most men want. But gol dern it, I just feel like somethin' is missin'. I suppose what she's doin' feels good enough, but it doesn't feel right to me. Something's definitely missin'.* Leo closed his eyes as he remembered Sean fondling him in much the same way.

Her gentle hands caressed his hairy bollocks and massaged his silky penis into a full erection. Muriel Anne remembered Sean's cute face wincing, grinning, and winking at her when he took her virginity. She closed her eyes, knelt up, then slowly slid down Leo's stiff member. Their combined lubrication allowed a smooth descent. When she hit bottom, her eyes flew open in surprise. She hadn't realized Leo sported a penis so much larger than Sean's. She found herself filled to capacity for the first time in her life.

Leo rested his hands on her hips and helped her lift, then slowly move back down. Murial Anne closed her eyes dreamily as she leisurely worked to give him pleasure. Her hand fell to fondle their connection. She instinctively caressed her love button, which sent her soaring higher and higher. But she didn't stop. She had just begun. Leo began flexing his long, strong legs, thrusting harder and harder. His muscular torso began writhing beneath her grasping hands. She had only known the love of a kind and gentle man, weakened by fever. For the first time, she felt the animal strength and masculine power of lust driving two healthy bodies together in increasing furor and fervor.

As Leo felt his passions increasing, his thoughts turned to his handsome, virile Sean. He remembered the incredible love they had shared, the joy they had taken from each other's ramming manhoods and lingering kisses night after night. As he grew closer to erupting, he leaned up and grabbed Muriel Anne in a hard hug. He gave her a ravishing kiss with a force she had never experienced. Leo closed his eyes and imagined he held Sean in his arms. He kissed her hard, holding nothing back. The stubble of his beard and mustache burned her delicate mouth and lips. The thrust of his tongue shocked her with its force and virility. Somehow that first thrusting male kiss felt more like her deflowering than Sean's gentleness the first time he had entered her.

She felt completely overwhelmed. And she loved it.

Her natural moisture made every movement lubricious and delicious. She returned Leo's kisses with a passion and fire she had never experienced or even imagined. They both soared to paradise simultaneously, lingering and lingering, frozen in ecstasy.

Only slowly did they begin returning to earthbound existence, coming back to their senses a little at a time. Eventually, they opened their eyes. They smiled timidly at each other, both shy again.

Muriel Anne collapsed over Leo's sweaty hairy chest. She twisted enough to slide off his body and recline along his side. She lowered her head onto his shoulder. She didn't want his maleness to leave her empty ever again. Her pelvis made minute, involuntary flexes, wave motions like little laps of water on the shores of a lake at night under a full moon. She smiled, completely satisfied. *Ah, so that's what Sean was talking about. He said he wished he could have shown me the pleasure of making love and finding marital bliss. Only I had no idea what he meant. But now I know. And I'm so glad. So glad.*

Muriel Anne leaned over and gave Leo a tender kiss on his cheek. She reached up and pushed his unruly bangs off his damp forehead. *Now I know.*

Leo lay relaxed after the efforts and release of their union. His thoughts returned to Sean. He recalled how he had always been so content to snuggle up to Sean after their joyous hard play.

He remembered losing himself in Sean's spicy male aroma overlaid with hints of smoke lingering in his hair.

He suddenly felt homesick and lonely in a flash of sadness, even with his new wife happily clinging to his side in their wedding bed. He turned towards Muriel Anne and took a deep breath. *She just doesn't smell like love and security to me. Not like my wonderful Sean did. She smells of milk and dried rose petals and something moist, musky, and dark. I guess it must be from her female parts. Oh, Sean. I miss ya so! Why did ya have to up and die and leave me all alone? Why?*

They both dozed off. The dry air cooled them off. They soon climbed under the quilts. They rolled together for a light good-night kiss, then moved apart. They slept with their backs touching, keeping each other's backs warm under the blankets. Leo turned off the lamp. The flame sputtered and died.

Even though exhausted, Leo lay wide awake listening to Muriel Anne's regular shallow breaths. He compared the difference between the thrilling, satisfying passions spent with Wen the past two nights to the less than fulfilling experience he had just shared with Muriel Anne. *Havin' sex with a man is just so natural, so good and satisfyin'. And now I know that havin' sex with a woman just isn't in my nature. Nope. That wasn't natural or happy or satisfyin' at all. How in tarnation am I gonna live with a girl when it goes against my nature?*

After a nearly sleepless night carousing with Wen and then a long hectic day, sleep finally allowed Leo's mind to stop worrying. He fell into an exhausted sleep.

Leo awoke before sunrise, crossed his arms behind his head, and stared at the ceiling. He compared his feelings after sleeping with Wenford to how he felt after sleeping with Muriel Anne. He looked over at Muriel Anne with her back to him. During the night, she had pulled most of the blankets over to her side of the bed.

He scowled. *Hell's Bells, but I got myself into a pack of trouble here. I know it's what Sean wanted, but gol dang it, it's not what I want. It's not what I need. I don't think this married to a*

337

girl stuff is gonna work, Sean. Oh, what am I gonna do now, Sean?

After a pause, Leo heard Sean's answer from the recesses of his mind, complete with his Irish lilt. *Now listen up, pardner. Ya gotta make the best of it, doncha know. When ya encounter a problem, ya just work on it till ya find a solution. It's as simple as that.*

Leo felt a sinking feeling in the pit of his stomach as he thought about sleeping with Muriel Anne every night. He began arguing with Sean. *I just can't do it, Sean. I'm sorry. Ya know I wanna do everythin' ya asked of me, my love, but this is askin' too much. It's so unnatural and dissatisfyin'. After sleepin' with y'all and then with Wenford, beddin' Muriel Anne just doesn't hold a candle. The thought of her pressurin' me fer romantic attentions night after night? Well, it's not gonna work. Sorry, Sean, but it's just not gonna work despite all yer good intentions.*

Leo heard Sean's rebuttal as if he were in the room. *I had me a problem, Little Lion. I didn't want to leave ya abandoned and all alone in the world. So, I worked on it till I came up with the solution of makin' a baby fer ya with Muriel Anne. We worked out how to do it in our handfastin' agreement, doncha know. We both faced the facts of the situation and figured things out together. Now, it's yer turn to do the same, me love. Face the facts and work it out.*

Wide awake, frustrated, and angry at himself, Leo climbed out of bed. He pulled on his blue jeans and boots and clumped down the stairs to stoke the furnace and start the day.

Muriel Anne slept through the noise of his shoveling coal and banging the cast iron furnace door closed down in the cellar. She even slept through Leo stomping angrily up the steps to the kitchen.

Leo made a pot of coffee in the new percolator. He thought about the problem of being saddled with a woman when he only wanted a man. He poured a mug of coffee and added plenty of sugar. Then he sat down at the kitchen table as he worried about his predicament. His thoughts slowly focused. *Fact one. Sleepin' with a girl isn't part of my nature. Fact two. I'm married to a girl of the female persuasion. And I'm afraid she's gonna expect me to give her attention pert near every night. And I just can't do it. Fact three. I've gotta come clean with her and let her know the reality of my situation. No, of our situation.*

Suddenly, Leo sat up straight. His eyes focused on the far distance. *I know. I'll make a contract with her that allows me to be true to my nature. That's it! She'll just have to understand.*

Happier now, Leo went outside to attend to his morning chores.

When he came in from the cold dark morning, he felt relieved to find Muriel Anne sitting in the kitchen in her bathrobe. Leo hung up his coat and hat, then poured himself a mug of coffee. He sat down directly across from Muriel Anne. He took a deep breath to calm his nerves and let it out slowly. Then he reached out and clasped Muriel Anne's slim hand in his cold, calloused fingers.

Leo looked her straight in the eye. "Muriel Anne, we have to talk."

Muriel Anne took a sip of coffee. "About what, dear?"

"Well, now. Ya see. I've got myself a big problem."

"Oh? What's the problem, husband?"

"Well, now, the problem is that it's my nature to like men."

She looked puzzled. She paused then nodded. "Yes, Leo. I knew that back when Sean told me the two of you were lovers as well as partners."

Muriel Anne gave him a long gaze, tilting her head to the side in a silent question.

"Well, now, Muriel Anne, I gotta face the fact that it's not my nature to desire women."

"Oh!"

Muriel Anne sat up and pulled back, worried about what Leo meant. "And?"

"And, well, Sean taught me years ago when we were mendin' fences on Dad's ranch, 'To thine own self be true.' I have to be true to myself. True to my nature. I can't live a lie and pretend that's all's well, just because we're doin' what Sean asked or what other people consider proper."

"Oh, dear! You don't want a divorce, do you?"

She shuddered internally. Her thoughts scattered, darting here and there in a panic. *Oh! How am I going to live? Where will I live? How can I raise a baby without a father? Who's going to support the baby and me? Father's dead. Oh my God! What will mother say? What will the neighbors say?"*

Muriel Anne became so worked up the coffee turned to a cold lump in her stomach.

Leo could see how his words upset Muriel Anne. He reached out and reclaimed her hand. "Nope. I'm not talkin' about a divorce, Muriel Anne. I'm talkin' about takin' a page from Sean's book. I wanna work out an arrangement we can both live with which lets me remain true to my nature and myself."

Muriel Anne frowned fearfully. "What kind of... of... arrangement?"

"Well, now. To start with, we're gonna have to face the fact that I won't be wantin' to repeat last night's activities in our bed, doncha know. We consummated our marriage as required by law and by custom. Fine. But I don't feel good about the idea of repeatin' it anymore. It would be dishonest of me."

Muriel Anne let out a deep breath as she understood Leo didn't want to sleep with her again. She had enjoyed herself last night more than she had ever dreamed. She wanted to share many more passionate nights with her handsome husband. She didn't want to taste such passion and then go back to living without it.

"But, Leo. We're married, now!"

"I know, wife. And that's precisely why we need to draw up our own contract. Even if it's only verbal words, doncha know. Just like y'all did fer yer handfastin'. First, we gotta acknowledge I'm a man who prefers men. And I know I'm gonna want to sleep with men, again, in the future."

Muriel Anne's eyes lit up in surprise. Leo rushed on. "But it doesn't have to change anythin' else in our marriage. It doesn't need to change any of the things Sean wanted for the baby and us."

Leo took a deep breath, struggling to express himself. "Ya see, Muriel Anne, we can still be married and live together in every way. Except for the part of sleepin' together fer carnal pleasures. And we can still be a happy couple to all appearances. We'll just have to keep this part private. Personal. Secret."

"Oh, Leo!"

"We'll eat together and live together. We'll be a perfect married couple fer all intents and purposes. And to all appearances. We can even share the bed at night if ya want. Who knows? We might even be happy together. I know I like ya an awful lot, Muriel Anne. And I still wanna be a good father fer Sean's love child. Whaddaya think, Muriel Anne? Do ya think we can make a go of it?"

Muriel Anne leaned back against the hard chair as she considered Leo's unexpected proposals. *Careful now, girl. He's being honest with you. He's not trying to cut you out of his life or out of his property. After all, what's one more secret on top of so many? Oh, but I'm beginning to hate secrets! Now that I think about it, all those men like Sean and Leo that I've read about over the years – men like Oscar Wilde and others whose scandals and private lives became gossip fodder in the newspapers – they were all married. So they must have had a working relationship with their wives to keep up appearances and remain socially acceptable. Why, Oscar Wilde even sired two children, as I recall. If others can do it, we can, too. Oh, dear. Secrets piled on top of secrets.*

Muriel Anne slowly shook her head. "But, Leo. You'll be wanting to bed men but not bed me. Correct?"

Leo nodded yes with a tentative smile. "Well, now. Just look at it this way. I'll never cheat on ya with another woman. I'll be true to our weddin' vows."

Muriel Anne acknowledged his comment with a soft snort of disapproval. "Huh! And what would you think if I said I wanted to sleep with another man? If you get to sleep around with men you find attractive, why shouldn't I? Why shouldn't I find pleasure and love in my life while pretending to be your ideal wife?"

Leo found himself taken aback. He hadn't considered her desires. He floundered for an answer. He hadn't thought of that side of the deal. "Well. Uh. I guess so long as ya didn't have someone

341

else's baby. Uh, I guess I couldn't really say much, now, could I?"

"So, let me see if I can sum this up for you in plain English, Leo. We can both sleep with any man we want, provided no children result from our dalliances. Correct?"

"Yep. I guess that just about covers it. Of course, after the birth of Sean's baby, if we decide we want another child, well, then I guess we could go about it in the normal way. Even though it's not natural fer me. Could ya agree to that?"

Muriel Anne took her time, reluctant to agree to live the way Leo proposed. But she couldn't see an alternative that didn't lead to her losing out in the long run. She reluctantly decided to agree. *All I'm giving up are the duties and pleasures of the wedding bed. I get to keep everything else. Heck, to hear mother and her friends talk about sleeping with their husbands, they complain it's an onerous duty they have to submit to. Especially as their husbands get older and fatter and develop bad breath. I remember overhearing Mother tell Hannah just a few days ago that submitting to one's husband, however much one might dislike it, is a wife's duty. She said it's just like cleaning house and cooking meals. Just something one must do. An unpleasant duty to be born. A duty and an obligation, she called it. So. Maybe I wouldn't be giving up too much, not really, not in the long run. Oh, but I so enjoyed last night.*

Murial Anne watched Leo nervously thumping his thumb on the tabletop. She placed her hand over his to stop the twitching. She struggled to smile but only partially succeeded. "Leo. Husband. I appreciate your honesty. I will not pressure you for sexual favors. Though if you are of a mind in the future, I will welcome you to my bed. I won't complain if you sleep with men. Provided you are both totally discreet, that is. And provided your affair doesn't come back to cause problems for our marriage or little family. There are sodomy laws, you know! I don't want to raise Sean's baby alone just because you were careless and got caught and sent to prison."

Leo nodded with a slight frown on his face.

Muriel Anne continued more emphatically. "I refuse to be a party to any scandals that besmirch our names and characters!"

Leo looked surprised. "Of course not!"

They sat looking at each other, looking away, gazing into the future, then looking back at each other.

"Well, then. I guess that says it all, doesn't it, husband?"

"Yes, wife. And I thank ya fer bein' so understandin'. I feel sure that Sean would approve were he to learn about our marriage agreement. It was his motto in life, doncha know. To thine own self be true. He said it more than once. To thine own self be true."

They both rose to their feet. They leaned in and shared a light hug, then kissed each other on the cheek.

Muriel Anne escaped to her wifely duties, preparing breakfast. She tried to ignore the turmoil in her mind as she digested this latest development. She sighed. *Another secret.*

Leo felt a great weight lift off his shoulders. He pulled his shoulders back and stood up tall, sure he had done the right thing. In his mind, he heard Sean telling him over and over again, 'To thine own self be true.'

Leo sat back down at the kitchen table, smiling gently.

Muriel Anne reassured herself, over and over again, *Everything will be all right, so long as Leo is discreet.*

Greenwich Village
End of December 2010

Art let go of Josh's hand and stretched. He leaned back over the leather sofa and spread his arms wide. He hunched his hips up and pushed his legs out in front of him in a big, long stretch. "So, that conniving Muriel Anne discovered what it was like to achieve an orgasm. But poor Grandpa Leo only felt homesick and sad for Sean, unsatisfied with having sex with a woman."

"That's right, Art. I can identify with Grandpa Leo. When you want a man, a woman just won't do."

Josh stood up and closed his laptop on the glass coffee table. "Have you ever dallied with a member of the opposite sex, Art?"

"Me? No. I was never interested in exploring. I dated girls, but only to have someone to take to the prom or double date with friends. I've had lots of good friends who were girls, but nothing romantic or sexual. You?"

"Nope. Me neither. I knew when I was still very young that I just wasn't interested in girls. And when I heard all the stories of gay men getting married and having kids, then coming out and divorcing their wives, breaking up their homes, leaving all those unhappy children, I was glad I never succumbed to social pressure like that. Nope, Art. You are exactly what I've always wanted. Strong, hairy, smart, and most of all, male!"

Josh leaped over and landed on Art. He grabbed Art's balls, making him flinch. "Male, I said!"

Laughing maniacally, Josh gave Art a sloppy kiss with lots of tongue.

Art happily returned the kiss. "That was brave of Leo. And rather honorable, too, wouldn't you say? He made an agreement with Muriel Anne so he could be true to himself and still keep their marriage intact. I rather admire him for being so honest with himself. It's not like he had any role models or support groups to help him figure things out like we have today. So tell me. What happened to Grandpa Leo? Did he settle into domestic bliss and learn to be a husband and father? Did he learn to be bisexual? People say it's possible to be bisexual. Though when I was younger, I thought it was only an excuse for staying in the closet."

"Well, Art, Grandpa Leo's story got real interesting after their wedding night. I'll tell you all about it. He found himself surrounded by women and girls. So he began going out of his way to meet and hook up with men. You'll see."

Leo's story continues in

DISCREET

Book Two: Growing Pains

Available now in paperback and on Kindle